IN THE MIDST OF PASSION

He kissed her then—hard and deep with an authority that was both savage and possessive. Soft moans rose from some place in his throat as his tongue thrust relentlessly into her mouth. When Topaz kissed him back, he squeezed his eyes shut even tighter and curved his hands over her hips to bring her closer. He cupped her chin and broke the kiss to tease the satiny skin of her jaw with his lips. Shortly, however, he was back—testing the sweetness of her lips with renewed intensity as he proceeded to kiss her all over again.

In The Midst
Of Passion

AlTonya Washington

Kensington Publishing Corp.

http://www.kensingtonbooks.com

DAFINA BOOKS are published by

Kensington Publishing Corp.
850 Third Avenue
New York, NY 10022

All Kensington Titles, Imprints, and Distributed Lines are avail-
able at special quantity discounts for bulk purchases for sales
promotions, premiums, fund-raising, and educational or insti-
tutional use. Special book excerpts or customized printings can
also be created to fit specific needs. For details, write or phone
the office of the Kensington special sales manager: Kensington
Publishing Corp., 850 Third Avenue, New York, NY 10022,
attn: Special Sales Department, Phone: 1-800-221-2647.

Dafina and the Dafina logo Reg. U.S. Pat. & TM Off.

First Dafina mass market printing: August 2006
10 9 8 7 6 5 4 3 2 1

Printed in the United States of America

*This book is dedicated to anyone who has
ever struggled to triumph over a ghost*

ONE

"You really should be bringing someone to this party, you know?"

"No one I could stomach spending an entire evening with."

"Well, if you'd ever just let me fix you up with one of my—"

"Hell no."

DeAndra Rice closed her eyes in response to her cousin's adamant refusal. Of course she knew better than to argue. "Just tell me you're on your way," she said instead.

"I'm fifteen minutes away," Alexander Rice assured the woman and clicked off his cell phone before she could utter another word.

A fierce scowl marred Alex's light caramel-toned face as he tossed the phone to the floor of the passenger side of his Navigator. For the fifth time that day, he found himself asking how he had allowed De to talk him into attending one of her uptight social get-togethers. Then, as if on cue, De's high-pitched nasal voice filled his ears: *As a respected newspaper publisher, you should be introduced to the people who will be welcoming you into their circle.*

Alex knew that was a "circle" he didn't care to become involved with. Still, he did realize that his attendance would be in the best interest of his paper. Besides, his managing editor and president, Clifton Knowles, would be out of commission until he recovered from a recent ski injury. Alex felt the smile tugging at his mouth as he anticipated the jokes Cliff would have to endure regarding black folks and skiing. Cliff would be the man in charge eventually, but tonight that job would fall to Alex. Though the paper was his brainchild, he chose to remain as far from the spotlight as possible.

"Come on, Zan. You're gonna be uptight enough once you get there," Alex told himself, deciding to push the aggravations from his mind. He hit the Play button of the CD changer and set his head back against the padded rest. The thriving combination of spoken words over rhythms filled the car as the sounds of MOP spilled from the high-tech speakers.

Again, Alex smiled as he imagined what his society-ensconced cousin would say about his musical tastes. DeAndra Rice would never believe one could actually enjoy the rawest hip-hop and possess a love of the classical genre as well. Alex, however, took great pride in his interests. He thought of how far he had come during the last three years. His newspaper had been little more than a neighborhood newsletter then. Now the small Charlotte-based paper had grown into a must-read piece of literature.

The *Queen City Happening* drew readers from all ethnic and social backgrounds. It covered the latest shows and concerts—for all musical tastes. There was coverage of local news pertinent to the arts and business crowds. The publication had most recently garnered several awards and had received a slew of recognition. This all made its thirty-two-year-old owner as pleased as he was successful.

Unfortunately, success carried its own share of unwanted elements. Snobs, gold diggers, and an overabundance of advice givers seemed to appear out of nowhere and gave Alex more reason to relish social hermitage.

Alex's extraordinary turquoise gaze suddenly narrowed behind the black sunglasses he sported, and he lowered the volume of the music. In the distance, a classic white Corvette sat along the side of the road. The captivating craftsmanship of the Anniversary Edition model beckoned more than a passing glance.

Alex was taken in only by the sensual appeal of the car. When he noticed its driver, he forgot about the sleek vehicle.

"My God," he whispered and pulled his black SUV to the shoulder of the road several feet ahead of the sports car. He shut down the engine and watched an incredible-looking woman leave the car. A moment later he exited the SUV.

Alex strolled closer to the distressed vehicle, taking note of the woman's provocative attire. The white evening gown teased the senses despite the fact that it reached her ankles. The hem flared about a pair of stylish, square, open-toed white wedge heels. The dress itself was a sleeveless number with straps that tied upon her shoulders and dipped low in the back. The bodice was secured by a row of strappy ties that offered fleeting glimpses of a full pair of firm breasts, flat tummy, and toned thighs and legs.

For a while, the intensely handsome, no-nonsense publishing entrepreneur was in awe. The piece of eye candy brought his male hormones to life like nothing he'd known. Still, Alex forced himself to shake off the pleasurable sensations before he approached her.

"Excuse me?" he called to her in a rough, yet seductively soft tone. He cleared his throat to quell the surge of arousal still coursing through his body. "Do you need any help here?" he managed to ask.

Topaz Emerson had just raised the hood of the sports car when she heard the man's voice. She turned, just as wind stirred the dust, which flew up around her like an entrancing mist. The rush of air lifted the long spiral curls that dangled from the classy chignon she wore. The man she found standing a few feet behind her rendered her speechless for several seconds. Her own devastating amber stare narrowed as she studied his shocking blue-green gaze.

"Oh no—no, thank you," she finally found her voice. "I, um, I have it under control."

Alex smiled at the clear, almost regal tone of her voice. His eyes raked her svelte, voluptuous body once again, before he nodded toward the car. "Looks like it's over-heated," he noted.

A grimace flashed on Topaz's lovely chocolate-toned face and she looked back at the engine. "Not quite, but if I don't get water in it soon, it will be."

"Well, I know a pretty decent mechanic. He's looked at my car a few times and I think he's a pretty good guy," Alex explained, hoping he wasn't coming across as condescending. "I don't think he'll jerk you around on the price or anything," he added.

Topaz chuckled, loving the sweet soft way he spoke to her. "I'm very thankful," she whispered, taking a couple of steps closer to him. "It's just that I know a shop that I trust with my life."

Alex's heavy, sleek black brows rose as he tilted his head. "Trust with your life, hmm? Maybe I should switch."

Topaz's shoulder rose slowly. "Well, I'm always in the market for new business."

Alex folded his arms across the front of the cream

shirt that molded to his chest and back. "You . . . are?" he inquired, obviously confused.

Topaz wouldn't allow him to see her amusement. "What I really need is a new water pump. I'm such a procrastinator. I haven't gotten around to putting it in my shop," she explained.

Alex, however, was still confused and tried to grasp her meaning. He watched her go to the trunk and return to the hood with a jug of water.

"*Your* shop?" he probed.

Topaz propped the jug against the mouth of the water tank and went back to the driver's side of the car. She handed Alex a gray business card when she returned.

TOP E TOWING AND MECHANICAL, it read. "Yours?" he asked.

"Mmm-hmm," she sweetly confirmed, emptying the jug and taking it back to the trunk. She was about to put the hood down when Alex stepped before the car and performed the task. Topaz felt her her eyes widen at the breadth of his torso and arms. "Thank you," she whispered when he was done.

"No problem, Miss?"

"Emerson. Topaz Emerson."

"Topaz," Alex repeated, smirking a bit as he thought how well the name suited her. There was something . . . a dazzling quality, shimmering almost, he didn't know. Whatever it was, it held him captivated.

Topaz blinked as the startling effect of the gorgeous stranger's eyes entranced her once more. Whoever he was, he was quite remarkable to look at. She would wager he stood almost seven feet tall, and he had a lean, chiseled frame that could rival the most fit basketball player's. Curly black hair was cropped into a close cut that flattered his very handsome, slightly angular, caramel-toned face, complete with a cleft in the center of his chin. Still, it was the unsettling quality of his deep-set turquoise stare that she could not shake.

"Well, I, um, I better get going," she told him when she shook herself from the spell his looks had drawn her into. "I'm already late."

"Yeah, so am I," Alex replied, though he made no effort to move. Instead, he watched Topaz walk back to the driver's side of her car. He couldn't help but admire her graceful stride and the manner in which her hands trailed the car; much like the manner a model would use as she displayed a prize. He tilted his head up in response when she wiggled her fingers toward him to say good-bye.

The car roared to life then and she zoomed away amid a flurry of dust. When the vehicle disappeared down the long back road, Alex studied the card he held.

Topaz angled the Corvette into an empty space far away from the majestic brick house, which seemed to span the distance of the entire block.

"Thank you," she whispered, pleased that she would be able to make a quick escape should the high-profile get-together become too much for her to handle.

"How'd I get talked into this thing?" she asked, once she was standing outside the car and gazing upon the stately house.

Clearing her throat, Topaz headed inside. Of course, almost everyone in attendance knew her well. Many had had their cars repaired at her shop. Once, she had also traveled in the same social circle. Long ago, she had turned her back on her affluent heritage. Her parents, Eric and Patra Emerson, were partners in their own law firm and had lavished their only child with every luxury. In spite of those trappings, Topaz had emerged as a compassionate, polite, and graceful woman who was loved by almost everyone who knew her. Summers spent at her aunt and uncle's Louisiana farm contributed to her love of the outdoors and cars. At an early age, Topaz knew what direction her life would take.

She accepted a glass of champagne from a passing waiter. She had taken only a small sip when two arms slipped around her waist.

"I was worried. Did you have trouble finding the place?" Simon Whitley asked as he hugged her close.

"I had car trouble," Topaz explained, patting her free hand against his white-tuxedo-sleeved arm.

Simon frowned, his dark brown face clouding with concern. "How'd you get here, then? You didn't have to ride with some stranger, did you?"

"No, no. Don't worry. The car just overheated. Nothing major," Topaz assured her friend.

"Come on," Simon instructed, pressing a kiss to her cheek and leading her farther into the house.

"So how long do you plan to be here?"

Simon chuckled. "What in the world is it with you and these parties?"

"I grew up around these parties," Topaz reminded him, taking another sip of her champagne. "I'd much rather get dressed up to get down than get dressed up to act stuck-up."

"Ouch," Simon teased, massaging the crisp dark hair at the nape of his neck. "Well, let's see if we can show our faces for at least forty-five minutes. Then we bounce. I promise," he drawled and pressed a kiss to her cheek.

"Simon, there you are!"

Topaz smothered a groan, recognizing the high-pitched nasal voice belonging to DeAndra Rice. *This should be interesting*, she thought.

"Hey, De," Simon greeted, leaving his date's side to take his hostess by the hand.

14 *AlTonya Washington*

DeAndra hugged Simon close and placed an overly gracious kiss to his cheeks. The bright expression left her face the instant her hazel stare moved past his shoulder. "Topaz," she said, through clenched teeth.

"De," Topaz replied in much the same manner.

"I must admit I'm surprised to see you here," De remarked, setting her frail-looking hands on her barely noticeable hips. "We never see much of you at my little gatherings."

Topaz folded her arms across her bosom. "Well, De, *one*, you never invite me to your little gatherings and, *two*, you know I hate coming to these things."

DeAndra's phony smile appeared to freeze on her face. "Have a good time, Simon," she finally said, then brushed an invisible speck of something from the severe-looking green tailored suit she wore.

"Oooh, that woman," Topaz whispered, clenching and unclenching her fists as DeAndra glided away. "Now I know we need to get out of here."

Simon chuckled. "Why do you always let that mess get you so uptight?" he asked, pulling her back against him again.

Frustration marred Topaz's lovely features. "Weren't you listening to what was being said?"

"Why do you hate this stuff?" Simon asked, looking around at the maze of well-dressed professionals strolling around the Charlotte home. "I thought most women loved going out for this sort of thing."

"I'm not most women, baby."

Simon couldn't argue with the simple reply. He could practically feel dozens upon dozens of male eyes spewing daggers of jealousy into his back because of the incredible chocolate beauty in his arms.

Of course, many of the secret admirers would have been less jealous had they known the true nature of the relationship. The onetime love affair had been over for many years, but Simon and Topaz had managed to remain friends. He rarely let himself revisit the memories of their troubles and was happy they were still in each other's lives. Simon didn't think any man could ever get a woman like Topaz Emerson out of his system.

"So what do you want to do after we get out of here?" Simon asked, nuzzling his handsome dark face against her shoulder.

Topaz sighed heavily. "I don't really care, just get me out of here," she urged, allowing her head to fall back against his shoulder. "I don't know why you always bring me to these awful parties, anyway."

Simon kissed her shoulder. "Part of your punishment for not marrying me."

"Mmm, I thought my parents were the only ones still punishing me because of that."

Simon turned her around to face him then. "You know I still love you, girl."

Topaz fixed him with her trademark dazzling smile and patted his cheek. "You better love me, look at what I'm putting up with because of you!"

"What took you so long to get here, Lex?" DeAndra was asking as she hurried toward Alex.

"You should be happy I came at all," he softly, yet firmly, replied.

De ignored her cousin's usual bad attitude and waved a hand toward the crowd. "Everyone's just mingling now, but dinner should be ready soon."

"Sounds good," Alex remarked, sounding as though he couldn't have cared less.

De watched him slip a cell phone inside his wine trouser pocket and rolled her eyes. "I hope you'll let your employees handle business tonight."

Alex smirked and shook his head. "Spoken like a person who's never worked a day in her life."

"Oh, Lex, come on. There're several single, lovely women here who would love to meet you."

"Mmm . . . and bore me to death."

Intent on keeping her cool composure, De raised her hands. "I give up," she whispered and walked away.

Alex celebrated the departure and strolled toward the full bar located near the rear of the den. He ordered a cognac and was sipping the pungent drink when he heard his name. He turned, letting loose a roaring bellow of laughter that drew several surprised looks from his cousin's more reserved guests.

"Xan!"

"Man, what the hell you doin' up in here?" Alex asked, shaking hands and hugging one of his oldest friends.

Trey Cooper's laughter was as rich and honest as Alex's. "Man, you know this haughty crap ain't my thang. My girl works for the city and got an invite, so I rolled up in here with her," he explained, tugging on the lapel of his tan sport coat.

Alex chuckled, his turquoise gaze twinkling with mischief. "Man, my cousin would have a damn fit if she knew she had the owner of Rump Shakas Plaza up in here," he said, citing one of the city's most popular gentlemen's clubs.

Trey laughed, patting one hand to his short Afro. "Hell, she'd probably faint if she knew I ain't got no college degree!" he teased in his usual outrageous manner.

The two friends had stood laughing and talking for a while longer when they were interrupted by the sound of someone calling Trey's name. They turned to see his girlfriend approaching.

"Trey, look who I found," Courtney Serens announced. Trey's brown gaze widened and his hearty laughter sounded again. "Topaz! Girl, what the hell . . ." he remarked as they shared a hug. "I know somethin's got to be wrong now, if they invited you!"

Topaz slapped his shoulder. "Hush, fool, a friend dragged me here. He was invited."

"Mmm-hmm, Trey got in on my coattails too," Courtney replied, joining in when everyone laughed over the remark.

Topaz's laughter softened. She noticed the devastating man standing a few inches behind Trey and smiled. "Hello," she whispered, her amber gaze narrowing.

"Oh, I'm sorry, Topaz," Courtney said as she stepped forward. "Topaz Emerson, Alexander Rice," she announced, settling her hands into the pockets of her spaghetti-strapped swing dress.

Topaz extended her hand. "I didn't get your name earlier. It's nice to meet you, Mr. Rice."

"Alex, please," he urged, smothering her hands in his warm, firm embrace. "It's nice to meet you too."

Courtney was curious. "You two met already?" she inquired.

Before anyone could respond, Simon Whitley found his date. Alex's striking blue-green stare sharpened when he noticed the man easing his arm around Topaz's waist. He glanced toward her hand for a ring. There was no wedding band, only a diamond thumb ring and an emerald cut on her pinkie.

Courtney introduced Simon to Alex and Trey; then the group indulged in a few more moments of idle chatter. A short while later, Simon whisked Topaz away for more dancing and Courtney went to speak with an aquaintance she'd spotted.

Trey accepted a glass of vodka from a passing waiter, before turning back to Alex. He could tell that his friend was quite interested in the dark leggy beauty who twirled around the dance floor with another man.

"Yeah, she is."

"She's what?" Alex asked, knowing to whom Trey was referring.

"As sweet as she is fine."

"How do you know her and I don't?"

Trey's wide shoulders rose beneath his coat. "You been a busy man. It's been a while since you been in town, right? Lot of functions you may've missed," he figured.

Alex drained the last of his cognac and grimaced. "I haven't missed that much," he argued, though silently he acknowledged there had been much *old* business to tie up.

"Maybe it just wasn't meant for y'all to meet yet. Everything happens for a reason, you know?"

Alex nodded, wondering if that was really true. "Who's the cat she's with?"

Trey shook his head. "I never met the man before tonight, but I do know she's not married or engaged or seein' anybody as far as I know."

"Hard to believe," Alex whispered.

"Hmph." Trey shrugged. "Tell me 'bout it."

"Sorry, baby," Courtney sang when she returned to Trey's side. "Alex, I'm stealin' my man."

"No problem," Alex replied with a grin and shook hands with Trey again. "All right, man."

"Drop by the bar sometime. You been away too long," Trey insisted.

"Count on it," Alex promised, clapping his friend's shoulder before they parted ways. He returned to the bar, deciding to enjoy the rest of the party from that location.

"Well, at least De has good taste in bands," Topaz complimented when the jazz group took five. "I think I need a drink after that workout."

Simon's brown stare was trained across her shoulder. "Baby, I see someone I should speak to. You mind?" he asked, cupping her face.

Topaz shook her head and sighed. "I don't mind, but make it snappy 'cause your forty-five minutes are almost up, mista."

Simon grinned and kissed the tip of her nose. "You're a doll, baby," he declared.

Topaz strolled toward the bar, stopping to speak briefly with old friends and acquaintances. When she found Alex nursing a drink, her smile brightened a little and she nearly forgot her desperation to leave the party.

"You don't appear to be enjoying yourself," she noted, taking a seat on the vacant stool next to him.

Alex smiled at the observation, his gorgeous gaze softening. "I shouldn't have let my cousin talk me into being here."

Topaz's smile lost a bit of its radiancy. "Your cousin? Not . . . DeAndra Rice?" she asked, unable to mask her displeasure when Alex nodded.

Of course, Alex noticed her reaction. He figured Topaz was just another person his cousin had rubbed the wrong way.

"I can't believe this," he said, setting his cheek against his fist. "You know my relatives, my friends. Why are we just meeting?"

"I don't know," Topaz coolly answered, leaning forward when the bartender approached. "Ginger ale please. I guess everything happens for a reason."

"And that's the second time I've heard that tonight."

Topaz smiled at his frustration. "You see?"

Alex found himself unable to respond. For a moment, he was almost in awe of the soft, innocently seductive gleam in her extraordinary amber eyes.

Topaz's smile transformed from one of amusement to one more knowing. "They're natural," she said.

The silky jet-black lines of Alex's brows drew closer. "Excuse me?" he whispered, leaning nearer. He hadn't the faintest idea what she meant.

Topaz motioned toward her face, her long French-tipped nails brushing the cool, creamy shade of her eye shadow.

Alex grinned then and nodded in understanding. "So are mine," he shared, before shrugging. "I would've been able to tell, anyway."

"Oh, really?" Topaz challenged, her full lips curving into a playfully doubtful smile.

Alex took a swig from his fresh drink and nodded. "Believe me, I've seen enough phonies in my day."

"Yeah," Topaz sighed, unable to mask her grimace over his remark, "hanging around *this* crowd, I find that easy to believe."

It was Alex's turn to grimace. "I assure you, these people aren't my crowd of choice. My cousin made me think I needed to be here."

Topaz sipped from the tall glass of ginger ale, letting the crisp strong flavor of the drink bubble against her tongue. "Sounds like her," she said, after swallowing.

Alex kept his eyes focused on his hand where it rested atop the bar. "You mind telling me why you two don't get along?" he asked.

Topaz set her glass aside and reclined against the metal-barred back of the stool. "It's a long story," she acknowledged simply.

"Well," Alex sighed with a glance across his shoulder, "you're the only person here I've enjoyed talking with this much, so you should feel free to share."

The translucent glow radiating from her dark face

dimmed for the first time that evening. "It's just old news, *very* old news, best left buried," she decided.

The reply was more than enough to tell Alex that Topaz Emerson's relationship with his cousin was a personal and painful topic. It surprised him to feel a partial urge to wring De's neck for causing a moment of sadness to the graceful beauty.

"So why are you here?" he asked, choosing not to dwell on such dark emotions. "I get the feeling you'd rather be doing something else."

Topaz folded her arms across her chest. "My friend got an invite. He and DeAndra are friends," she said.

Alex's stare followed the trail of her fingers roaming the length of her flawless deep brown skin. "Simon, right? Your man?" he slyly probed, his eyes still following the way she caressed her skin.

Topaz shook her head. "A friend. That's all," she said, excluding the fact that they used to be more.

Alex sipped more of his drink. He offered no further comment on the subject.

"Anyway, I grew up around this stuff," she shared, observing the staid crowd with unmasked disinterest.

"You're from Charlotte?"

"My parents are from Africa."

Alex's unsettling stare narrowed. "With a name like Emerson?" he noted.

Topaz laughed at his reaction. "Actually it's my mother who's African. She met my father when he visited during a college trip. She was in school herself, but had come home from the States to visit. They met and . . ." She paused to shrug. "The rest is history."

"So you were raised in Charlotte?"

"I spent much of my childhood in Africa," Topaz explained, recrossing her legs as she spoke, "but then we came here. My parents live in New York now."

Alex was intrigued. The look on his gorgeous face proved it. "That accounts for your accent," he said, when she noticed him staring. "Very distinctive," he added.

Topaz's trademark grin was so sunny, her eyes often narrowed to the point of closing. "Well, hopefully you'll never forget my voice."

"I don't plan to," he said.

Their eyes held far longer than necessary, each gaze appearing to look beyond the devastating attractiveness that lay on the outside, to something far more attractive beneath the surface.

Topaz was first to blink and look away as she cleared her throat. "So what about you?" she asked, reaching for her drink. "What are you really doing here? You don't seem like the type to let someone talk you into anything."

"Thanks," Alex conceded, lowering his gaze as he accepted her accurate observation. "I thought I could score a few more advertisers for my paper, use my attendance here to generate a bit more buzz at the very least," he admitted.

"Your paper?" she queried, intrigued and becoming even more interested by their conversation. "Care to elaborate?"

Alex took his drink from the bar and stood. "Only if we can take this outside." he suggested.

Topaz needed no coaxing and eased off the stool. They headed out of the den through one of the three sets of French doors skirting the rear. As they strolled the tree-, flower-, and bush-lined walkway, Topaz covertly studied her companion. Obviously, Charlotte was a much larger place than she'd always believed it to be. Alexander Rice was certainly a man she would have remembered meeting, but she never had. He knew many of her acquaintances, but they had never run into one another. She recalled her earlier words: *Everything hap-*

pens for a reason. She was more than a little curious about that reason.

" . . . and that's why I began the *Queen City Happening.*"

"The *Queen City Happening* is your paper?" she gasped, stopping midstride along the walk.

Alex pushed one hand into his trouser pocket and studied her. "You know the paper?"

Topaz rolled her eyes. "I read it all the time. Every week, to be exact. It tells me so much about the city and it's especially helpful when I have friends come visit. It's got the best articles about what's going on in *our* community. Must be an exciting job," she guessed.

Alex shrugged and looked away for a second. "It has its moments," he sighed, turning back to her, "but no way is it as exciting as owning a towing company," he said, preferring not to discuss the company where he was mostly a figurehead.

Topaz laughed and was about to respond when she heard her name. "Over here, Simon!" she called. "Excuse me, Alex," she whispered, stepping a few feet away to meet her date.

"Are you finally ready?" she asked.

Simon grimaced and reached for her hands. "Love, I got myself roped into having drinks with Shawn Eckards from Weston," he explained, referring to the senior representative at his firm.

Topaz pressed her index finger along his lips, silencing his speech. "It's all right. I have my car, remember?"

"I don't know, I don't want that thing breaking down on you," he said, patting his hand along the curve of her hip.

Topaz patted his smooth, dark cheek in turn. "I fix cars for a living, remember?"

"You're too much," he said, tugging on one of the tassles securing the back of her dress. "Too sweet," he whispered, kissing the corner of her eye. "I'll call or come by later, all right?"

"That would be nice," she accepted with a nod.

"Thanks for coming," he said, then looked over at Alex and waved. "Good to meet you, man."

Alex only nodded and watched Simon hurry off. "Business must be very important for him to leave you," he said, once Topaz returned to his side. He attempted to downplay his actual surprise—wondering how any man could leave such a beauty to go shoot the breeze with a stuffy business associate.

Topaz was inspecting a tie on her dress. "Ah, Simon's always been a workaholic," she lightly excused, sounding as though his departure was nothing to fret over. "Anyway, I'm glad. Now I can go on and get out of here."

Alex stepped closer. "Listen . . ." He paused then, hearing his cousin calling him from a distance.

"You better go," Topaz advised, her smile genuine.

Alex took her hand in his, not quite ready to let her leave. "It was nice meeting you *again*," he teased in recollection of their earlier encounter. "I enjoyed talking with you."

"Leeex!"

Topaz groaned that time in response to DeAndra's shrill voice. "I should go before she sees us together and we get into it," she decided, joining him in another round of laughter before silence reasserted itself. "Good night," she whispered.

Alex only nodded, his incredible turquoise stare following her, until she disappeared around a bend in the walkway.

"Lex? Didn't you hear me calling you?" DeAndra scolded when she found her cousin.

"What the hell is it, De?"

De halted at the stiffness in his voice, but she wasn't put off. "What's wrong with you now?" she asked.

Alex flexed his hand and dismissed the unexpected anger over his cousin's attitude toward Topaz. "What is it, De?" he asked in a softer tone.

"There're a few members of the City Council inside. They're very eager to meet with you if you can spare a precious minute. They have an idea they'd like to run past you," she explained.

Curious, Alex allowed her to escort him through the party. Inside the cozy, elegant sitting room were a group of men and one woman. They all shook hands with Alex while DeAndra made the introductions.

"So nice to be meeting with you finally, Mr. Rice," Josie Sharp was saying, her round, light honey-toned face illuminated by an interest that went far beyond anything professional.

He covered her small hand in his. "Call me Alex, please."

"Of course," Josie whispered, her smile very bright for the tall, handsome publisher.

"Why don't you all take your seats while I talk to the staff about your drinks?" DeAndra instructed.

"So, my cousin tells me you all have an idea to run by me?" Alex was saying as he settled into one of the armchairs circling the coffee table.

Redmon Cowan cleared his throat. "That's right, Alex. Because of the *Queen City Happening*'s relationship with the city's African-American community, we've decided your publication would be the perfect venue for what we have in mind."

Alex tugged on his earlobe. "And that is?" he asked, studying the older dark man with cool interest.

"We'd like your paper to begin a series of articles that spotlight local African-American entrepreneurs."

"A different one each week," Martin Cramer added, leaning forward to rub his chubby hands together. "In addition to congratulating these successful people, we'll also be informing the community about the very strong presence of black-owned businesses."

"Mmm, not to mention promoting the patronage of those businesses," Alex mentioned.

"You sound interested, Alex," Josie noted.

He favored her with a knowing grin. "I am. Tell me more."

The group discussed the idea in greater detail. Alex thought it had extreme promise and was a bit peeved that no one at the paper had suggested it before. Still, he informed the council members that he would discuss the matter with his managing editor and president and they would all agree to meet again.

"I'm out of here, De."

"You can't go now," DeAndra argued, her light hazel eyes widening in despair.

Alex shook his head. "I can't take it anymore. I accomplished what I came here to do, thanks to you."

The comment pleased DeAndra tremendously. "I'm glad their idea appealed to you."

"Very much," he said, leaning down to plant a kiss on her cheek. "Good night."

"De?" Josie Sharp called when the cousins parted ways. "Will Alex be joining us for dinner?"

DeAndra folded her arms across the front of her severe suit and sighed. "I'm afraid not. It was all I could do to get him to even attend the party. Oh well, at least he's interested in the entrepreneurs' spotlight."

Josie appeared crestfallen anyway. "Yeah, at least," she remarked.

DeAndra finally realized how taken the woman was by Alex and decided to probe a bit. "So I guess my cousin made an impression?"

"Definitely."

"Are you speaking professionally or personally?"

Josie's glossy berry-red lips pursed. "Come now, DeAndra. I know the man's your cousin, but do you really need clarification on that? He's absolutely devastating. Is he seeing anyone?"

DeAndra's oval, vanilla-toned face expressed pure cunning. "Oh, he's about to be," she said, believing she had finally found the perfect woman for her cousin.

"What do you think?"

"Sounds like you need a radiator flush, you may even have trash in your gas tank," Topaz explained, straightening up before the hood of the tan Mercedes. "That could account for the jerking you feel when it changes gears."

Jesus Jiminez shook his head, his pitch-black gaze narrowed in admiration. "You are incredible," he breathed. "When can you look at it for me?"

"Well, I'm leaving now," Topaz was saying as she rubbed her palms together. "Would you follow me?"

"I'd follow you anywhere, *bonita*," Jesus declared and kissed her cheek.

"Save the charm, J.J.," Topaz playfully advised. "Meet me at the shop in half an hour," she called as she headed off in the direction of her own car.

Halfway there, she ran into Alex along the walkway. He was checking his pockets and hadn't noticed her. Topaz smiled when she felt her heart jump to her throat.

She was around gorgeous, sexy men every day. What was it about this one that made her feel . . . so strange?

"Alex?" she called, having shrugged off the question. "Are you finally leaving?" she asked when he looked up.

"You better believe it," he wholeheartedly confirmed. "I thought you'd be gone already, though."

Topaz glanced across her shoulder. "I was looking at a friend's car," she told him. "What?" she asked when Alex grinned and shook his head.

He wouldn't answer. Inwardly, he was thinking how incredibly different she was. There was far more to the stunning goddess than her outward appearance revealed.

"Well, again, Alex, it was very nice meeting and talking with you. I hope we see each other again soon," she said, then turned to walk away. Clasping her hands to her chest, she prayed he would stop her.

"Topaz? How would you feel about talking more, over drinks?" he suggested.

"I'd like that," she accepted, just before her expression clouded. "Only, I already made an appointment to look my friend's car over at my shop. Um . . . can I have a rain check?" she softly requested.

Alex closed his eyes and nodded once. "Sounds good," he coolly accepted.

"Bye," Topaz whispered, wriggling her fingers before walking away.

Alex's gorgeous deep-set gaze raked over her curvaceous figure several times before he removed her card from his pocket. Rubbing his strong fingers across the raised black lettering on the gray card, he smiled.

TWO

"You just don't know how much money you could make doing this. . . ."

Topaz leaned back against the cushioned hunter-green armchair she occupied. Folding her arms across the front of the white crew-neck, open-backed T-shirt, she listened to Alfred Majors ramble on about his hopes for their businesses to merge.

"I just don't know how I can get you to realize how profitable this would—what?" he asked, when Topaz began to shake her head.

Topaz appeared relaxed and mellow, as the jazz band's airy tune wafted through the air. The aura of the sparsely filled club kept her cool and lovely when she felt the urge to scream in frustration.

"You're spending perfectly good money in this wonderful place to hear me turn you down, again," she said, fiddling with a bouncing curl as she spoke. "Hear me, Alfred. I have no desire to merge anything with you."

Alfred clutched his brandy snifter in a viselike hold. "Do you know what this could do for your business?"

"Nothing," Topaz sweetly answered. "My customers come to get their cars towed and fixed. They aren't thinking about having them washed in the finest wax or adorned with costly accessories."

"Maybe they should."

"Or maybe *you* should think about opening your *own* store," she softly suggested.

Alfred seemed appalled by the advice. "Do you know how expensive that is? I—"

"Ahh, so after all this time we finally hit the nail on the head," Topaz interrupted, her voice never rising. "You're just too cheap to get a building to sell that crap."

"Topaz. you've got a prime market, a prime location to make this a very profitable venture," Alfred continued to argue.

Topaz felt her lashes flutter from frustration. "You don't have to tell me how *prime* my location is, Alfred. That's one of the reasons my business is so successful. But you're wasting your time and you will continue to do so until you understand that I am not interested."

"Does it make you feel good to be so difficult?"

"Does it make *you* feel good to be so conniving?"

The frown darkening Alfred's light brown face turned more sinister. "Conniving?"

"Mmm," Topaz confirmed, sipping from her glass of spring water, "you don't care about making me money, Alfred, admit it. You want to sell your wares in my store, make your huge stash, and then leave taking a good portion of the new customers you'll bring in who'll patronize my shop as a result. No, thanks, I'm doing just fine with the loyal customers I have now. No need to get excited by a few new ones who'll only use my services because I just happen to be in the vicinity."

Alfred pounded his fist on the table. "You are extremely naive. I can't believe you've been in business so long. Who in their right mind would turn down the possibility of new customers, regardless of their *reasons* for utilizing your services?"

"One who knows how you operate," Topaz countered, tossing her heavy waist-length locks across her shoulder as she leaned forward. "Isn't it true that I'm your last shot? You've had plenty of opportunities to make this side store of yours a reality, but when talk of contracts or lengthy commitment is broached, you take your offer elsewhere. Isn't that true, Mr. Majors?"

Alfred was angry and guilty. Refusing to accept being bested by Topaz, he stood. "You were right. This has been a waste of my time," he decided, tossing his napkin to the table.

Topaz smoothed her hands along her bare arms and smiled. "Told you," she sang.

Alfred held a clenched jaw as he reached into his wallet.

Topaz barely raised her hand from the table. "Save it," she said, "I know how tight things are."

Alfred's small eyes narrowed dangerously. Visibly offended, he grumbled something inaudible and stormed away from the table. He stomped right past Alex, who had witnessed the end of the conversation.

Alex's light, uncommon gaze grew stormy as well as it followed the man who exited the soft-lit club.

Topaz sipped on a rum and Coke while humming in tune with the sax piece that played. She was reaching for a menu when she looked and saw Alex. Her smile instantly appeared.

"Good afternoon," she greeted.

"Are you all right?" he asked, his mood not so joyous.

"Sure, I'm— Oh. You saw that, huh?" she asked, glancing toward the exit Alfred Majors had taken.

Alex folded his arms across the front of his black knit

crew shirt. "Uh-huh. Didn't look like a nice conversation," he drily noted.

Topaz sighed. "It wasn't. I was turning down an offer."

"Ah . . ." Alex replied with a nod as he stepped closer. "Now I understand why homeboy was so mad."

Topaz giggled and wriggled her fingers. "It was business."

"I still can't get over that," Alex remarked with a slow smirk.

"Get over what?"

"You. Owning a garage," he admitted, watching her closely. "I hope that didn't offend you."

"Course not, but you know a woman owning a garage really isn't so uncommon these days."

"True," Alex acknowledged, as he reached for the remaining menu. "Still, I've never met anyone who owned a garage and looked the way you do."

"Ha! I assure you I can look *mighty* bad.

"I wouldn't believe it," he coolly disagreed, his light eyes focused on the menu.

"Besides, being a woman in the business does have its share of advantages."

"And disadvantages?" Alex guessed.

Topaz's arched brows rose a notch. "Oh yes, definitely those," she admitted, smoothing her hands over her formfitting flare-legged jeans. "Especially when people think they can run over or *get* over on you because of it."

"Like this guy?" Alex noted, jerking his head toward the direction Alfred Majors had taken.

Topaz nodded. "It's all worth it, though. I *do* love being my own boss."

"Same here," Alex agreed, leaning back in his chair. "In spite of all the headache, I wouldn't trade my 'boss' status for a thing."

"Headache?" Topaz repeated. "Your paper is where it's at right now. Everyone I know reads it more than the mainstream publications. How much of a headache could it be with success like that?"

"Have you ever heard of employees?" Alex inquired, simply joining Topaz in laughter.

The question launched an enthusiastic conversation about their respective job pressures. Their laughter resonated in the quiet club, which had yet to be mobbed by the scores of professionals who descended on the downtown establishment after the five o'clock hour.

"Xan! Topaz!"

The talking entrepreneurs ceased their chatter, turning in the direction of the shouts.

"What's up, Xan? Long time no see, kid!" Centron Holmes greeted, shaking hands with Alex while his twin brother kissed Topaz.

Alex blinked, his surprise mounting as he realized two more of his close friends were acquainted with Topaz Emerson.

"What's wrong, man?" Ronald Holmes asked, having spotted the man's expression.

"I see y'all have met before," Alex mentioned, his striking gaze shifting between the smiling threesome.

Centron and Ronald looked down at Topaz. They each planted a tender kiss on her temple.

"This our girl!" Centron bellowed.

"Best mechanic in town," Ronald added.

Topaz laughed. "I've never fixed your car."

"It's your presence," Centron explained, placing one hand across his chest.

"Anyway," Alex groaned, shaking his head once the laughter quieted. "So what y'all doin' up in here?" he asked the brothers.

"Aw, man, we always come to the Bay Club after work," Centron shared.

Alex snapped his fingers. "That's right, the firm is

across the street," he remembered, referring to the advertising agency the two men operated.

"Say, listen, y'all got plans tonight?" Ronald was asking.

Alex and Topaz exchanged a brief glance, but shook their heads.

"Cool, why don't y'all come on out to our cousin's club?"

"What club?" Topaz asked, folding her arms across her chest.

"The Limit."

"That's on the other side of town, right?"

"Mmm," Centron confirmed, with a nod toward Alex, "they're havin' a birthday party for Goldie Sims."

Topaz snapped her fingers then. "I knew there was something I needed to do," she said in a hushed tone. "I have to go get that boy a present."

"You know Goldie too?" Alex blurted in a knowing tone.

"I know Goldie's peeps sent out invites to everybody he knows," Ronald interjected.

Alex shrugged. "My damn office is such a disaster area, the thing's probably right in there," he sighed.

Topaz reached for her purse. "Y'all, I need to go get Goldie's present. See ya at the party," she was saying as she kissed Centron's cheek first, then Ronald's. "Hope to see you tonight," she told Alex, fixing him with a dazzling, lingering stare before she walked away.

Centron and Ronald noticed and fixed each other with knowing looks. Topaz had been gone a few moments when they realized Alex was glaring in their direction.

"What, man?" Ronald questioned.

Alex didn't mind his agitation showing. "How the hell all y'all niggas know this sista and I don't?"

The twins could see their friend was truly disturbed by the fact and let their smiles shine through.

"Finally got the upper hand on the Casanova," Centron chimed.

"Anyway." Alex grimaced, waving his hand in denial of the label. "She's just someone I'd like to know."

"I bet!" the twins said in unison.

Alex bowed his head. "She's fine," he acknowledged with a wolfish grin. "There's somethin' else, though."

"You just met her today, man?" Ronald wanted to know.

Alex shrugged. "Met her at a party De threw last night. Y'all know Trey Cooper?" he asked, watching his friends nod. "He was there too, told me how sweet she was and talked about how she was like one of the guys."

"Hell, she is," Centron confirmed.

"She's like a lil' sister," Ronald shared.

"A woman like that," Alex said, watching the brothers nod. "I don't buy it."

Ron smiled at his twin. "It took us a long time to get to that point," he told Alex. "Every man we know is in love with the girl."

"Damn right," Centron agreed. "Topaz is the kind of sista who appeals to a guy on *every* level, and that mess is rare. So, we cool with being friends if anything more is out of the question."

Ron chuckled. "Lex, man, you'd say or do anything to be around a woman like that."

Alex couldn't deny the truth in that statement. He had only met Topaz the day before and she'd been on his mind ever since.

"Trey told me she didn't have a man," Alex shared, taking another swig of his bourbon. "She was with this brotha named Simon," he added, spying the look passing between Centron and Ronald. "Y'all know him?"

"He had a thing with Topaz back in the day," Ron explained.

"Mmm," Alex grunted, stirring the ice cubes in his drink while he leaned back against the bar, "I figured they had a history. What's the story?" he prodded.

"They were engaged, right, Tron?" Ronald asked his brother, watching him nod.

Alex felt his hand tighten reflexively around the glass. An emotion he would not identify ripped through him at the sound of the word. "She break it off?" he asked, after several seconds of silence.

"*He* broke it off," Ronald revealed, waiting for Alex's surprised reaction.

"*After* they got back together," Centron provided.

"Elaborate please."

Ronald leaned forward. "Get this, man, *he* broke it off first. Then they got back together but I don't know, I guess it wasn't the same."

"He broke it off? Why?" Alex pried, his tone one of complete disbelief.

The twins shrugged.

"Damned if we know," Centron said, "but she's not with him or anybody else exclusively."

"Why, man?" Ronald slyly inquired. "You thinkin' 'bout tossin' your hat in the ring?"

"Hmph," Alex said, downing the rest of his drink. "Well, with y'all clowns for my competition, I shouldn't have a problem achieving success," he replied.

The boisterous laughter that followed was enough to turn the heads of several women.

Topaz rushed out of her car and headed up the curving sidewalk like a woman with a purpose. Her arms were loaded with shopping bags, one of them containing the birthday gift for Goldie Sims.

"Paz!"

Topaz was halfway to her front door when she heard the call.

Sprinting down his own driveway was Casey Williams, who lived across the street. Topaz laughed, happy to see her friend who had been out of town for the past two weeks.

"What's goin' on, girl?" Casey greeted as he kissed her cheek.

"Thank you," she sang, watching as Casey reached for her bags. "So tell me about Vegas," she requested, as they continued along the drive. "Did you win or lose big?" she teased.

"Funny," Casey drawled, his deep brown eyes twinkling as he spoke.

"Good thing you have a job to come back to."

"Tell me 'bout it. Especially after I dropped a bundle in that son of a bitch."

"A bundle, huh?"

"Hell yeah," he confirmed, waiting as Topaz located her keys. "I haven't even told you about my new job yet, have I?"

Topaz was surprised. "You mean you left the *Probe*?" she asked, citing the small weekly Casey had written for since graduating from college.

"I start writing for the *Queen City Happening* on Monday."

"Get out."

Casey shrugged. "It's true. They called the day I left for Vegas."

Topaz's arched brows rose a notch. "Well, I'll have you know I met the head man in charge yesterday."

"Who? The managing editor?"

"Hmm . . . I *think* he founded the paper."

"Alex Rice? You met Alex Rice?"

"I did."

"Damn," Casey whispered, sounding as though he was

awed by the fact. "I didn't meet him during my interview, but from what I hear, he's one intimidating brotha."

"Intimidating?" Topaz parroted, inserting her house key into the lock. "He didn't come across that way to me."

"Hmph, he wouldn't."

"Meaning?" Topaz drawled, turning to look at him.

"Never mind," Casey coolly replied, thinking how clueless his friend was about her effect on the opposite sex.

Topaz waved her hand. "Whatever. Listen, why don't you come with me to this party tonight?"

"Party?"

"Mmm-hmm, for Goldie Sims. It's his birthday," she explained, turning back to unlock the door. "It should be fun and you're probably still uptight from your flight. This'll help you unwind."

Casey debated the invite, then told himself he was crazy for doing so. What man in his right mind would decline a date with the lovely Topaz Emerson? "What time do we leave?" he asked.

Casey and Topaz stepped inside the house just in time to catch the end of a message being left on her answering machine. The friends silenced themselves when they realized the caller was shouting.

Topaz rolled her eyes and laughed.

Casey wasn't quite as amused. "Who the hell would leave you a message like that?"

"Alfred Majors," Topaz shared, having recognized the voice of her obnoxious menace. "It's nothing to be concerned about. Trust me," she tried to reassure him.

"Be careful," Casey warned, dropping the bags to the silver gray sofa in the living room. "How well do you know this fool?"

"Casey, please," Topaz whined, unfastening the straps on her heels, "the man's just a harmless bully."

"Mmm-hmm, he sounds greedy."

"Well, he's that too."

"And *that* can be a very dangerous trait."

Seeing how worried Casey was, Topaz pushed him down to the sofa and situated a burgundy throw pillow behind his back. "Now you listen to me, I promise to be careful, all right?" she prompted, waiting for his gorgeous smile to break through. "Now, let's get ready for this party."

Goldie Sims's party had been under way for two and a half hours and was just getting heated when Alex arrived. Of course, the moment the tall, devastating publisher stepped into the club alone, there were several lovely women ready to offer their companionship.

"You are truly a Renaissance man, Alexander Rice."

Alex smiled down into Tiffany Green's upturned face. "How do you figure?" he probed.

Tiffany's shoulder rose, allowing the wispy thin strap of her clinging magenta frock to slip downward. "The security business and now a successful publishing magnate? You're a man of many talents."

Alex fought to hide a grimace over the woman's mention of the now defunct security business. "You do know that I dissolved Rice Securities, right, Tiff?"

"And I really don't understand why. It was so successful. I mean, *everybody* called your company to handle whatever—"

"Tiff, can we not talk about this?"

Tiffany's full, rose-colored lips formed a pout. "You have to be the *only* man I know who doesn't like to brag about his successes," she complained, while stepping closer. "So whatever will we talk about?" she suggestively whispered.

Alex grinned at the woman's tenacity, as his brilliant

turquoise gaze drifted over her head. His eyes locked on Topaz Emerson.

Of course, it would have been impossible to miss her entrance when she stood at the top of the short stairwell leading down into the first floor of the Limit. She looked incredible dressed in a sable lace tunic with a mock turtleneck. The garment's fitted shape outlined every alluring curve with its flounce cuffs that almost shielded her hands from view. The sheer lining beneath the tunic gave a man the impression that he was seeing more than he really was. The black matte jersey pants, however, left nothing to the imagination. They fit like a scandalously snug glove and were coordinated with a chic pair of black platform boots.

"Alex? Alex, did you hear me?" Tiffany cooed, her fingers toying with the lapel of his sandstone sport coat.

Alex's eyes were riveted across the room. "Every word," he absently replied.

"I want to give him this gift before I start mingling around," Topaz was telling Casey as she scanned the crowd for Goldie Sims. Her stare located Alex Rice instead.

He stood close to the bar not far from the entrance. Topaz smiled, but couldn't resist a glance toward the women snuggled so close to his side.

"Paz!"

The bellow shook Topaz from her spell. She headed down the stairs with Casey close behind.

Goldie Sims was highly gregarious and lovable. The fact that he was only twenty-nine years of age had not stopped his closest friends from labeling him with the name Grampa. He set everyone at ease the moment they met him.

"Come on, gimme a hug, girl!" Goldie ordered as he

extended his arms toward Topaz. She happily obliged and they stood in the embrace for several moments.

"Gramp, you remember Casey, right?" Topaz asked when Goldie finally saw fit to release her.

"'Sup, man?" Goldie greeted with an extended hand.

"All right," Casey replied, enclosing Goldie's hand in both of his.

"Can I have my present now?" Goldie asked, his dark eyes slyly appraising Topaz.

"I got it right here," she sang, holding up the festive-looking gift bag.

Goldie took the bag. "I'm sure it's cool," he said and set the package on the table behind them, "but I'd prefer a chance to dance with you."

Topaz laughed. "Goldie . . ." she sighed, fixing Casey with a smile as she was whisked away.

Casey took the opportunity to speak with several acquaintances he recognized in the crowd. His mingling led him to the bar, where he decided to indulge in a drink from the impressive stock of beverages. While waiting for the bartender to return with his scotch and water, Casey noticed a familiar face a few spaces down the counter. He experienced a moment of hesitation, then decided to approach the stern-looking gentleman.

"Excuse me?" Casey called, watching the man turn. "Alex Rice? I—I'm Casey Williams," he announced, extending his hand. "Your newest employee at the *Queen City Happening*," he quickly added.

Alex's stony expression softened a bit as he accepted Casey's handshake. "What's goin' on, man? It's good to have you on board."

"Thank you, sir."

"But never call me that."

Casey froze, but soon relaxed when Alex grinned. "I'll remember that."

Alex took another swallow of his whiskey. "How long you known Goldie?" he asked.

"Thanks," Casey said to the bartender as he accepted the drink. "I only know Goldie in passing. My friend Topaz invited me. I live across the street from her."

"Hmph, figures," Alex muttered, a tiny smile tugging at his mouth. "So when's your first day at the paper?" he asked instead, launching a brief conversation with Casey regarding the job.

The music filling the dim, casually chic club had taken on a slower tempo. Those occupying the dance floor had the chance to catch their breath by taking advantage of the affecting ballads.

"I didn't know you knew the owner of the *Queen City Happening*," Topaz said.

"Who? Lex?" Goldie responded, as they swayed to a Keith Sweat classic.

Topaz's amber eyes were focused across the room. "Mmm-hmm . . ." she confirmed.

"Known Lex since the paper ran that story on the Gems," Goldie explained, referring to the jazz band he managed.

"He's got a good paper on his hands. Did he start it on his own or with help from his wife, friends . . . ?" she probed, hoping Goldie wouldn't realize how deeply interested she was.

"Wife!" he blurted, laughter just below the surface of the word. "Uh-uh. Neva'!" he declared. "That brotha is definitely single, much to the dislike of at least twenty women I know."

"So he's a playa?"

"Big time."

Topaz rested her chin on Goldie's shoulder, her lips

curving into a pout. The vintage slow jam faded into another and the lights grew dimmer.

"What kind of party you tryin' to throw, Goldie?" Topaz teased, moving back to fix her friend with a playfully accusing stare.

Goldie was undaunted, his chubby face alive with mischief. "The success of *any* party depends on how relaxed the ladies are. I plan on leaving after my presents are open, and I don't plan on leaving alone."

Topaz threw back her head and laughed. She sobered when she heard Goldie speaking to someone behind her.

"No problem, man," he called before kissing Topaz's cheek and leaving her alone on the floor.

Confused, Topaz turned and found herself staring directly into Alexander Rice's turquoise eyes.

THREE

"Do you mind?" he asked, his big hands spread apart as an expectant look brightened his handsome face.

After a moment, Topaz blinked. "No, course not," she softly accepted, her amber gaze holding a slightly awed gleam as she studied his exceptional height and incredible features. The tailored sandstone jacket, matching trousers, and collarless eggshell shirt flattered his complexion as well as his build. When his arms encircled her waist and he pulled her against his massive frame, she could have swooned. She could only focus on the deliciously hypnotic fragrance of his cologne.

"I promise not to keep you from your date too long."

Topaz was lost in the mesmerizing effect of his eyes. A few seconds slipped by before she tuned in to his words.

"Casey," she stated, realizing to whom he was referring. "We're only friends. He lives across the street from me."

"I heard. He starts working for me tomorrow, you know?"

Topaz was nodding. "He told me. You're getting a really good guy and a talented one, too."

"That's what I like to hear."

"Anyway," Topaz sighed with a wave of her hand, "he

should be getting out of here soon. We probably won't even leave together."

"You don't even have a clue, do you?" Alex whispered, watching Topaz with a look of probing disbelief.

She tilted her head. "What do you mean?" she inquired with a soft laugh.

Alex wasn't opposed to sharing his observation. "Topaz, there's not a man in this place who wouldn't want you on his arm when he walks out of here," he explained, his expression changing when she blinked. "Not that I'm implying anything would happen or that you're that type of . . . woman," he quickly added.

She was smiling. "I understand now and I'm flattered by your compliment. It's just that . . ."

Alex's gorgeous stare narrowed. "What?" he prompted.

Shrugging slightly, Topaz let her gaze waver. "Guys don't, um . . . tend to compliment quite that way. Usually they beat around the bush with it."

His smile deepened as he laced his fingers at the small of her back. The distance between them closed. Topaz almost gasped, but masked the gesture with a phony cough.

"I have a nasty habit of speaking my mind," he softly confided. "Whether the opinion is good or bad really doesn't matter."

Topaz made a face. "Must be hard to keep friends with an outlook like that."

Alex responded with a quick shake of his head. "I don't care too much for dishonesty and I try not to be that way. It's taken me a long time, but I've managed to distance myself from people like that."

"Sounds like you had a rough time doing that," she noted, observing the stony look in his gaze.

"I did." The response was flat and final.

Topaz pressed her lips together and nodded, deciding it was a woman-related issue. "Well, for the record, I always try to be honest," she shared, deciding to keep the conversation alive. "But if I feel it'll be too hard for the person to handle, I won't say anything."

Alex obviously disagreed. "It's impossible for me to keep quiet if I have a problem with something."

Topaz noticed the hard look returning to his extraordinary eyes. "I hope I never get on *your* bad side."

"You?" he queried, his stare softening as it caressed her dark face.

Topaz swallowed past the lump that had suddenly lodged in her throat. Somehow she managed to keep her eyes locked with his, in spite of the affecting power behind his intense stare.

"You must have excellent control over your staff," she noted.

"Meaning?" he challenged, enjoying their conversation.

Topaz tapped her fingertips along the iron ridge of his biceps. "Being on your bad side isn't a place I'd want to be."

"Do I scare you?"

"No," she answered without hesitation. Although the raw power the man exuded *did* send a shiver of . . . something through her body. "I *am* comforted by the fact that you like honesty, but I could see how you'd strike someone as . . . intimidating."

"Really?"

Topaz blinked. "Did I offend you?"

"Not at all," He responded with a slow shrug. "I like everything you just said."

"And he has a sadistic streak!" Topaz teased, her laughter rushing to the surface.

Alex joined in. "It helps for people to view you that way sometimes."

She closed her eyes. "Mmm . . . I know what you mean. I wish I could wield that sort of power on my guys every now and then."

Alex allowed his fingers to sample the softness of a heavy curl that dangled against her waist. "You have any women working for you?" he asked, though he couldn't have cared less. In truth, he was more involved with the feel of her body swaying against his. Clearly she was in fantastic shape—every limb was perfectly toned. Still, there was a supple quality that was purely feminine—purely intoxicating.

"I've tried getting women into the shop for a long time, but I haven't had any luck yet," she was saying. After a while, the lack of response caused her to clear her throat and take stock of their snug embrace.

"What's it like working around so many men?" Alex asked, now all ten fingers playing in her heavy, curled tresses. "Do you have a rough time in what's long been thought of as a man's business?"

Topaz's laughter was honest and unrestrained. "Actually, a lot of my headache has come from other women. Especially my mother, aunts, and such. Men treat me with a lot of respect. But then," she sighed, tilting her head back to fix Alex with an exasperated look, "I have to deal with younger women who don't like the fact that *my* business puts me in such frequent contact with so many men. Namely, *their* boyfriends."

"Uh-oh."

"Mmm . . . it's made having female friends a definite problem."

Alex's strong fingers flexed against the fabric of her top. He fought the urge to smooth the sadness from her face. Then he fixed her with a devilish smile. "From what I hear, having male friends ain't so bad."

Topaz giggled. "How would you know that?" she remarked, and their laughter heightened. "Hmph, I have to agree with you, though. Women are far too petty sometimes. Things that would break up a friendship between two women could be overlooked in a platonic relationship."

"Mmm . . . is that why you and Simon are still . . . close?"

Topaz blinked, her uncommon gaze narrowing. "What do you know about Simon?" she whispered.

For a second or two, Alex was so absorbed by her gaze, he hesitated with his response. "I know you were about to marry him," he finally confided.

Topaz wasn't angry that he knew, but she was more than a little curious. "Did our relationship come up in a conversation or something?"

"I asked about it after seeing you with him at De's party."

"Why?"

"Because I didn't want to step on his toes when I asked you out."

The cool admission sent Topaz's heart slamming against her chest. She could only pray that he couldn't feel it. Her stare faltered only a moment before she met his gaze. "Would it have mattered if you *were* stepping on his toes?"

"No."

"All right, all right, everybody! Give it up for the Jazz Scene!"

The boisterous instructions from the club's DJ intruded on the moment. Alex and Topaz joined the rest of the crowd in applauding the five-piece jazz band that had been performing live sets during the party.

"Sit with me?" Alex was asking, his hand brushing her hip as he spoke.

Topaz accepted with a short nod and hooked her index finger around his pinkie as she followed his lead from the establishment's lower level.

* * *

"Well, I have to say that I hope I won't be stepping on any toes by accepting an invitation from you," she was saying when they were seated at a small corner balcony table overlooking the dance floor.

"Meaning?" Alex prompted, reclining against the high-backed chair as he crossed his long legs at the ankles.

"Goldie told me what a playa you are."

Alex's laughter displayed a striking set of dimples. "Me? I promise you that's not true," he laughingly clarified.

Topaz propped her chin against the back of her hand. "Really?" she challenged.

He was shaking his head. "I'm way too busy to be out there like that."

"I don't believe you," she countered, her teasing tone belying her seriousness.

Alex sobered and folded his arms across his broad chest. "Why not?" he questioned, fixing her with a steady look.

Topaz let her eyes drift toward the champagne table-cloth. She felt too uncomfortable to tell Alex that he was far too gorgeous to be a social hermit. She shrugged, hoping the gesture would suffice as enough of an answer.

"Does that mean you won't go out with me?" he asked, while signaling an approaching waiter.

Topaz smiled and shifted in her seat. "You'll never know until you ask me."

"I'm asking."

"Yes, sir?"

Exchanging smiles, Alex and Topaz called a halt to their banter and placed drink orders with the waiter.

"Well?" he prompted, once the stout young man had moved on.

"It depends on what you have in mind," she replied.

Before Alex could enlighten her, they were interrupted again. This time, two short, handsome, smiling gentlemen stepped up to clap his shoulder.

"What's goin' on?" Alex laughed as he stood to greet Horace White and Stan Webster.

"Not a damn thing," Horace remarked, shaking hands with Alex, while Stan moved to kiss Topaz's cheek.

"Baby, you mind if we steal this brotha for a minute?" Stan asked Topaz, while his partner hugged her.

"Nah, but why don't y'all just stay here? I have a few people I need to speak to anyway," she was saying.

Horace and Stan took their places at the small table. When they looked up to find Alex watching them stonily, they exchanged knowing smiles.

"Sorry for the intrusion, kid," Stan said as he grinned.

Alex only waved. "I just can't get over how many of my boys know this woman and I only met her yesterday."

Horace shrugged. "Hell, man, you been caught up with that paper and stuff, you know?"

The reminder brought a tight grimace to Alex's mouth. "So what's up?" he asked, clenching a fist in hopes of warding off unwelcome thoughts.

The partners turned serious. "We had an interesting conversation 'bout two weeks ago," Stan explained, "with a guy who owns one of the other businesses on the block."

"The brotha had dropped a few hints that he was thinkin' of sellin' despite the fact that business was good," Horace continued. "Our side of town is a prime spot and the man was only in business lil' over six months."

Alex appeared disinterested. "What's strange about that? Maybe after six months he'd already grown tired of the grind."

"A week after that conversation, he sold," Stan announced. "Then we talked to another guy on the block who was speakin' the same stuff."

"He sold the following week," Horace explained. "And we'd just attended a party for him to celebrate his fortieth year in the family business."

Stan leaned forward. "The place had been passed down to all the firstborns or somethin'," he saw fit to add.

Alex shrugged. "I still don't see what's so strange. Maybe those cats got offers they couldn't refuse."

"We don't buy it," Horace and Stan said in unison.

"Look, Xan," Horace called, tapping on the table, "some fool's been sniffin' around our offices, askin' our people all kinds of crap. It's all been real laid-back, nothin' too involved. They just recently approached us."

Alex's easy expression slowly adopted its usually guarded appearance. "Why y'all comin' to me with this?"

"You know why."

"I hope not," Alex retorted, his gaze shifting out across the room.

Horace and Stan exchanged uneasy looks.

"Xan," Stan called, waiting for Alex to look his way, "we believe our neighbors were forced to sell. When we set a time to meet with this guy, we want you there so he knows he ain't dealin' with a couple of saps."

Alex muttered a fierce obscenity, clearly disapproving of his friend's reasoning. "Rice Securities is no more. I don't resort to that heavy crap no more. Y'all know that."

"We know that, man. We know," Horace soothed, stretching his hands across the table in a pleading gesture. "You don't have to say a damn thing. We just want you there for intimidation purposes."

Alex couldn't help but laugh then, his sour mood suddenly lightening. He groaned, massaging his temple while shaking his head. "Just tell me when you need me there, all right?"

The partners grinned broadly as they stood. Both

shook hands with Alex and promised they would be in touch when they knew more.

"You think we should tell Topaz about this?" Horace asked when they were leaving the table.

Stan thought it over, then shook his head. "I really don't think it's gonna be necessary once Marlon Sanders meets us."

Horace glanced across his shoulder. "Hmph, once he meets Alex Rice," he clarified.

At his table, Alex was thinking about the way he was still perceived—even by his closest friends. His infamous background began with a job he'd acquired as a bouncer at the age of nineteen. Soon, he began to accompany the club's owner on matters pertaining to the man's side business, which was loan sharking. Alex's new responsibilities included collecting on his boss's accounts.

Alex groaned as his mind clouded with memories of broken arms, legs, hands, etc. He had been determined, doggedly so, to push those acts as far from the forefront of his mind as possible. He hated the person—the animal—he had been in those days. The only payoff—if it could be called that—was the respect. People would always respect him. Of course, with the wisdom that comes with age, he now wondered if the respect people held for him was actually fear.

A throat being cleared nearby pulled him back into the present. He found Topaz standing next to the table Beside her was the waiter with their drinks.

"Let me get that," he sighed, reaching into his pocket for a few bills, which he placed on the waiter's square tray.

"Thank you, sir," the young man gushed, knowing the wad of bills meant a hefty tip was included. After setting the drinks down he bade them a good evening and headed off.

"You okay?" Topaz asked once they were alone. She'd reclaimed her seat and leaned back to watch him closely. "Horace and Stan didn't say anything to get on your bad side, did they?" she teased.

Alex only chuckled.

"Things looked pretty serious over here a minute ago."

This time, Alex shrugged. "If you know Horace and Stan, then you know how uptight they can be. Sometimes it wears off on you."

Topaz raised her hand. "Say no more. I know what you mean."

"Good," he said, taking a sip of the scotch and soda he'd ordered. "Plus, I rather discuss whether or not you're going out with me."

Topaz followed the line of her index finger as she traced the rim of her margarita glass with a nail. "If you recall, we never got around to discussing what you had in mind."

Alex grinned. "It's gotta be that good, huh?"

"Well, nothing *too* spectacular," Topaz cautioned with a wave of her hand. "Your usual first date stuff will suffice."

"Nah, I feel like I need to impress you."

"Why?"

Alex knew he wouldn't answer that. Not yet. "You like pool?" he asked instead, coolly dismissing the previous question.

Topaz wrinkled her nose. "It's not one of my best games, but I can hold my own."

Alex reached for his drink. "A new billiards place just opened up downtown. Supposed to have a good bar and grill. Care to join me?"

"Sounds like fun. When?"

"Good question," Alex responded with a grimace. "I've

got a dinner meeting tomorrow," he recalled, taking a sip of his drink. "What about the night after that?"

"Sounds perfect," Topaz accepted with a smile, even as her expression grew a bit wary. "I think I've made enough of an appearance at this thing," she decided.

"Ready to go?"

"Mmm . . ."

Alex scanned the crowd. "You seen Casey?"

"Actually that's who I went to talk to while you were with Horace and Stan," she explained. "He's already hooked up with somebody and they're going out for drinks."

"So he's just leaving?" Alex whispered, not bothering to mask his disapproval.

Topaz waved her hand. "It was my idea. I told him to go. Someone already offered to take me home anyway."

"Tell him to forget it."

"'Scuse me?"

"I'll take you home," Alex decided, already moving to stand.

"Alex, you don't have to."

"I know I don't have to," he acknowledged, tossing a few bills to the table. "Are you ready?"

Topaz sighed and stood as well. "I guess I'll go tell Goldie I have another ride."

Alex rolled his eyes. "Uh-oh, we gotta make the birthday boy cry."

Topaz's laughter turned many heads.

FOUR

Top E Towing and Mechanical was in its usual noisy, bustling state. The establishment stayed busy from open to close, much to the satisfaction of its owner and employees. The garage was a veritable hodgepodge of cultural and social activity. Customers who opted to wait for their cars to be serviced collected in the main lobby before a wide-screen TV. The proprietor of the establishment believed in keeping her patrons comfortable—there was always fresh coffee and Krispy Kreme donuts in the morning or chips and sodas for the afternoon crowd. Free of charge, of course. The air was filled with the meshing of pulsing rap music, smoother R&B tunes, passionate conversations, laughter, and the unmistakable clanging of heavy machinery.

"Is this gonna be a short job, guys?" Topaz queried as she peeked beneath the hood of her Corvette. "Or have I let it go too long?" she asked, looking up.

Darryl Groves and Stacy Merchants wiped the sweat from their brows in a syncopated fashion.

"We can get you rollin' in a couple of days, Paz," Stacy promised his boss.

"Yeah, two or three days," Darryl concurred. "We found a few things we wanna spruce up for ya."

"Spruce up?" Topaz parroted, her bright gaze filling with playful doubt as she eyed the two gorgeous giants. "Spruce up," she repeated, stepping away from her car. "I'm just happy I don't have to pay for this."

"Aw, Paz, you know we treat you right," Stacy chimed.

"Y'all just don't do too much *sprucing up* for your paying customers without their knowledge," she advised.

The dark hulks both raised their hands in the air as though they were taking oaths. "We never scam our customers," they simultaneously recited.

Topaz shook her head. "I don't even want to know," she groaned.

The threesome stood talking and laughing as a man strolled into the garage. It wasn't the fact that he looked like a salesman that set everyone on edge. It was the superior way he observed his surroundings and his obvious disregard for the countless signs that prohibited anyone other than Top E Towing and Mechanical personnel from being in the garage area. Topaz, Stacy, and Darryl eyed his short-sleeved olive-green dress shirt and the trousers that fit just a bit too snug.

When the man looked over at the silent trio, his gaze appraised Topaz in her low-rise jeans and long-sleeved shirt. Then he nodded toward Darryl and Stacy.

"Morning, gentlemen."

Darryl and Stacy mimicked the nod. "Morning," they replied.

"Looks like business is good, gentlemen."

Darryl glanced at Topaz. This had happened more than once—people were always surprised to discover the garage was owned by a woman. When Stacy looked over as well, Topaz smiled and turned away—a signal to the guys that they should continue the charade.

"Business is good. Business is real good," Darryl announced, hooking his thumbs around his overall suspenders.

"I been lookin' to start a business on this end, but the street seems filled up."

"Yeah, this is a real popular area," Stacy informed him.

"Y'all know anybody around who might be interested in selling?"

"There were two cats you might've tried, but they already sold," Darryl shared, propping his huge frame on the edge of Topaz's Corvette.

The slender, dark-complexioned man scratched his neck while eyeing the garage. "You two ever think about selling?"

"Uh-uh!"

"No way!" Stacy agreed with Darryl's boisterous response. "This place is a gold mine, too lucrative to sell out."

"Hell yeah, we got a great location, great customers, best mechanics in town," Darryl boasted. "No way we'd consider lettin' go of our place."

Topaz smiled and lowered her gaze to the oil-stained concrete. She never tired of listening to Darryl and Stacy play the roles of the proud proprietors. She focused in on the aspiring entrepreneur. Something about him heightened her suspicions and she knew he wasn't what he appeared to be.

"Think of the money y'all could get for this place. The fact that business is good now would only play in your favor."

"We know what you sayin', man, but sellin' is somethin' we ain't interested in," Stacy decided.

"At all," Darryl confirmed.

The slim man raised his hands while shrugging. "I understand. Hell, I wouldn't wanna let go of a place like this either."

"Good luck to you," Darryl called, easing off the car to follow behind Stacy.

"You brothas have a good one," the man called as he strolled out as leisurely as he'd arrived.

"Whatcha thinkin', Paz?" Darryl asked, as he continued to observe the man's departing figure.

Topaz shook her head. "I'm not sure yet."

"Think it could be Alfred Majors usin' a different approach?" Stacy asked.

Topaz folded her arms across her chest and grimaced. "Alfred only wants to go into business with me, he doesn't want me to sell."

"What you want us to do next time he shows up?" Stacy asked as he and Darryl turned away from the garage door opening.

"The next time he comes here, send him into my office."

"Earth to Alex . . . come in please . . ." Darby Cooper called out to her boss. She'd been standing in his office for almost three minutes.

Alex finally looked up to find his assistant towering over his desk. "What?" he whispered, the distant look in his light eyes a perfect match to his voice.

Darby's smirk was more of a full-blown grin. "What's her name?" she pried.

Alex's double-dimpled smile was like a ray of sun when he saw fit to use it. The dimples creased his cheeks and his incredible eyes crinkled at the corners in the most adoring fashion.

"Stop watchin' all them soaps, girl. Ain't nothin' goin' on here," he informed her.

"Whateva," Darby drawled, intentionally stressing her rich northern accent while she waved her hand around her head. "I always know when there's a new lady on the scene. What I don't know is if she's the one who'll help you shed that brooding serious image of yours."

"Darby—"

"One woman to make you more mellow," she continued, "to make you want to enjoy life."

"Mmm . . . and one to make me forget about work and all the other mess I have to do," Alex grumbled, the looming workload slowly souring his mind.

Sadly, his obligations to the *Queen City Happening* wasn't the only reason to dissuade him from becoming too attached. The soft mutter of familiar warnings began to surface, and he shook his head to ward off the memories they evoked.

"Anyway," Darby sighed, waving her hand as she scanned the clipboard she carried, "the budget meeting's in fifteen minutes and that new reporter will be joining us this morning."

"New reporter," Alex stated in a blank tone. His attention was already focused on the agenda Darby handed him.

"Casey Williams."

Alex was at ease again. Not from the mention of Casey Williams's name, but from the memories of Goldie Sims's birthday and Topaz Emerson. Again, Alex smiled as her image filled his head. She was so lovely and it was definitely more than skin deep. Clearly, her horde of admirers thought so too, Alex decided, recalling how many of his friends were acquainted with her. Their upcoming date leaped to the forefront of his mind then. He could only hope the time spent together wouldn't cause him to become even more attached to the chocolate-dipped beauty.

One by one, the reporters of the *Queen City Happening* began to trickle into the publisher's office. Under the instruction of Clifton Knowles, the daily budget meeting usually commenced at 10:00 A.M. With Alex in charge, the meetings had been pushed all the way to eleven thirty.

The writing team comprised seven segments: movies, music, the arts, business, sports, food, and news. One reporter with a staff of four headed each section.

"All right, everybody, let's get to it!" Alex called over the mix of conversation that stirred as more people entered the office. "Good morning," he greeted, nodding as the team returned the sentiment. "Before we get started today, I'd like you all to join me in welcoming our newest writer. He'll be working with Dominic Morris and the rest of the business team—Casey Williams."

The group clapped to welcome Casey, then began to cheer for Dominic, who'd constantly complained about being understaffed.

"Thank you all," Casey was saying as he waved to the group from his place at the long oval table. "I hope you all will find me a worthy addition to this fine team you have here."

"Aw, he's just bein' humble, y'all," Dominic revealed, fixing Casey with a sly grin. "He's already been burnin' our ears with ideas."

Alex leaned back in the navy swivel chair near the head of the table. "Care to share any with us, man?" he asked, spreading his hands as he spoke.

Casey hesitated only a moment, before leaning forward to share what he considered to be his strongest pitch. "I had an idea for a new subsection where we'll feature local African-American businesses and the owners."

The group listened intently as Casey explained his brainstorm. Clearly, they were all impressed. Even Alex was riveted on the man's proposal, his stare focused and narrowed as he jotted notes pertaining to the conversation at hand.

"What types of businesses do you have in mind for this feature?"

Casey cleared his throat and turned to face his boss. "Well, all kinds, Mr.—uh, Alex," he quickly corrected when the man's stare narrowed. "Everything from hair salons to investment counselors. If you give us the green light with the project, I'd like our first story to profile the business of a lady we both know—Topaz Emerson."

"Who's she?" someone asked.

Alex smiled, his gaze lowering to the table. "Finally someone who *doesn't* know her," he muttered.

"She owns a very successful garage and towing service on Briarcliff," Casey shared.

Sandra Morgan, the head music reporter, whistled. "Lady mechanic? Very impressive."

"She is," Casey confirmed. "And so is her business," he added, with a nod toward his other colleagues.

"Well, I already told Case I thought it was a good idea," Dominic announced in a definite tone.

"So do I," Alex concurred, pointing his pen in Casey's direction. "It's a damn good idea and I want you on this ASAP."

Casey nodded, barely able to contain his grin. "Yes, sir."

"But tonight, you join us at this City Council dinner."

Casey couldn't mask his confusion. "City Council, sir?"

"They're playin' around with an idea similar to the one you have. They're wanting to get some sort of charity ball going centered on an awards banquet featuring the city's entrepreneurs."

"Is that right?" Casey sighed, a rush of pride surging through him just then.

"Mmm," Alex replied with a slow nod while leaning back in his chair. "Maybe you can come up with a few more ideas on how we can make this a collaborative effort between the *QC Happening* and the City Council?"

Casey was determined to tone down his eagerness. "Yes, sir," he said.

Alex knocked his fist against the table. "Good. All right, people, let's keep this meeting rollin'. What's up next?"

Forty-five minutes later, the group of reporters trickled out of the publisher's office. Only two remained, Dominic Morris and Rossell Stanley.

"A tip?"

"Lex, man, we don't even know if the damn thing's worth investigating," Dominic sighed as he perched on the edge of the conference table.

Alex removed his heather gray woven sport coat and tossed it to an armchair. "Tell me about it," he said.

Dominic raised his hand toward Rossell.

"About a week ago, I got a call about two businesses that had been sold on Briarcliff," she began, smoothing the sage-green skirt beneath her as she took a seat on one of the armchairs before the desk. "The caller said the owners had been forced to sell."

Alex frowned and began to swivel his chair to and fro. His conversation with Horace White and Stanley Webster immediately surfaced.

"I know it could be a long shot, but it sounded like something we should at least check out," Rossell finished.

"The call came from a family member of one of the owners," Dominic supplied. "They flat-out confirmed that somebody forced their brother to sell."

"They know who's doing the supposed *forcing*?"

Rossell glanced at Dominic. "They have no idea," she said. "The owner was extremely tight-lipped about the whole deal—especially with his family. They *do* know that he got quite a bundle for his business, though."

Alex rolled his eyes. "Small consolation when you lose your life's work," he grumbled, gazing out at the view of downtown Charlotte. Suddenly, he turned to face his two reporters. "Get on it," he ordered.

"I just finished talking with Darryl and Stacy about this very thing. If he's a regular customer, you want him to stay regular. Fix the problem and *suggest* other improvements."

"But, Paz—"

"*Don't* go in fixing things without discussing it with your customer first."

Jacques Harris pressed his lips together and acknowledged his boss's firm advice. "The fool treats that Testarossa like crap," he couldn't help but remark.

Topaz pressed her forehead against her palm and smiled.

"He don't replace the wiper fluid, transmission fluid's always low, glops of mud underneath the body, and I bet the nigga don't even check the oil."

"So you're upset, why?" Topaz challenged, shrugging as Jacques pinned her with his deep-set chocolate gaze. "Sweetie, you *are* getting paid each and *every* time he pulls this stuff."

"But the car, Topaz . . ." Jacques moaned, shoving one hand through his thick Afro. "People like him shouldn't have cars like that."

"Jacques, listen, I appreciate your passion. I'm proud to have a mechanic like you on my staff, but you've gotta take a step back from it, okay? Why don't you try to *lightly* suggest to Mark the things you've noticed *before* you fix them? Open up the lines of communication just a little bit more," Topaz advised, spreading her hands apart for emphasis. "That just might get you a lot further with this guy."

Still exasperated, but somewhat pacified, Jacques nodded. "Thanks, Topaz," he sighed, then left the spacious back office.

Topaz was chuckling softly when the phone rang. "Top E Towing and Mechanical," she greeted.

"Hey, girl, how about dinner?"

"Simon?" Topaz blurted, surprised to hear the man's voice. "All right, now I'm suspicious. First the party and now a dinner invitation? What's up?"

Simon uttered an overexaggerated sigh, pretending to be offended. "I don't see the problem with one friend asking another one out to dinner. You got plans?"

"I guess I do. With you."

"That's what I wanted to hear. Pick you up at seven, all right?"

"All right. Uh, Simon?"

"Mmm-hmm?"

"You okay?"

Silence met the question. "Why?" he finally replied.

Topaz shrugged, tapping her fingers on her glass-topped desk. "Just wondering if there was anything wrong. You sound . . . funny."

"Funny, huh? I should take offence to that."

"Sorry."

"Baby, I'm fine. Okay?"

"If you say so," Topaz conceded, deciding to find out more during dinner. "See you later."

The connection broke and less than a minute passed before the phone rang again.

"Grand Central around here," Topaz whispered as she pulled the receiver off its hook. "Top E Towing and Mechanical," she greeted.

"Hey, girl."

"Well, hello," Topaz drawled, smiling at the light tone of Casey Williams's voice. "I haven't talked to you since we separated at Goldie's. So. How was the after party?" she slyly inquired.

"Hmph, obviously not *that* great. I made it to work on time," Casey lamented.

Topaz laughed. "Mmm . . . your lady friend wasn't up for overnight company in the middle of the week, I take it?"

"Nah, and neither was her man."

"Ouch."

"Don't worry 'bout it. Today more than made up for my night."

Topaz toyed with one of her pigtails. "Should I take that to mean that you're gonna be happy working for the *Queen City Happening*?"

"You should."

"So tell me about it."

"Well, actually, it had a lot to do with you."

"Me!" Topaz shrieked, bolting up in her mauve suede desk chair.

Casey was laughing as he spoke. "I had an idea for a new section featuring local businesses and entrepreneurs. It was a hit and our first story will feature Top E Towing and Mechanical and its beautiful proprietor— Topaz Emerson."

"Me?" Topaz sighed, a bit calmer this time. "I can't believe y'all would consider me."

"Why not? You're perfect," Casey assured her. "Smart, gorgeous lady makin' a killing in a, quote, 'man's business'? Girl, people are gonna eat that mess up," he predicted.

Topaz felt like she was being caught up in a whirlwind. "Damn, you just went in there and started runnin' things?" she asked, complimenting her friend.

Casey experienced a twinge of modesty. "I don't know 'bout all that, *but* my boss *did* invite me to a high-powered dinner meeting with the City Council tonight."

"Go on, Casey!" Topaz cheered.

"Yeah, it seems they had an idea that might work hand in hand with what I'm tryin' to do at the paper."

"I'm so proud of you," Topaz whispered, genuinely happy and pleased by the excitement she heard in Casey's voice. "So when is this entrepreneur's interview supposed to take place?" she asked.

"Well, Alex told me to get right on it, so . . . if you're free this weekend, we can set somethin' up."

Topaz shrugged. "Sounds good. Why don't we have breakfast at my house? Saturday morning?"

"See ya then," Casey accepted. "Look, I gotta get up outta here. I'll holla atcha."

After the call, Topaz allowed her thought to drift toward Alex Rice. She frowned when her heart actually fluttered as thoughts of their pending date came to mind.

"What's wrong with me?" she whispered. She knew far too many men to have this one make her feel . . . giddy. What was it about him? True, undeniably sexy and gorgeous were relevant arguments, but there had to be more. Perhaps, it was that quiet, unleashed power that was slowly drawing her in.

Alex Rice reminded Topaz of a lion at ease, but ready to pounce on demand. The way he watched her so intently, it was as if he were looking right into her soul.

"Stop it, Paz," she softly warned herself.

The phone rang once again and she celebrated the intrusion on her thoughts.

"Top E Towing and Mechanical," she greeted, her voice unconsciously lazy and seductive.

"You make me want to bring my car right over."

Topaz laughed when she heard Alex's remark. "Please do," she urged, "I could always use the business."

"With you as the spokesperson, I doubt you'd have any problems getting business."

Brief hesitation. "Thank you," Topaz whispered, knowing the shiver tickling her spine had resulted from his words. "So, um, I heard from Casey," she shared, eager to redirect the path of the conversation.

"I'm sure I can guess what the conversation was about."

"I'm sure you can. I was very surprised when he told me about it."

"Hmph. I don't know why. You know, you're unique."

"Stop before you give me a big head. Anyway, I'm sure you didn't call just to flatter me."

Alex stifled his response, wanting to tell her how easy she was to flatter. "I was actually calling about our date," he told her instead.

Topaz seemed to deflate a little. She wondered if he was about to cancel and couldn't stop the disappointment she felt.

"I wanted to know if you'd like to have dinner after we play pool."

"Dinner? Well, I thought that was the idea."

"I didn't like the thought of taking you to eat at a bar."

"Alex, it's fine," Topaz sighed. "Besides, I heard the food *and* the atmosphere were very nice."

"I don't like it."

Topaz snapped her fingers. "Damn, and I had my heart set on a burger."

"You can still have it."

"Oh? You know a better place?"

"Mmm-hmm. My Place."

Silence.

"Oh," Topaz replied after a while; virtually impossible, since her heart was still caught in her throat. "Umm . . ."

"Is that okay?"

Topaz twisted the end of her pigtail with shaking

fingers. "Alex . . . I don't know . . ." she breathed, feeling her cheeks flush with heat. She thought Alex was incredible—*more* than incredible. Still, the idea of spending an entire evening at his home unnerved her.

"Well, I guess we can go somewhere else," he was saying. "I've never eaten there, but I'd heard they have some pretty decent food."

Topaz pressed her fingers to her forehead. "Um . . . are you talking about the *restaurant* My Place?" she asked, frowning just a little.

"Yeah, what'd you—oh," Alex whispered before a round of soft chuckles erupted from his throat.

"What?" Topaz whined.

"Love, as much as I'd like to have you at my house, I wouldn't put you on the spot like that. Especially when we just met."

Topaz could only smile.

"So, tomorrow night?" he proposed.

"Tomorrow night," she accepted.

Josie Sharp raced around her quaint business district apartment. Her arms were filled with clothes. The City Council committee's dinner with Alex Rice was that evening and she'd been unable to choose an outfit for the date.

"Josie, girl, this is *not* a date," she softly reminded herself, deciding against the long border-striped wrap skirt and coordinating sweater set. "But that doesn't mean I can't look my best," she added, tossing a short chic dark tweed skirt and a curve-hugging cobalt turtleneck to the bed.

"Perfect," she decided, just as the phone rang. DeAndra Rice was on the other end of the line.

"How are you, Dee-Dee?"

DeAndra replied with an exaggerated groan, "Busy

beyond belief trying to plan this benefit for the African Heritage Preservation Society."

"Oh yeah, I forgot you were in charge of that this year."

"Mmm, and it's proving to be one large headache."

Josie laughed, deciding against the turtleneck sweater she'd chosen. "This can't be my old friend Dee-Dee Rice complaining about planning a party."

DeAndra responded with her usual staid laugh. "There's a first time for everything, dear. Anyway, I wanted to talk to you about getting Councilman Greene to attend the gathering."

"Councilman Greene?" Josie absently inquired as she tried to decide between a lovely V-neck floral-print sweater and a wine flutter-sleeved blouse.

"Mmm, I know he's voiced his opinion more than once regarding the importance of museums in the city. The benefit would serve as the perfect sounding board, and Councilman Greene's attendance may prompt the other guests to be more . . . generous with their donations."

"Well, you've certainly sold me," Josie drawled, choosing the flowing blouse and laying it next to a matching skirt. "I'll talk to him first thing in the morning," she sighed.

"Josie, is it my imagination, or did I call at a bad time?"

"What?"

"You sound distracted."

"Nooo," Josie whispered, stepping before the dresser mirror to fluff her curly locks, "I'm just getting ready for this dinner with Alex."

De's giggle resembled the delighted laughter of an evil witch. "Well, well, well, no wonder you sound so anxious. Trying to pick the right outfit for a date with my cousin."

"We're eating with the rest of the council, so it's not a date," Josie corrected.

"It could be," DeAndra countered. "Alex is a free man and he adores women. All *you* have to do is dazzle him."

"Dazzle him, huh?" Josie said, frowning at the way her natural curls hung in limp lifeless coils over her head. "Well, I could use some help, if you know what I mean."

DeAndra sucked her teeth. "Sweetheart, if you wanted me to fix you up, all you had to do was ask."

The two old friends dissolved into peals of laughter.

The Red Ribbon was an upscale steak house that boasted choice cuts shipped from its own farm in Salisbury, North Carolina. The restaurant resembled a lovely old farmhouse, while the parking lot was scattered with layers of crisp, golden hay.

Simon covered Topaz's hand where it rested on his arm. Pride shone on his handsome dark face as he escorted the statuesque beauty into the dining room. The seductive black jersey dress with its flaring, slitted sleeves and hem emphasized the stunning shapeliness of Topaz's long legs and lovely figure. Caramel and chocolate suede pumps added a few inches to her height, which surpassed Simon's.

"Why did I let you go?" he asked as the host escorted them to a table.

Topaz laughed. "You didn't have a choice," she sang. "Besides, we were just too different. You know that."

"But opposites attract, right?" Simon asked, while nudging her shoulder.

Topaz's expression took on a faraway look. "Sometimes, I think some things still have to jibe, though."

"You really know how to hurt me, sweet."

Topaz smiled at his solemn expression. "You know I still love you," she crooned and pressed a soft kiss to his cheek.

* * *

"This place has the best food. I don't know what to order," Simon was saying once they'd taken their seats and were scanning the menus. "I haven't tried their T-bones yet, but I'm hungry enough to try one tonight."

"Would you two care for drinks and appetizers?" the waitress inquired, holding her pen poised over a pad.

"Sam Adams for me. Topaz?"

"Oh, um, that's fine. I'll have the same."

"And bring us an Onion Blossom," Simon requested.

"Very well," the waitress said. "Are you ready to order your entrees?"

Simon's brows rose. "Topaz?"

"We'll wait. Thank you," Topaz decided, smiling up at the young redhead.

"Place isn't as crowded as I thought it'd be tonight," Simon was saying as he glanced around the dining room. "With fall coming on, people'll probably choose to stay in more. I know when it starts to get cold I—"

"Simon, stop. Stop for a minute, all right?"

"What's wrong?"

Topaz leaned closer to the table. "I'd like to talk about the way you sounded on the phone today."

Simon shrugged. "What about it?"

"Are you gonna tell me what had you so stressed?"

"I don't get how you figured I was stressed. We weren't even on the phone that long."

"Simon, please."

Simon smiled and raised his hands in defeat. "You still know me, don't you?"

"Very well."

"Hmph."

"Is it work related?" Topaz asked, tracing the rose pattern embroidered on the hunter-green tablecloth.

"There're some aggravations," he admitted, shifting in

the deep armchair he occupied. "It's just the same ol' same ol'. It did get me to thinkin' about you, though."

"I hope you're about to elaborate."

Simon reached out to capture one of her hands in his. "I just think you're too beautiful to let yourself get run down by a hectic business.

Topaz laughed. "My business is *not* hectic. I love it."

"But you don't take time to enjoy it," Simon argued, as he leaned back in his chair. "You should be chillin' on a beach somewhere."

"I took a vacation a couple of years ago."

Simon shook his head. "You just proved my point. You don't even realize how sad that sounds," he whispered, his dark gaze narrowing in its intensity. "Baby, you can stop tryin' so hard now, you know?"

"Meaning?"

"*Meaning*, you've proven that you can be a success runnin' a man's business. You should let this mess go now and enjoy yourself."

Topaz's smile tightened, her temper heating just as the waitress returned with their drinks and fried onions.

"Are we ready to place those orders now?" the young woman asked.

Topaz pushed her chair away from the table. "I need to visit the ladies' room," she decided, standing.

"Baby, you know I meant no harm," Simon called, realizing how upset she was.

Topaz could not manage a smile. "I think I need to go anyway. I'll be right back."

Simon watched her leave. His dark gaze was probing and uneasy.

Topaz felt much better after splashing a bit of cool water over her face. Unfortunately, she dreaded returning to her table. Smoothing one hand across her long, sleek braid, she headed back toward the dining room, thinking of Simon's words. Shaking her head, she dismissed his "advice."

Yes, some things still have to jibe, she told herself. Simon Whitley, like her parents and other family members, had never approved of her business. Regardless of her success, they had always deemed it beneath her—beneath them.

"Please give me strength to get through this dinner without slapping Simon senseless," she prayed.

Just inside the dining room doorway, Topaz scanned the sea of tables in search of Simon's. Instead, she glimpsed another familiar face and stared. Yes, it was Alex Rice seated at a nearby table with at least five other people. Thankful for an opportunity to delay returning to her own table, she decided to walk over and speak.

Casey Williams noticed his friend and neighbor as she approached. Alex's mouth curved into a soft smile as his vibrant stare raked Topaz's body with obvious desire. Josie Sharp, who had been eyeing Alex all evening, noticed the look. Intrigued, she turned to observe the woman who held his attention so thoroughly.

Casey was completing the introductions when Alex stood.

"How are you?" he asked.

"Fine," she replied, her tone soft and sweetly alluring.

"Join us, Topaz," Casey urged.

"Thanks, sweetie, but I'm here with someone," she explained, looking over at Alex in time to glimpse the narrowing of his gaze. The striking potency of the look sent her heart soaring to her throat.

"Well, um, I'd better be getting back," she decided, smiling shakily. "It was nice meeting you all," she said while squeezing Casey's shoulder. "Good night," she whispered to Alex, her lovely gaze lingering and unintentionally seductive.

Alex tugged at the edge of his maple suit vest as he resumed his seat. His eyes followed Topaz, until she had disappeared to the other side of the dining room.

FIVE

"We really want you to be there, girl."

"All this for an engagement party?"

"What can I say? My man wants to show me off."

"Well . . . Simon was just telling me I need to get away."

"Well . . . I'd say he's right. Besides, as one of the *few* female friends you have, I suggest you not disappoint me."

"Hush," Topaz ordered Cicely Grays.

"So? What do you say?" Cicely persisted.

Topaz leaned back in her desk chair. "An entire weekend, Cice?" she groaned.

"Girl, don't even try it," Cicely warned. "This party is gonna be so incredible. A weekend stay at Scott's uncle's cabin in the mountains?" she cried, referring to her fiancé. "It's gonna be quite the gathering," she boasted.

"Do I have to scrounge up a date for this thing?"

"We have it all planned. No pressure," Cicely assured her friend.

"Mmm-hmm. Why doesn't that set me at ease?"

"I have no idea, but you better get it together. We want everybody to have a fantastic time, and we mean *everybody*."

"All right, all right," Topaz sighed, jotting the date on her calendar. "It does sound nice."

"All right! That's what I wanted to hear before I got off the phone," Cicely blurted.

Topaz laughed. "So happy I could please."

"Seriously, though, girl. I gotta go. I'll talk to you soon, all right?"

"All right. I love you."

"Love you too."

Topaz settled the phone back on the receiver, just as the garage intercom buzzed.

"Yes?" she playfully drawled.

"This is Darryl. Your car is ready, lady."

"Yes!" Topaz hissed, clenching her fist.

"Does that mean you'd like to come and take it for a spin?"

Topaz had already grabbed her purse and sunglasses and was out the door.

"I thought this would take longer."

Darryl smiled as he watched Topaz peer over into the hood. "Other than a busted radiator hose, she's in prime shape. You take pretty good care of your car . . . for a woman," he teased.

Topaz grinned. "I know a good mechanic," she said, slamming down the hood. Her eyes focused on something across the street and she removed her sunglasses. "What the . . ."

Darryl followed the line of her gaze. "They been over there two hours already. Didn't you see 'em when you came in for work?"

"I came in from the back," Topaz absently responded, watching the three moving vans and over fifteen workers at the restaurant across the street. "What's goin' on over there?"

Darryl shrugged and set about wiping excess oil from his hands. "Guess Sallie's goin' out of business."

"Out of business? Why? I know things have got to be good—everybody in town stops by her place for lunch, and everybody who works on this block eats there."

"I ain't got a clue, honey," Darryl was saying as he glanced across the street with waning interest. "Probably just sick of the grind," he figured.

"I'm going to see what's up," Topaz decided, settling into her ride. "I hope I don't break down before I make it across the street," she joked, turning the key and revving the engine.

Darryl grinned, slapping the rear of the sleek white sports car. A second later, Topaz was zooming out of the garage.

At the opposite end of the block, Horace White and Stan Webster were preparing for a very important mid-morning meeting.

"More coffee, man?" Horace asked, holding the glass pot poised above the tray.

Alex waved his hand. "Do you two really need me to sit in on this thing?"

"My partner and I have a stinkin' suspicion that these people don't play by the rules."

"But forcing somebody out of business . . ." Alex trailed away, fixing Stan with a doubtful look.

"Aw, come on, man," Stan snapped, "you of all people should know a mess like this happens all the time."

Alex caught the true meaning of his friend's words and conceded with a nod. Of course, he took no offense since he could clearly recall the occasions on which he helped to "persuade" proprietors to relinquish their life's work.

In light of that, I'll stay. Maybe, in some way, I can make up for it all, Alex told himself, yet feared he would never come close to atoning for all the evil he'd done.

"Horace? Stan?"

"Go 'head, Jenny," Stan called to their executive assistant, who had buzzed in via speakerphone.

"Your eleven o'clock just arrived."

"Send him in, Jen," Horace instructed as he and Stan stood.

Alex remained seated in one of the armchairs near the rear of the office.

Marlon Sanders was a tall, solemn-looking fortyish gentleman with small green eyes and a thatch of dark hair that was styled to camouflage the baldness that was taking over his head. The conservative black suit and striped gray tie with polished wing tips lent to his staid persona.

"Mr. Sanders," Horace greeted.

Marlon extended his hand. "Mr. White. Mr. Webster. I'm glad we could finally agree on an amicable sit-down."

Stan nodded toward the back of the office. "Our associate," he announced, waving a hand toward Alex.

Marlon turned, his cool expression turning a bit apprehensive as he regarded the large man who had remained seated and offered no word or gesture of greeting. Marlon Sanders offered a shaky nod of acknowledgment before turning back to Horace and Stan. "Gentlemen, shall we get started?"

"This is only a meeting, Mr. Sanders," Horace reiterated as they took their places around the desk. "Don't take it to mean anything more."

Alex remained in the depths of Stan White's spacious office, lying in wait like a big cat. Meanwhile, Marlon Sanders presented an impressive offer to purchase the partners' firm.

"As you can see, gentlemen, we are quite interested in closing this deal," Marlon surmised.

"And just who is 'we'?" Horace inquired.

Marlon shook his head slightly. "I'm sorry?"

"This 'we' you keep referring to, Marlon. You've told my partner and me everything except who wants to buy our company."

"My people want to remain anonymous," Marlon coolly informed Horace.

The partners grinned and Stan placed his hand flat on the maple desktop.

"Well, until *your* people are prepared to step up to the forefront, we'll just reconfirm our decision to keep our little business," he said.

If possible, Marlon's solemn expression turned even more grim. "My people won't appreciate knowing I've wasted my time here."

"Too bad," Horace retorted.

Marlon returned his paperwork to the leather valise he carried and stood. "Are you gentlemen aware that almost half the businesses on this street have sold?"

Stan chuckled. "Well, Horace, at least we know everybody sold out to the same crooks."

Marlon stepped away from his chair so quickly, he knocked it to the floor. "The two of you *will* be hearing from me again. My people are quite intent on purchasing this property."

"That a threat?"

Marlon sneered. "Take it any way you like, Mr. White."

"That what you told Jarvis Cramer and Cooper Moss before they sold out?" Stan countered.

Marlon turned away. "Good day, gentlemen," he called over his shoulder, glancing toward the back of the office as he headed for the door.

"Whatcha thinkin', man?" Stan asked Alex once the office door slammed shut.

"Not sure," Alex said as he left his chair. "I think the man's just set on closin' a deal. I doubt there's cause for any real concern."

"You can't be sure, though?" Horace probed, watching Alex shrug.

"Sallie!" Topaz called. She parked her car and jumped out just in time to see Salamine Sentron leaving the restaurant.

Salamine waved, finishing her conversation with one of the movers. "Hey, girl!" she cried, rushing over to hug Topaz.

"Girl, what's this about you leaving? What's going on?"

Salamine managed a smile that didn't quite reach her exotic dark eyes. "The business was just taking up too much of my time," she explained with a small shrug. "I wanted more time with my family, anyway."

"Sallie, please, you don't even have kids," Topaz teased with a sly grin.

Salamine wasn't as amused. "Look, my parents are getting older, you know? I want to be with them more, all right?"

"All right," Topaz said, realizing how shaken the woman really was. "I *am* sorry to see you go, though. It's just that your place is always so busy. . . . Is there anything more going on here, Sallie?"

"No, Topaz, no," Sallie replied, her long black lashes fluttering as they spiked with moisture.

Topaz pulled her close. "You call if you ever need to talk, all right?" she ordered, feeling the woman nod against her shoulder.

Topaz made a move to end the hug, but Sallie held on. Then Topaz was certain. There was definitely more than family loyalties prompting Sallie into the sudden sale. Still, she didn't press for answers and, shortly, Sallie had walked away to continue her conversation with the movers.

Strolling back to her car, Topaz took a moment to survey the busy street. Her hands smoothed across the front of her hip-hugging, camel-colored pants while her gaze focused momentarily on each of the recently vacated businesses.

Something occurred to her then. Perhaps the time had come to do a little checking into the sudden sales. Before the day's end, she was determined to get some information on the real estate companies that had handled the sales.

Before Topaz could run with her ideas, a car horn caught her attention. Squinting out of curiosity, she recognized Alex when he exited the impressive navy blue Navigator. As usual, her heart beat double time in response to the undeniable sex appeal he exuded.

"What's up?" he softly greeted upon approach. His striking blue-green stare raked her frame encased in the curve-hugging flare-legged pants and chocolate cashmere sweater with its plunging V neckline. Chic black and camel pumps added several inches to her height and almost brought her to his eye level.

"You just eat?" Alex inquired, nodding toward the restaurant in the background.

Topaz pulled her eyes away from his to look across her shoulder. "No," she replied with a shake of her head, "I was just speaking to a friend. What are *you* doing here?" she asked, turning to face him again.

"Went by to catch up with Horace and Stan."

Topaz looked in the direction of White and Webster Consultants. "Yeah, I need to talk to them, too," she shared, then noticed the curiosity on Alex's face. "But first, I'm gonna take this bad boy out for a spin."

Alex grinned, looking over at the sleek Corvette. "You just get it back?"

Topaz giggled, rubbing her hands together. "I'm gonna see if my mechanic's worth what I'm paying him."

"Mind some company?" Alex requested, folding his arms across the front of the fitted black crew-neck T-shirt he sported with silver-gray trousers. He was more than a little interested to see her handle the impressive vehicle.

Topaz voiced no objections. She waved her sunglasses in the direction of the sleek, imposing SUV. "Park your ride and hop in," she instructed.

While Alex moved his vehicle, Topaz settled behind the wheel of her car. She couldn't resist observing his image through her rearview mirror.

"Damn it, Topaz," she hissed, closing her eyes against the reflection, "you've driven this car with a lot of guys. Don't get crazy over this one. No matter how hard your heart beats when you see him."

Alex tapped on the passenger window then, and she clicked the locks. "I hope you can fit," she teased, eyeing his long legs and powerfully athletic build.

"Funny," he replied, moving back the seat as far as it would go. Comfortable at last, he sent her a wink. "Let's see if you can move this thing," he taunted.

"Mmm-hmm," Topaz grunted, firing the ignition and revving the engine. "Sounds clean," she noted, referring to the vehicle. "Ride seems smooth," she added while merging into light traffic.

Alex made no comment. His unique stare was drawn to her toned thighs flexing beneath the fabric of her pants as she worked the clutch. He focused on her hand curved gracefully around the stick and smiled. Never before could he recall being aroused simply by the sight of a car being driven. Her fingers caressed the steering wheel and stickshift with the sweetness of a lover. The windows were down and the breeze lifted the tendrils of her hair left outside the loose chignon she wore.

Topaz reached a stoplight and took a moment to glance in Alex's direction. "You okay?" she asked, having caught his stare.

He nodded, his eyes never leaving her face. "Why?" he asked.

"I can get pretty wild behind the wheel," she warned, surging through the intersection once the light had changed.

"Don't worry. I'm enjoying everything about this ride."

Topaz cleared her throat. The sentence made her think his words held a far deeper meaning.

The drive continued in comfortable silence. Topaz drove outside the city in search of backcountry roads where she could really open the engine. Several times, she glanced over to observe her passenger's reaction to her stunt-driver-like skills. Alex seemed completely at ease. Taking advantage of the lack of conversation, she decided to replace the radio tunes with the CD. When the sounds of a vintage Redman track filled the speakers, Alex let out a yelp of surprise.

"What!" she called over the rapper's smooth metaphoric skills.

"Just when I think I can't be havin' a better time, you go and put on my music to drive to!"

Topaz laughed. "I'm glad you like the entertainment!"

"Sista after my own heart!"

Topaz squeezed the wheel tightly and tried not to become too heady over the sentiment. The drive ended a few acres outside a huge farm. Shutting down the engine, Topaz left the car, taking her cell phone with her.

"Top E Towing and Mechanical."

"Hey, James, put Darryl on the phone, will you?" Topaz asked, smiling as she waited for the connection.

"This is Darryl."

"Broken down out here in the middle of nowhere! Darryl, when I get back to the shop, I'm gonna—"

"Wait a minute, what happened? I know me and Stacy came correct on that job and—"

Topaz began to laugh, bringing a halt to Darryl's defense.

"If you wasn't my boss, I'd have to kill you," he calmly shared.

"I'm fine and the car is great. Y'all did a real good job."

"Thank you," Darryl indignantly replied.

"Tell everybody I'll be back soon," Topaz instructed, laughing again before she ended the call.

"Time to head back?" Alex asked as he leaned against the hood.

"Not for a while," she said, waiting to hear if he'd suggest other plans.

Alex looked behind him, studying the car momentarily. "Mind letting me behind the wheel?"

Topaz smiled and waved her hands. "Be my guest," she urged, already walking around to the passenger side.

Inside the car, they simultaneously readjusted their seats.

"Can I fit?" Alex drawled, recalling her earlier taunt. "You're almost as tall as I am."

Topaz rolled her eyes. "Please, *you're* seeing me in these high heels. I'm nowhere *near* your league."

Alex's stare scanned her long legs—unconscious of how intently he watched her. When she shifted beneath his gaze, he grinned and turned his attention to the car.

"Oh, I love this area!" Topaz cried sometime later.

Alex had taken the ride even farther. The remote housing development was home to many of the city's football and basketball players—not to mention other prominent figures in the Charlotte area.

"Sometimes I drive by the outskirts just to catch a glimpse of the houses," Topaz said.

"You've never seen any up close?"

"Only at night, if I attend a party out here."

Alex nodded. "Well, it's even nicer during the day," he said as they zoomed toward the gated community.

Topaz was very much like a little kid as she pointed, oohed, and aahed at the breathtaking mansions. When Alex parked the car in the cobblestone drive of one of the houses, Topaz grew quiet.

"Don't tell me you know who lives here," she whispered when he opened the passenger-side door and helped her from the car.

Alex glanced at the elegant, white brick mansion and shrugged. "Actually, I know the guy pretty well, since he's me."

Stunned, Topaz regarded the dwelling with increased interest. "I had no idea the newspaper business paid so well."

The teasing remark removed the softness from Alex's gaze. Topaz could see something rigid and guarded take its place in the bluish depths of his eyes.

"Would you like to come in?" he invited, having quickly masked the cold look he'd harbored. "I only stopped because we were close by," he explained. "If you feel uncomfortable—"

"Not at all," Topaz interrupted. Though pleased by his consideration, she wasn't about to pass on an opportunity to tour the incredible house.

Alex watched her bounce ahead of him. His extraordinary stare took on something tender and probing as he followed her across the drive.

"This is so incredible," Topaz breathed much later as she stood on a huge terrace overlooking the back lawn. The structure branched off from the kitchen and was furnished with a square glass-topped dining table and matching cushioned oak-backed chairs. Chaise longues were situated in cozy corners with huge umbrellas providing shade, while tall leafy ficus trees hovered nearby.

"Thank you," Alex replied for what had to be the twentieth time. He handed her a glass of lemon tea, then took in the view as well.

"I suppose a place like this comes in handy when you throw those wild weekend parties, huh?" she teased.

Alex chuckled. "I wouldn't know," he told her, smoothing one hand across his clefted chin. "I leave that stuff to everybody else. I like my privacy too much."

Topaz's gaze faltered and she sighed, setting down her glass. "Alex, I, um, I'm sorry if I implied something dishonest when I talked about the news business paying well. I didn't mean to offend you."

For a moment, Alex watched her inquisitively. Then the expression cleared and he smiled. "I'm sorry if I gave you the impression that I was offended."

Topaz could sense there was something nagging at him, but she did not probe. "So how long have you lived out here?" she asked instead.

"Since I started the paper," he shared, folding his arms across his massive chest as he leaned against the terrace railing. "It's always been real quiet out here—I like that."

"Yeah, that's important when you finish a hard day's work."

"So what about you?"

Topaz shook her head. "What about me?"

Alex grinned. "You know, I'm supposed to pick you up tonight and I don't even know where you live. Unless you want me to pick you up from your shop?"

"No, no, no," Topaz whispered, waving both hands as she recalled the night Alex had offered her a ride from Goldie's party. He had dropped her off at her shop where her rental car waited. "I forgot I hadn't given you my address. Tonight I'll be staying at my house."

"Tonight?" Alex inquired, his lips twitching against a smirk.

Topaz chuckled in spite of herself. "I have a condo in the city and a house in a *modest* neighborhood," she informed him.

"Modest, huh?" Alex drawled as though he didn't believe her. "I'd expect the daughter of two lawyers to be livin' high on the hog. Um, I hope that didn't offend you."

"Touché," Topaz replied with a soft giggle. "I just prefer simpler things. My parents can't seem to understand that; hence the condo in town."

"So that was their idea?"

Topaz nodded, her light eyes clouding with recollection. "I rarely stay there, but they foot the bills anyway. I think it's just that they prefer to think of me living in some fancy condo instead of a home that happens to be in what they call a 'lived-in' area."

"Hmph."

"Go on and say it. I don't mind."

Alex smiled. "Say what?"

"I come from a bunch of snobs."

"I wouldn't label your folks as snobs. Just caring parents."

Topaz braced her hands along the short brick wall of the terrace. "I know they care and they really are great people."

"But?"

"Sometimes they're just a bit too overprotective," she explained, giving him a skeptical look. "I don't guess guys understand what that's like, huh?"

Alex leaned over the wall. "What I understand is if I had a daughter like you, I'd want her to have the very best too."

Topaz blinked at the subtle intensity and complimentary tone to the statement. Her eyes met Alex's for a long while. Topaz was first to look away.

Alex cleared his throat. "We better get you back to your shop," he decided.

Topaz nodded, deciding it was time to head back as well. She couldn't wait until that evening.

SIX

When Alex arrived at Topaz's home that evening, she had a phone pressed against her ear and appeared completely stressed. When he greeted her with a wave, the look disappeared to be replaced by a vibrant smile.

"Hold on." Topaz spoke to the person on the other end of the line. "Come on in," she whispered, after placing the receiver against her chest.

Alex hardly noticed the warmth of the lovely two-story brick house. He was too taken by how incredible Topaz looked. Her black jersey dress was airy and sexy. Its V-neck and empire bodice called attention to her prominent chest, while the uneven ruffled hemline accentuated the stunning length and shapeliness of her legs. Black wedge-heeled, sling-backs completed the chic, sensual outfit.

"Can I get you anything?" Topaz asked as she ushered him into the den.

"I'm fine," Alex softly replied, his tone of voice belying the intensity of his gaze.

Still, Topaz made certain he was comfortable—even providing him with the TV remote before returning to her call. Alex crossed his trouser-clad legs and pretended to channel-surf while Topaz talked. For a while, he was so completely absorbed by her appearance, he couldn't focus on another thing. Then he tuned in to her conversation. It sounded as though she was turning down a date; then he realized she was trying to get out of attending a party. Obviously, the person extending the invite refused to take no for an answer. Alex smiled when he heard her complain about the boring people and "boogie" men with their "tired" conversations.

"Why are you so set on having me there when you know how I feel about it?" Topaz inquired of the caller, rolling her eyes as the person issued a response. "I'm sure they won't miss me," she added.

Alex could barely contain his smirk as he listened to Topaz plead her case. After a few more seconds of whining, she finally gave in and accepted the invite.

"You all right?" Alex questioned when she'd clicked off the phone and bowed her head.

Topaz clutched the cordless receiver, intending to hurtle it across the small oak desk. She decided against that and set it down gently. She leaned back her head and sighed, her hair rippling in a straight black cloud.

"Every now and then my background hits me in the face like a bucket of ice water," she solemnly stated, before turning to face Alex. "Please excuse my behavior. That was my aunt on the phone," she shared, setting the handset on its cradle. "My father's sister," she explained, "she's got this huge place out in the country. Like you're headed out toward Kannapolis."

Alex nodded, folding his hands across the front of his linen mocha shirt as he listened.

"My aunt Sophia's even worse than my parents. The woman's determined to see me married to one of her friends' rich, dry-humored, *boring* sons."

Alex chuckled. "Your aunt just loves you—wants the best for you," he argued, trying to play devil's advocate.

"Hmph, my aunt's just ashamed of me," Topaz corrected, her voice unusually rigid. "She just started to speak to me again, you know?"

Alex frowned a bit. "What happened?"

Topaz rolled her eyes and leaned against the desk. "Sophia wanted to kill me when I broke up with Simon."

The mention of that relationship caused the muscle to twitch in Alex's jaw. He stood from his chair. "So why are you stressing a party with the woman if she's so hard to handle?"

"Because she's my dad's only sister," Topaz explained, smoothing her hands across her bare arms. "She's got no kids of her own. Rich and lonely . . . I sort of feel sorry for her, you know?"

Alex didn't know. Sophia Emerson sounded like an aunt he'd write off no matter how pathetic her life was. Of course, this was Topaz and he was beginning to see how truly special she was. She had been treated coldly, but rose above it all to keep a callous aunt from being lonely.

Topaz noticed Alex staring and tilted her head a bit. "Everything okay?" she probed.

Alex pushed one hand into the pocket of his beige trousers. "You're too sweet for your own good," he admitted simply, regarding her with a narrowed blue-green stare. "I pray it never gets you into trouble."

Topaz shrugged. "I'm afraid it has. *More* than once. Anyway," she sighed, moving away from the desk, "looks like I've got another Sophia Emerson party to suffer through."

Silence filled the den for a few moments. Then Topaz turned to pin Alex with an anxious gaze.

Alex's mouth curved into a curious smile as he watched her. "What?"

Topaz glanced at the floor, then hesitantly took a few baby steps toward him. "Would you consider going with me to this party?" she blurted.

Alex blinked, momentarily surprised by the invite, but curious as well. "Don't you think you'd be putting yourself out there for more crap from your aunt? Obviously she's got someone for you to meet."

Topaz stepped closer, clutching her hands. "That's why I want you with me. My aunt's a very proper woman. She wouldn't be so crass as to push someone up in my face right in front of you. Besides, it would keep her other boring friends from holding my ears hostage all night," she decided, expelling a soft laugh.

Alex didn't appear quite as amused. "So are you saying you don't expect to be bored with me?"

Topaz sobered. "Not a chance. Please, Alex?" she whispered, raising her clasped hands in a pleading gesture.

Of course, Alex had no thoughts of refusing. When she moved closer and said, "Please," he knew in that instant he would move heaven and earth to make her happy.

"I'll be there," he promised, taking both her hands in one of his. "Just tell me when you want me to pick you up."

Topaz was so elated, she squealed and threw her arms around Alex's neck. Impulsively, she pressed a lingering kiss to the corner of his mouth, then gasped and moved away.

"I'm so sorry," she whispered. "It's just that you don't know how much aggravation your being there will save me. Lemme get you a Kleenex," she offered, never noticing the intensity of Alex's stare as she walked over to the end table.

"I can't wait for my aunt to see me walking in with you," she rambled, while wiping all traces of lipstick from his cheek. "This may be the first party she's given that I'll enjoy," she went on, glancing at Alex as she spoke. The undeniable emotion she glimpsed in the startling depths of his eyes drew a gasp past her lips. Before her nerves could get the better of her, she moved away.

"I'm ready if you are," she called, heading out of the den. "Just let me grab my jacket from the hall closet."

Alex made no move to follow, watching her walk away. He brushed his fingers against his cheek, then rolled his eyes and cursed his reaction to her. Silently, he berated himself for behaving like some young boy who had never been touched by a woman.

A soft chuckle erupted then, causing his dimples to flash. No, he was far from that. Topaz was just different—too different from the type of women he was used to. She had the face, body, and sensuality of an expert seductress. However, it was the sweetness that practically radiated like a beacon that threw him. *That* was the quality that held him utterly entranced.

"Alex? I'm ready when you are!" she called from the hall.

Snapping to, Alex clicked off the television and left the den. He found Topaz in the hall about to ease into a delicate chiffon jacket. Pulling the garment from her fingers, he held it for her and pulled her hair from the upturned collar. He allowed himself a moment's indulgence, immersing his fingers in the sleek black mass a bit longer than necessary. Then, clearing his throat, he stepped past her to hold open the front door.

Topaz locked up and waited as Alex checked the door behind him. She took note of his attentiveness—the way he cupped her elbow as they descended the front porch steps, the way he held open the door of the SUV before helping her inside, making sure her jacket never touched the step rail. Alexander Rice behaved more like a gentleman than any of the dozens of "cultured" young men she'd dated. Still, there was that . . . something . . . a dangerous aura that followed him like a mist.

Alex shut the driver's-side door as he settled behind the wheel and started the engine. Topaz shook her head and told herself she was reading too much into the demeanor of a sexy, rugged man who made her heart race and ignited the most intimate areas simply by looking her way.

My Place lived up to its name in every sense of the phrase. The restaurant was decorated just like a home. The lobby was fashioned like a comfortable den, complete with cushiony sofas, pool tables, televisions, and magazines littering the coffee tables.

The kitchen was in the rear and encased in glass. The dining room tables were round and the room itself was furnished with oversized shaded lamps and murals. Diners were afforded the luxury of having their meal served in personal casserole dishes, enabling them to dip their own food and eat their fill. Though a bit on the expensive side, the place was well worth it.

Alex and Topaz arrived to find the restaurant quite busy. Luckily, their table was almost ready so the wait would be brief. Topaz decided to pass the time inspecting the lobby. Alex followed.

"They've got a pool table," she announced upon entering the doorway.

Only two other couples occupied the lobby. The men actually ceased their game to watch Topaz, who strolled around the room. Alex lingered behind and watched the scene unfold. As he expected, the two angry girlfriends slapped the back of their men's heads to regain their attention. Topaz was still inspecting the room and didn't notice the arguing foursome a few feet away. The group had stormed out, several seconds before she even approached the table.

"Do you think we have time for a game?" she was asking Alex.

He glanced at the silver wristwatch he sported and grimaced. "I doubt it."

Obviously disappointed, Topaz looked back at the table and sighed.

"You that good?" Alex inquired, taking a seat on the table's mahogany trim.

Topaz propped one hand on her hip. "I told you I can hold my own. You should try me," she playfully boasted without taking note of the taunt's double meaning.

Alex smiled, trailing his index finger along his temple. *If you only knew how much I want to,* he silently responded.

"Rice, party of two. Rice, party of two."

"That's us," he announced, pointing toward the ceiling where the voice had originated. "How about a game after we eat?" he suggested.

Topaz smiled brightly and nodded like an eager child. Then, stepping close to Alex, she rested her hands on his shoulders. "I hope we can still be friends after I whip your ass."

Alex moved off the table, rising to his full height as he looked down into her lovely, smiling face. "I like your confidence."

Topaz shrugged, letting her hands fall away from his shoulders. "It's confidence backed up by truth," she said.

"Ah . . . so you really think you can whip me."

"I know so."

"Oh, you *know* so . . ."

The couple continued their banter as they went to claim their table.

"Okay, folks, that's the mixed platter with shrimp puffs, potato skins, mozzarella sticks, a Red Oak from the tap, and a banana daiquiri for the lady."

"That's right," Alex confirmed, leaning back to look over his menu.

The tall, thin young man gave a curt nod. "Be just a moment, folks," he announced before rushing off.

"I don't think I'll be able to walk out of here after I'm done eating all this food," Topaz remarked, scanning the pages of the thick, glossy menu.

Alex chuckled. "We only ordered appetizers so far," he mentioned.

"Mmm . . . but I'm a big eater and this place is known for heaping on the food."

The two studied their menus in silence for a while. Topaz began to frown and slowly raised her head when she heard what sounded like her name.

"Paz? Topaz Emerson?"

Turning, Topaz expelled a yelp of surprise at the sight of Wesley Dobbs approaching the table. She stood and rushed into his embrace.

"How long have you been in town?" she asked, pressing a kiss to the man's bearded cheek.

"Couple of days," Wesley explained, his deep-set brown eyes filled with adoration. "I was gonna stop by the shop. You still in the same place?"

Topaz nodded. "Mmm-hmm. You still drivin' that Escort?"

"You know it."

Topaz laughed and tugged on Wesley's sleeve. "Come on, I want you to meet my date," she whispered, pulling him the few feet to her table. "Alex Rice, this is Wesley Dobbs. We went to Clark together."

Alex was in the midst of shaking hands with Wesley when the innocent moment was brought to a sudden halt.

"Wesley! Wesley Dobbs! Wes-*ley*!"

Everyone turned to see a lovely, dark-eyed woman bounding across the dining room.

"Damn," Wesley muttered. "Daphne—"

"Who the hell is this bitch!" Daphne Johnson spat, folding her arms across her chest. "Answer me, Wesley!"

"Damn it, will you shut the hell up!" Wesley whispered in a furious tone, feeling dozens of pairs of eyes riveted in their direction.

"I ain't shuttin' nothin' till you tell me who this bitch is and why she all hugged up under you."

Wesley grimaced and moved his arm from Topaz's waist. "Daphne Johnson, this is Topaz Emerson. We went to college together, Daph."

Daphne raised her hands. "So what's up? Y'all tryin' to hook up or somethin'?" she interrogated, clearly threatened by the stunning woman who stood so close to *her* boyfriend.

Wesley took Daphne's hand in his. "It ain't even like that, baby."

"Then what's it like, Wesley?" Daphne retorted, wrenching her hand from his to smooth it along the wide expanse of her hip.

"Daph—"

"Aw, shut the hell up. I'm tired of your bull, Wes. I always got to find some bitch up in your face. You like bitches like this?" she accused, her eyes surveying Topaz's svelte form. "That what you like?" she repeated, her voice shaky with emotion.

"Nah, baby, you know it ain't like that," Wesley practically whined as he followed Daphne's departing figure.

Alex had regarded the entire scene from the comfort of his chair as he looked on with cool interest. When Topaz turned back to the table and bowed her head, his concern mounted. Instantly, he was on his feet.

"Are you all right?" he whispered, holding her elbow in a light grip.

"I'm all right," she barely whispered, trying to produce a smile. Tears appeared in its place.

"Damn it," Alex hissed, watching the water slide down her cheeks. "That foolish bitch," he muttered.

Topaz curved her hands over his forearm and squeezed. "Would you excuse me?" she asked, walking away before he could say anything.

Alex watched Topaz head in the direction where Wesley and Daphne's table was located. Judging from the group, it was to be a couple's night out. Obviously, Daphne had spotted her dinner partners.

Alex clenched his fists, silently ordering himself not to follow. He never lost sight of Topaz as she entered the "lion's den." He'd witnessed far too many similar scenes turn into nasty catfights. He saw Topaz touch Daphne Johnson's shoulder and begin speaking. After a few seconds, Topaz gestured across the room and Alex saw everyone at the table turn to look his way. After a few moments, Topaz was heading back toward him.

"Are you okay?" he asked, taking her arms in a firm hold when she was standing before him.

"I'm fine," she assured him, smiling when he pressed a brotherly kiss against her temple.

"What happened over there?"

Topaz shrugged and smoothed one hand across her sleek hair. "I just told Daphne that Wesley walked over to speak and I was just introducing him to my date when she walked in. I told her I rarely see anyone I went to college with and I was just excited to see a familiar face."

Alex shook his head, his disbelief more than apparent. "You're a brave lady," he finally complimented.

"Brave, huh?" Topaz replied with a smirk. "Nah, I just have a lot of practice with this stuff."

"Practice?"

"I have this problem a lot with other women," she clarified. "I guess that's why I don't have any female friends. Truth is, I only have one."

Though she spoke in a refreshing, airy tone, Alex could detect how much that upset her. Still, he couldn't tell her that he understood why she had such problems or that she was probably destined to have them for a very long time. He couldn't tell her that he understood why most women would feel threatened by her. A woman who looked the way she did—who practically radiated sweetness and compassion—could make any man look twice and, perhaps, want to stray.

Thankfully, the appetizers arrived.

"Are you folks ready to order your entrees?"

"Give us a while, man," Alex instructed when Topaz offered no reply to the waiter's inquiry. Smiling, he peered over at the platter of appetizers. "Damn, I've heard how good these things are," he said, selecting one of the grilled garlic shrimp puffs.

Topaz retained the smile, but only placed a few morsels on her saucer. She chewed on one of the delectables, but it was obvious that she wasn't tasting the food. After a moment, Alex leaned back in his chair and watched her.

"Sorry," Topaz whispered, feeling his eyes on her.

"Wanna talk about it?"

Topaz shook her head at first, then seemed to change her mind. "I just can't help but think about Simon whenever this happens."

Alex's jaw muscle tensed reflexively at the mention of her ex-fiancé. He dismissed his aggravation, though, knowing she needed to talk.

"It was why he broke things off."

"He broke things off?" Alex parroted, feigning surprise, though he already knew that part of the story.

Topaz was nodding. "He couldn't handle how uncomfortable other women were when I was around."

Alex's aggravation now mingled with anger. "Why was

he concerned about other women?" he snapped, without realizing how upset he was becoming.

"He was trying to make a name for himself in his company and . . . he was mostly concerned by the way his colleagues' wives related to me. . . ."

Alex needed no further explanation. He could tell how deeply hurt she'd been and wished he had Simon Whitley in striking distance.

"Sorry for putting a black cloud over the evening."

"Hush," Alex whispered, warding off her words with a wave of his hand. "You ready to get out of here?" he asked, gesturing for the waiter when Topaz graced him with a sweet smile.

"Ready to place your order, sir?"

"I'd like two cups of coffee—cream, sugar—and two slices of chocolate cake with the check," Alex requested.

Topaz was as surprised by the order as the waiter was. She didn't question him, however. Alex paid the check when it arrived and helped Topaz from her seat.

"Let's wait for dessert out front," he suggested.

"Alex, I'm so sorry about tonight," Topaz apologized again when they strolled into the deserted lobby. "I never thought our evening would be ruined like this."

Alex stopped her from walking any farther, his large hands curving around her chiffon-covered arms as he pulled her close. "For the last time, I don't want you to apologize. There's no need."

"We were gonna play pool," she noted in a tiny voice.

Alex shrugged. "Don't worry. You'll have plenty of time to get that ass spanked at pool."

Topaz laughed. "No, actually it's *your* ass that's in danger of being spanked."

The snappy retort melted the tension that had hovered. Shortly, however, they took note of their closeness.

"Thank you," Topaz whispered when she stepped back from the embrace.

"Dessert order for Rice. Dessert order for Rice. Please pick up at hosts' stand."

"Let's get out of here," Alex decided, pressing another kiss to Topaz's temple.

"So are you gonna make me finish this dessert by myself?"

Topaz's surprised expression was difficult to see in the dark. "I had no idea you were buying it for me. I figured since we didn't get past the appetizers . . ."

Alex shrugged. "I thought it might cheer you up," he said, bringing the SUV to a halt when the traffic light turned red.

"You're very sweet," Topaz whispered, turning to face him on the plum suede seat.

Alex graced her with a smile and could not resist the curve of her jaw with his index finger. "That would be you," he said, before returning his attention to the road.

Topaz cleared her throat and pretended to be interested in something outside the passenger window. "It's so nice out tonight," she remarked on the late summer evening, which was not warm, but comfortably breezy.

"We should find a place to have our cake outdoors," Alex suggested.

Topaz considered the thought, then snapped her fingers. "I know. There's a park in my neighborhood. It's pretty nice. I go out there lots of evenings—it's very peaceful."

"The park it is," Alex decided.

It was still quite early and Topaz hoped the park wouldn't still be crowded from basketball games or playing children. Surprisingly, the area was quite calm. When they left Alex's truck, Topaz was pleased to find that they had their choices of tables or benches. Alex set the restaurant bag on the table, and for the next ten minutes, they enjoyed rich chocolate cake and flavorful hazelnut coffee.

"So, when is this party?"

Topaz groaned at Alex's mention of her aunt's dreaded gathering. Suddenly, she raised her hand to her cheek. "I'm so sorry. I didn't even think to ask if you had other plans. The party's in a few weeks."

Alex only fixed her with a brief glance. "My plans are with you."

"I *did* put you on the spot, though."

"Will you stop?" he ordered, setting his plastic fork on the lid of the Styrofoam box. "I hardly ever find myself booked up on the weekends."

"Hmph," Topaz grunted, taking another bite of her cake. "I guess Goldie was wrong."

Alex pushed his cake aside and folded his arms across the table. "Goldie?"

"He said you were a real ladies' man," she explained with a soft chuckle. "'A real playa' is what he said."

Alex laughed then and Topaz likened the sound to a roar—a humorous roar, but a roar nonetheless.

"I think Goldie was describing himself, but just wanted to make me look bad," he decided.

Topaz was stumped. "Why would he do that?"

"Hell, Topaz, it *was* his birthday," he retorted, as though she should have realized. "If the brotha could've stepped out of there with any woman on his arm, my guess is his first choice would've been you."

"Me? Why?"

Alex didn't bother to mask his exasperation. "Topaz, you really have no idea, do you?"

Topaz clasped her hands to her chest and leaned forward. "I'm sorry to admit that I'm completely clueless. Would you please elaborate?"

Alex looked away, his gaze filling with weariness. "If I elaborate, I may offend you," he sighed.

Intrigued by what he *wouldn't* say, Topaz pushed her cake box aside and placed her hands flat upon the sanded, wooden table. "You once told me that you *always* say what's on your mind. I see no reason for you to change up now."

Realizing that he'd been trapped by his own words, Alex shook his head and smirked. "Just remember you asked for this."

"I know."

"You are extremely incredible to look at," he began, watching her extraordinary eyes widen in response. "Through no fault of your own you have the power to make a man want anything—any part of yourself—your time, no matter how minute. You can do this without even trying. That would probably explain why you have such trouble with your female counterparts. They hate you because they believe no one could look the way you do and not know how she affects a man. Personally, I don't think you have a clue and that only makes a man want you more."

The explanation rendered Topaz both speechless and motionless. She could feel her mouth hanging open and clamped it shut.

"Why don't we pack up this stuff and get you home?" Alex suggested, noticing how his words had affected her.

Topaz only responded with a jerky nod as she stood. They worked in silence for several minutes and were preparing to head back to the parking lot when a long whistle pierced the air. The couple turned in the direction of the sound and noticed three young men standing several feet away. Their grinning faces appeared more menacing than friendly. Topaz could feel her skin turn to gooseflesh beneath her jacket. She desperately wanted to look back at Alex, but she dared not move.

"Yo' wallet, nigga," one of the thugs ordered.

"Screw da wallet, send dat bitch," the second thug decided.

"Oh, she comin', no doubt," the final accomplice announced. "No way dat fine piece walkin' 'way," he added, cupping his crotch against the zipper of his ridiculously baggy denims.

Topaz was seconds away from breaking into a run, but she never had a chance to act on her own. Alex caught her arm and jerked her behind him in the span of a split second.

The menacing threesome was on guard and visibly shaken by the agility of the seven-foot giant. Alex didn't appear at all ruffled.

"Oh, we got a hero nigga out here, fellas," one of the hoodlums teased in an obvious effort to mask his unease.

"He ain't gone be no hero long," a second cohort decided, raising the hem of his oversized football jersey to flash the butt of a shiny handgun.

Topaz's gasp mingled with the young men's laughter. The threesome strolled forward, never extracting their weaponry as though its mere appearance would be enough to assure their success. At last, one of the grinning young men decided to lunge at Alex.

Topaz's amber eyes grew increasingly wide as she witnessed the man defending himself. It was like nothing she had ever seen before. Alex used the three thugs like punching bags—sending each one to the ground in howls of pain. He administered relentless high-powered kicks and punches to their backs, heads, and abdomens. The hoodlums' cries of pain only seemed to spur him on.

"This what y'all do?" he bellowed, circling the writhing threesome like a stalking cat. "This what y'all do!" he repeated, the tip of his black leather boot connecting with someone's neck. "Y'all hide out in parks and wait to attack, huh?"

"Nah, man! Please! Plea—"

"What!" Alex thundered, kneeling down to the man who had spoken. "Please? Please what? Whip yo ass some more?"

"No, man, man—"

"Gladly," Alex breathed, straddling the blustering man's quivering form. His massive hands curved into terrorizing fists as he punished the man's face with countless stinging blows. The man's nose appeared bloody and distorted—obviously broken, his lips were busted and his eyes were swelling shut. Alex did not quell his attack. Faintly, he thought he could hear his name and finally realized that it was Topaz screaming for him to stop.

Topaz watched Alex cease his punches as though a switch had been shut off inside him. He stood, staring down at the men who were barely moving and in need of medical attention. Their agony seemed to feed his anger and he landed a sadistic kick to the midsection of the man lying closest to his foot.

Topaz clutched her stomach as though she could feel the blow. She jumped when Alex took her by the arm and led her away from the scene.

SEVEN

"Do you need to stop by your house?"

Confused by the question, Topaz turned to face Alex across the gear console.

"I don't want you staying there tonight—not by yourself," he said, without looking her way.

Topaz had no desire to argue with his reasoning. "I have everything I need at the condo. It's downtown off Tryon."

Alex nodded, offering no further conversation as he reached for his cell phone."

"Yes, I'd like to speak with someone about filing charges against three men who tried to rob me."

Topaz froze, her light eyes widening as she listened to him relay his version of the evening's events.

"That's right, mmm-hmm . . ." Alex said in response to the lieutenant's questions. "If you send out a unit now, you should find them in the park. They'll need an ambulance . . . that's right, I said an ambulance. They underestimated me," he explained simply, then clicked off the phone and tossed it aside.

Topaz had to remind herself to breathe. She couldn't remember when she'd ever felt so uneasy.

"There was no need to put you in a position of having to see those jackasses again," he said, as though sensing her confusion. In the next instant, he was selecting a CD and shortly, the hard mixing styles of DJ Clue rose from the speakers.

Topaz relaxed against the headrest and closed her eyes. Her thoughts reeled back to what had happened. Alex . . . what he had done for her tonight—putting himself in the line of fire without a second's consideration for his own well-being. She would never be able to repay him for his heroism. Still, for all his gallantry, she knew it would never overshadow the image of the man she'd seen this night. Alex had appeared to her like a man possessed and she could not deny that it unsettled her more than she ever thought possible.

With the exception of the driving rhythms of the music vibrating in the speakers, the ride had been silent. Soon, Alex was pulling his truck beneath the huge canopied entrance to the condo Topaz kept near downtown Charlotte. He left the SUV's smooth powerful engine idling when he pulled to a stop before the double glass doors.

Topaz's hand paused on the door handle when she realized his intention was to leave. "Aren't you coming up?" she whispered, sure that he was, in light of what they'd just been through.

Alex kept his gaze averted while holding the steering wheel in a death grip. "You should be all right—there's security and your neighbors," he surmised, the muscle twitching in his jaw as he peered around her and past the glass doors.

Despite her newfound unease regarding this man and his abilities, Topaz knew she wasn't quite ready to be alone. "Please, Alex," she whispered, her stare beckoning in its intensity.

"Wait here while I go park the car," he said after a few moments of silence. "Damn," he muttered, when she eased out of the passenger side. Of course, his intentions were to drop her off and leave as quickly as possible. He had counted on her not asking him to stay, knowing he wouldn't refuse her if she did. What had occurred earlier tonight—his freakish loss of control—should have proven he had no business in Topaz Emerson's life. Yet, here he was and, against all the cries of advice from his better judgment, here he wanted to remain.

Topaz took Alex's arm when he met her in the lobby. Inside the elevator, she retained her grip around his massive biceps. Alex didn't mind, but kept his hands hidden in the deep pockets of his tailored charcoal trousers. He knew it was his only hope if he was to avoid touching her. He expelled a relieved sigh when the chrome doors opened on the fourteenth floor.

"Here we are," Topaz announced, when they stepped into the condo's small foyer.

"Nice," Alex complimented, taking note of the living room's cozy, artistic aura and colorful pastel murals. Black-and-white portraits, depicting events from the slave trade through the civil rights movement, decorated the walls, while incense burners and candles produced delicious, spicy aromas throughout the home.

Topaz tossed her keys to a chocolate suede sofa. She headed toward the brass bar cart located at the rear of the living room.

Alex moved farther into the room while inspecting his hands. He flexed them, making fists and wincing at the tightness he felt setting in. His gorgeous turquoise eyes frequently settled upon Topaz. She'd been relatively silent and calm, but he wanted to determine her true state of mind.

He watched as she poured a glass of vodka and gulped it down. He smiled—understanding how shaken she must have been and probably still was. Alex felt his smile fading when she poured and downed a second glass of the clear, potent liquid. A frown appeared when he spied her pouring a third. Then he rushed across the room and clutched her arm gently.

"Hey, hey . . . " he whispered, pulling the glass from her fingers. "This won't help."

Topaz fixed him with a doubtful look. "Believe me, it's helping," she assured him and turned to pour another glass, which she presented to him.

Alex hesitated only briefly before taking the drink. Topaz smiled while leaning down to unfasten the straps of her heels. Alex leaned against the bar while she prepared a pitcher of vodka and pineapple juice. Then with the glass and the pitcher in hand, she headed toward the sofa and set everything on the glass-top coffee table.

"I've got something to help that," she offered, noticing Alex inspecting the gashes across his knuckles.

"Thanks," he called, his bright gaze following her as she left the room. *What the hell am I doing here?* he asked himself, surveying the coziness of the room with unmasked skepticism. Being anywhere within a foot of Topaz Emerson was far too dangerous, given how powerfully attracted he was to her. Of course, there were other reasons why he should forget this relationship—reasons far too frustrating to think about.

"All right, this should help those hands," Topaz announced, returning to the living room with a small first-aid kit. She took a seat next to Alex on the sofa and pulled one of his hands into hers.

"Oooh," she remarked, wincing a bit as she lightly brushed her fingers across his bleeding knuckles. "I don't think anything's broken," she said, giving the hand a gentle squeeze. "At least I don't *think* anything's broken," she added, with a nervous laugh.

Alex was silent, his extraordinary stare tracing her face and body. Her lovely dark hair and cocoa skin held his attention as he focused on her gorgeous legs bared by the flaring hem of her dress. She glanced at his face, looking for any sign that she was hurting him. Alex cleared his throat and pretended to be concentrating on her treatment to his hand.

"Okay . . ." she whispered, using infinite care as she pressed peroxide-dampened cotton balls to his skin.

Alex smiled, in spite of the burn as the clear liquid fizzed over the wounds. Topaz was blowing cool air across the tops of his hands. He likened the gesture to a mother soothing her child as she treated him. His eyes narrowed when he smiled at her efficient yet tender bedside manner.

"Am I hurting you?" she asked in the midst of applying antiseptic ointment to his knuckles.

Alex simply shook his head. In actuality, the treatment Topaz provided completely took his mind off any discomfort.

"There," she announced, setting the kit on the coffee table and lifting Alex's hands to inspect her work. Sighing, she gave them a gentle squeeze and grimaced. "Tonight was a big mess and I'm so sorry," she whispered, looking down.

Alex nudged her chin with the back of his hand. "Hey," he called, waiting for her to meet his gaze, "I don't want to hear another apology from you, all right?"

Nodding, Topaz managed a smile and turned to the coffee table. "Fix you a drink?" she offered.

"I'm good, but thanks," he said, leaning back as he watched her help herself.

Topaz finished half a glass of the vodka-pineapple juice mixture, then prepared another full glass.

Alex leaned forward, about to advise her to slow down with the drinks. Before he could form the words, she began to speak.

"I still can't get over the way you handled those guys," she reminisced. "I've only seen fighting like that in the movies. How'd you learn to fight like that?"

Alex tensed, his jaw clenching when his hand tightened into a reflexive fist. "When you grow up like I did, you have to know how to defend yourself," he explained, having no desire to share the story of where and how he'd learned his fighting moves.

"Well, I'm sorry that you grew up in a rough neighborhood," Topaz was saying while adding more drink to her partially filled glass, "but I'm glad you were in control out there tonight."

"In control, huh?"

"Mmm-hmm," she drawled, the alcohol beginning to work on her faculties, "I'm so glad you were"—she yawned—"were there. I'll have to get you to show me some of those"—another yawn—"moves."

Alex chuckled as Topaz drifted off to a deep sleep. He knew their conversation was done for the evening, the vodka having worked quickly and silently. Gently, he removed the glass from her loose grip and set it aside. He stood, deciding it was well past time that he head out. Watching her there asleep, her head bowed as she sat slumped over the arm of the sofa, he debated on whether to leave her there. Surely, he knew she'd feel bad enough when she awoke the next morning. No sense making it worse by letting her sleep it off on the couch, he thought.

Exercising extreme care, he slowly pulled her against his chest. Her head fell against his shoulder and he smiled when the tiniest snoring sound rose from her throat. For a while, he stood there holding her secure in his arms. She felt incredible, as though she were meant to be there. Casting off the notion as silliness, Alex left the living room in search of the bedroom. The spacious one-floor dwelling housed an impressive master suite at the rear of the condo.

A soothing, musk aroma rose in the air the instant Alex stepped through the doorway. He hit the switch with his elbow and the room was suddenly bathed in the softest golden light. The king-sized brass bed was oval shaped and littered with pearl satin pillows and a matching comforter.

Alex placed Topaz on top of the cover, then went to move her feet to the center of the bed. He indulged in studying the shape of her foot—his fingers tracing the tops of her pretty French-pedicured toes. Of its own will, it seemed, his hand smoothed along the line of her calf and he marveled at its tone and shape. The touch was venturing higher toward her thigh when she shifted.

"Alex?"

He sat on the edge of the bed and caressed a lock of her hair. "I'm here," he whispered.

Topaz smiled, as though the sound of his voice further relaxed her. "Thank you," she sighed, her lashes fluttering closed as she dozed off again.

Her soft, trusting tone made him feel like a heel. She was so vulnerable then, and there he was with his hand beneath her dress. Grimacing over his loss of control, he left the bed and hurried from the condo.

"You think there's somethin' shady goin' on?"
"I have no idea."

"What does your gut tell you?"

"Hmph, I think I'm afraid to listen."

Casey Williams chuckled at his friend's reply. "Tell me what you have," he urged, reclining in his desk chair.

Topaz looked down at the pad she'd been scribbling on. "I ran with a hunch and discovered that the same real estate company closed the sales for each of the five businesses that have sold out on the block so far."

"Did you find out who the buyer was?" Casey asked, making notes from what she'd shared.

Topaz slammed her pen to her desk. "No—not a clue. Not one hint. They obviously wanna keep this thing a secret. There was a man who came to the shop a few days ago."

"He make an offer?"

"No, just fished around trying to find out if I was interested in selling. He made it seem like he was interested in opening a business on the block, but it was clear that he was only interested in my shop."

Casey frowned. "Did he give you any way to contact him?"

"Mmm-mmm. I doubt he'll even be back. I just know it's all connected somehow."

"Have you talked to any of the other proprietors?"

Topaz stood behind her desk. "Actually I'm on my way to see two of the other owners right now—see if they've had any *interested* visitors," she told him, slipping her keys into the side pockets of her gray flare-legged trousers. "You think maybe you could use some of your investigative expertise to find out anything on your end?"

Casey burst into laughter that told her he knew what she was up to. "Stop tryin' to butter me up."

"Is it working?"

"Always," he admitted with a phony, disgusted grunt. "I'll see what I can find out and we'll be in touch."

"Thanks, Case," Topaz whispered before hanging up. Without hesitation, she dialed another number. "Hey,

Jenny, could I speak with Horace or Stan?" she requested and waited for the connection.

"What's up, girl?"

"Horace, I need to see you and Stan later this morning if you're not tied up. It's important."

Horace frowned. "Somethin' wrong?" he asked, looking over at Stan, who was seated near the desk.

Topaz winced and scratched the hair matting her temple. "If it's okay, I'd rather get into it when I see y'all."

"No problem," Horace slowly assured her, more than a little curious. "We got the whole morning free—stop by anytime."

"See you guys in a few," she said, ending the call just as a knock sounded on her office door. "It's open!"

"Topaz Emerson?" the young deliveryman called as he peeked past the door.

Topaz waved. "Come on in."

"Package for you, ma'am," he said, trying not to ogle the lovely woman in his presence. "If you—you'd just sign," he awkwardly instructed, extending a clipboard.

"Thanks." Topaz smiled as she was handed a small envelope. Inside the package, she found a plastic card key with a note.

> *This will get you past the security gate in* my *neighborhood. Any time you get the urge to go to the park—go there.*
>
> *Alex*

Topaz felt her lashes fluttering while her heart beat double time. With trembling hands, she pressed the card against her lips and smiled. At first, she couldn't believe he'd done something so thoughtful. Then she remembered what he'd done the night before.

* * *

"Topaz, we need to talk!"

"You shut the hell up, it was my idea to come up in here!"

The moment of reminiscing effectively interrupted, Topaz placed the card in her purse and tuned in to the bellows of the two mechanics in the office. She promised herself she would thank Alex later that day. In person.

"I don't think so."

"Why not?"

"Busy."

"Lex, please, you *do* own the damn paper. Don't tell me you can't get away just for *one* evening."

Alex massaged the bridge of his nose and ordered himself not to tell his cousin what she could do with her dinner invitation.

"I won't take no for an answer, Lex."

"Well then, I guess I'm left with nothing to give."

"Lex!" DeAndra whined.

"De, I'm not interested, all right? I got a lot goin' on over here, so—"

"I was hoping to make this a very special evening," De interjected, deciding to reveal her true plans. "Josie Sharp is a friend of mine and she's interested in meeting you . . . again. I told her she was wasting her time, but she really wanted us all to get together and . . . well, it's only dinner, Lex," she drawled, hoping to underplay just how much she wanted to see her cousin involved with a woman like Josie Sharp.

Of course, Alex was all too aware of DeAndra's desperation. "I'll see if I can make it. I'll get back to you," he finally sighed, tired of arguing.

DeAndra squealed on the other end of the line. "Oh, thank you, Lex!"

Alex shook his head. "I said I'd get back to you," he sang before slamming down the phone.

A deafening thud sounded against the heavy cherrywood door and Alex looked up. An uncharacteristically bright smile crossed his face when he saw his managing editor, Clifton Knowles, wobbling on crutches into the office.

Alex stood and rounded the desk. His chuckles gained volume as he shook hands and hugged his friend/colleague.

"How were the slopes?" he teased with a straight face.

Clifton grimaced, shaking his head as he set aside the crutches and eased his six-foot frame into a nearby chair. "Save the jokes, brotha, I've heard 'em all."

Alex burst into full-blown laughter. "Aw, I bet I can come up with some new ones."

"Spare me, please," Clifton urged, massaging his bearded jaw. "I'd rather talk about this paper. I see it's still running, even with *you* in charge."

"What can I say?" Alex bragged, shrugging at the taunt.

"They sent me every edition while I was out. You did good, man."

Alex responded with a playful grimace. "Don't even try pullin' another week off, 'cause we need you back. Badly."

"Hmph." Clifton voiced his disbelief while propping his casted leg atop the edge of the desk. "So . . . anything big goin' on?"

Alex knew that Clifton was referring to his less than reputable "side" business. "Not yet," he remarked, reclaiming his seat behind the desk, "but there could be a possible takeover going on with the businesses on Briarcliff."

Clifton propped his elbows against the arm of the chair. "We covering it?" he asked, stroking his beard.

"Right now, we're just gathering information, but I think this is something we should try keeping *out* of the paper for now."

"You involved?" Clifton asked, fixing his friend with a steady, dark brown gaze.

Alex toyed with the open collar of his blackberry shirt and shrugged. "Two friends with businesses on the block asked me to sit in on a meeting. They believe there might be some shady dealings with the takeover and think they may need my . . . help."

Clifton needed no further explanation. "Looks like you might be pretty busy," he predicted.

Alex rubbed his fingers through his dark curls and squeezed his eyes shut tight. "Clif, I pray with everything in me that won't be the case."

Around eleven that morning, Topaz was being escorted into the president's office at White and Webster Contractors.

"Well, well, well, to what do we owe the honor?" Stan was asking as he pressed a kiss to her temple.

"Let's move this meeting down to the Cropsy," Horace suggested, referring to the delicatessen around the corner.

"Guys—"

"How's business, love?"

"Business is what I came to talk about," Topaz pointedly replied, sending Horace a stern look.

He and Stan exchanged glances, each one growing concerned.

"What's goin' on, love?" Stan asked, as he and his partner frowned into her lovely face.

"Something's going on with the businesses—the businesses closing on this block," she began, tossing her purse to Horace's desk. "I don't know if you two have noticed anything. Maybe you have and thought nothing of it."

"What's up?" Stan asked, perching his stocky frame on the edge of the desk.

"I got a visit from a man a few days ago. He was interested in knowing whether I was interested in selling—it got me to thinking. Why? All of a sudden, all at once, so many businesses gone, just like that?"

Horace looked over at his partner, who offered no response.

"It got me to thinking," Topaz continued, "I decided to do some digging and I found out that the same company handled the deals for all five sales."

Stan's interest was piqued. "You find out what company it was?"

Topaz shook her head. "Nobody would talk about who, but they definitely said they were aware they'd all been approached by the same group."

"How'd you find out all this?"

Topaz fixed Horace with a sheepish grin. "Just paid some friendly visits to a few people. Told them about the guy who'd approached me and I acted like I'd been thinking of selling, but wanted to find out about the deal they got first."

"And?"

"Everyone said they were sure the man was working for the company that approached them."

The partners inhaled deeply—each of them impressed by how much information Topaz had collected.

"You guys don't think I'm reading too much into this, do you?" she asked, suddenly appearing skeptical.

"You may be on to something."

"Yeah, Paz. The whole thing is kind of strange," Stan agreed with his partner.

The meeting proved to be quite productive. Topaz shared her suspicions and theories, while Horace and Stan listened and offered their own takes on the subject. Of course, neither was prepared to share his own facts just yet. They certainly weren't going to tell Topaz about Alexander Rice's involvement. They urged her not to do anything major without talking to them. She promised to keep them informed.

Female employees of the *Queen City Happening* attempted to downplay their intense appraisal of the two tall, incredible-looking men in their presence. Alex and Clifton were returning from a late lunch and were obviously in fine spirits. Their boisterous laughter, as they teased one another, exuded both masculine appeal and humor. Nevertheless, their looks and powerful builds were what drew the most attention.

"Mr. Rice, you've got a visitor waiting outside your office. Darby's already gone to lunch."

Alex was shaking hands with Clifton. "Thanks, Sherry," he said to the receptionist. "All right, man," he called, waving off his managing editor.

The wide, gorgeous grin Alex sported vanished when he rounded the corner and saw who was waiting to see him.

"Why are you waiting in the hall?" Alex whispered, not bothering to mask his anger.

"Your secretary was gone," Topaz explained as she stood from the comfortable armchair in the small lobby. "Your receptionist said you were out to lunch."

"Doesn't matter," he grumbled, taking her by the arm. "Someone should've had you wait inside."

Topaz smiled, appreciating his concern. "It was no

problem. Please, I'm fine and I only stopped by to say thank you."

Alex simply shook his head and guided her inside the office. "Thank me for what?" he asked, pushing the door shut.

Topaz pulled the card key from the front pocket of her quarter-length black angora cardigan. She waved it in the air and giggled when Alex closed his eyes and nodded.

"I was hoping you wouldn't think I was trying to put down your neighborhood."

"I didn't."

"I just felt good about doing it," he continued, massaging his neck as he walked farther into the office. "I think deep down you'll feel better too about enjoying a park with security."

"You're right," Topaz sang, slapping her hands to her sides. She sobered for an instant, thinking how much offense she would have taken if anyone else had made the gesture. "I only wanted to thank you," she repeated, shaking off the thought.

Alex rolled his eyes. "Not this again," he groaned, walking over to lean against his desk.

Topaz closed the distance between them before he could finish his complaint. "It was important to me to thank you," she said, taking his hand into hers. "Will you let me make you dinner?"

Alex fixed her with a look of playful doubt. "*Make* me dinner?"

"You're surprised?"

"I wouldn't peg you for a cook."

Topaz shrugged, acknowledging his insight. "It's something I do only on special, *rare* occasions. And *you* have certainly earned it."

"I've earned a dinner by Topaz Emerson," Alex remarked, his striking gaze tracing her face with unmasked appreciation. "You that good a cook?" he teased.

Topaz propped one hand against her hip and shrugged. "You'll probably want to kiss me when you're done eating."

The playful expression vanished from Alex's devastating features and he rose to his full height. "You don't have to cook to make me do that."

Topaz was speechless. Her amber stare faltered to the seductive curve of his mouth. When she looked back into his eyes, she gasped at the intent she found in his turquoise gaze.

He kissed her then—hard and deep with an authority that was both savage and possessive. Soft moans rose from some place in his throat as his tongue thrust relentlessly into her mouth. When Topaz kissed him back, he squeezed his eyes shut even tighter and curved his hands over her hips to bring her closer. He cupped her chin and broke the kiss to tease the satiny skin of her jaw with his lips. Shortly, however, he was back—testing the sweetness of her lips with renewed intensity as he proceeded to kiss her all over again.

The long-anticipated moment, though, was interrupted by the ring of the phone. The sound went ignored for a while. Alex's arms were like bands of steel around Topaz's waist as he fought to ward off any intrusions upon the moment he'd craved.

"Alex?" she whispered, when he released her mouth to nuzzle the softness of her neck. "It might be important," she cautioned as the fifth ring pierced the air. "Alex . . ."

A hushed curse passed his lips as he fought to restrain himself. He stood there, his forehead pressed against hers, as he inhaled large gulps of air.

"You better get that," she whispered, her fingers trembling as they toyed with the collar of his shirt. "Dinner's at seven. My house."

Alex was so affected by the kiss and the softness of her gaze, he had no thought to express his disapproval over her choice for dinner locations. He simply nodded and watched her collect her purse and walk out of his office.

When the door closed, he snatched up the ringing phone and growled into the receiver, "This better be damned good."

EIGHT

"Lex, man, I'm sorry to bother you."

Alex massaged his eyes and forced his agitation to subside. "Don't worry about it. What's up?"

Horace White sighed heavily over the line. "It's about the buyouts. Looks like the same real estate company's handling all the deals."

"Is that right?" Alex remarked, smoothing one hand across his jaw as he perched on the edge of his desk. "Who were they commissioned by?"

"We got no idea. It's still a mystery."

"And who's the real estate company."

"Another mystery."

"Damn."

"My exact sentiments," Horace replied with a grimace as he paced his office.

"So how'd you find out the same company handled all the closings?"

Horace hesitated, before blurting, "Topaz did some digging and found this out. She came to see us this morning."

Alex was rigid. "Topaz?" he repeated.

"We didn't like it either," Horace noted, sensing his friend's aggravation. "It was important to her, though, man. Like us, she's got some good friends who own businesses on this end."

"Yeah, I guess I can understand that," Alex said, though he still didn't approve of her investigating something with such dangerous possibilities.

"So where do you figure we should go from here?"

Alex smoothed one hand across the back of his neck and stood. "Well, y'all can either wait to see if there's anyone else on the street who can't be intimidated or go out and drum up support against the buyouts. Maybe it'll draw out whoever's behind this and they'll know what they're really up against."

Horace slammed his palm against his desk. "That's damn good. We're on it."

"Horace? You keep her out of this, you hear?"

Horace debated on whether to respond. "Lex, man, Topaz has her own way about stuff. I don't think keepin' her out of this will be possible," he finally said.

"You do what you have to and I'll do the same."

Topaz was on her way out of the *Queen City Happening* building. She was caught up in her own world—her mind on the kiss and Alex. She could feel her knees turn to water as she recalled the overpowering emotion that rose when he held her. After a moment, she rolled her eyes and grimaced. She was the last person to act like a girl who'd just received her first kiss. Still, she was hard-pressed to recall having ever been kissed that way before.

"Topaz, stop," she ordered, barely moving her lips as she spoke to herself, "it was just a damn kiss."

Of course, it *was* a kiss from *no* ordinary man. Alexander Rice was a man completely removed from anyone she'd ever known. It was maddening trying to determine why he captivated her so.

"Hmph, and if I could figure *that* out, maybe I could

treat him the same as any other man and he wouldn't occupy the majority of my thoughts. . . . Yeah, right," she grumbled.

It was then that Topaz heard her name. Turning, she found Casey Williams approaching her on the sidewalk.

"Mmm . . ." Casey said as they shared a warm hug. "I didn't count on seeing you today. Got time for lunch?" he asked.

Topaz felt her spirits lifting. "Definitely," she sighed, taking Casey's arm when he offered to escort her. "So what's going on? You seem to be in a great mood."

"You should know what's going on," he smugly responded.

Confusion marred Topaz's amber gaze; then it suddenly cleared. "You found out something?" she breathed, watching Casey send her another smug look.

"If it's what I think, girl, you've just dropped in my lap what could be the biggest story of the year."

"Lord, Casey, what'd you find?"

"After I got off the phone with you, I called a friend of mine who works for one of the local agencies in town."

Topaz felt a shiver that had nothing to do with the nip in the air. "And?" she prompted.

"We made a little small talk before I asked about the buyouts on Briarcliff."

"Was it his company?"

"Nah, but he was very eager to talk about it anyway since his company had lost out on handling the account."

Topaz squeezed Casey's arm and they stopped walking. "Are you trying to tell me all those businesses were looking to sell their shops at the same time?"

Casey stepped closer. "I'm trying to tell you that the real estate company is the one buying the shops."

"Wait a minute. I thought real estate agencies were like the middle man in selling property. I didn't think they bought it for themselves."

"That's what it *looked* like," Casey concurred, stopping

to take a sip of iced tea while waiting for their server to return. "Actually I was thinking the same as you, so I dug a little deeper."

"And?"

"Lockhurst Properties is the front man for another business."

"Who?"

"*That* I don't know," Casey sighed, leaning back against the high-backed wooden seat.

Topaz chewed on her thumbnail. "Damn," she hissed.

Casey leaned forward. "I'm not givin' up, Paz. I promise you that."

"You have any connections at this Lockhurst Properties?"

Casey's smile was confidence personified. "Not yet."

Topaz fiddled with a lock of her hair. "Why all the secrecy?" she whispered. "You think any of the store owners could've been *pressured* into selling?" she asked, watching Casey tug at the cuffs of his maroon shirt.

His expression was solemn. "That's exactly what I think. You be careful," he advised.

Across the dining room from where Casey and Topaz were having lunch, DeAndra Rice was seated with her newest love choice for her cousin.

"I'm telling you, Miss Sharp, if you play your cards just right, Alex will be all yours."

Josie fixed her friend with a doubtful glare. "Are you sure he'll be there?"

DeAndra rolled her eyes. "Would you calm down? My cousin fronts like he's cold and unapproachable, but he always gives in when it comes to me," she boasted.

"Mmm . . . because he loves you so much?" Josie asked, obviously believing differently.

"Hmph," DeAndra said, acknowledging the gibe, "because he doesn't want to hear my mouth."

The resulting laughter between the two friends ended when DeAndra spotted Topaz across the dining room.

"Damn," she hissed, her light eyes narrowing with hate.

Josie turned. "What?" she whispered, following the woman's stare across the room.

"I really can't stand her."

Josie offered a one-shoulder shrug. "She seemed quite nice the evening I met her."

"And just what evening was that?" DeAndra inquired, toying with a lock of her hair that rested against the high ruffled collar of her white cotton blouse

"The night the council had dinner with Alex," Josie shared, her small, lovely eyes regarding Topaz with an emotion somewhere between awe and envy. "She had the attention of every man at my table," she sighed, turning back to DeAndra. "Your cousin included," she added.

DeAndra sucked her teeth and frowned. "I knew Lex would be hooked. That bitch . . . I don't think there's enough paper in the world to hold the names of all the men she's slept with."

"Stop."

"It's true, darling," DeAndra drawled, disregarding the fact that she had no basis for the claim. "You can tell by looking at her—the way she flaunts and shows off. She's always in a different man's face."

"Oh, De, stop," Josie urged with a decisive shake of her curly bob. "She does run a garage. I'm sure *that* puts her in contact with *many* men."

DeAndra reached for her tea glass. "You're damn right it does."

"De—"

"Listen, don't worry about Topaz Emerson," she ordered, fixing Josie with a stony glare. "Respectable men or men trying to *obtain* respect don't want a woman like that on their arm. Trust me, after my little get-together, Alex Rice will be all yours."

"So we'll talk again when I have something."

"Sounds good to me," Topaz sighed, rising from her chair while Casey handled the check. She felt two arms ease around her waist and turned.

"Simon!"

Simon Whitley pulled Topaz close. "What's goin' on, girl?" he whispered, then extending his hand toward Casey. "What's up, man?"

"Here for lunch?" Topaz asked Simon as she stepped out of his embrace.

Simon helped her into the black cardigan sweater. "Mmm-hmm, but I wanted to stop by and see if you had a chance to think about what I suggested."

Frowning, Topaz waited for him to continue.

Simon chuckled. "Getting away? Taking some time off?"

"Oh, that . . ." Topaz remarked with an airy wave.

"Honey—"

"Simon, that sounds so good right now, you have no idea. But there's no way I can take time away right now. There's way too much going on."

"Am I gonna have to take it upon myself to see that you take a break?"

Topaz smiled, smoothing her hands across his shoulders as she stepped close. "Listen, I promise I intend to get away. If it makes you feel better to know this, I have two friends about to have an engagement party in a couple of months. It's supposed to be a weekend thing, so there."

Simon wasn't content. "You work way too hard for just a *weekend* off. What about something more extended?"

"Paz, I'll meet you out front, all right?" Casey called,

taking note of the fire brimming in her eyes. "Simon, man, I'll be seein' you," he added.

"Now listen," Topaz whispered, her expression still inviting, "I don't want to fight again over this."

"But?"

"But I am fine. I realize I need some time away and I'll take it."

"Just not now?"

"Just not now," she confirmed, watching Simon press his lips together. "Can we drop this? Please?"

Simon answered by placing a kiss to the tip of her nose. "I'll always care about you, honey."

"I know and I feel the same about you. So why not do yourself a favor and take your own good advice?"

"Me?"

Topaz giggled. "Here you are, getting on *me* for working too hard, when it's *you* who's the workaholic."

Simon laughed at once, nodding his agreement.

"Alex? There's a Beck Gillam on the line for you."

Alex froze, his back going rigid beneath the fabric of his tan shirt. The name never failed to produce the same reaction.

"Alex?"

"Uh, thanks—thanks, Sarah," he called to Clifton's assistant. "Put him through," he said, turning to stare out at his view of downtown. "Thanks for not putting the title before your name, man."

Dr. Beck Gillam chuckled over the line. "Just proving once again that I know how to keep the confidence of my patients."

"Well, I thank you. So, um, what's goin' on?"

Beck cleared his throat shortly. "I was concerned, Alex. You know you haven't been in touch in a while."

"I'm impressed," Alex drawled, managing to sound

as though he were teasing when in actuality he was quite perturbed at being tracked down. "You so interested in all your patients, Doc?" he asked.

"Only the seven-foot giants with anger management issues."

"Don't start, B.," Alex whispered, his teasing persona vanishing.

"I want to know how you're doing."

"Just fine."

"Still taking your medication?"

Alex's gaze faltered. "I started to slack off," he admitted, moving to sit on the edge of his desk. "I haven't had any problems. Now I'm completely off the stuff."

"Don't try to doctor yourself, man," Beck advised, making no attempt to mask his displeasure.

Alex let his lashes flutter closed. "For the last time, I'm fine." He spoke through clenched teeth.

"Fine, huh?" Beck challenged. "Anything stressful going on right now?"

"Nope."

"*That's* what worries me."

"Beck . . ." Alex warned, knowing full well what the psychiatrist was leading to.

"I truly believe you *are* feelin' fine right now—you're probably feelin' great now. But the minute something happens to stress you is when the problems will begin."

"Thanks for your optimism."

"If you won't stay on the pills, at least make an appointment to come see me."

Alex laughed. "I can't come all the way to D.C. right now."

"What do you mean, all the way? D.C. is nowhere from North Carolina."

Alex stood. "I'm hanging up now," he announced.

"Alex, man—"

"Hey. You want me to stay away from anything stressful, right?"

"Right."

"Then I need to end this call," Alex countered and slammed down the phone.

"Oooh, who got on *your* bad side?" Topaz asked when she opened her front door around seven that evening.

"You don't want to know," Alex assured her, stepping inside when she moved away from the door.

"Well, let's get you comfortable," Topaz decided, taking his arm and leading him out of the small foyer.

"Damn," Alex hissed, the moment they entered the hallway.

"What's wrong?"

"I meant to bring something," he explained, patting his hands against the pockets of his loose jeans, "a bottle of wine, beer, somethin' . . . I hate walkin' in empty-handed."

Topaz shook her head. "Please, Alex, I've got everything."

"Beer?"

"Killian's okay?"

Alex grinned. "I should've known you'd have exactly what I need," he said, laughter filling his words.

"So relax," she urged, taking his arm again and continuing their journey down the hall. "I'll get your beer and you can sit in the den and relax and forget whatever's bothering you."

"I don't think I'll have a problem doing that."

"I keep my CDs over here," Topaz instructed, smoothing her hand across the glass cabinet beneath the impressive stereo system. "Feel free to change the music if you want."

"I wouldn't dream of it," Alex sighed, dropping to the sofa. "I love Sarah Vaughn," he told her, closing his eyes as the allure of the woman's beautifully haunting voice soothed his frazzled nerves.

"Oh! I was just on my way back with your beer," Topaz said when she turned from the refrigerator to find Alex leaning against the kitchen doorway. "Here you go," she whispered, handing him one of the frosty brews.

"Smells good in here," Alex commented after taking a swig from the longneck bottle. "What'd you make?"

Topaz clasped her hands, eager to share the evening's menu. "We've got collard greens with rice, macaroni casserole, corn bread, fried chicken, and sweet potato pie for dessert."

Alex watched her in disbelief, his gorgeous stare widening in appreciation. "All this just for givin' you a card to use my park?"

Topaz laughed and peeked in on her corn bread. "It's for a lot more than that," she assured him, turning to fix him with her bright eyes. "Alex, I don't know what would've happened in the park that night if—"

"Don't," he ordered, suddenly raising his hand. "Can we just stop talkin' about that mess altogether?" he pleaded, unable to admit how much it angered him just to think of those men threatening her.

"You won't hear about it again," she promised, fiddling with the flaring sleeves of her buttercream button-front blouse.

Alex enjoyed another swig of beer and watched her working at the stove. He ordered himself not to grow fixated on the provocative fit of her hip-hugging jeans. A smile triggered his dimples when he noticed her feet were bare.

"So which one of your parents taught you how to cook?"

"Neither!" Topaz called, stirring the steaming pot of greens. "I learned from my aunt."

"The uppity one?" Alex blurted, his bottle poised for a drink.

Topaz burst into laughter. "No! No, no . . . my father's brother owns a huge farm in Louisiana. His wife is a great cook. I spent most of my summers there," she told him, turning the heat down under the collards.

"Did you go because you wanted to or because you *had* to?" Alex teasingly inquired

"Oh, I wanted to go. I love that life," she admitted, then shook her head. "My parents really would disown me if they knew I plan to have my own farm someday."

Alex could only shake his head, enjoying all the interesting facets to her personality. "I guess your farm-girl mentality is what helped you to escape the privileged lifestyle with your goodness intact."

Topaz leaned against the counter and regarded him curiously. "Why are you so against privileges, when you seem to come from a family that's obviously well off?"

"I don't know very many people in my family with half your decency," he replied without hesitation, his striking eyes never leaving her face.

Topaz was first to look away, her eyes tracing the breadth of his chest and shoulders beneath the gray and burgundy football jersey he sported.

The oven timer sounded before the moment had the opportunity to become too electric.

"The bread's done," Topaz announced, pulling the thick, golden creation from the middle oven rack. "Time to eat."

"Can I help with anything?" Alex offered, tossing the empty bottle to the trash can near the back door.

"No need for all that," she told him, pouring the greens into a glass casserole dish. "I'll just set out everything and we can help ourselves. The plates are in that cabinet behind you," she instructed, already setting the casserole dish on the counter.

They worked together in silence preparing the marble-topped kitchen island for dinner. In the midst of it all, Alex's hands slowed over the silverware.

"Um, Topaz . . . I wanted to talk to you about today . . . when I kissed you."

Topaz felt a shiver shimmie up her spine, but she maintained her self-control.

"I just wanted to tell you I was sorry . . . I never meant to do that," he softly admitted, his gaze soft and sincere. "I don't want you to think I was taking advantage or anything," he went on to explain when she turned to look at him.

"You didn't do anything wrong, Alex."

He shrugged and finished up with the silverware. "Well, I just thought it needed to be said."

Topaz stepped closer to the island. "Why?" she asked.

"I like what we have here," he said, his gaze steady and intent. "I don't want to ruin it."

Topaz turned away, not wanting him to see the reaction she was unable to hide. She thought she could've sunk beneath the floor—knowing that he only wanted them to be friends.

"You don't find a woman who can cook, likes rap, and looks the way you do every day, you know?"

Topaz's spirits instantly lifted and she turned to grace him with a dazzling smile.

"You're really making me miss my mother right about now," Alex was saying later while they enjoyed pie and the sounds of Ella Fitzgerald in the living room.

Topaz smiled and set her saucer on the end table. "Well, I must say that I feel flattered to be placed in such high company. I only started making sweet potato pie about two years ago."

"Well, it's incredible."

"So tell me about your family," she urged, tucking her legs beneath her on the sofa.

Alex felt the muscle tighten in his jaw. "What about 'em?" he asked.

Topaz shrugged. "I don't know, um . . . do you have any brothers, sisters, where are you from . . . ?"

"I'm an only child."

"Ah . . . mommy's little man?" Topaz teased.

Alex nodded. "I think I broke her heart when I got mixed up with the wrong crowd and didn't go into business like all her nieces and nephews."

Topaz was shaking her head. "You and De are so different, but I see she's not the only one from an affluent background."

Alex rolled his eyes. "I always hated that whole scene," he grumbled, massaging the back of his neck. "I don't even know how me and De managed to stay in touch all this time."

"It's because you're a real gentleman and you can't be mean to a woman no matter how much of a bitch she is."

Alex's roaring laughter rumbled to the surface. "That must be it . . . which reminds me . . ."

"What?"

"I find myself in need of a favor."

Topaz clasped her hands to her chest. "*Finally* I get to pay you back."

Alex responded with a playful, warning look.

"Sorry," she whispered, then leaned back against the sofa. "Go on."

"She's havin' a dinner party tomorrow night."

"What's the problem?" Topaz asked, propping the side of her face against her palm.

"I'll go crazy if I have to go there without another sane person to talk to."

Topaz leaned her head back against the sofa. "I don't know how sane I am, but I'd love to go," she sighed.

"I'll pick you up at seven."

Alex and Topaz were dozing on the sofa when the final CD on the changer started to play. Smokey Robinson's soulfully angelic voice resonated throughout the house and set the stage for relaxation.

Alex's eyes drifted open and he smiled, thinking of how relaxed he felt in that moment. Then he realized Topaz was lying snuggled against him and he attributed that to his tremendous feeling of contentment. He watched her, tracing every lovely inch of her face while treating his fingers to the silky thickness of her long locks splayed across her back and his chest.

He pressed a whisper-soft kiss to her forehead, then slowly brushed his lips across the area. The sweetness of the moment darkened with the memory of his earlier conversation with Beck Gillam. Alex squeezed his eyes shut, but the man's advice would not be silenced. The warnings swirled through his mind like hummingbird wings—fast and furious. He assured himself that they were unfounded. Still, there was that night in the park. . . . Had Topaz not called out for him to stop, he might have killed those boys. The memory triggered his reflexes and his hand tightened around Topaz's upper arm. She blinked and lifted her head to take stock of their position. Alex watched as she tried to get her bearings and silently vowed that he was fine. He would never allow the ghosts in his past to put anyone in danger—ever again.

Topaz had dozed off again and he used the opportunity to ease out from under her. This time, her hold on him tightened and she sighed. Her features were relaxed and she appeared completely content and trusting in his arms.

Unable to resist taking advantage of the moment, Alex buried his face in her hair and inhaled the soft scent clinging to the tresses.

Topaz's head snapped up again, and this time she was fully awake.

"Sorry," she whispered, feeling her cheeks burn when she saw how close they were.

Alex gave her arm a gentle squeeze. "No problem, but I better get goin'," he decided, pushing himself into a sitting position when she began to move away.

Her stunning amber stare remained fixed on his face—tracing the sensual curve of his mouth

"Am I picking you up here tomorrow night?" he asked, standing from the sofa.

"Mmm-hmm," she confirmed, taking note of his displeasure. "I'll be just fine. Don't worry."

Alex chewed his bottom lip for just a moment as he studied the classic coziness of the lovely house. "Thank you for tonight," he eventually remarked, looking down at her. "I enjoyed this."

"Thank you, Alex. Good night," she whispered, wishing with all her heart that he would kiss her good-bye.

In spite of her wishes, the front door closed with little more than a click. She leaned against it momentarily, before ordering herself to take her head out of the clouds. Thankfully, the ringing phone assisted her efforts.

"Yesss?" she playfully drawled.

"Well, hello, I was hoping to get the voice mail."

Topaz's smile widened as she shook her head. "Why, Mommy? Because then you could hope that I was spending the night at the condo?"

"Hmph," Patra Emerson grunted. "Don't shoot down an old woman's dreams, little girl," she urged.

Topaz laughed. "How are you doing?"

"I'm wonderful as always, but I called to ask how *you* are."

"I'm just fine . . . why?" Topaz challenged, knowing her mother had an eerie sixth sense where she was concerned.

Patra sighed. "I don't know . . . just thought I should check in, that's all," she said, the regal quality of her voice softening with love for her only child. "Your father and I miss you very much. Any hope for a visit in the near future?"

Topaz perched on the arm of the sofa. "You to me or me to you?"

"Makes no difference as long as I get to see my baby soon."

"I love you, Mommy," Topaz sighed, feeling a familiar warmth surround her. "And a trip to New York would be nice. Simon's already been on me about working too hard."

Patra's doe-shaped brown eyes widened. "Simon?" she parroted, her ears perking at the mention of her hoped-for son-in-law. "Love? Is there something going on that we should know about?"

"Nothing at all," Topaz sang, happy to dash her mother's hopes.

"I don't know . . ." Patra breathed. "There *is* something, I'm sure of it. Something in your voice . . . and you didn't even get upset when the condo was mentioned."

"Mmm, you just caught me in a good mood, I guess."

"I must have . . ." Patra conceded. "I guess I'll be more certain once we see each other. Any idea when that might be?"

"Not too much longer. I'll try to make sure of it. There's just a lot going on with the business," she added, without going into more detail. "Anyway, Aunt Sophia's having a party soon and I already promised I'd be there, so you don't have to worry about me not getting out."

Patra reclined in her black suede desk chair in her home office and tapped her nail against a high cheekbone. "Sounds like you have things well in hand," she noted.

Topaz laughed softly. "I'm trying."

Patra, however, was definitely suspicious of her daughter's sunny demeanor. Especially when she was well aware of how detestable Topaz found Sophia Emerson's parties. Patra decided not to probe further, leaving Topaz to think she accepted the fact that there was nothing more "interesting" fueling her wonderful mood.

NINE

"Nine o'clock on the dot," Stan Webster announced when Topaz opened her door that morning.

"Thanks for coming, guys," she replied, her smile as dazzling as her eyes.

"Unexpected invitation to your house early in the morning," Stan drawled, a lopsided grin on his handsome round face. "Should we have worn our good underwear?"

Topaz chuckled, reaching out to pat both men's cheeks. "Sorry to disappoint you both, but I won't be seeing your underwear this morning. Come in," she urged, lowering her gaze when they stepped past her. "I'm sure y'all know everyone."

Horace and Stan stopped in the living room doorway, where they saw several business owners from their block.

"What the hell?"

Stan turned to ask. "Topaz, what the hell's goin' on here?"

"Sit down, guys," she insisted, pushing them on into the room.

The group of entrepreneurs appeared to be among the toughest on the boulevard. They had openly refused to be intimidated by the unseen force that had closed so many other businesses.

"Now. Does anyone have *any* ideas about the identity of this mysterious buyer?" Topaz questioned, her eagerness dimming as the men in the room all shook their heads. "All right then, this is what I know. A real estate company by the name of Lockhurst Properties has been closing the sales. I've discovered that Lockhurst is actually purchasing these businesses on behalf of someone in shadow. This is our buyer and they're going to great lengths to keep their identity a secret."

Topaz's enlightening presentation sparked a lively discussion among the group. Horace and Stan watched the heated talks with uneasy gazes. They waited until the group was embroiled in conversation for at least ten minutes, before pulling Topaz to a quiet area.

"Baby, do you think this is wise?" Horace asked when they were all closed off in the kitchen.

"Just how deeply have you involved yourself in this thing? Have you talked to these Lockhurst people in person?" Stan was asking.

"I haven't talked to them yet."

"Well, good.

"Keep it that way."

Topaz's eyes narrowed with knowing intensity. "Why?" she asked anyway.

Horace raised his hands. "Paz—"

"It's just better this way."

"Why?"

"We want to keep you safe."

"Oh . . . " Topaz sighed, crossing her arms over the front of her V-neck T-shirt. "You wanna keep *me* safe. So I suppose that goes for everyone here and y'all are gonna tell everybody in the living room the same thing?"

Horace and Stan exchanged blank looks.

"Why would we do that?"

"Why wouldn't you!" Topaz blasted Horace.

"Paz, we just don't want you involved."

"Why not? I got just as much to lose as the rest of you. Why don't you want me interested in this?"

Stan shrugged. "We didn't say you couldn't be interested."

"Well what *are* you saying?"

"All right, Topaz," Horace said, snapping his hunter-green suspenders as he approached her, "the truth is, you're the only female entrepreneur left and we intend to keep you safe."

Topaz shook her head. "I knew it. I can't believe you."

"Well, believe it," Horace snapped. "In fact, let's see how the rest of the group feels about it."

"Horace!" Topaz called when he stormed out of the kitchen with his partner at his heels.

"Stan!" she cried, racing out behind them.

In the living room, Horace was already asking for everyone's attention.

"I think we should all thank Topaz for all the info she's brought to us this morning. If it weren't for her, we probably wouldn't know half as much as we do about these bastards."

Topaz gave a weak smile as she watched each man come to his feet in applause.

"But now I think it's time we gave her a rest and handle these fools ourselves!" Horace went on, fixing the crowd with his most serious expression. "Let's face it, y'all, these people don't play fair. They fight dirty. I say we keep Ms. Emerson away from the rest of our meetings and we definitely agree never to meet here again for this reason!"

"Wait a minute!" Topaz bellowed, feeling sick inside when she noticed the group agreeing. "Now just hold it!

In case y'all just forgot, *I* was the one who brought this thing together. You wouldn't be sitting here to discuss anything if it weren't for me!"

Unfortunately, each man had made up his mind. Topaz was powerless to do anything as they passed by— squeezing her hand or kissing her cheek on their way out the front door.

"I just want you people to know I'm not settlin' in around here. I was just bored . . . had nothing better to do."

The unexpected teasing from their publisher produced hearty laughter from the budget meeting attendees.

Alex cleared his throat and leaned closer to the polished conference table. "I'm actually here to find out what more Mr. Williams has on the Briarcliff buyouts. Let's see if his suspicions have any merit."

"Why don't you go on and get us started, Casey?" Clifton Knowles instructed.

"Well, something shady is definitely up," Casey began, opening the file folder he'd brought into the meeting. "I've been looking into Lockhurst Properties. My source connected with the case can confirm they are the Realtor handling the buyouts. Lockhurst, however, is actually purchasing the businesses on their own behalf."

"Buying it for themselves? There's no other client?" someone asked.

Casey smiled. "There is, but we got no other name to tie them to. . . ."

Alex listened as Casey shared his findings. The young reporter mentioned a source and Alex didn't need long to guess who that was. Obviously, the mysterious buyer was more than a simple company looking to expand its holdings. Someone was going to great lengths to ensure secrecy. Clearly, they wanted that property badly enough to do anything to get it. Topaz certainly didn't need to be involved, he thought to himself. Unfortunately, he had no idea how to convince her to step aside.

Casey's presentation was brought to a halt when the distinctive ring of a cell phone pierced the air. Alex grimaced, pulling the tiny machine from the inside pocket of his moss-colored suit coat.

"Sorry for not shutting this thing off, guys," Alex apologized as he stood. "Go on, Casey," he urged, crossing the conference room and pressing the phone to his ear. "Alex Rice."

"Alex?"

At the sound of his cousin's distinctive nasal tone, Alex muttered a curse. "I'm in a meeting, De," he softly informed her, though his aggravation was clear.

"Don't get in a huff," DeAndra quickly urged. "I'm only calling to confirm your attendance at the party."

Alex bit his tongue, knowing it was the only way he could resist telling the woman what he thought of attending the gathering.

"You remember Josie Sharp, right?"

"What?"

"Lex, please pay attention. Josie Sharp? You remember her from my party? She's with the City Council. I think you all had dinner recently—"

"Yeah, yeah, yeah, I remember her. Why?"

"Well . . . she's going to be at the party."

"And this is important to me because . . ."

"Lord, Alex!" DeAndra hissed, her cousin's unapproachable mood finally testing her patience. "I only thought you'd like to know there'd be someone there that you already know."

"I wasn't worried about that, since I'm bringing someone."

DeAndra was silent almost a full minute. "Bringing someone?" she repeated, her voice dropping on the last word.

Alex smiled.

"Who?"

"You'll meet her at the party."

"Well, thanks for telling me at such a late date, Lex. The caterers are already prepared for a specific number of—"

"So have 'em set one more place."

"It's not that simple—"

"Well, that's why you're the great party hostess you are. Figure it out. I gotta go."

"Lex—"

"Bye . . ."

"Lex? Lex? Damm it," DeAndra breathed, slamming the cordless to her white oak desk. Her mind racing with suspicions, she leaned back in her chair and concentrated. Within seconds, a devilish smile tugged at her thin lips.

"DeAndra Yvonne Rice, sometimes you're just too smart for your own good," she whispered, reaching for the cordless. "Hello there, how does a party sound to you?" she asked when the connection was made.

"Hmph, sounds good right about now but—"

"No buts. I want you there Saturday ready to have a good time."

Simon chuckled. "I appreciate the invite, De, but I got a ton of stuff goin' on at the office. Saturday's gonna be a full day of work for me."

DeAndra studied her bloodred-polished nails while Simon declined attending. "I think a break would do you good. I know Topaz would love to see you."

"Topaz."

"Mmm. She'll be there."

"What you up to, De?"

"What!"

"You're the last person I'd ever expect to try and get me and Topaz back together."

"True. But no offense, Simon, I'd rather see her with you than my cousin."

"Oh."

"Mmm-hmm. Alex is getting just a little too close to her—I know it. Besides, you've never gotten over her, in spite of all my sage advice against a relationship with her."

"Hmph," Simon grunted, shaking his head at the woman's blatant dislike. "You're somethin' else, De."

"So I'll be seeing you then?"

"You'll be seeing me."

To a passerby, Topaz would look to be in some sort of trouble, but she was the one causing the disturbance. Two of the proprietors from that morning's meeting, along with Horace and Stan, had arrived at Top E Towing and Mechanical to recruit one of the owner's top men to sit in on their meetings.

"I don't believe this! You actually expect me to go for this?"

"Your business should be represented at the meeting—"

"Horace, you actually expect one of my men to report back to me like I'm some sort of feebleminded woman who can't take care of her own business?"

"Don't you wanna know what's going on?"

"I already know what's goin' on, Stan!" she fumed, folding her arms across the plunging ruffled neckline of her wine flyaway cardigan. Closing her eyes, she counted to five. "What kind of message will it send not to see me there? They'll immediately figure me to be one of the poor fools they've been forcing to sell."

Horace and Stan exchanged glances, silently acknowledging the merit of her argument. Still, they would not allow their feelings to be swayed.

"I don't need representatives for my business when I'm able to be there."

"And we want to keep you *able*, Topaz. Now you go along with this and keep yourself in the loop, because you won't be there. The location will be kept secret and—"

"You know you guys are just as vulnerable in all this as I am!" she threw back, stepping right up to Stan.

Someone snickered and soon the four men were chuckling.

"Take it or leave it, Paz," Horace finally challenged.

Topaz curled her fists so tightly, her nails could have drawn blood from her palms. She knew there was no way to change their minds, so she grudgingly conceded.

"Stacy!" she called, waving toward one of her two best men. She eased her hands into the back pockets of her dark denims and waited. Horace and the other men watched her, hating that they had to bully her but believing it was for her own good.

"Stacy Merchants, you know Horace and Stan. This is Gary Green and Banyon Brown from G and B Air and Heat," Topaz announced, watching as Stacy shook hands and greeted each man. She was about to explain the situation, but Horace was already taking care of that.

Topaz stood fuming. Faintly, she recalled that she still had some control over the situation. She would still be in contact with Casey Williams. In her opinion, her connection with him was far more valuable. With that in mind, she felt more comforted by the knowledge that she would be able to offer her help in some way.

Alex arrived then and noticed the scene on the gravel drive in front of the garage. From inside his Navigator, he could sense that the situation was heated and voiced a silent prayer that nothing negative had happened to affect Topaz. He shut off the SUV's powerful engine and stepped out with a determined glint in his stunning gaze. The group had left Topaz standing alone on the drive. She was glaring after them when Alex approached.

"You all right?" he asked, smiling when she whirled around to face him.

Topaz's glare only deepened. "Men are at the bottom of my list right now."

Clearing his throat, Alex bowed his head to hide his expression. He found her words pleasing, in light of how many men she knew. Deciding to test the waters further, he stepped closer.

"*All* men?" he asked.

"Yes. Unless you tell me you see nothing wrong with me wanting to be involved in the meetings regarding the buyouts."

His gaze narrowed. "What's going on?"

"Every man on this block is hell-bent on keeping me completely cut out of anything related to the subject," Topaz snapped, dragging both hands through her lengthy tresses. "I mean they've all forgotten the fact that it was *me* who gave them what little they have to go on."

Alex smoothed one hand across the dark denim shirt he wore and prepared himself for her reaction to what he was about to say. "The last place I want to be is at the bottom of your list, but I think that's probably a good idea."

"You actually agree with those fools?" she hissed, pointing in the direction the other men had taken. "After all the information I gave them about this mess? They weren't even thinking about getting together to discuss this before I got involved."

"I know."

"But you don't care?" Topaz accused, fixing him with the same scathing look she'd used on Horace and Stan earlier. "You're all a bunch of chauvinists. You all probably get together and have a good laugh behind my back over the fact that I own this garage."

Alex closed what distance remained between them. His hands folded over her upper arms, effectively silencing her. He watched her for a second or two, then lifted her chin with his index finger. "Laughing at you would be the last thing we'd do," he said when she met his gaze, "but I understand where the guys are coming from and why. It's obvious these people are willin' to play dirty, and it's even more obvious how dead set you are against selling your shop. Things could get real messy and the guys are probably feeling bad about the fact that you're putting yourself out there like that when they have no leads at all. Maybe we're a bunch of chauvinists, but we just want you safe. One less thing for us to have to worry about."

Topaz rolled her eyes and smiled. "How can you say the same thing and not sound like a pig?" she asked, her bright eyes focusing on the cleft in his chin when he grinned.

"A gift," he decided.

Slowly, they took note of their cozy embrace. Alex released Topaz and smoothed his hands over her arms.

"So what are you doing here?" she asked.

"Lunch. Unless you've eaten?"

Topaz smoothed one hand against her stomach left bare by the design of the two-button sweater. "I probably couldn't keep anything down."

Alex laughed. "Well, if you decide not to eat, you can just soak up the atmosphere."

Intrigued, Topaz smirked. "What have you got in mind?"

Alex raised his hands. "You have to come with me to find out."

"Oh, I love Goofies!" Topaz was saying fifteen minutes later when Alex parked his truck in the parking lot of the popular jazz club. "How'd you know?" she asked, watching him shrug.

"A gift." He boasted for the second time that day.

Topaz shook her head. "I should've known. I don't think they're open, though," she noted as they walked closer to the establishment.

"They're open for us," Alex assured her with a mysterious wink.

Sure enough, when Alex knocked on the side door, it opened. The man who answered was as tall and well built as Alex. Topaz felt exceptionally tiny as she stood next to the two giants.

"Topaz Emerson, this is Cammie Reynolds."

"Cammie?" Topaz repeated, smiling at the name, which seemed completely unsuited for such a huge man.

Cammie grinned and smothered Topaz's hand in his. "Short for Cameron. Man, I told you not to call me that in front of the ladies," he playfully admonished Alex.

Laughter followed, and then Cammie escorted them into the partially deserted club.

"I don't believe I actually found a man in this town who doesn't already know you," Alex whispered to Topaz as they headed down a softly lit corridor.

She would have laughed, but they entered the main area of the club then. Topaz let loose a delighted scream and sprinted out onto the huge, empty dance floor. "I can't believe I'm here when the place is *this* quiet," she raved, twirling around like an excited little girl. "Do you know the owners?"

Alex waved one hand near his head. "One of the guys owes me a favor."

Music drifted down from a state-of-the-art sound system, and Topaz stopped twirling and extended her hands.

"Dance with me," she urged.

"Mmm-mmm."

"Come on," she whined, moving closer to Alex, "you know we're goin' to De's party and you're gonna have to dance there."

"Wanna bet?" he argued, allowing Topaz to pull him onto the dance floor. When she turned and pulled his arms around her waist, he silenced his arguments.

Topaz smoothed her hands across Alex's wide chiseled chest and savored the fact that they had the entire floor to themselves. She moved sensuously, loving the seductive rifts of the trumpet and sax piece.

In spite of his initial hesitation to dance, Alex was a natural leader. Soon, his masterful skill emerged and he enjoyed the beautiful woman in his arms. His hands ventured beneath her sweater's flyaway hem and his fingers caressed the satiny expanse of bare skin he found.

"I'm impressed," Topaz breathed, as his fingertips played a sensual melody along her spine. The music had slowed to a more mellow groove and she felt completely relaxed.

"Too much for you?" Alex teased.

"Please," she teased back, though secretly she tingled from being caressed, held, and handled by such an incredible man.

Suddenly, Alex cleared his throat. "De knows I'm bringing someone to this party of hers."

"Me?"

"I didn't say."

Topaz groaned. "This will definitely be interesting."

"I can't wait."

"Hmph, I can."

Alex set his hands on her hips and watched her intently. "What happened between y'all?"

Topaz shook her head, clearly wanting to avoid the subject. "De's hated me ever since I started seeing Simon."

"Why? She have a thing for the brotha?"

"I don't know," Topaz sighed, massaging her neck momentarily, "I just figured they'd always been close friends and she was just very protective of him. *That* and the fact that she's never approved of me."

"Does she know y'all just about have the same backgrounds? Hell, yours is probably even more lucrative."

Topaz grimaced. "It's more than a money/background issue with your cousin, Alex. De doesn't like the *image* I project."

"Mmm," he grunted, needing no further clarification as he thought about Topaz's image. It could easily instill insecurities in another woman.

The remaining time on the dance floor was enjoyed without further conversation. Afterward, Alex led them to a small table set for two.

"Order anything you like," he urged while studying the menu he held.

"The chicken fettuccine is my favorite," she told him.

Silence settled again. When Topaz looked away from her menu, she found Alex watching her. "What?"

"I have something else to say about your involvement with this whole buyout situation."

Topaz slammed down her menu and closed her eyes. "Why did you have to bring that up when we were havin' such a good time?" she asked, strained laughter following her words.

"I'm about to make another decision for your own good," he announced.

Topaz did not respond. Her eyes clouded with confusion as they narrowed.

"Casey Williams is working on a story about the buyouts. He's got a source he's not naming, but I don't have to ask who she is, do I?"

Topaz leaned back in her chair. "What are you gonna do?"

"I don't want you involved with his investigation in any way. I don't even want him discussing it with you."

"You can't do that!" she blurted, gasping when Alex's striking stare sharpened dangerously. "Why?" she whispered.

"You know why. I don't want you getting hurt over this."

"Bullshit. You think I'm some helpless, silly woman who can't handle her own business," she accused.

"I don't have to explain this to you, Topaz."

"The hell you don't," she argued, leaning forward. "What's goin' on with these buyouts *is* my business."

"And that paper is *my* business. Casey works for me, remember?"

"So you'll *order* him not to tell me anything?"

"I won't have to."

Topaz fixed him with an incredulous gaze. "Why, Alex? Because you know I'll do as you've dictated?"

"I'm not being a dictator here," he said, returning his attention to the menu. "I hope it won't come to that and I hope you'll let it go."

Somehow, Topaz maintained her regal composure. The only clues to her true emotions were the slight trembling of her bottom lip and the minute flaring of her nostrils. Knowing it would be unwise to let her anger show, she stood and left the table. After no more than five steps, Alex's hand closed over her elbow. She gasped at his hold and he released her.

"I think our table's this way," he said and waited for her to precede him.

Topaz studied his expression, which revealed nothing. Finally, she abided by his unspoken request and headed back to their table. The waiter arrived shortly to take their orders.

"I'll have a steak and cheese, fries, Heineken. Topaz?

Topaz?" he called, waiting to gain her attention. "You ready to order?"

Topaz passed the menu to the waiter. "House salad's fine."

Alex nodded toward the waiter, then looked back at Topaz. "Are you upset with me?" he asked, propping his handsome face against his palm.

She shook her head.

"Can't you say so?"

"I'm not upset. I'm just not in the mood to talk, okay?" she retorted, running her hand through her hair as though the gesture were calming her. In truth, nothing could take her mind off the man who just sat across the table watching her. "Could you stop staring at me please?" she finally whispered.

He did not stop. "Does it make you nervous?"

"Uncomfortable," she admitted, feeling her stomach tighten in response to his bright, observant gaze.

"I'm sorry," he said, smiling at the disbelieving glare she flashed him.

The rest of the lunch date passed without conversation.

"Maxine! Thanks for returning my call."

Maxine Cafrey, office manager for Lockhurst Properties, checked the call off her to-do list and smiled. "Casey, how are you?"

"I had no idea it was my old spades partner from the yard!" Casey raved, referring to their college campus.

Maxine chuckled. "Man, that seems like so long ago."

"Not that long."

"So what can I do for you today? The *Queen City Happening* paying you enough to afford a bigger house?"

"Not yet, but that may change if I can break this story I'm working on."

"What's it about?"

"Lockhurst Properties," Casey replied, waiting a few seconds before he continued. "Are you guys handling all those buyouts on Briarcliff?"

Maxine chuckled. "I'm sure you already know that we are, Case."

"All right . . . well, I also know Lockhurst is acting on the behalf of another interested party."

"That's what we do, Case. That's what selling real estate is all about."

Casey's smile was reflected in his voice. "I know that."

"But what you *really* want to know is who that 'interested party' is?"

"If you'd be so kind . . ."

"Casey, why's the *Queen City Happening* so interested in a simple real estate deal?"

"We do cover local business, Max."

"Well, why the interest in who our client is?" Maxine countered, her uncertainty evident.

Casey decided to come to the point. "We find it very interesting that so many businesses on the same street have closed their doors so suddenly."

Maxine chuckled again. "We found it interesting too, which is why we took the job. Perhaps those proprietors were just ready to move on to other things."

"Maybe that's because they were being forced to move on."

Maxine's wide brown eyes narrowed as she leaned closer to her desk. "Now you hold on a minute," she breathed, all traces of friendliness gone from her voice. "Lockhurst has never done anything illegal for *any* reason."

"Does that go for your client as well?"

"You're going too far now, Casey. I thought the *Queen City Happening* was a respected and honest paper. Here you are, accusing us of illegal dealings, or is it more than an accusation? You probably already have the story primed for tomorrow's front page!"

"Max—"

"Weston Enterprises has never been accused of such a thing, and for you to insinuate—"

"That's *Weston* Enterprises?" Casey coolly inquired, while scribbling the name on a pad next to the phone.

"Good-*bye*, Mr. Williams," Maxine hissed, before slamming down her phone.

"Weston Enterprises," Casey repeated, drawing a circle around the name.

"I never heard of them," Topaz was telling Casey when he called her later that evening. "So what's next?" she asked.

Casey held his phone against the crook of his neck while testing the temperature of his shower water. "I'm gonna dig a little deeper. Find out who Weston is."

"Well, I'll keep my ears open in case someone mentions the name."

Casey turned away from the shower and sighed. "I want you to be careful with this, all right?"

"Here *you* go," she groaned, flopping back against the sofa cushions. "I have had enough of every man telling me to be careful like I'm a frail damsel waiting for someone big and strong to come save me."

Casey laughed on the way back into his bedroom. "Who's been givin' you flack?"

"Besides you? Let's see . . . Horace and Stan, all the other male proprietors on the block. Even my own guys are *advising* me to be careful. Then, there's your boss."

"My boss?"

"Mmm . . . he'll probably demand that you not tell me anything more about the story."

"Alex just cares, Paz. We all do."

"Well, at least I can depend on *you* to keep me in the loop, right, Casey?"

"Listen, Topaz," Casey sighed, leaning against his navy-blue-tiled bathroom counter, "besides my not wanting to do anything to jeopardize my job, Alex Rice ain't a brotha I got the urge to anger."

"What are you saying?" Topaz asked, bolting up from the sofa.

"The guy makes me uneasy," Casey said after debating on how to phrase the reply, "strikes me as a dangerous guy—friend *or* foe."

"Has he, um . . . done anything to make you feel this way?" Topaz asked, anticipating Casey's response.

"Nah . . . it's just a vibe I get from him. I don't know. Maybe it's just 'cause the nigga's big as hell."

Topaz laughed. "He's a great guy, you just don't know him very well. You're probably just reading too much into that intense personality of his."

"Well, whatever," Casey responded with a shrug. "Anyway, girl, I need to go take this shower 'fore I lose all my hot water."

"All right, sweetie, talk to you later. Bye." Topaz set her phone down and replayed Casey's opinion of Alex Rice in her head. She was reluctant to admit that she was somewhat inclined to agree with him.

"Enough of this, Paz," she groaned, leaving the room. She was headed for her own shower when Casey phoned. Now she tightened the belt on her short, blue silk robe and strolled toward the staircase.

This time, she was interrupted by the doorbell. She changed directions and set off for the foyer. A look through the peephole brought a gasp to her lips. She pulled open the door to find Alex on her porch.

"Did I get the time wrong?" she asked, pressing one hand to her chest.

Reflexively, Alex glanced at his watch. "No, I'm just early," he explained, stepping past her.

Topaz's light eyes followed Alex as he headed out of the foyer and toward the living room. She took her time closing the front door, then followed him into the house.

"Um . . . did something change with the party?"

Alex was perched on the arm of the sofa. "I came to see if you were still interested in going."

Topaz didn't bother hiding her confusion. "Why would you question that?"

"Do you remember what happened at lunch?" he asked, folding his arms across the front of his nautical-blue crew-neck shirt.

Her gaze faltered. "I remember," she whispered, stepping past him.

Alex studied Topaz as though he was trying to figure her. "I hope I haven't ruined anything," he softly probed.

The uncertain, boyish look he wore melted what remained of her frustration. Her eyes began to twinkle then. "Well . . . it *was* your fault."

A second passed, and then Alex's uncertainty cleared and his devilishly sexy smile returned. "So am I forgiven?"

Topaz tapped her nails against her chin. "I guess . . . I certainly wouldn't feel right about leavin' you hangin'. Especially with De," she teased, watching Alex leave the sofa to step in her direction.

"Thank you," he sighed, toying with her fingers when he pulled her hand into his. "I knew there was somethin' I loved about you," he whispered.

All teasing vanished in that moment. Their bright, extraordinary gazes locked for countless moments. Alex was still holding her hand, his fingers stroking the center of her palm with such sensual slowness that she gasped.

"What?" he inquired, tilting his head as he stepped even closer.

Topaz could only lower her eyes to his mouth.

It was an effective response. Alex read her thoughts easily and dipped his head to kiss her. Topaz gasped again, allowing him adequate access, which enabled the kiss to deepen. They moaned in unison as their simmering attraction suddenly reached a furious boil. Alex held her impossibly tight, allowing her to feel every chiseled inch of his incredible body. Topaz shivered when her fingers trailed over the unyielding surface of his muscular fore-arms and powerful biceps left bare by the short-sleeved shirt he wore.

Alex was torn between wanting to massage her back and to indulge in the gorgeous softness of her hair. He had unraveled the loose braid she wore and threaded his fingers in the waist-length locks. When she wound her arms about his neck and arched herself closer, he sud-denly broke the kiss.

"You should go get dressed," he advised, though he still held her captive in his arms and his forehead was pressed against hers.

"I have to take a shower," she whispered.

Alex muttered a hushed curse, his long lashes falling over his eyes.

Topaz looked up into his face, having heard the muf-fled obscenity. "What?"

Alex looked everywhere but at her face. "I should leave."

"Why?"

"Because I can't sit down here while you're up there . . . showering."

The confusion cleared from Topaz's dark, pretty face as she realized what he was telling her. "I don't want you to leave," she admitted.

"Topaz . . ."

"Help yourself to anything in the kitchen, go to the den and watch TV or listen to some music. I'll be back before you know it," she promised, smiling at the look he sent her. She stood on her toes, intending to press a quick kiss to his mouth.

The "quick kiss" turned deep and lengthy. Alex's tongue thrust savagely past her lips and he could feel the familiar tightening below his waist.

"De'll hurt me if I don't show up to this thing," he groaned amid the kiss, knowing he couldn't have cared less. He was consumed by her lithe, voluptuous form, pliant and eager in his embrace.

Topaz kissed him back with sensuous abandon. "She won't hurt you, she'll hurt *me* for keeping you away," she whispered, her fingers swirling through his close-cut wavy hair.

Alex's fingers curves around the belt securing her robe. He felt compelled to see what lay beneath it. He broke the kiss instead. "Topaz, please go get ready," he urged, dropping a kiss to the corner of her mouth.

Topaz moved away, smoothing the back of her hand across his caramel-toned cheek. Alex waited until she disappeared up the stairs, then covered his face in his hands and groaned.

"Well, I must admit I didn't think I'd hear from you again. Ever."

Alex grinned. "Cool it," he warned his doctor.

Beck Gillam chuckled. "So does this mean you've reconsidered coming in for a session?"

"I have a question first."

"Shoot."

Alex glanced toward the doorway, hoping Topaz wasn't on her way down just yet. "Do you think I could, um . . . hurt someone like that again?"

Beck was surprised by the question. "You mean while you're—"

"Yeah."

"It's a definite possibility, Zan," the psychiatrist confirmed. "Someone with a condition like yours . . . fatigue, headache, even hunger are only a few of the many triggers that could set off your rage. For that kind of anger to attack you in an unconscious state—"

"Well, what if I started on the pills again?"

"Zan, the pills will pacify those urges but they're only a *temporary* solution," Beck explained, the tone of his voice relaying the seriousness of the situation. "Therapy, Zan—discussion and feedback. *That's* what will 'cure' you."

Alex's blue-green gaze focused on the stairway. "Hmph. A temporary solution sounds good right now."

"Alex, what's really going on here?" Beck questioned, hearing the faint despair in his patient's voice.

Alex squeezed his eyes shut and rubbed his fingers through his hair. "I met somebody. She's . . . she's unreal, Beck. I know that sounds extreme, but, damn . . . I never met anyone like her. I honestly don't think I will ever meet anyone else like her."

Beck stared at his phone, more than a little shocked by the words coming through the receiver. "You're in love with her, aren't you?" he asked, knowing the man had never spoken about anyone with such obvious care and passion.

Still, Alex would not allow himself to admit to the emotion. "I care about her and I very much want to be with her."

"Then my advice is that you continue the therapy."

"All I need are those pills."

Beck shook his head. "Zan, this is a deep-seated problem that goes back years. If you care about this lady, like

I know you do, you'll do everything you can to work through this problem."

"Hell, Beck, this is just some damned imbalance," Alex snapped, his hand constricting around the delicate cell phone.

"Zan—"

"If you won't help me out here, I can always find someone who will," Alex decided, ending the call with the softly voiced threat. He was tucking the cellular into the inside pocket of his gray sport coat when Topaz walked into the den.

She was sexy, chic, and classy in a pair of fitted, heather chocolate cuffed pants with matching platform boots. The creamy mocha silk cashmere ballet wrap blouse was fitted with a V-neckline that drew attention to her full breasts, while elegant bell sleeves almost shielded her hands from view.

Alex stood, his fantastic stare raking her body with unmasked desire. "Damn clothes you wear tease me more than that skimpy robe."

Topaz was about to laugh, but suddenly her glee faded. Alex noticed and immediately regretted his words.

"I'm sorry," he whispered, pressing one hand to his abdomen, "I shouldn't have said that."

"No, no, it's—it's not that. I . . . I just don't want you thinking . . ."

"Thinking what?"

Topaz chewed her bottom lip, then slapped her hands to her thighs and decided to speak up. "I have a lot of male friends and . . . I consider you a friend too, but . . ."

"But . . . ?" Alex prompted, as he strolled closer.

"But we've gotten very close and I don't want you to think I behave the same way with my other friends as I did—do with you," she said, grimacing at her stammering explanation while wringing her hands.

Alex couldn't believe she'd said such a thing. A look of complete surprise covered his handsome face. Finally, he closed what distance remained between them and cupped her face in his massive hands. "I'd never think that," he uttered in a fierce whisper.

Topaz wasn't convinced. "De will say things—"

"Shhh. Baby, De's opinion means very little to me. We're cousins, but the girl only wants me around so much now because now I'm a bit more socially acceptable."

Topaz searched his deep-set gaze. "You say that now, but she's very persuasive. I mean, she persuaded Simon to break up with me and—"

"Wait a minute, wait a minute," he interrupted, closing his eyes briefly. "Didn't I once tell you that I never say things I don't mean?" he asked, waiting for her nod. "And I'm *nothing* like Simon Whitley."

"I know that," Topaz replied without hesitation, her gaze clearly flattering.

Alex refused to give in to the enjoyable urges she aroused in him. He shook his head and took her by the hand. "Let's get out of here," he decided.

TEN

"Well, well!"

"Simon?" Topaz called, seeing her ex-fiancé approaching her with outstretched arms. "I didn't know you'd be here," she was saying as he hugged her close.

Simon shrugged, keeping his arms around her tiny waist. "De just called and invited me."

"Out of the clear blue?"

"Not exactly."

"Right," Topaz retorted, knowing DeAndra Rice definitely had an agenda. Silently, she commended the woman's intuition. Obviously she knew her cousin better than he realized.

Alex regarded Simon Whitley with an ice-blue glare, despising the familiar way the man touched Topaz.

"Lex!" De called, having spotted her cousin at the top of the stairway leading down into the living room.

"Damn," Alex grumbled, just as the bartender passed him an icy mug of Heineken. DeAndra's shrill voice had sounded across the living room. He and Topaz turned to find the woman rushing toward them.

"I second that," Topaz muttered, taking a swig from her bottle of Red Stripe.

"Lex, I have someone I'd like you to meet. Oh! That's right, I almost forgot you two already know each other," De-Andra rambled as she smiled at the woman standing next to her. "Alexander Rice, you remember Josie Sharp?" she drawled, sending Topaz a look that was clearly dismissing.

"How you doin', Josie?" Alex was saying as he shook hands with the City Council executive.

Josie was beaming. "I'm wonderful," she remarked, her dark eyes twinkling as they traced his devastating features.

DeAndra was still regarding Topaz with her coldest stare. "You know, dear, I'm sure there's a free man around here for you to latch on to," she spat.

Topaz regarded DeAndra's bland attire, then took another long swig from her beer bottle and stood. "Tell me something, De, are you upset that I attract more men in one night than you can in an entire year or is it just plain old sexual frustration that makes you act like such a jackass?"

People standing nearby heard the exchange and somewhere, a burst of laughter was heard. Topaz slammed her beer bottle to the bar and walked away.

"She had it comin'."

Topaz shook her head and smiled at the couple she was speaking with. "Plato, why'd you even come to this thing? You don't even like De."

Plato Rogers shrugged, running one hand through the fat, reddish brown dreads covering his head.

"Girl, he just had to tag along behind me," Felicia Cooper, Plato's longtime girlfriend, remarked.

Topaz fixed the lovely, full-figured schoolteacher with a knowing look. "You don't like her either," she blurted, setting her hands on her hips.

Felicia shrugged as well. "Free food."

The threesome burst into hearty, uninhibited laughter. They were still chuckling when Simon approached.

"Hey, y'all," he greeted, nodding toward Plato and Felicia. "Topaz, can I talk to you a minute?" he whispered.

Topaz followed Simon to the French doors near the dance floor. "What's up?" she asked.

"Pretty strong words between you and De," he noted.

"I didn't know you heard that."

Simon pushed his hands into his khaki trouser pockets. "Word travels fast at a party like this."

Topaz rolled her eyes. "I am *so* ready to get out of here. *But,*" she sighed, "I promised Alex I'd stick by him."

"What is it with you and that guy?"

"He's just a friend," she replied with a flippant shrug.

Simon seemed to accept the explanation. "So how are Patra and Eric doing?" he asked, referring to her parents.

"Crazy as always. Impatient for me to come and visit soon."

Simon's dark eyes brightened with approval. "I hope you won't leave 'em hanging. They *are* your parents."

Topaz shook her head at his authoritative tone. "I promise not to keep them waiting much longer."

"Good. Listen, I'll catch up with you later," Simon was saying, suddenly appearing rushed.

Topaz watched him hurry away, her expression darkened by a frown. She felt a hand at her elbow and found Alex at her side.

"Are you all right?" he asked at once, his gorgeous eyes raking her body as though he expected to find her injured.

"I'm fine, but I apologize for getting nasty with your cousin."

Alex rolled his eyes. "She had it comin'," he decided as laughter crept into his voice. "She could barely talk to me and her friend—she was so embarrassed."

Topaz found that she wasn't gleeful over the news. "I still feel bad. I mean, this is her party—her house."

Alex's smile faded and was replaced by a stern look.

"You're somethin' else. You know that, right? Here you are, feelin' bad about hurting someone else's feelings, when they don't give a damn about yours."

Topaz managed a weak smile. "You'd think I'd have more female friends in light of my sunny disposition."

"Let's check out this dance floor," Alex suggested, hoping to coax her out of the somber mood.

They stepped onto the dance area just as the tempo of the music changed. A cool, seductive jam was drifting through the speakers. Alex brushed his lips across her forehead and temple while thoughts of their kisses filled his mind.

"So who was De's friend?" Topaz asked when they had been dancing awhile.

"She's with the City Council. We all had dinner a while back—about the entrepreneurs' spotlight stories we're about to start running."

"Yeah, with everything going on, Casey and I have had to reschedule our interview about three times. He just reminded me that we need to get a firm date down to get it done."

Alex was tapping his fingers against the small of Topaz's back. "I hope that whole scene earlier didn't make you feel too uncomfortable."

"Why should it?" she innocently inquired, smoothing her palm across his chest before he could respond. "Plus, you're gonna be put in the same position when we go to my aunt's party this weekend."

Alex smiled, acknowledging the fact. "I only hope I'll be able to remain as dignified as you've been tonight," he complimented in a tone of playful haughtiness.

Topaz waved her hand. "I'm sure you won't have a problem."

"You know, your aunt will probably tell your parents you brought a date to her party."

Topaz's gaze wavered as though the thought had just

occurred to her. "I don't know . . . she'll probably be too aggravated that she couldn't push all her boring friends, *more* boring sons up in my face. I think we'll be safe."

"You think your parents would be pleased if they met me?" he asked, appearing uncharacteristically uncertain as he spoke.

She smiled. "I'm *sure* they'd be pleased. I know my mother would be."

"Why?" he queried, fixing her with a knowing look.

"She has a weakness for handsome men."

"Handsome? Is that what you see me as?"

"How could I not?" she challenged, her exquisite gaze trailing his face with unmasked appraisal.

Alex pulled her closer then, burying his face against the crook of her neck and inhaling the softness of her perfume. Topaz steeled herself against shivering in his arms.

"Get the hell off my back! I didn't have to come here tonight, you know."

"Save it, Simon! The moment I told you Topaz would be here you couldn't wait to show up!" DeAndra hissed.

"I don't have time for this mess." Simon retorted, eager to end the heated conversation and return to the party.

DeAndra caught his denim shirtsleeve. "You were supposed to keep your ex away from my cousin!"

Simon stepped close, his index finger poised inches from her cheek. "Remember, De, if it weren't for you buttin' in, I'd be married to her by now."

"I think it's you who needs a memory check, Simon. Don't even try to put all this on me," DeAndra countered, her light eyes blazing with anger. "You had just as much to do with all that. You had plenty of problems with the way Topaz carries herself."

"She *carries* herself like a lady," Simon snapped.

"But she has an *un*-ladylike job and too many male . . . acquaintances."

"What you want from me, De?" Simon blurted, his voice growing hoarse from all the shouting he'd done in the deserted wing of the house.

DeAndra stepped so close to Simon, her nose was but a hairbreadth from his chin. "I want you to keep her away from Alex. Every man who meets her seems to fall in love, and I don't want that bitch in my family."

Simon slammed his fist against his palm, struggling to control his temper as DeAndra stormed off. *I don't need this,* he told himself. *Not now.* He stomped all the way back to the party and found Topaz in the den. She was obviously involved in a conversation, but that didn't faze him.

"We need to talk," he told her, taking her by the arm and escorting her none too gently from the room.

Topaz glanced across her shoulder as she jogged to keep up with him. "What are you doing?" she whispered.

"Why the hell did you have to come here with De's cousin when you know how she feels about you?"

Topaz wrenched her arm from Simon's punishing hold. "How *she* feels? What about how I feel, Simon? That's the one thing you never seem to consider!"

Simon stepped closer, taking both her arms in another tight grip. "You knew this would be a big mess."

"Alex asked me to—"

"You should've turned him down."

"Who the hell are you supposed to be!" Topaz spat, pulling herself free of his embrace. "Certainly not my fiancé and definitely not my husband. De saw to that quite nicely."

"You played a part in it too, Topaz," Simon reminded her, wincing at the look she sent him.

"Oh?" Topaz replied with a start, her expression clearing. "How so? As I recall, *you* ended things because she told you to."

"You know what? Let's not get into this," he decided.

"Fine!" Topaz threw back, turning to walk away. "I don't have time for this anyway," she added.

"Too busy with work, I suppose?"

"And what does that mean?" she whispered, turning back to face him.

Simon pulled her into another punishing grip. "Would it make a difference if you knew? Would it!"

"Simon!" Topaz hissed, attempting to break free of his hold. "Simon, let go!"

Unfortunately, Simon had no chance to respond to Topaz's fevered request. He was suddenly jerked away from her. Topaz's eyes widened to small moons when she saw Alex. She watched as he handled Simon Whitley like a rag doll. His massive hands wrapped around the man's neck as he shook him violently.

An image of the night in the park flashed in her head when she saw Alex's hand clench into a fist. Memories of the three men in the park brought a gasp past her lips and she rushed to grab his arm.

Alex was ready to deliver his blow when he heard Topaz softly coaxing him to calm down. He realized what was happening and seemed to snap out of the rage. Turning the tables on Topaz, he took her by the arm. "We're leaving," he muttered, pulling her through the silent, astonished crowd.

The walk to the sleek, dark Navigator was void of conversation or laughter. Alex helped her into the passenger side, before taking his place behind the wheel. Only the hum of the SUV's engine filled the silence. The radio did not play. Topaz relaxed against the butter-soft suede seat, until she noticed them bypass the exit to her home. Her concern mounted when they also passed the downtown exit toward her condo.

"So where're we headed?" she asked, keeping her voice light.

"My place," he pointedly replied.

"The restaurant?" she queried, purposefully misunderstanding. When Alex fixed her with a stony glare, she nodded.

The SUV stopped. Alex left the truck and walked around to assist Topaz from the vehicle. When her feet left the step rail, he prevented her from moving any farther. One of his hands clutched the passenger door while the other braced against a side window.

"I didn't mean to scare you."

"You didn't," she assured him, her lashes fluttering madly. "I just didn't want you to kill Simon, no matter how much he deserved it," she teased.

Alex's smile was not forthcoming. "I don't plan on staying long."

Topaz watched him closely. "I don't mind," she whispered, the soft look on her lovely dark face relaying the true meaning of her words.

Alex looked away, then turned away completely and walked toward the house. Topaz followed, taking note of the tension in his broad shoulders. The house was dark, with the exception of the track lighting that shed shallow golden light into the lower-level rooms.

In the lounge, Alex grabbed a palm-sized remote from one of the bookshelves. After he pressed a button, Billie Holiday's haunting, sensual voice colored the silence. Alex tossed the remote to a chair and headed toward the bar with long purposeful strides charting his path. He took a cooler glass from one of the shelves of the built-in bar and reached for a bottle of whiskey. He was in the midst of pouring the stiff drink when he looked up and saw Topaz standing in the doorway. His probing stare rested on her for a moment, and then he set the drink aside without taking a sip. The same purposeful strides closed the distance between them. His massive hands folded over her hips as he pulled her into a kiss. The act was hot and commanding as his frustrations and desire were released in an erotic mixture.

Topaz shuddered, her arms encircling his neck—her fingers splayed across the back of his head. She arched closer to him, eager to feel every chiseled inch of his powerful form. Faintly, she heard him utter a low, guttural sound and she gasped at the increased pleasure it brought her. Alex deepened the kiss, his tongue slowly thrusting and caressing the dark sweetness of her mouth. When she suckled his tongue, in a scandalous fashion, he broke the kiss and lifted her against him.

Topaz felt herself being lowered to one of the long, overstuffed sofas. Alex's massaging touch moved from her hips to her waist and back, as his lips suckled her earlobe and the diamond stud she wore. Her lashes fluttered, her breathing gaining more volume.

Alex's attention was drawn to her full bosom, heaving seductively against his chest. He buried his nose in the deep cleft there and inhaled the scent of the soft perfume clinging to her chocolate skin. One hand covered her breast and squeezed gently, his thumb brushing across the nipple straining against the material of her blouse. Slowly, he began to ply the exposed skin of her cleavage with soft, moist pecks.

"Alex . . ." Topaz moaned, her nails searing his back through the material of his shirt. Unconsciously, she nudged her chest against his mouth—desperate to feel him there.

The kisses slowed, then stopped completely. Alex

rested his head against her chest and inhaled deeply as though he was struggling to control his need.

"I should get you home."

His deep voice sounded muffled against her skin, but Topaz heard every word. Smiling, she caressed his flawless light caramel skin. Her fingers stroking his brow, the sides of his face, then his jaw, she urged him to look at her.

"I don't have a curfew," she softly informed him.

Alex brushed his thumb across her mouth, before helping himself to another taste. He suckled her bottom lip, his fingers moving to the wrap tie around her blouse.

Topaz gasped again, this time feeling the material of his shirt against her bare skin. Alex pulled the blouse from her shoulders, but didn't remove it completely. A soft, helpless sound passed his lips as his eyes feasted upon her nude form.

"I knew you'd look like this," he whispered, caressing the firm dark mounds of her breasts with his eyes, then his mouth.

Topaz snuggled deeper into the burgundy cushions and smiled in appreciation of his lips tracing the tops and undersides of her breasts. She chewed her bottom lip when his thumb and forefinger manipulated one nipple with teasing strokes and squeezes. She felt the tip of his nose encircle the other rigid nipple.

"Alex, please, please . . . " she begged, enticing him to put his mouth on her. "Please . . ." she whispered, when he did not oblige.

Alex, however, was battling a war within himself. Desperate to take what he wanted—what she offered—he squeezed his eyes shut tight to silence the warnings screaming inside his head. Suddenly, he moved away, pulling her arms from around his neck. "Topaz, fix this," he ordered, referring to the loosened tie that had secured her blouse. "I should take you home," he told her again, his tone signaling that his decision was final.

"What about the garage? How's that workin' out?"
"Well, she hasn't really been heavily recruited."
"Well, get her recruited!"
"She and those two contractors are gonna take time. They aren't as easy as some of the others."
"Well, make them easy or make them irrelevant."

Alex arrived on Topaz's doorstep promptly at 8:00 p.m. When she answered the door, his seemingly translucent gaze narrowed sharply as he took in the devastating cut of her gown. The black beaded leaf dress was floor length with deep side splits. The V neckline drew attention to her provocative bustline. Black roses and leaves trailed a diagonal path across the silky creation. Double spaghetti straps emphasized the graceful curve of her neck and shoulders while dipping low to meet at the small of her back.

He cleared his throat softly, bringing his gaze to her face. "Are you ready?" he asked.

"I only need to get my jacket," Topaz whispered, trying to take her mind off how incredible he appeared in the finely tailored tuxedo. The silk bow tie was still loose and hanging around the shirt's unfastened collar.

"I'll just wait out here," Alex decided, already turning to leave the porch.

"Would you come in please?" she called from the doorway.

Alex hung his head. "Topaz—"

"I insist . . . please," she whispered, stepping aside and waiting.

He slowly complied, strolling into the foyer with both hands hidden deep within his trouser pockets.

Topaz smoothed her palms across her gown and took a baby step toward him. "Alex did I do something wrong? Last night? Was I . . . too forward?"

Alex could have laughed had it not been for the uncertainty he saw on her face. "Baby, you didn't do a thing wrong," he quietly reassured her, "you did everything right." *Too right.*

"Then why didn't you make love to me?"

Alex bowed his head, grinding his teeth as thoughts of that night flooded his memory. The way she responded to his touch and whispered his name when he . . .

"Baby we better make a move if—"

"Alex, wait," she urged, moving before him when he would have walked past her. "Can't you just answer my question first?"

He looked everywhere but her face. "Honey, you know we shouldn't be too late," he cautioned.

Topaz could see he was struggling to contain his emotions. She searched his gorgeous face, her eyes tracing the angular curve of his jaw and his magnificent gaze. Finally, she turned away, deciding to let the subject drop.

Alex watched her collect her things. He studied every inch of her body, appraising the graceful length of her neck bared by the upswept style of her hair. Curled tendrils bounced against her shoulders. The dress molded to every dip and curve she possessed. The deep split bared one leg almost to her upper thigh and he could feel himself responding physically and emotionally.

Topaz turned to find Alex already holding open the door—a silent message to hurry. The drive to the outskirts of Charlotte was silent.

* * *

"Listen, thank you for coming here tonight," Topaz was saying later, when Alex parked his SUV on the front lawn amid scores of other vehicles. "I promise we won't stay long," she added.

"I don't mind being here, Topaz," he told her in a soft voice.

She offered no reply and left the truck without his assistance.

Alex caught up to her, keeping his hand at the middle of her back as they headed up the steep front stairway leading to the stately home. He could feel Topaz stiffen beneath his touch and silently cursed himself for creating the wall between them. He was moments away from pulling her into his arms and confessing all, when the double doors opened and they were greeted by a tall, middle-aged dark man.

"Topaz!"

"Hey, Samuel," she greeted, favoring her aunt's butler with a warm hug.

Samuel Moore grinned, stepping back to inspect the young woman he'd known since she was an infant. "Lovely," was all he could say.

"Thank you," Topaz replied with a slow nod. "Where's Miss Rita?" she asked, referring to Samuel's wife and her aunt's head cook.

Samuel rolled his eyes. "Where else but in the kitchen? And she'll kill us both if you don't stop in there and speak to her before you go."

Topaz smiled and kissed Samuel's cheek. "I promise."

"Topaz? Darling! Is that you?"

Everyone turned toward the petite, beautiful honey-toned woman who crossed the spacious foyer. Her hands were outstretched and the graceful chiffon train of her gown floated behind her. Alex smiled, watching the woman place overexaggerated faux kisses on Topaz's cheeks.

"Aunt Sophia—"

"Now come on, dear," Sophia Emerson was already telling her niece. "I have so many people for you to meet."

"Auntie—"

"Car and Tessia's nephew came into town today and . . ."

Topaz grimaced and looked across her shoulder. "Alex?" she called.

Sophia stopped talking and turned as well. When she spotted the devastating tuxedoed stranger standing a few feet away, she gasped and cast a quick glance toward her niece.

Topaz was extending her hand toward Alex and smiled when he accepted it. "Auntie, I'd like you to meet Alexander Rice. Alex, this is my aunt, Sophia Emerson."

Sophia's brown eyes roamed Alex's face and frame with unmasked approval. "Topaz," she breathed, "I had no idea you were bringing a young man to . . . meet the family. What does this mean, if I may ask?"

Topaz shook her head, fixing Alex with a knowing glare. "It means, I wanted you to meet my friend, Auntie."

"Mmm . . ." Sophia returned, though it was clear to her that the feelings between the devastating couple ran deeper than platonic. Deciding not to pressure her niece further, she took Alex by the arm and led him into her exquisite Spanish-styled home. Chatting away, she took less than five minutes to obtain Alex's vital statistics and other choice bits of information—including how he and Topaz had met and what he thought of her. At last, she nodded and turned toward her brother's child, who had been following along behind them.

"I like him. Make him happy," Sophia instructed her niece.

Topaz appeared shocked, watching her aunt glide into the crowd. "That's never happened," she breathed.

Alex shrugged. "I suppose I passed the test."

"No one ever has."

"Let's hope it keeps her too occupied to bother with matchmaking."

Topaz's expression regained its earlier somberness. "That may not have been such a bad idea after all," she whispered.

Alex heard her quite clearly. "Let's dance," he suggested, his tone brooking no argument.

Topaz dreaded the impending contact, but knew it would be useless to argue. She wanted to melt when he pulled her close, but managed to remain steely.

"Will you tell me what's wrong?" Alex asked, after he'd held her rigid form close to four minutes.

"Nothing. Why?"

"You're stiff as a board."

"It's better this way. Don't you think?"

Alex grimaced. "Not better for me," he admitted.

Topaz felt her lashes flutter. "I don't want to give you the wrong idea."

"How could you do that?" he asked, pulling away to look at her.

"I've been asking myself that question for the last few nights."

"Topaz . . ." Alex groaned, closing her eyes.

She pressed her hands against his chest and stepped out of his arms. "I need to get some air."

"How long has she been seeing him?"

"Does it look serious?"

Sophia fielded the questions from her brother and sister-in-law with firm precision. She'd dialed their number shortly after leaving Alex and Topaz in the ballroom. "She claims it's just one of her friendships, but I could tell . . . the way she leaned into him and held his hand . . ."

"What about him?" Eric Emerson probed.

Sophia's lashes fluttered like a young girl's as she rested one hand across her heart. "Oh, that gorgeous young man is definitely around the bend for Miss Topaz. He looks at her like she's the only woman in the room. Listen, you two, I need to go now, but I'll keep you posted."

"Sophi, wait—"

"Bye, bye . . ."

Topaz had ventured out into the flower garden, her favorite place at her aunt's home. She stood in the middle of the lily field and inhaled the fragrant air. Several minutes had passed when she felt a soft caress against her bare arms. She whirled around, finding Alex just behind her.

She was opening her mouth to speak when he kissed her. His hand cupped the side of her neck as his tongue thrust past her lips with feverish intensity. His free hand squeezed her breast through the beautiful material of her dress.

Topaz gasped and pushed him away. "Women don't like to be teased either," she told him.

Alex voiced no response, he simply stepped forward and pulled her back into his arms. Intent on keeping her close, he let one hand venture beneath the split and curve over one lush thigh to cup one buttock cheek.

"Alex . . ." she moaned, when he began to massage her there. She arched her neck, aching to feel his lips against her skin.

"I want to take you home," he was saying, while showering her jaw with tiny kisses.

Topaz groaned her disappointment. "Alex . . ."

Alex chuckled, pulling away to look down into her face. "I want to take you home and make love to you," he clarified, watching her light eyes snap to his face. Without a word, he took her hand and led her from the garden.

* * *

Alex pulled the keys from Topaz's shaking fingers and unlocked the front door to her home. The house was dark except for the one lamp that had been left burning in the corner of the living room. Topaz followed him through the foyer, removing the linen jacket from her shoulders. She set it on a chair just as Alex dropped the keys to an end table. His back was toward her and Topaz watched as he pulled his bow tie loose and unfastened his shirt collar. Her heart raced frantically as she studied the magnificent breadth of his back and shoulders when he removed the tuxedo jacket and pulled the shirttails free of his trousers.

When he turned to face Topaz, she gasped. The stark-white shirt was unbuttoned, revealing the devastating expanse of his chest. Massive pectoral muscles appeared to have been sculpted—they were so perfectly formed. His abdomen was simply a mass of chiseled cords of muscle that flexed with every breath he inhaled.

Topaz blinked, watching him like a schoolgirl viewing a man's body for the first time. Alex slowly closed the distance between them, undoing the cuffs of his shirt and slipping the links into his pockets. When he stood before her, his fingers brushed upward along her arm, pausing at the strap on her shoulder. With maddening slowness, he eased it down, then focused on the other shoulder.

Topaz fought to control her breathing, but it was no use. The rapid breaths made her chest heave so rapidly, the lush mounds grew increasingly visible above the bodice of her gown.

Alex's extraordinary gaze was drawn to the movement; then his fingers drifted. He peeled the material away, exposing more and more of her body until the straps hindered the action. He stepped closer, tugging the straps farther down her arms and removing what remained of the dress—leaving Topaz clothed in nothing but black lace panties and strappy heels.

Alex bowed his head to outline her neck and collarbone with the tip of his tongue. The caress lowered to the valley between her breasts and charted a straight path to her navel.

Her gasps pierced the silence when she felt his tongue probe the sensitive area. Now he was on his knees before her. Tentatively, Topaz slid her fingers into his silky hair, feeling the luxuriant curls caress her palms. She whimpered and retreated from his kiss into her belly button, but he gently eased her back, holding her close with his powerful grip.

Eventually, the grip loosened and his hands curved over her buttocks, squeezing as his tongue traced the lacy waistband of her panties. His thumb ventured to the middle of the undergarment, caressing the dampness he felt on the fabric.

A tiny, tortured cry passed Topaz's lips when his thumb delved beneath the garment to tease the most sensitive spot she possessed.

"Alex . . ." she moaned, her legs weakening to syrup. He simply forced her to remain standing with a warning squeeze to her thigh.

Alex looked up to judge her reaction to what he was doing to her. He increased the speed of his thumb's caress, smiling when she gasped unashamedly and arched against his finger. He felt the moisture increase next to his skin and relished the jolt to his ego at how powerfully the simple caress had affected her.

"Alex! Alex . . . Alex, please, I—I can't . . . " she breathed, smiling when he stood and pulled her into his arms.

He took the stairs two at a time, kicking open two doors before locating the room he knew had to be hers. Track lights lined the edge of the fluffy peach carpeting. Alex whipped back the covers and placed Topaz in the center of the bed. His mouth began a slow ascent up the shapely length of her leg. He kissed the tops of her toes, her feet still encased in the sexy heels. The kisses gained moisture and intensity until he was lying at the joining of her legs. He favored her inner thigh with a slow tongue kiss that ventured closer to her panties. Topaz's hips rose from the bed when his nose nuzzled the fragrant softness of her femininity still shielded by the lingerie. He pressed her back to the brass queen-sized bed, his teeth fastening around the waistband of the panties and tugging gently. Finally, his fingers curved into the crotch and he ripped away the material.

Topaz's fingers curled into the linens when she felt his mouth against her body. At first, he simply pecked at the satiny, chocolate petals of her womanhood. Her scent drove him mad with need as his tongue bathed her with devastating languid strokes.

The soft, helpless cries Topaz uttered were at once lusty and breathless. Alex showed no mercy, simply separating the sensitive petals with his fingers and driving his tongue deep inside her. Topaz felt her body turn completely limp as he loved her in the most intimate fashion, his tongue thrusting and rotating with shocking intensity. Her thighs began to quiver uncontrollably and she couldn't even cry out.

Alex ended the devastating kiss so quickly, Topaz slammed her fists against the bed out of sheer disappointment. He had moved over her, bracing his considerable weight on his forearms, and watched her succumb to the effects of her second orgasm.

"Alex, please . . ." she moaned, her hands trailing the length of his massive thighs beneath the material of his trousers. Her eyes widened when she realized the extent of his sex. Her lips parted in surprise at his impossible length and girth.

Alex pushed himself up and pulled the shirt from his back. Topaz tugged her bottom lip between her teeth, eager to test the powerful chest that rippled and flexed with muscles. He buried his gorgeous face between her breasts, then wasted no time tugging one nipple between his perfect teeth. He soothed the firm bud with his tongue before suckling it with unnerving expertise. He switched to the other breast, favoring it with the same treatment as he worshipped the rich dark chocolate tone of her skin with possessive strokes of his fingertips. . . .

Topaz was desperate to have him inside her. She unfastened his trousers and slipped her hand inside the waistband of his black boxers. Alex rested his head against her chest, squeezing his eyes shut to relish the sweet strokes of her hand. Topaz moaned as she massaged him. The feel of the steely, silk-covered shaft against her palm was an erotic treat in its own right. She smiled with glee when he suddenly bolted from the bed to remove his socks, trousers, and boxers. With protection in place, he returned to the bed. He took time to appreciate the feel of her chocolate-dipped body lying deliciously nude and eager beneath him.

Topaz threw her arms above her head when Alex settled between her legs. He invaded her body in a torturously slow manner. She turned her face into a pillow to muffle the scream that was a mixture of pain and pleasure.

Alex pressed his lips against her ear. "Too much?" he whispered, even as he continued to press forward.

"Don't stop."

Alex's lashes closed over his eyes and he thrust hard and deep, burying himself to the hilt. Topaz's sharp gasps as she chanted his name increased his arousal.

Soon, he was thrusting in reckless abandon, his face hidden against the crook of her neck. Topaz met the powerful lunges of his hips with a fire of her own. They rode the erotic tidal wave forever, it seemed. Near the culmination of the sensual romp, Alex was gasping Topaz's name. He pressed her arms to the bed and took her with ravishing intensity—as though he were determined to carve his place deep inside her.

When Topaz woke, it was still dark outside, but in the soft lighting she could see Alex looking down at her as he stroked her face. She smiled, pulling him into a wanton kiss of which he was an eager participant.

She pushed herself up and moved to straddle him once a second condom was in place. Alex removed what pins remained to confine her hair, then wound his fingers throughout the gorgeous locks to pull her into another kiss. Soon, his hands were cupping her hips to dictate the speed and direction as she rode him. Topaz braced her hands across the elaborate design of the brass headboard, tossing her head back in delight of the virile giant beneath her.

Topaz smiled up at Alex when he woke her the next morning. "Mmm . . . more?" she purred, snuggling deeper into the bedcovers. She reached out to tug on his hand, but he resisted. "What's the matter?" she whispered, vaguely noting that he was dressed.

A tortured look tightened Alex's magnificent features. He knew what he had to do, but one look at her expressive, sweet amber stare and he was speechless—incapable of bringing any sorrow to the luscious gaze.

Topaz did begin to frown, though, as she sat up in the middle of the bed. "Alex, what's wrong?" she probed.

He reached out to toy with the lock of hair that lay across her shoulder and disappeared beneath the sheet that covered her chest. "Last night was incredible," he said, watching her with unmasked desire. "You have no idea how much I needed that, how much I needed you."

Topaz reached out to smooth the back of her hand against his flawless light caramel-toned skin. His words made her feel as warm and soothing as a creamy cup of cocoa. "But?" she prompted, still feeling as though things weren't quite right.

Alex looked away then, his hand leaving her to lie limply against his thigh. Topaz inched closer, her fingers toying with the row of silver buttons along his shirt.

"Remember when you told me that nothing could keep you quiet if you had a problem that needed to be discussed?"

Nodding, Alex smiled and grudgingly acknowledged her fantastic memory. "I can't keep seeing you," he said.

Topaz straightened. "What?" she whispered, her hands leaving his shirt. "Why?"

"Baby," he sighed, cursing inwardly at his inability to tell her the entire truth.

"Alex?"

"It's not fair to you."

"Fair?" she whispered, her eyes narrowing.

"I never want to hurt you," he said, his stare solemn and unwavering.

Topaz ignored the chill grazing her skin. "You don't want to hurt me, but you're telling me you can't see me anymore after—"

"Love, I know you don't understand this."

"It doesn't make any sense."

Alex took both her hands in one of his. "Honey, if we continue to see each other, you *will* get hurt. I can't let that happen."

Suddenly, the confusion in Topaz's eyes cleared and she wrenched her hands out of his. She could barely look at him as a wave of humiliation washed over her. While Alex's explanations had been vague, they were telling enough. Obviously there was someone else—another woman he'd . . . forgotten to mention while they were growing closer.

"Oh God," she breathed, bringing her hand to her mouth as the reality increased her humiliation tenfold. "I was so . . . so wrong about you. . . ."

"Topaz—"

"Would you leave? Please? You've said what you had to say, just go."

Alex hesitated. When Topaz averted her face, he could see a lone tear stream down her cheek. He left the room quietly, his heart aching when he heard her breathless sobs through the closed door.

Later that morning, Topaz was seated on her front porch enjoying a cup of tea. She had taken a long shower where she'd tried to wash away all traces of Alexander Rice's touch. Sadly, she could not erase the events of the previous evening from her memory.

"Paz!"

She looked up, seeing Casey Williams leaving his house. Forcing a smile to her face, she returned his wave. Casey tossed his briefcase into the flatbed of his navy blue Nissan truck, then walked across the street.

"What's up, girl?" he greeted, taking his place on the white rocker next to Topaz.

"I should be asking *you* that."

Casey sighed, understanding her meaning. "I've been told not to talk to you about the story, Paz."

"And you're planning to accept that?" she blurted, her eyes wide with disbelief.

"Baby, what do you expect me to do? The guy's my boss and your—"

"Nothing. I won't be seeing him again, so . . ."

Casey was obviously thrown by the news. He could tell the subject was a sore spot with Topaz and decided not to push. "So what are you doin' tonight?"

Topaz shrugged beneath her oversized fuzzy lemon sweater. "I'm doing it."

"How 'bout we get on that interview this evening?"

"Sounds good."

"Cheer up, huh?" Casey urged, concerned by the faraway look in her eyes. He pressed a kiss to the part running down the middle of her hair, then started to leave the porch. He changed his mind to leave, though, and turned back toward her. "Topaz, have you talked to anyone about Weston? The other business owners?"

She shook her head. "I haven't been in touch with them since you told me about it," she said, just as something occurred to her. "But I'll be seeing them soon and we'll definitely get into it."

"Be careful, all right?"

"Bye, Casey . . ." she sang, her pensive stare twinkling as she imagined the surprise on her associates' faces when she would arrive at their "secret" meeting.

ELEVEN

"I can't believe I'm hearing this."

"Don't embarrass me, Doc. You don't know what it took for me to call you."

"Well, I'm pleased that you did," Dr. Beck Gillam admitted. "A sit-down appointment is exactly what you need. So . . . what changed your mind?"

"I broke things off with Topaz."

Beck was silent for a while as he digested the information. "Well, Alex, you do need to get well for yourself. First and foremost. Otherwise, no amount of talk or medication will help."

"Topaz is the best reason I've ever had to get better," Alex decided, tapping his fingers against the secluded table he occupied for lunch. "Can you help me?" he asked.

"I'd certainly like to try, man."

"I wouldn't even allow myself to fall asleep next to her, Beck. I was afraid I'd—"

"Let's not dwell on that right now," the doctor advised. "I don't want you upsetting yourself unnecessarily. What we need to do right now is schedule these office appointments."

Alex listened to Beck as his gaze scanned the dining room that was gradually filling for the lunch rush. He did a double take, his hand tightening around his cell phone, when he saw Topaz enter the dining room on the arm of another man. "How soon can I get back on the pills?" he asked, interrupting his doctor in midsentence.

"After our first session. Give me a second while I check my calendar."

Alex waited, leaning back against his chair to watch Topaz walk across the dining room. Immediately, his thoughts went back to the breakup and the events that had led to it. Memories of them together had tortured his mind for days. He'd dreamed of having her that way for so long, and that night surpassed all his fantasies. He knew she was confused and felt hurt and used. Unfortunately, it would be far more cruel to remain in her life as he dealt with so many dangerous ghosts.

"What the hell?" he muttered, seeing a group of men stand when Topaz and her "date" approached their table.

Topaz arrived on the arm of Stacy Merchants, who'd been selected to represent Top E Towing and Mechanical during talks regarding the buyouts. Head held high, she strolled into the dining room looking stunning in a chic white-on-black suit. The fitted, single-button jacket accentuated her prominent bustline and minute waist. The skirt stopped midthigh and flattered the breathtaking length of her legs.

"What the hell—"

"Don't even try it, Stanley," she ordered, her index finger slicing the air. "Y'all are not gettin' rid of me this time. I'm through being treated like some fragile thing that can't get her hands dirty like the rest of you."

Stan braced his hands on the table. "This is about a little more than gettin' hands dirty, Topaz."

Topaz returned the man's glare. "Don't talk to me like I'm a child."

"Damn it, Topaz, we don't have time for this!" Horace

snapped, stepping closer. "We're expecting to meet with someone from Lockhurst Properties in a minute."

"That's right, Paz," Stan said, confirming his partner's statement. "We just want to feel the guy out and we don't need you flyin' off the deep end and tippin' our hand."

"Tipping *your* hand?" Topaz spat, her eyes firing amber darts at every man around the table. "*I'm* the one who found out what Lockhurst was up to and told you deadbeats about it. You fools are tryin' to play junior detectives and cut me out of the loop when *I'm* the one getting you all the goods."

"Topaz—"

"Why don't you ask your lunch partner if he knows anything about Weston Enterprises?"

"Who?"

Topaz fixed Stan with a smug smile. "That's who Lockhurst is working for," she announced, smoothing one hand across her neat chignon as she took a place at the table.

Before anything more could be said, a short, stout Caucasian man arrived at the table.

"Good afternoon, gentlemen—and lady. I'm Beaumont Harris, Lockhurst Properties," he announced, smiling as the group turned to greet him.

Topaz was silent, observing the order of the meeting as introductions were made. Things progressed quite nicely, until Beaumont Harris announced that his people were prepared to up their asking price. Topaz watched her colleagues' jaws drop when they heard the new figure. Even those most adamant about not selling appeared to be floored by the more lucrative proposal. Their reactions zapped what little self-restraint she had left.

"I don't believe I'm seeing this," she said, speaking softly but with a slow tone that harbored fierce determination. "Are you people gonna let yourselves be suckered by these crooks after they forced everyone else we know out of business? And you," she said, turning to pin Beaumont Harris with her angry glare, "you think because you've added a few more zeros to your offer, it makes you a reputable businessman instead of an unethical son of a bitch?"

"All right, Topaz, that's enough!" Stan Webster said as he stood.

"After what these jackasses did? That's not nearly enough!"

"Get her out of here!" Horace ordered. He, Stan, and Stacy rounded the table to circle around Topaz.

She began to struggle the instant Horace and Stan caught her forearms. "Get your damn hands off me!" she ordered, unmindful of the attention she drew.

The three men hustled her from the dining room and didn't stop until they'd ushered her none too gently up the stairs that led to the washroom corridor.

"I said let . . . go!" Topaz demanded, wrenching herself free of her captors.

"Hell, girl, do you want these people to win!" Horace bellowed.

Topaz smoothed back the hair that had fallen loose of her chignon. "Don't give me that! The minute that runt voiced that new offer you jackasses responded like a bunch of pigs droolin' over a trough of slop!"

"Topaz, you stupid little—" Stan stopped himself, taking a few deep breaths before he continued. "This is the way we've all agreed to handle it and you bouncin' up in here with your ass on your shoulders is the last thing we needed!"

Topaz raised her chin defiantly. "You will not stand there and try to make me feel guilty for comin' here! Not when it's you and your little amateur detectives in there making a pure mess of this whole thing!"

The situation went from bad to worse. Even Stacy Merchants, who was basically acting as a figurehead, joined in the melee of raised voices as he defended his boss. The shouting match vibrated throughout the entire upper level of the establishment.

"What the hell is this!"

The unexpected roar drowned the volume of the other four yellers. Everyone quieted and turned to see Alex Rice standing at the end of the hall. Topaz provided no response, but Horace and Stan were quick with their explanations. Alex barely made any indication that he heard the two men. His eyes followed Topaz while she kept her distance. It was a jolt to his system when their gazes finally locked. Alex knew the anger he saw in her eyes had more to do with him than with anything going on at that restaurant. Topaz didn't break eye contact. Instead, she strolled toward the end of the hall.

"You know, Alex, your only stake in this entire mess is a story. So why don't you just stay the hell out of our business?" she advised, regarding him with a look of extreme distaste before fixing Horace and Stan with the same expression. "I'm sure one of these fools will be happy to give you an exclusive when this is all over."

Horace, Stan, and Stacy watched in stunned surprise when Topaz stormed off.

"What the hell got into her?" Stan pondered.

"Damn it, let's go talk to her," Horace decided.

Alex clapped his shoulder. "Don't bother. I'll handle it," he said, leaving them in the corridor as he went after her. He caught up to her easily on the carpeted staircase leading down toward the lobby and dining room.

"Let's talk," he said, clutching her wrist and guiding her through the restaurant.

Topaz strained against his hold. "Let go," she ordered through clenched teeth while attempting to jerk herself free of his iron grip. She gasped in surprise and faint discomfort when his hand flexed briefly around her upper arm.

"Now, I'm not Horace *or* Stan," he whispered close to her ear. "Don't try that with me again," he advised.

In the parking lot, Alex released her. "Don't do this, Topaz. You have no idea what you could be getting into."

"Hmph. That seems true of a lot of things lately," she retorted.

"Situations like this can get messy, baby," he warned, his eyes ablaze with a look of foreboding. "People like this don't play fair."

Topaz stepped right up to him and poked her index finger against the lapel of his sienna sport coat. "Don't you dare pretend to be concerned about me after what you did," she ordered, her lashes growing moist with tears.

"This has nothing to do with that."

Topaz wanted to hit him. "What the hell does it have to do with? Or should I ask, who?"

"What?" he hissed, tilting his head as his eyes narrowed.

"I have to go," she was saying with a wave of her hand.

Alex watched her sprint across the parking lot, settle into her Corvette, and speed away. He was so frustrated, he didn't trust himself to return to the dining room and remained in the parking lot trying to calm himself. He was still outside when the group left the restaurant and waved off Beaumont Harris. Alex waited for the man to drive away before he approached the others.

"What's his story?" he asked Stan and Horace.

"Lockhurst came back with a new figure. A bigger one."

"Huge," Stan indicated.

Alex watched them closely. "Is that right?"

"Hell yeah, that's right," Horace confirmed. "Our jaws damn near hit the floor when we heard it."

"Topaz was mad as hell," Stan recalled. "Guess she thought we were actin' too impressed."

Horace waved off the comment. "Hell, man, she knows we ain't 'bout to sell . . . she knows that, right, Lex?" he inquired, concerned by the man's quiet.

Alex only shrugged.

"Makes you wonder, though," Stan whispered, "what's so special about our property to make these folks shell out all this cash?"

"Y'all should look into it," Alex absently suggested. "Maybe that strip of land is worth more than you know," he added, his mind still focused on Topaz.

The group thought it was a wonderful idea. As they discussed the particulars, Alex reached for his phone and dialed Beck Gillam's number.

After a very long drive, Topaz returned home to indulge in a soothing bath in hopes of soaking away all remnants of the stressful luncheon. The aggravation with Horace, Stan, and the others drifted away easily. The run-in with Alex, however, wasn't so easy to dismiss. Her lashes fluttered closed as she slid deeper into the fragrant tub of water. It seemed almost inconceivable that a relationship that bloomed so perfectly had become such a frustrating situation.

"Damn you, Alex," Topaz grumbled, reaching for the remote resting along the oak-trimmed edge of the tub. She raised the volume of the slow groove being played by a local jazz and R&B radio station. A content smile touched her lips as the mellow song further relaxed her.

"And that was Bony James featuring Dave Hollister on your favorite place for smooth jazz and R and B. Coool 94.7. This is your host Dan Sweet. We're gonna interrupt the mood just briefly here and take you to downtown Charlotte. We've got our 'eye in the sky' newscaster Shauna Wells touching down on Briarcliff Drive. What's goin' on, Shauna?"

"Thanks, Dan, I'm here on the corner of Briarcliff and Elm standing across the street from a spectacular sight."

Topaz barely listened as the woman's stern, authoritative voice boomed through the speakers. She hoped the broadcast would be brief and that the music would shortly resume.

". . . once again, Top E Towing and Mechanical is ablaze and drawing quite a crowd of spectators."

Topaz's eyes snapped open and she jerked into an upright position.

". . . this major fire is still going strong, Dan. Fire crews are working doggedly to control the blaze that only seems to be spreading . . ."

Water sloshed outside the tub when Topaz stumbled out. Her heart raced as she ran into her bedroom and flipped on the television. Turning to one of the local channels, she received an eyewitness view of the story. She stood rooted to the spot, shaking her head in disbelief. Her knees weakened momentarily, but she resisted crumbling to the floor. Instead, she moved quickly. Choosing a pair of wrinkled jeans, T-shirt, and sneakers, she dressed and stormed out of the house.

Fire crews, EMS personnel, and news vans crowded the corner and side street along Top E Towing and Mechanical. Topaz had to park her car several blocks away and run to the scene. Once there, she stood, not blinking—unmindful of the smoke, ashes, and fumes blowing into her face.

Someone grabbed her arm and Topaz turned to find several of her employees there. Her facade crumbled and she fell into their arms, accepting comfort from the burly men.

"Was anybody hurt? Was anyone inside?" she began to question, her light eyes settling on each of their faces.

"Shh . . . shh . . . 'sokay . . ." Darryl Groves reassured her, pulling her into a comforting embrace. "I was the only one there. I was in the office when I smelled the fumes. Everybody else was either on the road or out for lunch."

"Oh, Darryl, how'd this happen!" she cried, turning back to observe her thriving business being reduced to a charred heap of wood and brick.

Darryl pulled her back against his chest. "I can't answer that, love. I was makin' some calls from the office when I smelled the fumes. I didn't think much of it till I noticed the smoke outside the window and heard people yelling 'fire' outside."

"'Scuse me? Mr. Groves? Could I speak to you a minute, sir?"

Darryl kept his hands around Topaz's shoulders and guided her toward the man who had called out.

"Actually, this is the lady you should be speaking with. Topaz Emerson, this is crew chief Larry Silver. Chief Silver, Ms. Emerson is the owner of the garage."

"Good to meet you, ma'am," the chief greeted as he removed his hat and extended his hand.

"Can you tell what started this?" Topaz questioned after they'd shaken hands.

Chief Silver glanced across his shoulder toward the blaze, which was finally showing signs of abating. "Hard to say right now, ma'am. We'll know more after the investigation is complete."

"Investigation?"

"Standard procedure, ma'am," the chief explained with a lazy shrug. "I'm sure you know a business like this is prime for sudden blazes," he said, watching her nod. "Ms. Emerson, I want you to take my card, should you have any questions before I get back to you."

Topaz was looking across the street. "How long will this investigation take?"

"I don't anticipate it'll take very long," the man predicted, using a dingy handkerchief to wipe the soot from his red face.

Topaz wanted to scream. "Is there *anything* more you can tell me?"

The chief stepped closer to pat her hand reassuringly. "Ma'am, I'm almost positive there was no foul play at work here."

Just then, Alex's earlier words came to mind. *"People like this don't play fair."*

"Thank you, Chief Silver," Topaz whispered, watching the older gentleman turn and leave. "Guys, thanks for stickin' around," she said to her employees.

"Why don't you come with us, Topaz?"

She shook her head. "I should stay. See if they need me . . . for anything," she sighed, looking back toward the garage.

Stacy Merchants kissed her cheek. "They not gone need you round here, Topaz. You only gone make yourself miserable lookin' at all this."

Topaz wiped at the tears clinging to the corner of her eyes. "Thanks, y'all, but I wouldn't be any good company right now."

"We don't care 'bout that," someone said and the group voiced their agreement.

"Seriously, I'll be fine," she tried to assure them. She couldn't tell them how much being around them made her realize all she'd lost.

Slowly the group acknowledged the wishes of their boss. Topaz smiled, relishing their kisses and hugs as they moved on. Free of their concerned gazes, she let the tears water her eyes.

"Looks like you'll have to rebuild."

Despite the noise and mingled conversation, Topaz heard the comment. Anger and suspicion illuminated her dark face when she saw Alfred Majors at her side.

"What the hell are you here for?" she hissed.

Alfred folded his arms across the money-green de-signer T-shirt he sported. "Heard about the fire on my car radio. Decided to come see what was happening."

"Mmm . . . to view your handiwork?"

Alfred appeared stunned. "You actually think I'd do something like this?" he questioned, laughter following the words. "No, Miss Emerson. I came by hoping you'd be more open to the idea of including my accessories shop when you rebuild this place."

Topaz's mouth fell open in surprise.

"That is," Alfred continued in a tone of exaggerated doubt, "if you have any interest in rebuilding after a catastrophe like this."

Topaz couldn't believe the man's nerve. She could only watch as he winked, smiled, and strolled away. Groaning then, she buried her face in her palms.

"Topaz?"

"What!" she hissed, whirling around.

Simon raised both hands, his eyes widening with sur-prise. "I'm sorry," he replied.

Topaz was already shaking her head. "No, Simon, I'm—I'm sorry. It's just . . . I'm sorry for snapping."

"Don't apologize to me. I can certainly understand," he said, glancing around. "How you holdin' up?"

The simple question caused the heavy ball of emotion to burst inside her chest. The tears rushed forth again. Simon muttered hushed words to console her as they hugged.

"Want me to take you home?" he whispered against her windblown hair.

Topaz nuzzled her face into Simon's shoulder. "Home's the last place I want to be," she told him, inhaling the scent of cologne clinging to his maroon shirt.

He pressed a kiss to her cheek, then made her look

at him. "How about I take you home and you can change your clothes so I can take you out to dinner?"

Topaz managed a smile when he tweaked her chin. "Sounds perfect."

"You think she'll sell the property after this?"

"I don't see why she wouldn't. However . . ."

"However . . . ?"

"She's tough. Beau says she has a lot of power over that group."

"Hell, of course she does, look at her!"

"I have. . . ."

"Mmm-hmm, listen, I'm counting on you all to handle this. Otherwise, we'll have to make our presence more known."

"We understand how badly your people want this land. We simply want as little bloodshed as possible. Especially since they already know who *we* are."

"I understand your concerns, but I want that property."

"You'll have it."

"Thanks for making the trip, man."

Beck Gillam shrugged and recrossed his long legs at the ankles. "Hop, skip, and a jump from Columbia," he explained.

Alex grinned. "What the hell were you doing in South Carolina?"

"Visiting my mama," Beck said, removing the short plastic straw from his club soda. "I try spendin' a few days or so with her every month."

Alex leaned back in his chair and smiled. "Damn, that sounds good right about now," he admitted, thinking how nice it would be to see his own mother.

Beck took note of his patient's melancholy demeanor.

"I hope this won't be a onetime get-together," he pointedly remarked.

"It won't. I want to keep every appointment."

"She must be somethin' else."

Alex focused his penetrating gaze on Beck and grinned. "She is," he confirmed, losing a bit of his cool. "But I hurt her when I broke it off. I don't know if she'll forgive me."

Beck cleared his throat, his green eyes narrowing. "Did you . . ."

Alex tilted his head in confusion, then grimaced upon realizing what the doctor was asking. "It wasn't like that. I told her I couldn't see her anymore and she was hurt."

Beck sipped his soda. "Are you going to tell her?"

"Tell her? Tell her what, Beck? That my dreams affect me so violently, she could wake up to find my hands around her neck?"

"Alex—"

"I won't tell her that. I can't even *think* about tellin' her that. Not until it's a thing of the past."

"It'll never be a thing of the past, Zan."

"You know what I mean."

"Zan—"

"I won't tell her that!" Alex snapped, his voice a fierce whisper as he slammed a fist down on the table. "I never want her to see me as that person. Ever," he confided, the pain in his eyes blatant and unrelenting.

Beck focused on the pattern in the tablecloth. "So you'll settle for losing her instead?" he asked, raking one hand through his wavy brown hair when he looked up.

Alex only reclined in his chair and folded his arms across his chest. He fixed his doctor with a sour expression, before his blue-green stare focused across the dining room. "I'll be damned . . ." he breathed, watching Topaz standing in the arched doorway.

"What?" Beck inquired, setting his glass on the table.

Alex grinned, shaking his head as he massaged his jaw. "Not long ago, I'd never heard of Topaz Emerson. Now, every time I look up, there she is."

Beck turned to follow the line of his patient's gaze. "Topaz Emerson, I presume?" he remarked, his jade-green gaze observing the devastating chocolate-skinned beauty across the room. "And you've decided to cut things off with her?" he asked, still looking toward the doorway. "Hmph. If you can walk away from a dime like that, you're a better man than I could ever *hope* to be," he declared, turning as he spoke. "Don't take that as a professional viewpoint," he advised, grinning at the look Alex flashed him. "I'm speaking as a man, not a psychiatrist."

Alex chuckled and smoothed one hand across the lapel of his stylish olive-green suit coat. "I hear ya, but I'm not a better man, B. Just a dumber one," he corrected, continuing to stare at Topaz. His eyes narrowed further, but there was now a more probing element within the depths.

For some reason, Alex felt Topaz wasn't herself. The glow she usually possessed seemed somewhat dimmed. She was as lovely as ever, but there was definitely a more solemn aura surrounding her this evening.

Topaz smoothed her hands across the bell sleeves of the peach cashmere sweater she wore with fitted cream pants and matching low boots. The evening had turned quite cool, but she acknowledged her chill had little to do with the weather.

The reality that her business was gone still had her reeling. More unsettling, however, was the fact that it might not have been an accident.

Simon met Topaz at the dining room entrance and pulled her back against his chest. "You up for this?" he asked, rubbing his hands along her arms.

She nodded, turning to pat his cheek. "I needed to be out tonight. Thank you."

He kissed her cheek. "I agree," he murmured against her ear. "Let's go," he instructed when the hostess arrived to escort them to the table.

Beck Gillam had turned to take another look at Topaz. He saw the couple strolling arm in arm across the room and reluctantly turned to observe his patient's reaction. As he feared, Alex's face was a picture of sinister intent. Beck watched as his hand curved into a massive fist.

"Let's start confirming those sessions, huh?" Beck suggested, reaching for his electronic planner.

Alex continued to watch Topaz holding hands with Simon Whitley. He faintly heard someone say, "There she is." It took a few moments before he realized they were referring to Topaz. He couldn't hear many details, but it was clear that something had happened. It involved Topaz and it was something terrible.

"How do those dates sound to you, Zan? Zan?" Beck called, watching his patient stand. "Zan? Zan!"

Alex didn't look back as he closed the distance between himself and the table Topaz and Simon shared.

"Let's see . . ." Topaz sighed, her gaze scanning the heavy, leather-bound menu. She was about to give her order when someone took her by the arm. Her chest constricted when she looked up to find Alex at her side.

"Can we talk?" he asked, though he was already urging her from her seat.

Simon stood. "Man, she's been through a lot—"

Alex's murderous glare quieted Simon instantly. Topaz noticed and reached out to squeeze Simon's hand.

"It's fine," she assured him. "Go on and order for me," she added, leaving him with an easy smile.

Alex didn't speak until they left the dining room. "What are you doing with him?" he softly inquired as they walked.

"Like it's any of your business," she snapped, almost feeling his ice-blue glare when he looked at her. Finally, she sighed. "He didn't want me alone after . . . what happened."

Alex found a semiprivate area just off from the bar. "After *what* happened?"

Topaz searched his face intently. "Haven't you heard?"

"Would I be asking if I had?"

"I—it's just that it was all over the news and I . . ." She trailed off, tears beginning to pressure her eyes for what had to be the thirtieth time that day. "My . . . my business—the garage, it's gone. There was a fire—"

"What!" Alex exploded, releasing Topaz's arm when he felt the rage beginning to simmer in his gut. "You tell me what happened."

Topaz folded her arms, hiding her hands inside the wide sleeves of her sweater. "I don't have many details yet. The fire chief said he'd be calling . . . there's gonna be an investigation . . . please don't say 'I told you so,'" she implored, looking up to see him staring down at her.

"I would never say that to you," he whispered, stepping closer to cup her face against his wide palm. "Are you all right?" he asked.

"I'm okay," she confirmed with a nod. "I admit, I'm a little shaky and I'm a whole lot mad."

Alex smiled at her toughness, loving the silken texture of her dark skin as his thumb stroked her cheek. "So you don't think it was an accident?"

"Not at all, *but* I'll wait. See what the fire chief has to say about it."

"Thought about rebuilding?"

Topaz shrugged. "Maybe. I really haven't had time to dwell on it," she sighed, her eyes clouding with distaste as she looked around. "Right now I just want to get as far away from this town as possible."

Damn, man. I think you're more interested in the news biz than you're lettin' on," Clifton Knowles teased his publisher when the man arrived shortly after the budget meeting began.

Alex chuckled softly so as not to disrupt the reporters. "I guess I do miss the grind. I really just wanted to hear what Casey's come up with so far."

Of course, Alex had voiced the desire of almost everyone in the room. After all, the young man had emerged as the lead reporter regarding the hottest topic in town: the Briarcliff buyouts and the fire that had ruined one of the area's most lucrative businesses. Casey Williams was a veritable well of information and garnered most of the meeting time. During his briefing, he mentioned the connection between Lockhurst Properties and Weston Enterprises. Alex jotted both names on the pad he held and enclosed them in a dark circle.

TWELVE

"This is nice, man," Alex sighed, savoring the strong flavor of the cognac that warmed his bones. "Think your uncle would mind renting it out for another weekend?"

Scott Woods fixed his oldest friend with a look of phony agitation. "Please, kid, you practically family. Uncle G. would knock my skull in if I asked how much he'd charge to *rent* this cabin to you."

Alex chuckled, picturing Scott's gregarious uncle Gary in his mind. "Well, tell him to be expecting a call from me," he sighed.

"Considering the deal *he* got on this place, I doubt he'd even consider *renting* to anyone," Scott remarked, his deep-set brown eyes feasting on the extensive spread of land visible past the glass of the French doors. The two-story, eighteen-bedroom cabin was snuggled deep in the picturesque mountains of Boone, North Carolina. The hilly landscape was already sprinkled with a light frost, while the towering tree leaves reflected vibrant autumn colors.

"I gotta admit, I didn't think you'd take the invitation," Scott was saying after downing the remnants of his bourbon.

Alex shrugged. "I really hadn't planned to, but everything got so crazy back there, I figured I could use a break. It's only a weekend, right?"

"Exactly, my brotha," Scott drawled, deliberately overexaggerating the statement. "I promise you a feast for your eyes," he added, smiling as they clinked glasses.

Alex turned back toward the view. "Yeah, I can believe that."

Scott was shaking his head. "Not out the window, yo. I mean inside these very walls. Cice's got some friends, man . . ." He trailed away, emphasizing how impressed he was by his fiancée's friends.

Alex rolled his eyes. "Not interested," he said, downing what remained of the cognac.

"Sorry, brotha, but you know how she is."

"That's right!" Cicely Grays called as she entered the room. "I don't want nobody mopin' around on my engagement party weekend," she told Alex while pulling him into a warm bear hug and kissing his cheek.

"I just need some rest, Cice. I needed to escape Charlotte for a little while."

"Mmm-hmm," Cicely acknowledged, propping her hands over her hips. "City's a real hotbed these days, so I understand how you feel. No pun intended," she added, realizing the way her expression might have come across.

Alex was clearly confused. He exchanged glances with Scott, then looked down at the voluptuous five-foot-three beauty standing next to him.

"What are you talkin' about?" he finally inquired.

Cicely smoothed her hands across the sleeves of her mocha sweater. "The fire," she whispered.

Alex stepped closer. "Y'all heard about that all the way in Raleigh?"

Scott shrugged. "We'd have heard about it anyway, since Topaz Emerson is a friend of ours."

"Yeah, she owns the business." Cicely explained.

"Topaz Emerson?" Alex slowly pronounced.

Scott grinned. "Mmm . . . one of Cice's girls. Talk about fine, man," he sighed, chuckling and grunting when Cicely punched his side.

"Anyway," she drawled, "she owns the place and has run it successfully for years. They say the fire started there at the garage, but spread to some of the other businesses. Topaz was hit the hardest, though."

Alex appeared in a state of shock. "I can't believe y'all know Topaz."

"Wait a minute. *You* know her?" Scott asked.

"Very well."

Cicely and Scott exchanged glances.

"This is perfect!" Cicely cried, clasping her tiny hands together. "I couldn't have planned it better. Y'all are gonna have a great time."

Alex didn't have the heart to tell her he disagreed.

Alex asked Cicely not to tell Topaz he was there. Of course, Cicely obliged, loving the mystery. Meanwhile, Alex used the rest of the afternoon to survey Topaz without her knowledge. Clearly she wasn't completely herself, but with so many interested suitors vying for her attention, she had little time to dwell on her woes.

Alex waited until nightfall to make his presence known. He found her just before dinner, near the boat dock. Her attention was riveted over the crystal lake and towering mountains with peaks dotting the skyline like skyscrapers.

"Topaz?" he called, noticing her stiffen in response.

Topaz bowed her head. "Don't tell me you know Cice?" she asked, looking back at him.

"Actually, Scott's my boy. We go back since nursery school," he shared, strolling closer.

Topaz's laughter seemed to echo in the crisp evening air.

"You mind?" Alex whispered, gesturing toward the spot next to her.

Topaz waved, urging him to take a seat. For a while, they enjoyed the silence. Both stared out at the view. Only the sounds of swaying branches, falling leaves, and animals in the distance filled the air.

"How are you?" Alex asked sometime later.

Topaz hugged herself, savoring the feel of the oversized black cotton sweater that enveloped her in warmth. "I'm all right, I guess . . . considering my life's work went up in flames last week."

Alex grabbed a stick and tapped it against the toe of his boot. "Heard anything from the fire chief?"

"Not yet. It may be a few more days," she said, toying with the braid dangling from her ponytail. She tried to remain cool and focused, but the facade did not last.

"Shh . . ." Alex whispered, pulling her close when he heard her taking shuddery breaths.

Topaz didn't want to accept the comfort, but her emotions overruled the anger she felt toward Alex. Her tears flowed freely and almost soaked the front of his sweatshirt.

Alex squeezed his eyes shut tightly and tried to focus on consoling the woman in his arms. Unfortunately, he could feel the rage just beginning to heat someplace deep within him. Just the thought of anyone causing her one moment's despair was an easy trigger to his anger.

"It's okay," he whispered, kissing her face, temple, cheek, and forehead, "it's okay, shh . . ." The sweet kisses slowed, growing softer in their delivery. When his lips touched the corner of her mouth, Topaz turned into them.

The moment was sensual and feverish as their pent-up desires and frustrations boiled over. Alex cupped her face and deepened the kiss. His moans mingled with hers, just as he ordered himself to break away.

Topaz jerked out of his embrace, cursing herself for being a fool for him. She made a move to stand, but he caught her wrist. "Leave me alone."

"Topaz, wait. Please. I'm sorry," he whispered, his gaze boring into hers.

"Don't bother apologizing, Alex. Why don't you save it for the poor woman you're betraying?"

"The . . . woman I'm betraying?" he asked, his eyes narrowing as a frown formed.

Topaz rolled her eyes. "Do not play me for a fool," she ordered through clenched teeth

Suddenly, he understood. "You think I'm pushing you away because there's someone else?"

"Aren't you?"

"Topaz . . ." he groaned, realizing just how hurt she was—how betrayed she felt. "Baby, I'm sorry, so sorry. I never meant for you to think that."

"You mean, you thought I was too stupid to figure out what was really going on?"

"No, no, that's not what I meant—"

"Forget it, Alex," she hissed, jerking out of his loosened hold. "I don't want to talk about this again. As far as I'm concerned, that night is in the past. I'll never think about it again and it will *never* happen again!" she promised, prepared to bolt away.

Alex moved fast. He caught the hem of her sweater. "I need you to listen to me now. What I said . . . wanting to end things, it had nothing to do with another woman, because there isn't one."

"Then what *is* it? What's going on? Why can't we see each other?" she whispered, knowing from the look on his face that he wasn't ready to tell her. "I just don't understand why you'd do this when we—we've been so close," she said, hating herself for begging him to confide in her.

Alex kissed her temple and nuzzled the side of her face. "I know this is confusing . . . it's just—Topaz, for me, this thing is so scary. I can't even talk about it."

"Scary?" Topaz whispered, stunned that he would be so affected by anything.

Alex grinned. "Do you have any skeletons in your closet?"

Topaz shrugged. "Some," she admitted.

"Well, trust me, sweetness, a skeleton in a closet is better than a ghost in your head."

"I don't understand."

"A skeleton is something hidden," he said softly, staring down at her fingers entwined in his. "You can't hide from ghosts—they float around your head, drivin' you crazy, making you do crazy things . . ."

Topaz could hear the helplessness in his deep voice and knew he'd been struggling to deal with the mysterious situation. She decided not to pressure him for more clarification. "I pray you'll come to me," she whispered, cupping the side of his face. "We started off being pretty decent friends, remember?" she said, nodding when he smiled. "Sounds like the only way to exorcise this ghost is to get it *out* of your mind. Maybe talking about it, acknowledging it, so you can fight it, is the only way to do that." She stood on her toes and pressed a kiss to his jaw. "Think about it," she urged, then left him alone.

Morning began brisk and airy outdoors, warm and cozy indoors. The group gathered in the living room to mingle and enjoy the blazing fire while indulging in coffee, tea, and pastries. Though the affair had been organized so that there was a girl for every boy, Topaz had managed to attract more than her fair share of admirers. Several arrived downstairs to find themselves disappointed by the fact that her attentions were being required by another.

Topaz found Greg Vickers charming in spite of his talkativeness. He was the type of person who knew something about everything—at least he thought he did. He kept her laughing, though, and that, she admitted, was the thing she needed most. Still, when Alex Rice walked into the room, Topaz found that even the extensive charms of her present admirer grew paper thin.

If Topaz drew the attention of every male in the room, the same could be said of Alex with regards to the women. Of course, Topaz couldn't fault one of them for being drawn to him. After all, who could resist his cool intensity, magnetism, strikingly handsome features, and those eyes . . . ?

"Topaz?"

"Hmm?"

"Your stance?"

Topaz was slow to look away, but eventually returned her attention to Greg. She realized that the conversation now focused on golf.

"My stance?" she inquired, pushing her hands into the back pockets of her hip-hugging denims.

Greg nodded. "I think many people are so unsuccessful when it comes to the game because they have a poor stance."

"I see. You play often?"

"Every few months or so."

Topaz hid her smile.

"I'd be happy to help you work on your swing. Maybe show you some putting techniques I've picked up."

Topaz had no desire to spend her morning "benefiting" from Greg's golf lessons, but decided it would be far better than wondering when or if Alex would decide to really talk to her.

"Why don't we meet outside after breakfast?" she suggested, fixing the man with a dazzling smile.

Greg appeared stunned for a moment, looking as though he couldn't believe she'd accepted his offer. "Okay, um, why don't I get you a plate of something to eat?"

Topaz smiled and nodded. When Greg hurried off, she strolled over to stare out at the gorgeous view past the French doors leading to the patio. She hadn't been there two minutes when she sensed him behind her.

"Good morning," Alex greeted, one hand patting her waist while the other rested on her hip.

"Morning," she whispered, happy he'd approached.

"Thank you for last night—our talk," he clarified, resisting the urge to pull her back against him. "You gave me a lot to think about."

Topaz nodded, her gaze still focused past the large windowpanes. "I'm here to talk whenever you're ready."

"I appreciate it," he said, before chewing on his bottom lip as he debated. "Um, Topaz? . . . Who was that guy?" he finally asked, looking and sounding every bit like an uncertain little boy.

"I'm having a golf lesson with him later," she shared, reading nothing into the question.

Alex smirked, smoothing one hand across his cobalt-blue sweatshirt. "Doesn't look like prime terrain for golfing this morning."

"It's not a game or anything. He's just helping me with my stance."

I'll bet he can't wait, Alex silently remarked.

"I'd better get going," she decided, turning then to smile up at him before she hurried from his side.

Alex clenched his jaw, his eyes narrowing in agitation.

Topaz met Greg Vickers toward the back of the room. She accepted a plate he offered as well as a mug of cocoa. Greg kept his arm around her waist as they strolled from the living room. Alex wasn't far behind.

"Now you want to keep your shoulders and feet in perfect alignment. Your stance is the most important aspect of your swing."

"All right . . ." Topaz breathed, her mind focused as she prepared to swing the iron.

She accepted Greg Vickers's instruction like an apt pupil, enjoying the lesson far more than she'd expected. She was happy that something had managed to shift her every waking thought from Alex Rice.

Alex's attention, however, was completely centered on Topaz Emerson. He stood watching the lesson from his position against one of the trees in the distance. He appeared cool, but a closer look showed the steely frustration dwelling in his startling blue-green eyes. A muscle danced wickedly beneath his square jaw as he witnessed Greg Vickers's hands cup Topaz's hips as he guided her movements.

Topaz made a perfect putt and laughed in glee. Greg laughed as well, both hands patting her hips before smoothing across the waistband of her denims. He pressed a kiss to her cheek, then another to her shoulder covered by the chic, embroidered quarter-length sweater coat.

Alex lost the feather hold on his temper and stormed across the yard. Topaz was still laughing over her newfound skills when she felt a hand around her arm.

"I need to talk to you," Alex said, without acknowledging the man at Topaz's side.

Greg moved to intervene. "Hey, brotha—"

"Um, Greg, it's okay. I need to talk to Alex anyway,"

Topaz explained, desperate to reassure the man lest he be the victim of a painful fate. "I'll catch up with you later!"

"Are you gonna tell me what's goin' on now?" Topaz inquired, once they'd walked in silence almost three minutes. "Alex?" she called, when he shared no response. Finally, she focused on keeping up with his long strides as they made their way to a remote area of the property. Topaz felt her heart fly to her throat when she noticed the tiny isolated structure where they were headed.

"Alex?" she whispered.

Still silent, Alex continued to walk on. Approaching the small, stone cottage, he pulled open the heavy oak door and tugged Topaz inside behind him.

"What the hell are you doing?" he asked at last, once the door was shut tight.

Topaz blinked, her sparkling gaze dimming with confusion.

Alex grimaced, looking down at the carpeted floor while massaging his neck in hopes of cooling his temper. "How could you stand there and let that nigga feel all over you like that?" he asked, the question directed toward the floor.

Topaz uttered a short, surprised laugh. "It wasn't like that. We—he was giving me a golf lesson. I told you that."

"Goodness, you can't possibly be *this* clueless," he hissed, his stare narrowing sharply when he looked at her.

"Damn it, Alex, he only offered to help me with my swing!"

"Hell, Topaz, the fool looked like he was ready to screw you right there. You had to know that," he whispered.

"I don't have to take this from you," she decided with a flippant wave.

Alex caught her arm when she stomped past. "I'm not done," he told her.

"Who do you think you are?" Topaz snapped, wrenching free of his hold. "What right do you have to question anything or anyone I'm involved with?"

"What are you tryin' to say?"

"I said it! You have no right to come at me like this. I don't have to justify a thing to you!"

"Topaz—"

"Especially when it's about somethin' as innocent as a golf lesson!" she raged.

Alex, however, seemed calm. "A golf lesson?" he almost whispered, a wicked smirk triggering deep dimples near his mouth. "A golf lesson. And I suppose if he'd stuck his hand down inside your pants, you would've thought he was just tryin' to give you a better stance?"

Topaz slapped him and didn't stand around to witness his reaction. Again, she prepared to storm off, but again, she was hindered. Alex's reflexes were swift. He caught her arm in one hand while the other curved around her neck. He punished her with a deep kiss. Of course, the "punishment" simply belied the sensual, heated thrusts of the kiss.

Topaz kept her hands curled into fists, which she pounded against his chest. The blows had little power as the seeking, caressing lunges of his tongue soon left her gasping his name.

Several moments passed, and then Topaz felt Alex's touch venturing to the button securing her jeans. Her anger was rejuvenated, her fists slamming against his chest and shoulders. His kisses were impossible to resist, but she would not allow her desire for him to overrule all rational thought.

Of course, Alex was unfazed by her resistance. He ignored the refusals and suavely unfastened her pants, removing them and her shoes. He lifted her as though she were weightless and carried her despite her kicking and punching, to the sofa. There, he made her straddle his lap, keeping her wrists locked in his grasp as he unraveled her ponytail.

"Damn you." She sneered, desperate to free her wrists. An angry tear slid from the corner of her eye when she felt her body respond to his touch, which ventured beneath her sweater. Her lower lip trembled in a mix of frustration and desire. "Don't." She weakly resisted when he pushed the sweater from her shoulders and went to work on the bra hooks.

The straps gave way once the fastenings were loosened. Alex released her wrists in order to free her of the lacy garment. Immediately, Topaz responded with a cracking slap to the side of his face.

Alex grimaced at the sting before jerking her close. "Stop fighting me," he ordered, tightening his hold on her upper arms.

His striking stare drained her refusal and Topaz averted her face when he leaned close to ravish her neck with his attention. Her lashes fluttered with a will of their own. Her fingers curved into the neckline of his sweatshirt and she pulled him closer.

Alex's massive hands smoothed down her back and hips, savoring the feel of her silken dark chocolate form bared to his gaze. His hold firmed upon her waist to settle her closer. One hand moved to cup a breast for his mouth. Topaz let her head fall back as his lips traced the plump circumference of her breast. His tongue stroked her infrequently, finally closing around one nipple and suckling as the bud grew more rigid with his manipulations.

Topaz watched as his mouth worked across her skin. She observed the way his sleek brows drew closed as he focused on her body. When he turned his attention to the other firming bud, she wiggled herself across the incredible ridge straining beneath his jeans.

"Alex," she moaned, only to have him push her down on the sofa to further indulge himself in the pleasures of her body.

Leaving her clothed only in the inviting wispy panties, Alex began a devastating assault against the uncovered areas. Topaz squeezed her eyes shut, determined not to lose herself in such overwhelming pleasure. Of course, that would be impossible to accomplish as he began to satisfy her through the barrier of her only undergarment. She could feel his nose nudging her—his tongue feverishly thrusting against the drenched middle of her panties. Her breathless cries filled the tiny cabin and eventually she sought to free herself from the confines of the lingerie.

Alex pressed her hands to her sides and held her in place while he continued the erotic torture. At last, his perfect teeth tugged away the panties. He loved her with his lips and tongue until she screamed his name. When at last protection was in place, he pleased her with the delights of his incredible body. Desire left Topaz both drained yet unashamedly wanton. They spent the entire day making love. Alex only allowed Topaz brief intervals of sleep between the rapacious love sessions that zapped her strength while invigorating her erogenous zones. It was approaching dusk when they finally walked out of the hidden cottage.

THIRTEEN

Horace White and Stan Webster sat stone-faced and speechless as they watched the short, thin, balding man who had just completed his report.

Horace leaned forward, bracing his elbows on the top of his desk. "You're kidding, right?"

"A joke before he gives us the real story?" Stan guessed.

Raymond Jolzon shook his head while closing the silver briefcase he'd brought into the meeting. "I assure you both that we are not mistaken," he said, fixing both partners with his steadiest gaze.

Horace and Stan looked at one another. After almost a full minute, grins simultaneously creased their faces.

"Damn, Ray, when we asked you to do the survey, we were just covering our bases. We never expected you to find somethin' like this."

Raymond shrugged, but appreciated Stan Webster's astonishment. "What will you do with this information?" he inquired, chuckling when the partners responded with dazed looks. "You both realize, you all are now very comfortable financially."

Horace slowly spread his hands. "Ray, we've *been* very comfortable *financially*."

"Yeah, but now you're *filthy* comfortable," he clarified, pulling his briefcase off the table and turning for the door. "Call me when you get over the shock."

"Did you expect this?" Horace whispered, when he and his partner were alone.

"Not in *two* million years. . . . It all makes perfect sense, though."

"You mean the buyouts?"

Stan only nodded.

"What do you think we should do?"

"I think it's time to have another meeting."

Topaz attempted to smother another yawn, but failed at the task. "Simon," she groaned, leaning her head against the man's shoulder.

"Just a little longer, sweetheart," he whispered, smiling down at her.

"I don't believe you," she grumbled, feeling his shoulder when he chuckled.

"Simon, my man, you plan on takin' advantage of Weston or Graeme when you play the market again?"

Simon shrugged. "I don't plan on getting too excited. I'm content with my employee stock options. As for the other . . . I'll have to tread carefully. They're the competition on several points."

"Smart man," someone commented.

Talk of business and politics continued to filter through all conversations. Topaz shifted her stance and, this time, managed to smother another yawn. Simon had asked that she accompany him to the party and she accepted despite her lack of energy. Since returning from the weekend gathering several days earlier, she'd been unable to catch up on the sleep she desperately needed. She hadn't seen

Alex since the evening of their day together. He left that very night, taking all her hopes for the possibility of their relationship righting itself. Grimacing over the intrusion of unwanted thoughts, Topaz cleared her throat and tried to focus on the current topic of discussion. Someone was saying how good it was of Clifton Knowles to organize such a gathering in their honor.

"Well, the *Queen City Happening*'s new entrepreneurs' page has gotten a lot of positive buzz."

"Not to mention the increased business we small businesspeople have gotten as a result."

Topaz felt her lashes grow spiky as tears began to pressure them. Thoughts of her own business filled her mind to capacity. She smoothed damp palms across the navy blue bustier-style camisole and the short matching straight skirt she wore. She was tossing her head back in an effort to keep the tears at bay when she noticed Alex arriving at the party. He didn't arrive alone. Topaz smiled, taking note of the woman at his side. Josie Sharp practically beamed with happiness and pride as she gazed up at Alex with adoring eyes.

"Simon, I'm going to get a drink," Topaz whispered, walking off before he could respond.

Clifton Knowles had joined Simon and Topaz's group. He too had spotted Alex and was calling the man over just as Topaz rushed away. Once introductions were made, the conversation returned to talk of stocks and future outlooks.

Alex allowed his attention to wander. He'd seen Topaz hurrying away and just managed to hide his grimace when he saw her. He knew she'd seen him walk into the room and he couldn't blame her for heading in the opposite direction.

"Josie, would you excuse me a minute?" he whispered

down to the woman who'd been eagerly participating in the heated business discussion.

Alex found Topaz at the bar. He brushed the back of his hand along the line of her arm covered by the sheer fabric of a quarter-length navy blue chiffon coat.

Topaz didn't bother to turn. She didn't need to, able to sense his presence—sight unseen.

Alex was cupping her elbow in his palm. "Can I talk to you?"

"There's no one around, go ahead."

He tilted his head closer to hers. "I prefer someplace more private."

"Why?" she blurted, muttering a curse at her reaction.

Alex's hold around her elbow tightened just slightly. "Do you have a problem being alone with me?"

"Course not," she curtly responded, setting her drink on the bar and allowing him to lead her to a more private area.

Once they were far away from the crowd, silence captivated their would-be discussion. Finally, Alex balled a fist to his mouth and cleared his throat.

"I'm sorry about what happened before we left the mountains," he said.

Topaz felt her cheeks burn as those explicit memories returned. Her lips parted as a wave of heat washed over her.

"I'm very sorry, Topaz," he was still apologizing. "I never should have treated—kept you there like that in that cabin all day. I just, um . . ." He trailed away, frowning as he fought to find the best words.

Topaz smiled, feeling the honesty lacing the words he did speak. She smoothed her hand against the front of his tan suit coat. "Greg was just someone I met and struck up a conversation with. I didn't take his . . . friendliness to mean anything more. I never would have slept with him."

"Slept with him?" Alex retorted, blinking in surprise. "Love, I never thought you'd actually do that. I was just angry over the way he was touching you—*his* motives," he clarified, sudden laughter rising to the surface. "Hell, I probably would've tried to kill him if I thought you'd actually let him . . ."

Topaz felt her mouth fall open. It was now her turn to be surprised. "Why would you care about that when . . . you told me nothing more could ever happen between us?"

"You know why I said that."

"Not really. I don't."

Alex stepped closer, caressing her cheeks with his thumbs. "Topaz, if you don't know by now how much you mean to me, take this as notification. I care about you so much that it scares me. And for a man like me, that can be a dangerous thing."

Topaz's eyes narrowed to amber slits. "What do you mean, 'a man like you'?"

"Damn," he whispered, his stare faltering as he realized his mistake.

Topaz smiled. "Does it have anything to do with those ghosts you were talking about?"

Alex chuckled then. "Somethin' like that," he admitted, watching her shake her head.

"Why won't you talk to me, Alex? I wouldn't betray your confidence."

"I know that," he whispered fiercely. "It's all just too complicated and I—I don't think you can handle it."

Topaz rolled her eyes. "I run a garage, man. I can handle most anything."

"Maybe I don't want you to have to handle this," he countered, his thumb brushing her mouth before he planted a kiss there. Placing another on the crop of curls atop her head, he walked away from her.

Returning to the party, Alex located Josie Sharp, who was still talking with a group of other financiers. Completely disinterested in a discussion of appealing stock opportunities, Alex forced himself to appear involved.

". . . I certainly plan to take advantage. Now, before the price goes even higher," Josie said.

"And you know it's only gonna go up, up, up . . ."

"And I plan to be riding that wave, you can count on it."

"I can't believe how quickly the stock shot through the roof. They were relatively unknown a few months ago."

The weary expression Alex wore disappeared when Topaz rejoined the group.

She could feel his penetrating gaze follow her every move, but commanded herself to disregard it.

"Simon, I'm leaving," she whispered, hooking her hand through the crook of his arm.

"You okay?" Simon asked, turning to face her.

Topaz responded with a nod, but clearly she was drained.

"I'll take you home," Simon decided.

"Oh, Simon, no," she declined, pressing her hand to his forearm, "you don't have to do that. I have my car, remember?"

"Well, I'm worried about you."

Topaz regarded him closely. "Why?"

"Topaz, this is me," he reminded her, laying one hand against the center of his chest. "I know how much you loved that garage and we're here at a party to honor the entrepreneurs . . ."

Topaz couldn't mask her sadness. "I've thought about the fire every day since it happened."

Simon kissed her forehead. "I know you have and I'm concerned by it. Now why don't you let me drive you home?"

"It's important for you to be here. I don't want you to leave."

Finally, Simon grimaced and bowed his head. "I'm at least walking you to your car."

Alex's stare was trained on Simon and Topaz as they left the party. He made a silent decision that it was time for Simon Whitley to excuse himself from Topaz's life. Alex shook his head then. He certainly had no right to decide such a thing when he couldn't even be honest with her about his past.

"Guys, please forgive me. I'm so sorry for being late," Topaz feverishly apologized when she entered the president's office at White and Webster Contractors.

Horace waved toward his partner and the other remaining owners from the block. "It's no problem, Topaz. We weren't gonna start without you."

"Well, since Ms. Emerson is here, we can begin," Stan announced.

"What's this all about, y'all?"

"Yeah, why this emergency meeting?"

Horace waved both his hands, urging silence. "Y'all give us a minute and we'll answer all your questions. We've discovered why the property on this block is such a hot commodity."

"Well, don't keep us in suspense."

"To make a long story short, we're sittin' on a gold mine."

Silence followed Horace's announcement as everyone fixed him with blank looks.

"What the hell are you talkin' about?"

"This ain't no time for jokes!"

Stan stood and pushed his partner aside. "We decided to investigate!" he shouted over the mixture of raised voices. "We decided to investigate our own land. We hired a surveyor. He was able to conclude from the condition of the soil and other tests he ran that there's a wealth of petroleum flowing beneath us."

"Petroleum?"

"In *this* area?"

Stan nodded. "Which could very well explain why that fire at Topaz's shop was so destructive."

"Do those bastards tryin' to buy the land know about this?" someone asked.

Horace shrugged. "There's a chance they've already done their own study of the property."

"What in the world made you guys look into this?" Topaz asked, fiddling with a lock of her hair as she spoke.

"After that sit-down with Beaumont Harris, a friend suggested we look into why these clowns were willin' to shell out so much cash," Horace explained.

"So what do we do now?"

"Horace and I think we should all take time to reevaluate this Weston deal," Stan slowly stated.

Of course, everyone was a bit more eager to "reevaluate" their options in light of what they now knew. Still, no one could deny what they knew of Weston Enterprises—the strong-arm tactics they'd used with their former colleagues. Amid the melee of conversation, Topaz waved her hand and stood.

"Guys, I have an idea. It's kind of out there, so . . . hear me out, before you form an opinion."

Intrigued by her mysterious tone, everyone exchanged glances. Finally, Horace clasped his hands and leaned forward.

"All right, Ms. Emerson, let's hear it."

"I'm glad you kept your appointment, man," Beck Gillam was saying as the session drew to a close.

"I told you I was serious," Alex reiterated, deep chuckles following the statement.

"I wouldn't mind an introduction to the lady who put this fire under you."

Again, Alex chuckled. "Well, I realized it was somethin' I needed to do for a long time."

"But she was the catalyst?"

"She *was*."

Beck nodded, his green eyes narrowing. "Is it definitely over?"

Alex's expression hardened. "I don't want to hurt her, B."

"I understand that, but it may do you a world of good should you decide to confide in her."

Alex groaned, standing from his chair. "And how would you suggest I do that? How do I tell her somethin' like that?"

"*That* I can't tell you. I do think you'll know when the time is right and I think you'll know just what to say," Beck decided, as he also stood. "In light of that, I want to go on and give you your prescription."

Alex followed his psychiatrist across the sparsely furnished, spacious, dim office. He didn't bother masking the dread that darkened his face.

Beck handed Alex the prescription slip but did not release it. "I want you to be careful with these new meds, man," he warned. "They're powerful and you may not like the way they make you feel."

"Can I get a few more details here, Doc?"

Beck focused on the gray carpeting, searching for the best explanation. "You're a take-charge kind of guy, Xan. This medicine can make you kind of . . ."

"Passive?"

"Good guess."

"Damn," Alex groaned, tugging the slip from Beck's hand.

"Fill it, Xan," Beck advised, waving a hand before Alex turned away. "Just think twice before you take them. You'll feel a lot better if you try to beat this thing on your own."

Alex nodded. "Thanks, man," he whispered, shaking hands with Beck before leaving the office.

Alex's thoughts were filled with his therapist's cautions and advice. Still, he acknowledged for the first time he felt slightly hopeful and less doomed. For the first time he felt as though he had a chance of triumphing over the ghosts he'd lived with for so many years. Topaz came to mind then, and he muttered a foul curse at how terribly he'd handled things with her. He remembered her at the party—so open and willing to listen to him in spite of the way he had treated her.

"I can't believe I let her leave that damned party with Simon Whitley," he muttered seconds before his steps slowed to a halt. "Damn it," he hissed, his eyes narrowing as he stormed off.

Topaz relaxed at home that evening. She was lying on her living room sofa-pad, pencil and calculator in hand. Her eyes widened as she scanned the numbers that appeared across the calculator's display panel.

"This may not be such a crazy idea after all," she admitted, looking toward the front door when the bell rang. "I could even rebuild the garage . . . maybe," she considered, on her way to answer the ring.

"Sorry for dropping by like this, Topaz."

"Simon?" Topaz started, watching the man walk inside. "What's wrong?"

"We need to talk."

Topaz smiled. "Well, I'm glad you stopped in," she said, eager to tell him what was going on, "I can't wait for you to hear about my meeting with Horace and Stan and—"

"Speaking of which, where do things stand with the shop?"

"The shop?"

"Yeah, Topaz, the shop. Have you made plans about rebuilding yet or what?"

Topaz walked up to him, her hands clasped. "Well, that's what I'm trying to tell you—"

"Because I think you should consider doing it somewhere else—a completely different location," he decided, his voice turning hoarse as it gained volume

"Simon?" Topaz whispered, tilting her head at the urgency to his words.

"Honey, I think you can agree that too much has gone down on that end of town."

Shaking her head, she stepped closer to smooth both hands across the front of his light beige suit coat. "Simon, calm yourself. Now, what you've said is very true and I do realize that too much has happened on that side of town. I also know *why* so much has happened

Simon's dark eyes searched her face. "Why?" he parroted.

"The owners left on the block have just realized how 'special' our land is. I don't think any of us want to let go of it in spite of the fact—"

"What do you mean—none of you wants to let go of it?"

"Simon—"

"After all the crap you've gone through, you still haven't had enough?"

"Simon?" Topaz treaded softly, backing away from her former fiancé's advancing figure.

"People have been seriously hurt over there and y'all still aren't convinced. You keep playin' on the edge and nobody'll be able to help you. Any of you."

Topaz stopped retreating, her mouth opening in surprise and discovery. As Simon ranted, she finally acknowledged what had been right before her eyes. She thought back to a conversation with Casey Williams when she denied ever hearing the name Weston Enterprises. She had heard it, though. Once when Simon obtained his new position, once at a DeAndra Rice party, and again at Clifton Knowles's get-together the evening before.

"Do you understand what I'm trying to tell you, Topaz? Topaz?"

"Yes, yes, yes, Simon, I understand," she gasped, desperate to remain calm. "I understand and—I agree."

Simon's glare appeared to fade. "You agree?"

"It's what I was trying to tell you before you exploded," she explained, walking away as she spoke. "We've started to reconsider our adversity and, um, we're planning to contact the interested buyers this week."

Simon's relief was now more evident. He seemed to utter a relieved sigh before approaching Topaz and placing a sweet kiss against her forehead.

"I'll call you later," he decided and brushed past her on his way to the door.

Topaz quietly yet quickly slid the dead bolt in place when he exited. Leaning against the cool oak door, she eased down its length, her hands covering her face. Her mind reeled from the discovery. So many things—events came to mind, coincidences she'd dismissed as nothing more. Her heart raced, threatening to impede the steadiness of her breathing.

She'd been huddled next to the door for quite a while when a harsh pounding threatened to knock it from its hinges. Topaz jumped and flinched away. Crouching on the floor, she looked at the door—hoping that her silence would prompt the unwanted visitor to leave.

"Topaz? Topaz, it's Alex! Topaz!"

"Alex," she whispered, moving to her feet and whipping open the door. "What are you doing here?"

"Are you all right?" he counterquestioned, bending a little to look directly into her eyes.

"All right? Why? Why would you ask something like that?"

"Have you seen Simon?"

Topaz tucked a lock of hair behind her ear. "You know, don't you?"

"That he works for Weston?"

Topaz felt her legs weakening and turned away. "He came here. I thought he wanted to talk about how things were going with the shop. Then he—he just got so angry when I told him everyone on the block was still unsure about selling. I never saw him so angry," she whispered, then turned quickly. "Oh, Alex, do you think he could've had anything to do with the others being forced to sell?"

"I can't be sure," he admitted, slowly shortening the distance between them. "I'd be willing to say it was a safe bet, though."

Topaz hugged herself, feeling chilled beneath the folds of her cozy pink terry cloth robe. Alex could hear her breathing become labored and he knew she was weeping.

"Shh . . ." he soothed, enveloping her in his strong arms. "Don't do this, Topaz . . . it's gonna be fine," he promised, brushing his mouth across her temple. "Shh . . ." he continued, his soft kiss falling to her jaw, earlobe, and neck.

Topaz turned then and they shared a hug.

"Alex, do you think Simon could've had anything to do with the fire at my garage?" she asked, her voice sounding muffled against his chest.

"Shh . . . don't think about it."

"You do, don't you?"

"Topaz . . ." he sighed, wanting to ease her mind but unable to deny that Simon Whitley might have been involved with the blaze. He felt her shudder against him and knew her tears had returned.

"Honey, don't do this to yourself," he urged, holding her impossibly tight as he kissed away the tears sprinkling her lashes and cheeks.

Slowly, the feathery kisses caressed the tip of her nose and the corner of her mouth. Topaz nuzzled into the softness, her lips pressing against his, until their tongues were engaged in a sweet duel. Alex massaged her back as he moaned his appreciation. It was some time before he realized she was pushing him away.

"What?" he asked.

Topaz wouldn't meet his gaze. "You should go."

"Why?" he whispered, tilting his head to obtain a better view of her face. "Topaz?"

"Alex, I can't handle you—this right now."

He straightened, reluctantly admitting that it was best that he did leave. He cleared his throat to quell the rise of emotion in his chest, then nodded and left the house.

Topaz watched the door close behind him. She stared at it for a while, desperately wanting to go after him. Instead, she headed for the phone. Punching in ten digits, she waited for the connection and smiled at the sound of the brisk, deep voice that answered.

"Hey, Daddy, it's me. Um . . . I'm gonna come home for a while, okay?"

"So you guys are sure you want to take my advice on this?" Topaz was asking her remaining colleagues the following evening when they all met at her home. She was on her way out of town, but wanted to get things squared away regarding the buyouts.

"We're positive," Monroe Farmer, of Farmer's Farmer's Market, assured her. "Your idea puts us in the position of making even more money."

"Not to mention givin' us leverage to put a rip in Weston Enterprises' shorts by sellin' to someone else," Horace White mentioned.

"But not before we make it clear to our potential buyers that we expect certain regulations to be set in place," Topaz warned, clasping her hands against the herringbone tweed skirt she sported. "Toxic dumping, et cetera. We gotta do everything in our power to stifle that. We don't want an even bigger mess than the one we already have."

Stan Webster rubbed his hands. "Looks like we're basically goin' with the lesser of two evils."

Darnell Sands eased his index finger along the line of his shirt collar and cleared his throat softly. Obviously, he was quite stunned by the proposal he and his colleagues had been presented with.

"And you're all in agreement about this?" he slowly inquired, his gray eyes shifting over the group of thirteen well-dressed men.

"We are," Horace confirmed, clasping his hands atop the conference table. "Ms. Emerson is out of town, but we are able to speak on her behalf and this was actually her idea."

Darnell inhaled deeply while flashing his associates a quick glance. "Mr. White, you all understand that we'll need to discuss this. We'll need time to go over your concerns, which are quite valid and most relevant to the community. If your schedule permits, we'd like to meet back here with you all next week."

"So this means you're interested?" Stan asked.

Darnell and his colleagues stood. "Oh, Mr. Webster, we are definitely interested. We'll be in touch. Gentlemen."

The instant Darnell Sands and his associates from Mecklen Gas and Power were out of the office, Horace reached for the phone.

"Now to put the second nail in the coffin."

"Beaumont Harris."

"Mr. Harris! Horace White."

Seated behind his desk at Weston Enterprises, Beaumont Harris snapped his fingers to gain the attention of the four men in the office.

"Mr. White, it's good to hear from you," he said, hearing Horace chuckle on the other end.

"You may not feel that way for long."

"Oh?"

"The deal's off."

Beaumont frowned. "I'm sorry, I don't quite under—"

"We're not selling. Not to you."

"Mr. White, I must say this is quite a change from our previous discussion. May I ask what made you change your mind?"

"We *are* going to sell, Mr. Harris."

"But you just said—"

"A friend suggested we find out just why our property was so special. You can imagine our surprise when we discovered we were sitting on top of massive amounts of petrol."

"Petrol," Beaumont gasped, watching the men in the office all storm over to his desk.

"That's right, sir. Perhaps you should've gone after the businesses on the other side of the street first since that's where the gold mine is. Of course, you guys got some prime land for parking lots should you wish to—"

"This is unacceptable!" Beaumont snapped, his heart beating double time.

"No, Mr. Harris. What's unacceptable are your tactics, and since your company has seen fit to use force to get your way in this deal, we've decided that this opportunity isn't something we'd feel right offering to you. Good day."

Beaumont gently replaced the receiver and stared at it.

"Son of a bitch!"

"Beau, please tell me that conversation wasn't about what I think."

Beaumont leaned back in his silver swivel and fixed his associates with a defeated look. "We won't make another sale off that block. They've discovered the *true* value of their property."

"Damn!"

"We'd have been better off using our usual methods to get that deal closed!"

"No!" Beaumont thundered, rising from his chair. "We had a deal that there would be nothing that sinister!"

"We also had a deal that the land was as good as ours."

"Cheer up, Beau. This mess hasn't gone public. Besides that fire, there's been no other press. No one knows what's going on. No one except the proprietors, who will soon be dealt with."

"Casey, you still holdin' out on us, brotha?"

Casey chuckled in response to Clifton Knowles's boisterous inquiry. The *Queen City Happening* was in the midst of its daily budget meeting. Of course, the buyout story was still the hottest topic. Everyone eagerly awaited its appearance on the paper's front page.

"The story is solid, my sources have been confirmed and reconfirmed, but I'm inclined to wait a little longer. I want to present a beginning, a middle, *and* an end to this piece. I'd like to wait a little longer and see what the owners do."

"Is that wise?" Clifton asked. "This is a hot story. We wait too long, we may find it on someone else's pages."

Mmm-mmm," Casey replied, with a slow shake of his head. "This is a hot story that hasn't been leaked. Why is that? This story was in the works long before I ever got wind of it. No, boss, there's a lot more to this story than we realize and I think a few more weeks may make *all* the difference."

* * *

Brooklyn, New York

Topaz stood on her toes to reach a box of one of the flavored teas that filled the cupboard above the kitchen sink. She was reading the box of one when she heard her name.

"Hey, Mommy. You want some tea?"

"No, my dear . . ." Patra Emerson declined, trailing her fingers through her glossy, shoulder-length tresses. "That stuff will put you to sleep. Quick," she warned.

"Good," Topaz sighed.

Patra tapped her nails to the peach marble counter, then relieved Topaz of the tea box. She pushed her daughter onto one of the stools surrounding the kitchen island. "You've only been here a short while and I can still tell that you aren't your usual sunny self."

"Mommy . . . it's probably just the trip."

"I don't think so," Patra stated, setting a kettle on to boil.

"And the fire . . ."

"Hmph, nice try, but I don't think that's it either."

Topaz realized the sixth sense her mother possessed where she was concerned was building up to full steam.

"Talk to me," Patra ordered, finishing with the kettle and turning to lean against the counter.

Topaz slumped in her chair, her mouth forming a pout as she toyed with one of her pigtails.

Patra smiled, glancing down at her small, spice-polished toes. "Does this have anything to do with a certain young man I heard about?"

Topaz's amber eyes darted to her mother's face, and her expression registered with shock and realization. "Aunt Sophia!"

"Tell me everything," Patra urged, folding her arms across the front of her elegant mauve silk lounging gown.

"Mommy, I wouldn't know where to begin."

"Sophi said he was quite handsome," Patra remarked, taking a seat on a stool across from Topaz. "Is he as attractive on the inside?" she asked.

Topaz smiled, closing her eyes as she pictured the man. "He's even more attractive on the inside, Mommy," she confirmed, fixing her mother with a dreamy look. "I mean, I have a lot of male friends, but Alex . . . it's different. I knew that from the first moment I met him."

Patra eased off the stool to remove the whistling kettle from the stove.

"If only he weren't so complex," Topaz moaned, cradling her forehead in her hands.

Patra placed two steaming mugs of the fragrant tea on the countertop. "Is he worth the heartache, baby?" she whispered.

"He most certainly is. There's just something eating away at him. I know he wants to talk about it, but he won't allow himself to share it."

"So what will you do?"

Topaz shook her head and began to stir her tea. "I have no idea . . . that's why I came home. I just needed to escape, you know?

"I take it you didn't tell him you were leaving?"

"I thought it best not to, Mommy. I would've gone crazy had I stayed there any longer."

Patra raised her mug and blew softly against the surface of the berry-colored liquid near the rim of the cup. "Do you feel he'll soon tell you what the problem is?"

Topaz didn't restrain her tears. "God, Mommy, I hope so."

Patra set her mug aside and leaned over to grasp her daughter's hands. "Sweetheart, have you thought that maybe he doesn't think you'll feel the same about him after he tells you?"

Topaz shook her head. "No," she denied amid the sniffles. "Nothing could change how I feel. I know that."

Patra's expressive, almond-shaped eyes narrowed as she cupped Topaz's cheek. "You love him, don't you?"

Topaz nodded. "So much."

Alex lounged in his home den. The house was silent—he wanted nothing to distract him as he pondered the decision he had to make. In his hand, he held a vial of pills—the prescription from his therapist. Silently, he read the label: *Take one pill per day following meal. Hmph, may cause passive, punkish tendencies to arise,* he added with a cynical smirk.

His stare narrowed as he thought of Topaz. She wanted to be with him in spite of everything he'd said and done to keep her away. She was so very special and he knew she'd stand by him at any cost.

"But these pills will keep me sane," he said. *Sane, but dead inside,* a silent voice added.

The phone rang, its shrill sound breaking his train of thought. He welcomed the interruption.

"Alex Rice," he curtly greeted.

The voice on the other end of the line seemed laced with humor. "Alex Rice, Calvin Fines."

Alex's hand clenched reflexively around the pill bottle. Of course, he would have recognized the man's voice even if he hadn't offered the name. His suspicion mounted quickly and steadily.

"So how are things down there in N.C.?"

"Good."

"Paper doin' well?"

"Very well."

"So I hear."

"So why don't you tell me what's goin' on?" Alex

requested, losing his patience for small talk. He could hear Calvin Fines chuckle on the other end of the line.

"Man, you ain't changed a bit. You still all business."

"And this call *is* about business, right?"

"It is. We have a situation I'd like you to handle. You're the only one we trust with this."

"Why?"

"Well, we know you tryin' to go to the straight and narrow these days, but I had to try. Besides the fact that you live in the vicinity, we don't need a softie on this."

"What you mean, livin' in the vicinity?"

"The job we want you to handle. The target lives in Charlotte."

"Charlotte?"

"Yeah. It's a woman and she's a real dime. A lesser man could be persuaded not to carry out his duties."

Alex straightened in his chair, his heart beginning to race as his breathing grew labored. "What's this about, C.? he asked, his hands shaking as the man explained what Alex already knew.

"Anyway, it needs to be done before they complete the sale. If she's killed, it'll persuade the others to sell. It's a moot point to kill her afterward. Besides, killin' a woman would show these country niggas we mean business."

Alex felt nauseated inside and regretted the fact that Calvin had always trusted him so. The man's unnerving calm as he discussed ending Topaz Emerson's life filled Alex with a murderous rage.

"Lex? You there, man?"

"Yeah, yeah, C., but I'm afraid I'm gonna have to turn this down. I'm handlin' somethin' in the Caribbean. Payment's already changed hands, you know the drill."

"Yeah . . .damn. I really wanted you on this. But hell, everybody knows you the best. I just caught you too late."

"Sorry, man."

"Screw it. Handle your business, brother. I'll holla."

"Mmm-hmm," Alex muttered, setting the phone aside. Then, slowly, he leaned close to the end table and extracted a tape from the answering machine that had recorded the conversation. He stared at the tiny cassette, then put it on the table. Focusing on the pill bottle, he grimaced and shook one tablet into his palm.

FOURTEEN

Topaz had been visiting with her parents for two weeks. The time away had given her the chance to rest and think. She realized that she was ready to let go of the garage and start fresh elsewhere. She thought about how crazy the last several months had been. She didn't want to deem herself a quitter, but she'd had enough. Besides, throwing a huge wrench into the plans of their mysterious buyer was consolation enough, she thought.

Then, there was the matter regarding Alexander Rice. Topaz recalled the conversation with her mother. Patra Emerson had asked her daughter if she thought Alex would think she wouldn't feel the same about him if he told her everything. Hearing that said made Topaz feel, for the first time, that Alex's ghosts were truly eerie.

The doorbell buzzed and she finished with her braids. The two pigtails she had taken to wearing during her stay gave her a delightfully girlish look. Topaz flipped off her bedroom light and hurried downstairs. Exercizing caution, she took a quick look out the front door peephole and gasped.

She stepped away from the door and waited, but after a few seconds the bell rang again . . . then again. Topaz grimaced, inspecting her clothing. Snug denim cutoffs and a T-shirt emblazoned with the well-known bunny across her bosom wasn't her first choice of entertainment attire.

"Please go . . ." she whispered, closing her eyes and praying that Alex would leave.

However, he must have sensed someone was home, for he continued to press the bell. Finally, his calls were answered.

Topaz whipped open the door to find Alex leaning against the doorjamb. He watched her as though he knew she'd been just on the other side all along—debating. His incredible eyes narrowed as they studied her appearance.

"Can I come in?" he asked.

"What are you doing here?"

"I came to talk to you."

"About what?"

"Let me in and I'll tell you."

"Alex—"

"May I come in?"

"My parents aren't home," she blurted, the first excuse that came to mind.

Alex's lips twitched a bit and he glanced toward the floor to hide his amusement. "Does that mean you can't have company?"

Topaz almost laughed as well, realizing how silly she sounded. She stepped aside, her lashes fluttering and her nostrils flaring at the scent of his cologne. Her stare lingered on the breadth of his back and shoulders. The entire package appeared ruggedly devastating in a pair of sagging light blue jeans, navy suede hiking boots, a lightweight hooded sweatshirt under a navy blue and gray flannel shirt. The black tobagan covering his head completed the ensemble.

When Alex turned to fix Topaz with an expectant stare, she cleared her throat and pushed the front door shut.

"Um . . . can I get you anything? I don't think there's any coffee made, but I could make some, or even tea if you—"

"Is there someplace we can talk without being interrupted?" he asked.

Topaz blinked and glanced around the spacious, softly lit sunken living room. "We—we're all alone here . . . so anywhere's fine."

"Topaz, I don't want us to be interrupted at all. Will we be alone all night?"

She smoothed both hands across the seat of her shorts, then bowed her head and stepped past him. She led the way to the wing that housed her suite.

"Nice place," Alex noted, taking in the flawless luxury surrounding him. The two-story brownstone encompassed a massive space. Inside, its coolly elegant Mediterranean style created an atmosphere that was completely Old World.

"My parents may be out all evening. They usually are when they attend those lawyers' association dinners, but just in case . . ."

Alex motioned for Topaz to precede him when they approached her bedroom door.

"Have a seat," he urged.

"Alex, what's going on?" she asked, facing him with both hands on her hips.

"Sit down," he softly, yet firmly, requested.

Topaz took her place on the edge of the brass four-poster queen-sized bed. Clasping her hands, she watched Alex step farther into the room, where he shrugged out of the flannel shirt and tossed it to a chair. He perched against the stately oak wardrobe, his hands hidden deeply inside his pockets.

"You're scaring me," Topaz remarked, when he simply stared at her.

"That's the last thing I want to do, but it's time I told you everything," he said, his gaze never wavering. "I can't hide from this anymore."

"I'm listening."

"I should start from the beginning," he decided, pulling away the hat to rub his fingers across his silky hair. "De's my cousin, but last names are all we have in common. Our lives were completely different. The family—my mother's side—practically disowned her when she married my father. Because he worked a low-paying blue-collar job and because his . . . complexion was darker," he explained, looking up to judge Topaz's reaction.

Her eyes were wide. "Well, that might explain a lot. Maybe that's always been De's problem with me."

Alex cleared his throat and stepped away from the wardrobe. "When things didn't last between my parents, the family still shut her out—saying it was what she deserved for runnin' off with someone they'd deemed a no-good hoodlum. She didn't even bother to tell 'em she was pregnant with me."

"But they found out?" Topaz whispered.

"They let the wall down," Alex confirmed as he nodded. "Mama wasn't havin' it, though."

"I don't blame her."

"Yeah, neither could I. Still, it made things rough, real rough, and growing up that way made me hate seein' my mother run-down from work. When I got older," he sighed, "and more able, I took an after-school job delivering groceries for the corner market. The owner's brother liked me right from the jump and I thought he was cool as hell. Eventually, he asked if I'd like to run errands just for him." Alex laughed. "The money was incredible, but

Mama didn't buy the fact that there were no strings attached and she made me quit."

"Did you stop?"

"I told her I did, but the quick cash and easy assignments seduced me," he admitted with a lopsided grin. "Unfortunately, the older I got, the more difficult the assignments became."

Topaz smoothed a loose lock of her hair behind one ear. "What did the, um, assignments involve?"

Alex's eyes narrowed. "I was labeled a bouncer, but my duties sometimes extended to arm and leg breaker," he confessed, turning away when he heard Topaz utter a quick gasp. "I think I was like a machine then," he continued. "I couldn't even see what a monster I was turnin' into. Later, I tried to justify what I did by reminding myself that I was hurtin' some people who'd done some real foul shit to others anyway, so what the hell?"

Topaz's emotions went out to Alex at the lost hollow tone to his words. She watched as he took a seat on the edge of the bed and braced his elbows on his knees.

"All I knew was, I was makin' enough cash to keep me and my mother living well," he said. "I was able to invest some and I even paid my way through college."

Topaz turned to face him. "At least you did something good with the money."

"Hmph. A college degree wasn't enough for me to change my ways. My pursuit to become as wealthy as possible as quickly as possible made me resort to some pretty heinous things."

"I can't believe that," Topaz whispered, her light eyes wide and probing. "What about the paper?" she asked, refusing to believe he could ever have been so heartless.

Alex shrugged. "The paper came later. Much later, *too* late, I think sometimes."

Pressing her lips together, Topaz debated a moment

before asking her next question. "When you say you resorted to 'heinous' things, what did you mean?"

Alex leaned forward to cover his face with both hands. He had no desire to further the discussion, but knew he'd gone too far to suddenly develop a case of cold feet. "Do you know what it means to take out a contract on someone's life?" he asked, looking over at her.

A chill brushed her bare arms and legs. "I've heard the phrase," she whispered.

"But do you know what it means?"

"To have them killed. Alex, what are you trying to tell me?"

"I think you know. I made a good portion of my money carrying out those very contracts."

Topaz began to shake her head wildly. "No," she mumbled, almost stumbling to the floor in her haste to leave the bed.

"It's true," Alex softly confirmed, his eyes filled with regret as he watched her covering her mouth while shaking her head. "Topaz—"

"No! Alex, please, stop. Just stop, okay!" she cried, waving her hand to further emphasize her words.

"Baby, I need to tell you everything," he said, rising from the bed.

Topaz was nearing hysterics. "I know you do, I know you do," she chanted, "but not now. Not now, please."

"Honey, shh . . ." he soothed, stepping close to cup her dark lovely face in his big hands. "Honey, I know about the petroleum."

Topaz's expression cleared, her eyes searching his face. "How . . . ?"

"Weston Enterprises acted as the front for the company owned by the man I used to work for," he explained, watching despair fill Topaz's wide, exquisite eyes. "They thought it'd be better to have a local company acting in the forefront instead of making their presence known. Weston, in turn, felt it would be *better* to have a front for themselves—hence Lockhurst Properties."

"So everything we suspected about the others being forced . . . ?"

"It was true."

If possible, Topaz appeared even more wary. "The fire . . ."

Alex brushed his thumbs across her cheeks. "Honey, I'm so sorry . . ." he whispered, pulling her close when the sobs shook her body.

Topaz was unable to supress her sobs and almost soaked the sleeve of Alex's sweatshirt with her tears. She wouldn't allow herself to remain content in his embrace, though, and jerked from his hold.

"Did you have anything to do with it?" she questioned, her gaze accusing.

Alex's stare never wavered. "On my life, I didn't. I promise you that."

"So how did you find out?"

Alex hesitated, but only for a moment. "These people want you dead," he revealed, making her face him when she would have bolted off. "They know what you're planning with the gas company and they want you out of the picture before the papers are signed. . . . Getting rid of you— a woman—would show the others they mean business."

Topaz finally succeeded in wrenching out of his hold. "Why are you saying this?" she blasted.

"Baby, it's true—"

"How do you know that!"

"I told you I used to work for them."

"And they just laid it all out for you!"

"Yes."

"Why?"

"Damn it, Topaz, because they want me to do it!" he

roared, muttering a low curse at the horror on her face. "They want me to do the job," he clarified in a softer tone.

Topaz shook her head, slowly backing away from him. "They—they—they want you to—to . . ."

"They want me to kill you."

Topaz appeared faint, but instead of fainting, she raced to her bedroom door. Alex got there first, simply pressing his shoulder next to the door to prevent her from leaving.

"Alex, stop," she hissed, scratching at the doorknob, desperate to open the door. "Get out of here!" she ordered, when he pulled her close. "Get away from me," she cried, her voice losing volume as the tears returned.

"Baby, shh . . ." he urged, rocking her until her breathing began to calm. He could still feel her trembling and knew the anger she tried to display was simply a front for her fear. "Baby, listen," he said, turning her around to face him, "I never had any intentions of doing it. I told 'em I couldn't take the job."

Topaz sniffed, blinking the moisture from her lashes. "You did?"

"Yes, of course I did. I could never do that to you. I could never do that to anyone again," he said, smirking as he looked down at her hands. "It was a lesson learned late, but a lesson learned."

Topaz smoothed both hands across her forehead and groaned. "I'm so scared," she admitted.

"I know," he said, favoring her temple with soft kisses while he massaged her back. "I'll never let anything happen to you. I'd die before I let anyone touch you. Do you believe me?" he asked, pulling back to look into her eyes.

Slowly, Topaz nodded. Unfortunately, the uneasiness was far from gone. "I'm still scared. What am I going to do?"

Alex's expression hardened. "I don't want you to

worry about that. I'll take care of everything," he swore, cupping her face as he spoke. "Do you trust me?"

"Yes," she whispered, melting into his arms when he pulled her into a hug.

Topaz savored the powerful embrace; still, her eyes relayed mixed emotions. Burying her face into his chest, she forced the unsettling thoughts from her mind. The soothing massage Alex applied to her back began to deepen and she shivered. His hands smoothed away her worries for a time and she focused on his touch.

Alex pulled her back to the bed. He took a seat on the edge and had Topaz sit between his knees on the floor. He continued the massage, his fingers stroking the nape of her neck and shoulders. Topaz smiled when she felt him unraveling her braids. She let her head rest on his thigh, her lashes fluttering as he rubbed her scalp. She turned then and looked up into his eyes. Alex's fingers slowed, then stopped moving as his head lowered. The kiss was slow in coming, but just as sweet. At first, their lips met in soft, brief pecks, which lengthened as the kiss deepened.

Topaz moaned helplessly and turned to face him, bracing on her knees as she kissed him passionately. Alex was reluctant to break the kiss, but realized she needed her rest after such a dramatic evening. His hands tightened around her arms and he pulled her to her feet. Topaz watched him turn down the bed; then she took the hand he extended toward her. They settled beneath the heavy covers enclosed in a romantic spoon embrace as sleep arrived.

Topaz woke with a jerk, bolting upright in bed the next morning. A split second later, the memories came flooding back and she buried her face in her palms. She heard movement and looked over at Alex, who had moved to sleep in one of the armchairs, sometime during the night.

She smiled, her eyes tracing his magnificent features relaxed in his unconscious state. The horrible aspects of his past, she thought with a shudder. He was such a wonderful man that hearing him tell her what he had been shocked her to her soul.

A knock sounded on the bedroom door and Topaz rushed from her bed to answer.

Patra Emerson stood on the other side of the door. The stunning fifty-seven-year-old appeared full of energy as she snapped her fingers and shuffled back and forth.

"There are bagels and coffee downstairs, baby," she announced. "What's wrong?" she asked in the next breath, instantly sensing her daughter's mood.

Topaz managed a laugh. "Nothing, Mommy, I'll be down shortly, all right?"

Patra nodded, her hazel eyes narrowing when they shifted toward the door. "Bring your friend when you come down."

Topaz smothered her gasp, but kept her gaze focused on the floor. When the door closed behind Patra, Topaz turned to find Alex leaning against the wardrobe.

"Ouch," he said.

Topaz grinned, but shook her head. "My parents aren't like that, but they *have* been a lot more concerned about me lately. Especially since the fire and now . . . I don't know how I can pretend everything's fine when I know someone's out to kill me."

"Shh . . ." he ordered, reaching for her hand and pulling her close.

The soothing rocking and soft raspy words of assurance were Topaz's undoing, and soon she was weeping again.

"Is there anywhere else you can go besides here or Charlotte?" he asked.

Topaz pulled back, her eyes searching his face with heightened urgency. "Are they safe?"

"They are. I'm certain of that," he confirmed, patting her hip as he spoke. "I know how these people operate, but I don't want you here," he said, deciding not to frighten her more by revealing that the Fines Group operated out of New York.

"After I left here, I'd planned to go see my aunt and uncle in Louisiana. If I back out now, I'm afraid there'll be too many questions," she reasoned.

"Your aunt and uncle," Alex said, smiling as he remembered, "the ones responsible for your fierce cooking and love of cars."

Topaz giggled. "You have a fantastic memory."

Alex closed his eyes, bowing his head in acknowledgment. "Give 'em a call, tell 'em you're on your way."

"On one condition."

"Which is?"

"You come with me."

"Topaz? Are you sure?" Alex whispered, watching her closely.

"I'm positive. I can't be alone with this hanging over me."

"I figured you'd want me as far away from you as possible after what I told you last night," he said, appearing surprised and uneasy.

Topaz nodded. "The things you said to me last night . . . they were frightening. *You* were frightening," she admitted, watching him take a deep breath as he winced. "Alex," she called, stepping closer when he would have moved away, "these ghosts of yours are scary, but I'm not ready to let them win yet."

Alex caught her wrist and pulled her close. Closing his eyes, he buried his handsome face against the side of her neck. *Will you feel that way when I tell you the rest?*

Topaz snuggled deeper into the embrace, smiling when Alex's hands roamed her back and hips. Their cheeks and noses brushed before their lips met briefly.

"I love you." Alex whispered the hushed phrase he'd been afraid to utter. His dimples flashed when he heard Topaz voice a surprised sound. Pulling away, he smiled down at her. "I don't expect you to say—"

"I love you too," she replied, standing on her toes to grace him with another kiss. "Now will you come with me?"

Alex squeezed her tightly. "Anywhere you ask," he said.

Eric Emerson pounded his fist to the kitchen table and grinned. "Now that's the attitude more people your age should have," he told Alex, who had just finished speaking of the paper he published.

"It's a lot of hard work, Mr. Emerson," Alex cautioned.

Eric waved his hand. "More young black people should be in business for themselves," he declared, looking over at his daughter when she burst into laughter.

"As long as those businesses don't get their hands dirty, right, Daddy?" she challenged.

"Oh, you can get your hands dirty," Eric countered, "long as you wash 'em good and leave the mess at the office."

"Ah . . . the way you do?"

Patra waved a bagel at her daughter. "Don't get smart."

The bantering continued, but it was all in fun. When it was over, Alex had to admit that he had never laughed so hard.

"So, Alex, how long will you be in town?" Eric asked.

"Only a couple more days, sir. Just taking a few days off. I'm not sure of my plans after that," he told Topaz's father.

"I'll be leaving in a couple of days too," Topaz announced, "I want to relax a little longer before I head back."

Patra smiled over at her husband. "Well, at least she's finally taking some time off," she told him.

Topaz looked over at Alex and he read the unspoken question. He nodded, assuring her that she'd handled the situation properly. The Emersons spoke with the couple only a short while longer, before they excused themselves to catch up on the sleep they'd missed the night before.

"That went well," Alex commented, once they were alone in the kitchen.

"Do you believe it was really necessary?"

Alex knew what she was really asking. "Topaz, I meant what I told you before. I know these cats, they don't operate that way. I'm positive your people are quite safe."

"But it never hurts to be cautious?" she sighed, spreading her hands across the table. "I'm still scared," she admitted, smirking when Alex covered her hand with his.

"This trip to Louisiana is just a pit stop," he informed her. "We'll be movin' in a couple of days after we get there."

Topaz turned in her chair. "Why so soon?" she asked, watching him closely.

"I'm taking you to Seattle."

"Washington? Why?"

"I own a home there."

Topaz blinked and focused on the polished oak tabletop. "I can't believe you're doing all this."

Alex squeezed her hand and waited for her to look at him. "I told you I love you. You think I'd say those words lightly?"

Topaz leaned close, her light eyes tracing his face as she stroked his jaw. "If we weren't involved, you wouldn't have to go through this."

Alex closed his eyes, turning his face into her palm and

kissing her there. "Topaz . . . if we weren't involved . . ." He trailed away, choosing not to complete the thought.

Topaz looked away. "I'd be dead by now," she finished.

Alex pulled her close and they hugged across the table.

Alex decided they would travel to Louisiana via train. It would take longer to arrive, but he wanted to spend more time with Topaz.

"This is your only carry-on?" he was asking when their boarding call was announced.

Topaz only nodded, pulling her fuzzy hat farther down over her head. She followed Alex through the crowded terminal, clutching his hand like a lifeline. Alex draped his arm about her waist as they walked to the platform. He could feel her shivering and began to rub her back.

"What's the matter?" he queried, keeping his eyes focused straight ahead while he spoke.

"New York autumns . . . winters . . ." she remarked with a soft chuckle, "they're no joke."

"Mmm-hmm. Can I have the truth now?"

Topaz remained silent. They reached the platform, taking their place in the line of passengers waiting to board. Alex looked down at her then and she knew he was waiting for an explanation.

"I know it's stupid . . . I just feel so suspicious of everyone, like any one of them could be the one who's been hired to . . ."

"Damn," Alex hissed, hating that he'd pressed her to put her fears into words. "This'll be over soon," he vowed. "I don't want you to feel threatened by anyone."

Topaz curled her fingers around the lapels of his heavy tan suede jacket. "I feel completely safe with you," she declared.

Alex wasn't satisfied. "I don't care," he snapped, his gaze scanning the length of the silver train with unmasked distaste. "You're too special. Too good a person to be goin' through this crap. I'll do what's necessary to put this mess behind you."

"Alex, listen to me good. I don't want any more violence over this," she said, waiting until they'd taken their seats before voicing her thoughts. The set look on his face filled her with a sense of foreboding.

"I'm afraid more violence is necessary," he callously remarked, not realizing how serious she was. "Only way to deal with these fools," he added.

"I don't want *you* resorting to that. Just let the police handle it."

"The police," Alex parroted, smiling at the cuteness of her naïveté. "Baby, the police are no good at this. Trust me, you'd feel even more unsafe than you do now. What's needed here is—"

"I don't want to hear about what's needed here!" she whispered fiercely. "I'm serious, Alex" she emphasized, leaving her seat and storming out of the car.

Alex found Topaz a short while later. She was nursing a cup of hot tea at a table in the dining car. She stared out at the stunning late afternoon view past the huge windows. Alex watched her for a moment, before he squeezed next to her in the booth she occupied.

Determined not to acknowledge him, Topaz kept her face turned. Alex propped his chin on her shoulder and nuzzled his handsome face against her neck.

"What's the matter?" he whispered.

"Not worth going into," she retorted.

Alex focused on the passing view. "Well, considering

you just snapped at me and stomped off, I'd have to disagree. Now talk."

Topaz enjoyed another sip of the delicious berry tea and continued to observe the picturesque view. She was all set to take another sip when Alex took the cup from her hand. With a frustrated sigh, she turned her angry glare toward him.

"There's been enough violence," she declared. "I don't think we need any more. You're not that young thug anymore, Alex. You're older, a respected publisher and businessman. You should be able to handle things better now."

Alex looked down at the white oak table where he'd begun to tap his fingers. "I've struggled a long time tryin' to do just that, Topaz."

"Alex, this is dangerous," she warned, facing him more fully as she rested one hand against his chest. "I don't want you getting hurt or worse because of me."

Alex cupped her chin and brought his face closer to hers. "I can't think of a better reason to get hurt."

Topaz slapped away his hand, rolling her eyes as she did so. "That doesn't make me feel better. You're gonna mess around and get your ass killed!" she hissed.

Alex chuckled while pressing a soft kiss to her cheek. "Baby, I honestly appreciate your concern, but I've been taking care of myself for quite some time. I think I got this."

"Alex—"

"Shh . . ." he ordered, leaning in to kiss her more thoroughly. "Now," he called, breaking the kiss as it grew more heated, "you need to get some rest."

"Are you coming with me?" Topaz asked, smiling when Alex nodded.

He read her thoughts easily. "I have my own compartment," he told her, hiding his grin while watching the disappointment creep into her amber eyes.

"A separate one?" she parroted, her fingers loosening around the neckline of his Hampton sweatshirt.

"We need sleep, Topaz."

"We can sleep together."

"No, we wouldn't," he assured her with a lazy smile as he caressed the flawless dark skin of her face.

Moments later, their heated kisses had resumed. Several interested stares were cast toward the gorgeous couple locked in the sensuous embrace at the rear of the car. Alex and Topaz had no concern for the outside world. Their lips met in waves of fiery emotion, their tongues battling passionately.

"Topaz . . . we need to go. I mean it this time," Alex managed to say.

Topaz pouted when he pulled away and eased out of the booth. She was reluctant to follow, but knew his mind was set.

Alex met Topaz the next morning as she made her way down the aisle of one of the passenger cars.

"How'd you sleep?" he asked, his hands closing over her hips when they stood before one another.

Topaz uttered an exaggerated sigh. "Unfortunately, I slept the entire night."

Of course, Alex understood the underlying meaning and pulled her close. "Hungry?" he said next to her ear.

Topaz shivered. "Starved," she admitted.

"So what do I tell my aunt and uncle when we get to Louisiana?"

Alex set his menu on the table and debated. "I think it'd be best to tell them the same thing you told your parents."

Topaz pressed her lips together and focused her gaze on her own glossy picture menu. "So what persuaded you to buy a home in Seattle?" she asked, her eyes still on the menu.

"Tryin' to escape," Alex admitted with a chuckle. "The climate there, the rain . . . helped me focus more on what I wanted instead of what I'd done."

"Sounds like a relaxing place."

"It is," Alex promised, his gaze staring off as though he was envisioning the place. "I've never taken anyone there," he shared, looking back at her.

Topaz hugged herself. "I feel so honored," she teased.

Alex remained serious. "I love you and I want to share what I have with you."

The firm tone to his sweet words brought a questioning gleam to Topaz's sparkling stare. She fixed Alex with a narrowed glare. "I'm not sure I know how to take that."

Alex shrugged. "Why not take it for what it is?" he suggested, deciding to keep the rest of his feelings muted.

Topaz could see that he was emotional and thought it best she not inquire further about his telling words. "I think you'll like my aunt and uncle's place," she said, smiling as she focused on the gorgeous setting of trees below as they crossed a bridge. "Have you ever been there?"

"Louisiana?" Alex asked, glancing up to see her nod. "Never."

"I think you'll enjoy yourself."

"I never doubted that," he told her, winking to emphasize the suggestive tone to his teasing words.

A freezing rainstorm had rocked Louisiana since early the previous evening. All weather reports indicated the inclement conditions would only worsen. There had already been talk of numerous train delays and cancelations.

Alex and Topaz huddled close together as they exited the train. Bundled warmly, they trudged through the mass of bodies on their way inside the station. Someone jostled

Topaz from behind and she shrieked, losing her fuzzy blue hat in the process. The scene was so chaotic, she almost passed right by her uncle, who had been shouting her name. Catching sight of the tall, ruggedly attractive dark man, she screamed and rushed toward him.

"Uncle Sherm!" she cried, hugging the man tightly when they met just inside the station.

Sherman Emerson was older than his brother, Eric, by three years. Like his younger brother, though, Sherm was a believer in the entrepreneurial spirit. He had taken a small thatch of land, cultivated it, and acquired more property over the years. Now Emerson Livestock produced some of the choicest beef in the country, with several high-end restaurants patronizing its products.

"I wouldn't have seen you without this hair flyin' everywhere!" Sherm teased his niece, keeping one arm around her waist as he kissed her cheek.

"Uncle Sherm . . ." Topaz sighed, hugging the man again.

"Let's get you out of this mess." Sherman decided, already leading the way to one of the exits.

"Uncle Sherm, this is Alex Rice. I told you he'd be joining me."

"Ah . . ." Sherm noted, his deep brown eyes twinkling in recognition. "The new boyfriend."

"Uncle Sherm!" Topaz chastised.

Sherman feigned confusion. "Huh? Fiancé?" he tried, chuckling at the exasperation on his niece's lovely face. "I'm just messin', good to meet you, man."

Alex grinned. "Same here, sir," he said, shaking the hand Sherman extended.

The threesome rushed out into the blinding rainstorm. The parking lot was just as chaotic as the inside of the station, but Sherman led them right to his majestic Suburban. Topaz opted for a rear seat, anxious to stretch out and close her eyes. Sherman and Alex didn't mind, as they had conversed nonstop since leaving the station. Topaz smiled, a bit amazed by how quickly they'd connected. Especially since her uncle was known for his strong, silent demeanor. There was actually quite a bit of her uncle in Alex, she thought. Topaz drifted off to sleep amid their conversation and laughter.

Louisiana

"Baby . . . you gonna get out of there and gimme a hug?"

Topaz opened her eyes, realizing the Suburban had stopped. The rain still raged, but she could make out the face of the lovely, honey-complexioned woman peeking in at her from the driver's window.

"Aunt Rica . . ." Topaz sighed, easing out of the backseat and into her aunt's arms. Closing her eyes, she relished the embrace that was almost as secure as her own mother's.

"Let's get you warmed up," Rica decided, already pulling her niece toward the porch.

"Alex—"

"He and Sherm are already inside. I told 'em I'd take care of you," Rica explained, her full lips curving into a sultry smirk. "He sure is a sight to behold. I'm sure your mother would be quite pleased to have a specimen like that for a son-in-law."

"Auntie . . ." Topaz warned, as they walked into the house.

"He seems very nice and not just because he's gorgeous beyond belief."

Topaz was sipping creamy coffee when her aunt spoke.

The woman's words made her burst into laughter. "Does Uncle Sherm know you talk like this?"

Rica's hand rose in a lazy wave. "Please, that man knows I think the sun rises and sets on him. So? How serious are the two of you?"

For the first time that day, Topaz's expression clouded with uncertainty. "Auntie, would you understand if I told you I was too afraid to say how serious we are?"

Rica smiled, leaning forward to smooth the back of her hand against her niece's cheek. "I'd understand perfectly. . . . Do you love him?" she asked, watching Topaz nod. "Then that's all that matters, baby."

Topaz squeezed her aunt's hand, savoring the warmth her words provided.

"We better get these muffins and coffee out to the boys," Rica was saying as she placed napkins and spoons on the food-laden tray.

"I'll be out in a minute," Topaz called, lingering behind to enjoy the sight of ice crystals along the window. The shimmery glow captivated her so, she didn't realize how long she'd remained in the kitchen, until a pair of arms encircled her waist.

"Your aunt and uncle are great people," Alex whispered, setting his chin against her shoulder.

"Mmm-hmm, you know you've charmed the both of them in record time?" Topaz revealed.

Alex smiled. "I think it's the other way around," he admitted, focusing on the wintry view outside the windows. "I wish we could stay longer than a few days."

"Why can't we?" Topaz blurted, turning in his arms. Her eyes closed in regret when she remembered.

"It'll be over soon," he promised.

"I pray we live to see it," she said, sniffing as they hugged.

* * *

The freezing rain ended sometime during the night. By late afternoon the following day, unexpected and uncommon snow began to fall, covering the ice that had formed. Topaz set out for a walk around the ranch. The place resembled a wonderland, with a seemingly unending expanse of land. The livestock had been tucked away in one of the many heated barns dotting the landscape.

Alex joined Topaz on her walk, eager to take a closer look at the incredible property. Dusk had set in by the time they reached the horse stables.

"Damn, it feels good in here," Alex noted, rubbing his gloved hands when they walked into the spacious building.

"We always keep it heated for the animals," Topaz explained, brushing away the snow that clung to her suede jacket and matching hat. "It's a bit cooler up in the loft. Warm, but comfortable," she told him, already heading across the hay-covered floor.

A narrow stepladder led the way through the loft floor. There, Topaz removed her hat and coat and plopped down onto the hay that served as a heavy cushion.

"I had the best times here at this ranch," she reminisced, her stare traveling around the space as though she was envisioning those times.

"Helpin' your uncle wrestle cattle?" Alex teased, removing his own suede jacket and white hat before sitting next to her in the hay.

"Not quite, no matter how much I begged to help," she revealed, giggling softly as more memories flooded to the surface. "Usually, I just followed the guys on my horse, observing but rarely participating."

Alex nodded, his gaze soft as he watched her. "I'll bet you still had fun, though?"

"Are you for real?" Topaz blurted, rolling her eyes toward the ceiling. "Makes you wish you never had to grow up, you know?" she sighed.

Sensing the dark turn in her mood, Alex moved behind her and began to massage her neck and shoulders. Topaz leaned her head back, causing her hair to cascade down her back and cover Alex's hands.

He smiled, immersing his strong fingers in the healthy locks. Eventually, he resumed the massage, applying increased pressure to the nape of her neck and the area between her shoulder blades.

"Alex . . ." Topaz sighed in response to the heavenly caresses. She felt his hands tighten around her upper arms and allowed him to guide her down into the hay.

He dropped kisses to her forehead and temple, before trailing his lips down the side of her face. To her mouth, he pressed quick, soft pecks that traveled over her cheek and jaw, then on to her neck. Meanwhile, his hands disappeared beneath the hem of the fuzzy crimson sweater she wore. Topaz assisted him in pulling the garment over her head. She was so absorbed in the man's touch, she didn't realize he'd removed her remaining attire, until a slight breeze whisked across her skin.

A tuft of hay served as an effective stimulator. Alex trailed the hay between her breasts, encircling the dark mounds once before applying the same treatment to the firming nipples. The simple caress left Topaz urging Alex for more. He finally replaced the hay with his mouth and the scene turned lustier. They made love in the middle of the hay-covered loft.

Much later, the couple slept cuddled close together. The contented smile Topaz wore began to fade as she awakened.

"Alex?" she whispered, trying to move in his evertightening embrace. "Alex?" she called again, attempting to turn in his arms. Faintly, she thought she could hear him moaning. His hold continued to tighten to the point that Topaz felt her breathing grow labored. "Alex," she tried once more to rouse him. Unfortunately, his crushing hold left her breathless and her voice was barely audible.

Thankfully, Alex soon awoke. He jerked, his arms loosening around Topaz's slender frame. She rolled to her back, inhaling deep breaths. Alex frowned, knowing that something was wrong and that he was to blame.

"What did I just do?" he whispered, watching as she focused in on his face.

"What?"

"What'd I do? What'd I do to you?" he questioned, sitting up to glare down into her face.

"Nothing—"

"Topaz, please don't lie to me. I can tell. Just answer me."

"All right," she snapped, sitting as well, "it was nothing. You were just holding me a little tight. I called you, but you were sleeping so hard and—"

"God . . ."

"Alex? What?" Topaz breathed, reaching out to touch his forearm. "Alex, talk to me now, you're scaring me."

Alex draped his arms across his knees and bowed his head. "Last thing I want to do is to scare you, but it seems like that's all I've been doin'."

"I wanted you to talk to me. I still do," Topaz said, pressing a kiss to one of his massive biceps.

"How can you say that?" he probed, turning to fix her with his startling gaze. "After everything I told you, how can you say that?"

Topaz looked away briefly, then met his gaze again. "I honestly don't know. All you've told me . . . I should be terrified, but something won't let me be."

Alex covered his head with his hands. "Maybe you should hear more," he muttered.

"Alex?"

"There's more I need to tell you."

"Another ghost?"

"Oh, yeah." he confirmed, his gaze narrowing when he looked up at the ceiling. "And this one scares me more than the others ever did."

Topaz sat on her knees and leaned closer. "Why don't you tell me about it?" she quietly prodded.

Alex stood then, completely oblivious of his nude state. Topaz forced herself to look away from the fantastic view, fearing she would be unable to focus on what he had to tell her. "Alex?" she coaxed, when he'd stood in silence for nearly two minutes.

He grimaced and began to massage his neck with both hands. "When I told you about what I'd been . . . the things I'd done . . . I was sure you'd be out the door so fast."

Topaz reached out to stroke his calf. "I'm still here, though."

"Hmph, and *that* I still find hard to believe," he mused, managing a light smile. "I never want to lose you," he said, the brief easiness fading from his demeanor.

"Obviously I've shown you there's nothing you can't say to me."

Alex looked back at her. "I know that, but it's . . . your reaction to what I have to say now that scares me."

Topaz rose to her knees. She reached for his hand, pressing a kiss to his palm, then his thigh.

Alex smiled, then resumed his place next to her in the hay. "Unless you're a complete monster—a machine, perhaps deranged—there's no way you can take the life of another person and not feel something, a little piece of yourself dying with them. No matter who they are—whatever they'd done—you know it's a human life you've just ended. It sticks with you, Topaz," he said, averting his face. "Until a few years ago, I was that machine—that monster. The fact that I never served time for any of it put more than a bad taste in my mouth once I started to face the sickness of it all."

"What happened then?" Topaz whispered.

Alex shook his head. "It started with a serious case of guilt. Remorse came later. I even started a side business—offering security, if you can believe it—to friends, acquaintances who were being threatened—physically threatened." He frowned. "I guess I thought it would help me cope, like in some way I was makin' up for all the evil. . . . I soon realized I was only making it harder on myself."

"How?"

"I started to have these daydreams—really they were flashbacks of actual violent episodes I'd carried out," he recalled, rubbing a hand across his arm as though he were chilled. "Then the dreams came—then much worse," he whispered, looking directly into her wide eyes as he spoke. "I began to—to act out those episodes in my sleep."

Topaz shook her head once. "Act out?" she probed.

Alex focused his eyes on the floor. "If I . . . envisioned myself squeezing someone's neck, I'd wake up and find myself sitting up in the middle of the bed with my hands out."

Topaz gasped, her gaze riveted on Alex's hands. They were poised in the air as a visual accompaniment to his words.

He grinned humorlessly. "It gets worse," he warned.

"Go on." She spoke in an uncertain, breathless voice.

"My psychiatrist's name is Beck Gillam," Alex shared, leaning back against one of the massive beams supporting the roof. "We'd gone to school together and when I decided to become his patient, I looked at it as though he were just a friend I was confiding in."

Topaz drew her knees up to her chest and rested her

chin there. "What did he say about what you were going through?"

"The problem I suffer from affects my ability to control my anger. When I feel the emotion, the easiest method of overcoming it is to vent the frustration," he explained, shifting his gaze to hers. "That night with those guys in the park was as much about them threatening you as it was about what had happened earlier in the restaurant."

"The restaurant?" she questioned, her stare turning blank as she watched him. Then the memory returned and she raised her hands. "But . . . that was such a petty thing," she said, recalling the scene with her old college friend and his hot-tempered girlfriend.

"Don't take much," Alex said.

Topaz looked away, clenching a fist when she noticed how badly her hand shook. "Can't anything be done? I mean, is the therapy helping at all?"

Alex pushed away from the beam. "There're times when it seems to, my doctor even prescribed medication."

"But?"

"I haven't taken it," he admitted, fixing her with a wavering smirk. "It has a nasty little side effect that, for a time, may render me passive mentally and . . . in other ways."

Topaz's brows rose and she offered a tiny smile. "I see," she said.

"If I can't even turn to the medication, then I really am up a creek."

"But this isn't a hopeless issue," she argued, while shaking her head. "You've managed to grab on to that part of yourself that's sweet, gentle, caring. You can't give up, Alex. I won't let you," she decided, raising her chin when he fixed her with a skeptical look. "You'll get past this. I'll help you as much as I can. All you need is someone to be there."

Alex's expression hardened. "I won't put you in danger, Topaz. I can't do that."

"But I feel safe with you," she countered, scooting closer to massage his forearm. "A lot has happened and there've been times when I have felt uneasy, but you need me. This thing is eating away at you and I won't let you go through this alone."

"Damn it!" he hissed, squeezing his eyes shut as he massaged the bridge of his nose. "Topaz, don't you get what I'm tryin' to tell you? I could kill you!"

She blinked, her expression clearing of compassion and clouding with a hint of doubt. "You couldn't. You couldn't do that."

"I've done it before."

"What?"

Alex moved then, grabbing his jeans and jerking into them. Topaz reached for her coat, draping it across her chest and legs.

"Five years ago, I was in another relationship," he shared, leaning against a far wall with his hands hidden into his front pockets. "It ended the night I woke up and found myself choking her."

Topaz's startled cry reverberated in the loft.

"I didn't kill her, but I came damn close."

Topaz couldn't speak. She swallowed several times in hopes of finding her voice, but it would not come. She wouldn't have known what to say if it had. She tried to mask her shock and horror when Alex looked her way, but he had already glimpsed the telling expressions on her face.

He had finally done it, he realized. No matter what she said, he knew she would never see him quite the same. She would never feel truly safe around him. He was a murderer, how could she?

Alex reached down to retrieve his shirt, lying close to

where Topaz was seated. She reached out to take his hand and he took it, craving the gesture.

"One night you put your life on the line for me," she said. Her eyes focused on her fingers entwined with his. "You say it was about more than those guys threatening me, and I believe you. But you see, this . . . monster who you're telling me you used to be or still are . . . I don't know him. I only know you. Those fools could have done more than simply flash that gun, they could've used it without a second thought. And still, you stayed," she said, sniffling softly as her eyes pooled with tears. "So you see, I'm not ready to let you go yet. Besides my being incredibly attracted to and in love with you, you saved my life. Now let me help you save yours."

Alex bowed his head. "This won't be easy," he whispered, rolling his eyes toward her.

"I know."

"You may not feel this way tomorrow."

She closed her eyes, acknowledging his point of view. "I may not. But I feel this way today."

Leaning forward, Alex cupped her face in his massive palms. "How'd you get to be so sweet and so blind?"

"I love you."

"You know what they say about love?"

"Alex—"

"Topaz, can we not talk about this anymore right now?"

She smiled, scooting closer to kiss his mouth. "We don't have to talk at all.

FIFTEEN

Alex and Topaz left Louisiana by train and arrived in Washington State to find the weather conditions less than favorable.

"So, it's true what they say about Seattle," Topaz remarked, her sparkling eyes alive with humor.

"Mmm," was Alex's only reply to the tease. Clearly, he wasn't in the best mood.

Topaz had been walking under a cloud herself. Alex had definitely pulled away from her. His emotions had seemed to shut down since he had shared the incident involving his former lover. They had remained at her aunt and uncle's place a few more days. Around Sherman and Rica Emerson, he was charming and talkative. Alone with Topaz, he found little, if anything, to say.

Alex turned the rugged Ford pickup into the steep driveway that led to a breathtaking home atop a hill. The two-story burgundy and white ranch-style was practically hidden by dense fog, heavy rain, and trees. Still, Topaz could tell it was nothing less than spectacular.

Alex hit a remote located somewhere along the dash. One touch of a button illuminated the spotlights along the roof and tracklighting outlining the lawn. Topaz gasped at the effect.

"This is incredible," she breathed, her eyes riveted on the calming picture of rain blowing around the cozy dwelling.

Alex barely grunted at first. "Yeah, I guess if you break enough legs and end enough lives, two houses on two coasts is easily attainable."

Topaz closed her eyes. "Alex . . ."

He was already leaving the truck. Topaz watched as he moved to the rear of the vehicle and began to collect their things.

"I can take something," she offered, after leaving the passenger side.

"I got it," he grumbled, hefting the straps of their heavy garment bags across one shoulder, then grabbing two duffel bags from the flatbed.

Topaz settled her white tobagan more snugly across her head, then followed Alex as he led the way up the stone porch steps. He deposited their belongings in the foyer, then secured all the locks along the cherry-wood front door.

"I'll show you to your room," he announced, once again collecting the bags.

Topaz followed silently, observing the beauty of the polished hardwood floors, vibrant green plants, brick fireplaces, and glass doors. The room Alex took her to was cozy yet spacious. From the deep, fluffy peach carpeting to the king-sized bed cluttered with matching pillows, the place took her breath away.

"Where will you sleep?" she asked, watching him place her bags on the polished oak platform that supported the bed.

"My room's just down the hall," he explained, before turning to leave.

"I thought we'd share a room," she said, not bothering to hide her disappointment.

"Not a good idea," he said on his way past her.

"Alex?" she called. The rest of the question, however, was interrupted by a shrill ring.

Alex left the bedroom and headed toward the office at the opposite end of the long corridor. The ring had come from his fax machine. There, Alex found a message from Horace White and Stan Webster. Of course, they knew he'd been seeing Topaz, and the message to him was a part of their attempts to locate her.

Alex sighed, grimacing murderously as he stared at the paper.

"Everything all right?" Topaz asked from the office doorway.

"Message from Horace and Stan," he said, waving the page in the air. "They're tryin' to find you, but that's not what has me concerned."

Topaz didn't need him to explain. "You think your friends may track us here too," she guessed.

"They're not my friends, Topaz," he quickly snapped, his expression hate-filled.

"Damn it, Alex, I'm sorry, all right!" she hissed, her temper and tolerance stretched as thinly as they would go. She watched him draw the paper into a wad and slam it into a nearby wastebasket. "Why're are you acting this way? Shutting me out again, when you know your past doesn't faze me?"

"It does. You just won't admit it."

Topaz balled her hands into fists and rolled them in the hem of her oversized lime-green sweater. "Why are you so afraid to let me in, all the way in, Alex?" she whispered, her captivating stare glowing with emotion. "Are you more content living in the past?" Does it *really* help with all that guilt you're carryin' around!" she spat, then stormed down the hall.

Alex waited an hour or so before approaching Topaz. When he looked into her bedroom, he found her relaxing along one of the L-shaped cream-cushioned window seats. She appeared content, not pensive while observing the blinding downpour.

After a moment, Alex strolled across the room. Pulling one hand from the deep pocket of his loose-fitting navy blue sweatpants, he reached out to stroke the top of her head. He could feel her stiffen beneath his touch and let his hand fall to her shoulder.

He leaned down to whisper against her ear, "I made us some soup. Are you hungry?"

Topaz shrugged. "I'll eat later."

"I'd like it if you'd eat with me."

"Why, Alex?" she blurted, brushing his hand from her shoulder. "So you can ignore me or snap when I ask you to talk to me?"

Alex closed his eyes. "Topaz, please . . ." he murmured, pressing his handsome face into her hair.

Topaz let her lashes flutter against the need tingling through her body. She wanted to melt against him, but told herself to pull away.

"Fine," she whispered, inching off the window seat and leaving the room.

The house was silent with the exception of the rain pelting the rooftop. Topaz didn't realize how hungry she was until she pulled the lid off the deep soup pot and inhaled the aroma of the rich, beefy creation. Armed with a bowl of the fresh vegetable and beef soup and a saucer of hot corn bread, she moved to the small round dining table set near the French doors that led to the back patio.

Alex held her chair, then prepared his plate and took a seat across from her. Not once did his entrancing stare leave her face. Topaz could almost feel the unsettling intensity from his gaze. She prayed for an escape and jumped when her cell phone rang sometime later. She smiled at the forethought she'd used in turning it on and bringing it down with her.

"Topaz Emerson."

"Girl, where the hell you been? We been lookin' all over for you. You had us scared to death!"

"Stan? Stan! Calm down, calm down. I'm fine. I'm all right."

"Where are you?"

Topaz looked over at Alex, who was leaning back in his chair and listening intently. "I'm just taking some time off. Some much-needed time off. So what's happening back there?" she asked, eager to move the discussion from her whereabouts.

"Everything's a go, my sista," Stan proudly announced. "Well . . . almost. The company is interested and they've already started on all the research, testing, and whatever the hell else they do. All's needed now is your signature on the documents to make it a done deal."

Topaz twirled a lock of her loose hair. "Can they be faxed?"

"Well, they're gonna need your mark on the originals. Sorry."

Topaz closed her eyes. "No, no, I understand."

"What?"

She looked up at Alex, who had spoken. "They need me to sign the original papers for the sale. They can't be faxed."

After a moment, he nodded. "Tell Stan to have 'em

messengered. He can check with Clif Knowles at the paper tomorrow morning and get the address."

"All right," she whispered, then passed the instructions on to Stan. If the man was curious about the cloak-and-dagger feel to obtain the address, he never mentioned it. When the call ended, she pushed her chair away from the table and stood.

"I've had enough," she said and left Alex alone in the kitchen.

He had tossed for most of the night. Knowing Topaz was right down the hall and wanting him as much as he wanted her made sleep a hopeless wish for Alex. Around 3:00 a.m., he threw back the covers and left his bedroom. Topaz's door was ajar and he pushed it farther open. He stood there, arms folded across his wide chest, as he leaned against the doorjamb and watched her. He knew he would do anything to keep her safe. Anything. He had come to love her more than he thought he'd ever love any woman aside from his own mother. If keeping her safe meant keeping his distance, then so be it.

Topaz shifted in her sleep and the new position placed her dangerously close to the edge of the bed. Her head rested along the side, her long hair brushing the carpet. Alex went to set her back in the middle, his hands brushing the silver-blue sleep shirt that barely covered her thighs. Alex sat next to her for a long while and simply stroked her face and hair.

"Get the hell out of here," he told himself, moving to leave the bed, when he heard her whisper his name in her sleep. With a sigh, Alex pressed a kiss to her forehead and she awakened.

"Don't go," she called as he stood. "Alex," she whispered, taking his hand when he didn't acknowledge her request. Tugging gently, she silently urged him back, scooting to make room for him to join her beneath the covers.

They held on to one another as sleep revisited.

Later that morning, Alex woke to find himself alone in Topaz's bed. He rubbed the heels of his hands against his eyes when he heard the shower stop. Topaz stepped nude from the bathroom a few moments later, drying her hair with a small towel.

"Hey," Alex called, leaning against the headboard when she turned to face him.

Topaz read his expression easily and reached for his hand when she approached the bed. He pulled her across his lap and she straddled his powerful frame, her lashes fluttering when she touched his arousal, which was just as evident in spite of the black sleep pants he wore.

"What's wrong?" Topaz whispered when he only stared at her.

"Nothing at all," he assured her, his bright intense gaze lowering to her chest. His hands rose to cup the dark brown mounds and he buried his face in their fullness.

Topaz leaned her head back and moaned. She began to ease across the breathless extent of his manhood, growing orgasmic from the simple friction. Her moans gained volume when he tugged a nipple between his lips and manipulated it to a hard bud. He alternated between suckling and licking the sensitive peak, while his thumb caressed the other.

"Alex . . ." she breathed, whimpering when his hand settled between her shoulder blades to hold her close to his mouth. "Alex!" she gasped then.

He was silent, focusing on the sweet, chocolate beauty sitting astride his lap. Eventually, he gripped her hip and lifted her slightly while he freed himself from the loose confines of his pants.

Topaz let her forehead fall to his shoulder and smiled at the increased sensation. "Alex, please . . ." she whispered, unashamed to admit her need.

Surprising her, he switched the tables and rose above her, kicking away his pants as he followed her down. Determined to extend the pleasure as long as possible, Alex resisted her attempts to pull him close. He held her captive against the bed, her wrists trapped in his grasp while his nose outlined the shape of her breasts. Topaz's lashes fluttered like hummingbird wings when she felt his tongue dart out to tease one firm nipple. Her fingers flexed above his hold about her wrists and she moaned when he suckled the rigid bud between his lips.

"Alex . . . please . . ." she begged him again. Still, he continued to ply her with the torturously erotic mastery of his lips and tongue.

His attention ventured to the valley between her breasts, then along the flat plane of her stomach. He held her hands against her sides while he ravished her belly with sweet kisses. Her legs tensed, then trembled when his mouth brushed the spot that yearned most for his attention.

Topaz could scarcely respond. She was so weakened by pleasure, she knew she would have been unable to raise her arms even if Alex had freed them from his grasp. His tongue stroked the petals of her femininity before delving past the satiny folds to seek the treasure inside. Topaz pressed her head deeper into the down pillow, feeling her inner walls relax and contract around his tongue. Her thighs trembled so, Alex released her wrists to hold them steady as he feasted.

Much later, Alex suggested they take a shower. Topaz, unable to move, happily allowed him to assist her. In the sleek, spacious, black-tiled stall with its brass fixtures,

Alex held her at his mercy. One hand cupped her hips firmly while he suckled her earlobe and the sensitive area below it.

"No strength in my legs . . ." Topaz sighed, gasping repeatedly as his fingers worked one nipple to a protruding pebble.

Alex simply positioned his knee between her thighs and continued to have his way with her. Later, he lathered her dark form with a scented soap and bathed her as his mouth had done moments earlier.

"You have incredible stamina," Topaz noted, watching him on his knees as he massaged a soapy cloth across her thighs.

Alex shrugged. "Nothing to do with stamina."

"Incredible restraint, then."

"You think?" he asked, rising to his full height.

Topaz's eyes widened at the extent of his aroused manhood. Pressing her lips together, she reached for the cloth before treating him to the same pleasure he had just provided her.

"I don't want you to leave me," Alex admitted, stroking her damp locks as they lounged on the floor of the dark shower.

Topaz snuggled her head against his chest. "I never want to," she whispered, hearing him sigh over the water trickling down the drain. "Does that upset you?" she asked, turning over to face him.

Alex's stare was focused on her damp hair lying in wavy ribbons across her back. "No, I like the sound of that. Doesn't mean it's for the best, though."

"Alex," Topaz called, rising to her knees, "you told me everything, right? Everything you were holding back?" she asked, watching him nod. "See? And I'm still here. So please stop this. I'm not afraid," she fiercely assured him, drawing him into a tight hug.

Alex closed his eyes while silently admitting that he was afraid enough for them both.

"How does it look?" Alex was asking later. He had decided an evening out would do them a world of good. He took Topaz to one of his favorite seafood eateries.

Topaz had been engrossed in the contracts since they had arrived a half hour before she and Alex left the house for dinner. With a resigned smile, she shuffled the documents back in order. "It looks fascinating. I especially like the part with all the zeros," she added, favoring him with a teasing wink and smile.

Alex's hearty laughter turned the heads of several women. "So how are your guys gonna handle it?" he asked, referring to the employees of Top E Towing and Mechanical.

A bit of the light dimmed in Topaz's shimmering eyes. "They won't like it, but . . . I believe they'll agree it's a good idea. Plus, once they receive their cut of the sale . . ."

"Say no more," Alex drawled, chuckling as his cell phone began to ring.

Topaz was smiling as she inhaled the aroma of the delectable appetizers the waiter was setting on the table then. Alex checked the ID of the caller and cursed, drawing a look from both his dinner date and their server.

"Yeah, De?" he briskly greeted his cousin.

"Lex!" DeAndra breathed. "Do you know how frantic I've been trying to contact you!"

"I'm in the middle of somethin'. Could you get to the point?" Alex curtly requested.

"Where are you? When are you coming back?"

"I'm out of town," Alex tiredly responded, reaching out to select one of the mozzarella sticks from the platter. "Don't know when I'll be back," he informed her.

De replied with another overly dramatic sigh, "Well,

I'm giving a party in a few weeks for the City Council. Josie will be there of course and—"

"Hold up, De. Don't push Josie up in my face again, all right? She's a fine person and deserves a man who's all about *her*. I'm not interested in you tryin' to hook me up with any more of your girls, you hear me?"

"But, Alex, you and Josie make such a—"

"De. De? I'm with Topaz Emerson. I'm looking at her right now as a matter of fact," he revealed, sending Topaz a devilish wink. "No more matchmakin', all right?"

Silence met the order and finally DeAndra cleared her throat. "Of course, Alex."

"Ouch," Topaz remarked, watching Alex click off the phone and ease it to the inside pocket of his purple sport coat.

"I think she got the point," Alex said.

Topaz shrugged. "No, I think she'll save the *point* for me," she groaned, shaking her head when Alex began to chuckle. "You know she's not gonna approve."

"To hell with her."

"She's your family," Topaz pointed out, raising her hand when Alex opened his mouth to retort. "Hush," she softly commanded. "You think you can handle the drama?"

Alex leaned back against his chair, a contented smile on his face. "I'm just thankful Beck gave me such a hefty prescription."

Topaz placed her elbow on the table and propped her chin in her palm. "Have you started taking them yet?"

"Not yet. Too leery about the side effects."

"Mmm," was Topaz's only reply as she decided to keep her concerns unspoken.

Alex reached out to trail his index finger down her forearm. "What?" he probed, urging her to speak her mind.

Toying with the wispy mauve ties at the bodice of her

clinging dress, Topaz debated. "I know . . . the medicine is to help you, but I like you the way you are," she said, looking right into his eyes. "Faults and all, Alex, and while I understand how important it is for you to control your rage, I'd hoped you could do it through communication instead of medication." She shook her head then and smiled sheepishly. "I'm sorry, that's just me talkin'. I'm not a doctor or anything, so . . ."

Alex looked down at her hands sliding restlessly across the table. "I remember once I told you that I hoped your goodness never got you into trouble," he sighed, covering her hands with his own. "I hope you really know what you're getting into here. Exorcizing these ghosts hasn't been easy, let alone pretty."

Topaz leaned across the table and patted his cheek. "I'm willing to take the chance."

The rest of the week was like something from a fantasy. Alex delighted in showing Topaz why he had fallen in love with Seattle, while she was simply elated to be with the man she was falling more in love with. When Alex mentioned them having to return to North Carolina soon, she cringed at the thought of the magic coming to an end.

"I'm hungry," Alex growled, his deep voice muffled but audible as his handsome face lay buried between Topaz's breasts.

She smiled, raking her hands across the sheet where it covered his buttocks. "Mmm . . . and what are you going to cook?" she purred, enjoying the feel of his heavy frame still covering her body after another incredible session of lovemaking late that evening.

"Me?" Alex argued, his body beginning to shake when he chuckled over her question.

"Well, I'm nowhere near as good a cook as you are," she tried.

"Flattery will get you nowhere," he countered, moving his weight off her. "Up," he ordered, pulling her into a sitting position.

Topaz left the bed in pretend outrage. She headed to the bathroom, where she washed her face and pulled her hair into a loose ponytail. She retrieved her bathrobe from the bed and was slipping into it while stepping out into the hall. Suddenly, she was wrenched into an iron embrace.

Alex had grabbed her from behind, his hand clamping across her mouth. "Don't make a sound. We're not alone," he murmured against her ear.

Eyes wide, Topaz nodded quickly. She was almost afraid to breathe when he moved his hand and turned her to face him. "What is it?" she whispered, her light gaze searching his closed expression.

Alex was looking past her shoulder. "If my guess is right, and I know it is, my *friends* have tracked you here through me."

"How?" she cried, glancing across her shoulder. "How'd they find us?"

Alex went back into the bedroom, heading toward the spacious walk-in closet. "I have no idea," he grumbled.

Topaz began to wring her hands, gasping when she saw him leave the closet. In his hand, he carried a semiautomatic with a laser sighting.

"Let's go," he ordered, slapping a smaller pistol into her palm before pulling her out of the room behind him.

They crept through the darkening house. Topaz clung to Alex, whose attention was wholly focused on confronting the intruder with nerve enough to step into his home. They took the back stairway and spotted a dark figure ascending the front staircase through the living room.

Alex motioned for Topaz to stop where she was; then he continued onward. She leaned against the banister and closed her eyes to pray for courage. Alert, yet anxious, she crouched close to the carpeted stairs, watching as Alex tracked the intruder. She pressed her lips together to smother a scream when Alex ran up on the man and pounced. A struggle ensued as the two large males danced a brutal waltz. Punches were thrown and landed, furniture was broken, and portrait frames crashed to the floor beneath the pressure of their bodies slamming against the walls.

Topaz was trying to make out who had the upper hand in the tussle when, to her horror, she saw a third figure enter the violent performance. Ordering herself to her feet, she pressed the gun close, then raised, aimed, and fired as the second intruder pointed his weapon toward Alex. She was too late, as the man fired his gun just as her bullet pierced his shoulder.

"Alex!" Topaz cried, dropping her gun as she watched him clutch his calf where the bullet hit.

From then on, the events occurred in a dizzying fashion. The first intruder was aiming for Topaz when Alex managed to reach his arm. Again, they struggled until Alex wrestled the gun from his nemesis, squeezing the man's wrist until it crunched. Howling in pain, he dropped to his knees, but he was not quite ready to surrender

"Topaz! Grab the guns!" Alex called.

She snapped to and did as he had ordered. In seconds, she was aiming both weapons at their attackers.

"Good girl," Alex whispered, trudging over to take one of the guns. "Are you all right?" he asked, dropping one arm around her shoulders.

Topaz offered a jerky nod, smiling when he kissed her temple. Her eyes narrowed when he left her side to cross the other side of the room. "What are you doing?" she whispered, watching him push a button on the stereo.

Alex didn't respond. Instead, he inserted a cassette tape into the appropriate slot and pushed PLAY. In seconds, Calvin Fines's voice filled the room—it was the discussion of the contract on Topaz's life. The two intruders appeared faint at the sound of their boss's voice, and Alex smiled. While the tape continued to play, he reached for another, which he dropped into the lap of the man whose wrist he had broken.

"Here you go. I've got plenty," he whispered, standing over the cowering man. "You tell Calvin to cancel the job on this lady or I send one of these to every TV and newspaper in the country—starting with my own. Oh, and I'll be sure to get one to the FBI as well. They've been trying to pin somethin' on Cal and his pops for over two decades," he added, reaching down to wrench the man's jacket collar into his fist. "Now get the hell out of my sight before I forget that I'm tryin' to quell my murderous tendencies," he growled close to the man's face, before shoving him off.

Of course, the men did not hesitate. With the duplicated tape in their possession, they raced out of the house, using the beveled glass doors through which they had entered.

"Alex?" Topaz called in a tiny voice, when they were finally alone. He turned and opened his arms. She didn't hesitate to run right to him.

"Are you all right?" he murmured against her forehead.

She snuggled deep into his embrace. "No, but I'm getting there fast."

SIXTEEN

Alexander Rice and Topaz Emerson were the stars of DeAndra's party. Of course, it had been much the same scene since the story on the buyouts hit the newspapers. No one could believe such corruption had existed in their town. Though all the evil elements had not been revealed, the story, covered in perfect detail in the *Queen City Happening*, had sent several tongues wagging.

"Are you sick of this yet?" Alex was asking, looking down at Topaz while they danced.

She beamed, winding her arms about his neck. "No, this is something people should never forget. Not that they ever could. I'm just glad it's over," she sighed, nuzzling her forehead against his chin.

"You feel that way even though the real culprits haven't been brought to justice?"

Topaz offered a rueful smirk. "Sometimes things just have to be a certain way, I guess. Besides, those tapes are our insurance, right?"

Alex grimaced, absently trailing his fingers along her shoulder bared by the cut of the mint-green strapless dress she wore. He knew she couldn't feel half as content as she was letting on. "I don't want you feeling like you have to look over your shoulder every second."

"Well, if I look over my shoulder and see *you* there, then . . . well that's something I could definitely live with."

"I love you," Alex whispered, kissing the tip of her nose.

"I love you," Topaz sighed, closing her eyes when they hugged. Her lashes fluttered then and she gazed out over the elegantly attired crowd. She caught sight of Alex's cousin DeAndra huddled close to Simon Whitley. "Wonder what they're cookin' up," she teasingly inquired. A gasp touched her lips then and she pulled away from Alex as though she'd been burned.

"What?" he asked, frowning at the dazed look on her face.

Topaz smoothed her hand across the chignon at the nape of her neck. "I need to go speak with an old friend."

Alex pushed one hand into the pocket of his mushroom trousers and turned to watch Topaz head to the other side of the spacious living room. Something told him to follow.

Topaz had seen Simon and DeAndra part company a few moments before she reached the other end of the room. She followed her ex-fiancé to a remote den, where she greeted him in a calm, reserved voiced.

"Paz!" Simon cried, appearing overjoyed to see her as he rushed over with outstretched arms.

Of course, Topaz could detect the trace of unease in his dark eyes. "You're surprised to see me, aren't you?" she asked.

Simon stopped short, his unease becoming more obvious. "Well, yeah, yes. I—uh, I know how you hate De's parties."

Topaz clasped her hands together behind her back and stepped inside the room. "But that's not why you're surprised, is it?"

"I don't understand."

"Weston Enterprises."

Simon appeared to shudder, averting his gaze for one brief moment.

"You work for them," Topaz continued, bowing her head as she strolled through the room. "You work for them. Or at least, you did before all this bad publicity hit them."

"Topaz, what—"

"Simon, *please*, please don't ask me what I'm talking about."

"Even if I don't know?" he challenged, slapping both hands to the sides of his black trousers

Topaz shook her head. "For once in your phony life, can't you tell the truth?" she asked, folding her arms across her chest. "You can tell me the truth, you know? Even though I know what you did, I guess I want to hear your side."

Simon would not speak, at first. He simply stood across from the woman he had once planned to marry. He fixed her with a look he reserved for his toughest business associates. When she met that gaze with her own intense, unwavering one, he turned away.

"Simon?"

"I can't say it, Topaz," he croaked, raising one hand as though he'd had enough. "Whatever you're thinking . . . what the papers said, it's all true. Just leave it at that."

"De must've told you I was with Alex," Topaz guessed, blinking unexpected tears from her eyes. "I'm sure she knew about the place he keeps in Seattle and all it would have taken was a bit of crack detective work to find it—especially once those documents were messengered."

"I don't know anything about documents," Simon said, swallowing as though a sob were rising in his throat. "De was so upset after she talked to Alex. I was over here all night tryin' to calm her down. She figured Alex would take you to Seattle since he always disappeared there when he wanted to get away."

"Why?"

Simon understood the context of the whispered word. "Topaz, I had a chance and I took it," he admitted, rubbing the back of his hand across his eyes. "I've always wanted to get ahead. You knew that when we met. This was my chance. Mine. My opportunity to come out big, so maybe one day my name would be on the front door. But you wouldn't understand that," he spat, fixing her with an accusing glare. "You wanted a business and voilà, there is was."

"Son of a bitch. You know it was never that easy for me," Topaz hissed, stepping closer to him.

"May as well have been," Simon threw back with a flippant wave. "Hell, even if you had never made a go of that damn shop, you wouldn't have been hurtin'. Mama and Daddy Emerson woulda been right there to front more cash for your next idea."

Topaz blinked, shaking her head as she watched him with a probing gaze. "I never knew you were so hostile about that. I guess that was probably the *real* reason you ended things, huh?" she whispered, inhaling deeply to retain her calm. "Had nothin' to do with De or jealous wives at the company. You couldn't handle the fact that money seemed to come to me so easily, while you had to scrape and struggle for it."

"Money?" Simon laughed, massaging the back of his neck. "You think that was it? To hell with money. Money can come and go like the wind. Without power to back it up, you may as well stand on the street and give it away.

No, Miss Emerson, what I wanted was power and I would've been set if . . ."

"Power," Topaz repeated, watching him turn away again and bang a clenched fist to his thigh. "I guess that'll keep you more warm at night than friendship, hmm?"

"Topaz—"

"Leave it. Just leave it alone, Simon," she urged, allowing him to see the drained look in her eyes. "I shouldn't have bothered trying to get you to make me understand why, when there really is no explanation good enough to justify what you did. You sent a murderer after me, Simon!"

"Damn it, Paz, all you had to do was sell!"

"And all *you* had to do was be human!" she cried, slashing the air with a raised index finger. "All you had to do was be human. But I guess you never were."

The soft words cut Simon deeply and it showed. Topaz turned away as he leaned his head against the wall and cried. She was on her way out of the room when DeAndra entered through a side door.

"Simon, we—oh! Topaz. Alex did say you'd be joining him, didn't he?"

A dazzling smile in place, Topaz met DeAndra in the middle of the room. Taking the woman's hands, which were extended in a phony gesture of greeting, she leaned close.

"I'm going to enjoy being a member of your family," Topaz announced. Her smile grew brighter when she heard DeAndra gasp.

"Alex—Alex asked you to—to . . ."

"Talk to you soon, De. We should get together for lunch!" Topaz called across her shoulder as she sprinted from the den.

"Hey."

Topaz stopped and turned, finding Alex partially hidden in shadow where he relaxed against a remote wall.

"Did you . . . hear everything?" she inquired, her steps slowing as the distance closed between them.

Alex nodded. "I knew Whitley worked for Weston, but I never thought he'd send those fools after you like that. I can't believe I didn't piece all this together."

Shrugging, Topaz glanced toward the den door. "You would've needed a lot of pieces to be able to do that."

Alex reached out to brush his thumb across her chin. "I'm sorry anyway. I know how much you wanted to be friends with the man. To find out he was behind somethin' like this must hurt."

Again, Topaz shrugged. "One of the many things I'll have to get over, I guess," she sighed, her expression growing uneasy. "Um . . . about what I said to De. Alex, I'm so sorry, I was just so angry with her and it was either that or curse her out in her own house."

"I would've gotten a laugh out of either one."

Topaz searched the easy expression he wore on his handsome honey-toned face. "You're not upset?"

He leaned even closer, pressing his thumb to her mouth. "You didn't say or do anything wrong. Just beat me to the punch is all."

Her eyes narrowed. "What are you saying?"

"Well, she would've had to be told sooner or later."

"Told? Told what?"

Alex pushed his massive frame from against the wall and curled one arm about Topaz's waist. "I think we should have this conversation someplace else. I hope you're in the mood to discuss it."

Topaz's gaze sparkled with anticipation as she rested her head against his chest. "Oh, believe me, right now my mood is definitely shaping up."

Eric and Patra Emerson held an incredible dinner at their lawyer's waterfront club in Rhode Island, New

York. The event was in honor of their daughter and her fiancé. The guest list included close friends and a few family members. The Emersons had even arranged for Alex's mother, Lynetia Rice, to be in attendance. The wonderful seafood menu complemented the lively conversation and gregarious toasts to the engaged couple.

"You think they'll be all right over there?" Topaz asked, casting a sly gaze toward their loud dinner companions at the table near the huge bay windows.

Alex smoothed his hands across her hips and grinned. "We'll make this a short dance," he playfully decided, then brushed his lips across her forehead.

Topaz sighed her contentment, turning her face into his neck. "Not too short," she urged, feeling Alex's chest vibrate beneath the rumble of his laughter.

The lovely couple simply held each other, barely swaying in response to the sweet jazz drifting overhead. The show of peace and happiness on their faces was an added testament to how utterly blessed they felt in light of all that had passed. Even to those who were unaware of their relationship, let alone their engagement, it was more than obvious that the two were deeply in love.

The soft sound of a throat clearing roused their interest sometime later. The waiter standing nearby squeezed his hands as he smiled uneasily.

"So sorry to disturb you. Mr Rice, you have a call at the bar," the young Puerto Rican man announced.

Alex grimaced. "Who the hell tracked me down here?" he whispered.

Topaz reached up to tap her fingers against the muscle twitching along his jaw. "Shh . . . it must be important."

"Still . . ."

"Listen, go take care of it and we'll meet back at the table, all right?" she urged, slipping her hands beneath his maroon suit coat and stroking his back. "All right?" she repeated, slowing the strokes against the crisp material of his shirt.

Alex's gorgeous gaze narrowed with desire as he traced her exquiste dark chocolate face. His lips followed the path of his eyes and soon he was kissing her thoroughly.

"Mmm . . ." Topaz moaned, eager to experience more, but deciding not to give in to her desire just then. "Go," she ordered, turning him in the direction of the bar.

Alex didn't bother to remove the frown from his face or voice when he answered the call.

"Mr. Rice, thank you for taking the call. I realize this is a bit unorthodox."

"'Unorthodox' wasn't the word I had in mind."

The caller cleared his throat, realizing he would be better suited in getting to the point. "Sir, the purpose of my call is to inform you that your fiancée is not safe."

Alex's frown deepened into a murderous scowl. "Who the hell is this?"

"I work for someone who has an interest in the situation."

"What the hell do you know about 'the situation'?"

"Mr. Rice, please, I urge you—"

"And I urge you to pray I never find out who you are."

"Mr. Rice, *please*. You must listen to me. The threat against your fiancée is still in effect. Her life is still in danger."

"Who—"

"I promise you, steps are in place to remove this danger. We believe you'll be pleased to be made aware of them."

Alex closed his eyes, massaging them with one hand, while the other threatened to break the receiver in two.

"You listen to me. I'm in no mood for games, riddles, or anything even remotely similar."

"I understand, Mr. Rice. Mr. Carlos Fines would like to meet with you tonight and discuss the matter further."

"Fines," Alex repeated, his lips twisting at the bile rising in his throat. "Tonight is no good," his voice grated.

"Mr. Rice, I understand your reluctance and Mr. Fines does realize the inconvenience this poses, but in light of what's at stake—"

"Where and when?" Alex questioned, checking his wristwatch as he listened to the instructions.

When Alex returned to the table, the exciting mood there had not diminished. He kissed his mother, then excused himself and asked Topaz to walk with him.

"It sounded like you were saying good night back there," Topaz noted, her voice light with the happiness she felt.

"I was."

"What?"

"I have to go," Alex told her, smiling sympathetically at the disappointment in her gaze.

"Well, why? What happened?"

Alex kissed her temple. "Business."

"What's wrong? Is it, does it have anything to do with the call?"

"Yeah."

"Well, do you want me to come with you?"

"No, I want you to stay right here."

Topaz couldn't stop the thoughts of dread from creeping into her mind. Her fingers tightened around his wrist. "How long will you be?"

"Don't wait up for me."

"Alex—"

"Listen, this is something I need to handle. Tonight," he snapped, allowing his frustration to show.

Topaz's eyes misted with tears as she watched his magnificent features harden with emotion. "Are you all right?" she asked in a meek tone.

"I am, but I need you to cease the questions, okay?" he whispered, pressing a hard kiss to her mouth when she nodded. "Make an excuse for me," he said against her lips, then left her standing alone in the lobby.

Topaz hugged herself when she realized she was trembling.

Carlos Fines had requested Alex meet him at the penthouse he kept in Manhattan. Alex knew the place well. There, he'd received dozens of "orders" during his employment with the Fines Group.

Taking the elevator that opened in the foyer of the split-level penthouse, Alex was greeted by Reynolds. The forty-something Jamaican gentleman acted as Carlos Fines's executive assistant, valet, butler, driver, etc.

"Been a while, Rey," Alex greeted the man who took his coat.

Reynolds responded with a regal nod, but his expression was one of pure approval. "Quite a while," he said, turning to hang the black leather three-quarter-length coat in the closet. "Still on that Tanqueray?" he inquired.

"Always," Alex confirmed with an easy grin.

Reynolds nodded, then extended his hand. "It's good to see you, boy."

Alex nodded, his eyes narrowing in the appreciation he held for the man.

"He's in the study," Reynolds announced, then headed off to prepare Alex's drink.

* * *

Carlos Fines was a short, rotund man in his early six-ties. The son of two music teachers, Carlos used the education he obtained from school as well as the one he obtained from the streets of Harlem to build his organ-ization. He utilized a mixture of fear, intimidation, and cunning as well as a fair amount of undeniable charm.

To the naked eye, the Fines Group appeared most rep-utable as a retailer of mechanical and industrial equipment. The group also maintained various holdings in the corpo-rate world—including banks, investment firms, and oil companies.

"Alex . . ." Carlos sighed, approaching the younger man with his arms outstretched. He appeared every bit the adoring father greeting his favorite son.

"Carlos," Alex greeted, leaning down to accept the hug.

Carlos stepped back, his dark eyes sparkling as he studied Alex's face. "It's been a long time."

Alex didn't attempt to retain his smile. "It has, but I'm sure you didn't ask me here for a social visit."

Carlos nodded, turning away to resume his place behind a long, pine desk that occupied an entire corner of the dim study. "I can certainly understand the urgency to return to your fiancée. She's quite a beauty," he com-plimented, glancing up in time to see the blue-green daggers Alex's gaze fired toward him. "I promise you, boy, I have no intentions of harming anyone so lovely," he remarked, fixing Alex with a firm look before he sighed. "My son, on the other hand . . ."

Alex tilted his head and stepped closer to the desk. "You sayin' this foolish order on her life is not your doing?"

"It's not, my boy. Not the order or even the forced sales down in North Carolina."

"Carlos, I need you to tell me what the hell is goin' on

here," Alex wearily requested, smoothing one hand across his soft hair in an attempt to calm himself.

Carlos unbuttoned the salt-and-pepper tweed vest he wore and reclined in his desk chair. "Over the past two years our natural gas and oil holdings have taken a real beating. Cal was in charge of those holdings to a great extent. In his *eagerness* to prevent a total loss, he started to search for a new cash cow."

"And the search led him to Charlotte?" Alex supplied, settling into one of the deep leather armchairs before the desk.

Carlos was nodding, his youthful brown face appearing tired and harried. "He found out about those businesses by dumb luck. His desperation led him to believe the boast of an acquaintance who believed in some poor fool's granddaddy. The man said his family business had been successful for so many years because it sat on rich soil."

Alex leaned his head against the chair, his eyes closing as he realized how the situation began. "Hmph, Cal was always a sucka for a get-rich-quick scheme," he chided.

Carlos nodded, but he was far from amused. "He's a misguided soul and determined to keep this family drowning in illegal activity," he said, slamming his palm to the desk as he stood. "I never apologized for the way I handled my business. I did what I had to do because then it was the *only* way I felt I could do it and I had a family to support. I did those things so Calvin wouldn't have to . . . " He trailed away, rubbing both hands across his balding dome. "He's never understood it. I've actually seen him turn giddy from the possibility of violence. There've been times when I've wondered if he's my son at all. I know I'll never be able to entrust my life's work to my only son," he admitted, turning toward Alex.

"On the phone, your contact said 'things' were in the

works to remove the threat to my fiancée's life. Can you clarify that?"

The worn look of a disappointed father left Carlos's face and was replaced by a more stoic expression. "If something isn't done, there will be no more Fines Group," he said, coming to take the armchair next to Alex. "I'm an old man, Xan, but many young fathers depend on me to feed their families. My . . . son is spoiled, selfish, and evil with no desire or intent to change."

Alex leaned forward, knowing he had to be misreading what he saw in the older man's eyes. "He's your son."

"He won't live to see the beginning of the week. It's been decided. The only question now is: Who will see it through?"

"So you called me?" Alex queried, his light eyes intense and mercilessly probing.

"You're surprised?" Carlos argued, spreading his arms as he stood. "Cal's never cared for you, because *I* cared for you. He's always known you were the better man and when you walked away . . . he knew you'd only gained more of my adoration. I could sit here for hours reminding you of all the things that transpired between the two of you. But the most damning reason for you to handle this is wearing your ring on her finger. His threats on her life have to be eating away at you."

Alex stood. Suddenly, the rush of rage's bile threatened to bring him to his knees. The anger built steadily inside him as his hands curled into massive fists aching to strike.

"You have no idea how much it eats away at me," he said when he was able to turn and face Carlos. "To do this would give me a satisfaction you can't imagine. But I don't want that life anymore."

Carlos leaned against his desk. "Who said anything

about that? You would be ridding yourself of the man who threatened the life of the woman you love."

"And it's because of her that I can't do this," Alex decided, knowing Topaz had much to do with it. Moreover, he knew that to resist so powerful an urge would be the greatest step in triumphing over the anger that had ruled his heart for so long.

Carlos folded his arms across his chest and nodded. "Topaz Emerson must be a remarkable lady and not just on the outside."

Alex cleared his throat. "She is and if this was all you wanted to discuss, I'll be saying good night to you."

Carlos studied Alex's extended hand momentarily, before he accepted the shake. "All the best to you, son," he whispered.

Lynetia Rice left the ladies' room to find her soon-to-be daughter-in-law seated on one of the brick-red-paneled benches along the corridor. Lynetia's captivating heart-shaped face softened with adoration for her son's choice and she strolled across the hall.

"Looks like you're hiding," she observed, smoothing a lock of Topaz's hair behind her ear.

"Is it *that* obvious?"

Laughing softly, Lynetia settled her petite frame on the short bench. "Family gatherings can be a lot to take. Especially when something else is on your mind."

Topaz's smile belied the confusion in her eyes. "Something else?" she asked.

"Mmm," Lynetia confirmed, smoothing her small hands along the silky gold sleeves of her blouse.

"Lynetia, nothing's wrong. I'm sorry if I upset you."

"Oh, hush," the little woman playfully scolded, brushing her fingers against the flaring plum hem of Topaz's dress. "I know my son well enough to know when he's in a mood, and I believe you know it too. Besides, you were completely changed when you came back to the table."

"Oh, Miss Lynetia," Topaz moaned into her hands, "I love Alex so much, but it's so hard to deal with him when he shuts me out this way."

"It's something I've had to deal with for years, baby," Lynetia shared, hugging Topaz. "My son has gotten himself into some things that have haunted him terribly. I think he may always be haunted by them."

"How did you handle that? Him shutting you out that way?"

Lynetia's smile only increased the youthful radiance of her honey-toned complexion. "Well, sweetie, I did have an edge. I'm his mother and I couldn't walk away no matter how much I sometimes wanted to."

Topaz laughed, blinking away her tears as her mood lightened

"My son is very, very adamant about protecting and providing for those he loves. Sometimes I think he actually obsesses about it. The way we struggled when he was so very young played a huge part in the decisions he made later on. Then, when he realized what he'd gotten into, he felt he had no one to turn to and no way out."

Topaz turned to face Lynetia more fully on the bench. "But he had you," she pointed out.

"And getting him to confide in me was like pulling teeth and it still is at times. Even as his mother, I have to keep pressing until that iron will of his caves in," she confided, reaching out to cup Topaz's cheek against her palm. "It's an exhausting process, but he always gives in."

Topaz reached up to pat Lynetia's hand. "Some mothers would have given up. Cast Alex off as a worthless son."

Lynetia smiled off into the distance as though she were picturing her son just then. "Alex is a man worth saving. I've always believed that and I'd like to think I'd feel that way even if he weren't my son."

"I believe he's worth saving too and I also believe you've worked alone in doing that for too long," Topaz whispered, pressing a kiss to Lynetia's cheek before they hugged.

Alex could not shake his furious mood despite his firm decision to not take part in Calvin Fines's demise. He couldn't return to the hotel. Topaz was there and he wasn't ready to face her. Instead, he opted for lodging in a New York City hotel and a call to his therapist.

The talk with Beck had calmed him, but his reaction to Carlos Fines's request concerned him. Scared him. Clearly, he was still easily riled—murderously so. For that reason, he refused to go to Topaz. The last thing he wanted was to hurt her, in *any* way.

Alex grimaced at the bourbon bottle on the nightstand next to his bed. After a moment, he twisted the sealed cap and took a lengthy swallow. "Damn it," he hissed, knowing what he had to do.

Topaz awoke suddenly, her head jerking from the pillow. She had taken a nap, hoping Alex would be there when she got up. He wasn't. She hadn't seen or talked to him since his hasty departure from the engagement party two nights earlier.

Urging herself not to overreact to his lengthy absense, she reached for the television remote and leaned against the headboard. For a while, she listened absently, her attention mainly focused on the front door. When at last the lock clicked, she shut off the TV, moved to the middle of the bed, and waited.

* * *

Alex didn't head straight for the bedroom once he stepped into the hotel suite. First, he stopped for two drinks from the bar cart in the living room.

"What's up?" he greeted his fiancée as though he'd said good-bye to her only moments earlier.

"Hey," she barely whispered, taking in his wrinkled clothing and whiskered jaw. "Did you handle your business okay?" she asked, ordering herself not to bombard him with the questions she really wanted to ask.

Alex's broad shoulders tensed visibly beneath the wrinkled cream shirt he wore. "It worked out fine," he said, his back toward her.

"It seemed pretty serious," she noted, looking down at the sheet twisted between her fingers.

"Worked out fine."

Topaz nodded, still looking down at the sheet. "Anything you need or want to talk about?"

Alex's deep voice was muffled as he walked into the closet. "No time to talk. We need to pack."

"Pack?" Topaz parroted, confusion replacing the unease in her light eyes. "I don't . . . understand."

"And I really don't have time to explain it to you, but we need to get back to Charlotte tonight.

"*We* need or *you* need?" Topaz snapped, tiring of his attitude.

"Take your pick," he countered.

"What is going on with you?"

"Topaz—"

"Wait a minute," she called, raising her hands above her head. "You leave me at our engagement party to go . . . handle some business, you're gone all night *and* the next day and night without even a phone call, and I'm just supposed to go along with that?"

Alex slammed his fist against the closet doorjamb and fixed her with a warning glare.

Topaz refused to back down. "So now you're mad?" she retorted.

"So I have to answer to you now, is that it?"

Topaz gasped, the surprise and hurt evident in her exquisite gaze. Alex blinked to mask the regret in his own eyes. He turned away, knowing what he'd said had been unfair and completely without merit. Instead of explaining himself, he slammed his suitcase to the bed and began to toss his belongings inside.

"Stay if you want to, but I'm on a plane that leaves in three hours," he told her.

Topaz watched him for a while, hoping the rigid set of his shoulders would soften and that he would turn and talk to her. Finally, she acknowledged that would not happen and left the bed to collect her things

Topaz had accepted this decision as her only option. She didn't necessarily agree with it. In fact, she dreaded going through with it. She had no choice, however. Alex had as much as told her where things stood between them.

Almost a week had passed since they'd returned to North Carolina from New York. Topaz had not seen or spoken to Alex once since then. From the airport, they went straight to her home. He set her bags just inside the foyer, pressed an almost obligatory kiss to her forehead, and said he would call her later. About three days passed before Topaz acknowledged that "later" meant never.

When she'd mustered as much courage as she could gather, she visited the *Queen City Happening*.

"I'm sorry Ms. Emerson, he's not in just now, but—"

"All right then, I'll just come back," Topaz hurriedly decided, her courage fading fast.

"But wait," Marci Evans called, standing behind her

desk. "He was in a meeting, but it's over now. He should be on his way back. I know there were some letters he wanted me to get out," she explained.

Topaz debated, chewing her bottom lip while fidgeting with the long, flaring sleeves of her silver-gray dress. Steeling herself against the urge to back down, she nodded and let the woman escort her down the hall.

Alone in the sparsely equipped office (Alex wouldn't allow his staff to place him somewhere more suitable), Topaz set her purse on a chair and began to pace. Her thoughts of New York, the engagement party, returned to the forefront of her mind. They were so happy . . .

Then, like clockwork, Alex began to shut down his emotions. It had happened before, but this time . . . after all they'd been through, all the things they'd said to each other . . . Alex turning his back on her now was too much to take. A soft curse escaped her lips then. She still didn't want to let him go. In spite of all that had happened, in spite of her hurt feelings, she wasn't ready to let him walk out of her life.

Maybe he just needs a bit more time alone to think, she tried to convince herself. *Maybe I shouldn't—*

The office door creaked open and Alex stepped inside. The expression he wore silenced all her doubts.

"How are you?" he greeted, speaking to her as though she were a business associate instead of friend, lover, future wife . . .

Topaz swallowed her emotions and watched him stroll to the desk. "I won't take up much of your time," she promised, watching as he began to thumb through a stack of mail, "there's just something I need to say."

Alex's startling gaze narrowed and he looked up. His expression relayed complete concern as he watched her. "Did something happen?" he asked.

Topaz smiled, tucking a glossy lock behind her ear. "Nothing like that. I don't need you to rescue me again," she said, watching him return his attention to the mail, "and you don't need to be rescued by me either."

Alex looked up again, his pretense at shuffling through mail effectively stifled by her comment. This time, his expression was both inquisitive . . . and guarded.

Topaz cleared her throat, determined to say her piece quickly and get out of that office.

"It's so obvious that you're pulling away . . . again. If you can't see that—you *have* to see that."

"Topaz—"

"Alex, just let me say this please." She kept her eyes downcast as she spoke. "I have no hope of getting through to you this time and I don't want to."

Alex blinked, obviously surprised by her candor. He set the mail aside, then rounded the desk in a slow, uncertain manner.

"Time and time again, I've urged you to talk to me—to be honest about what you were going through. But you chose to silently go through this hell on your own."

"Topaz."

"Don't," she softly commanded, stepping back when he made a move to approach her. "Alex, I understand. I know that it's impossible for you to open up just like that when you've been handling this for so long on your own. I mean, it's one thing to open up to your therapist, who's also your boy and an old friend, it's another thing to bare your soul to a woman you've known just short of a year."

"Stop this, Topaz. I love you," he swore.

She responded with a sad smile and slow nod. "I believe you. I love you too. I love you enough to let you go and do what you need to, to handle this—to try and live with what eats away at you and prevents your love from being all that it can be."

Alex began to shake his head as she spoke. He could barely hear a thing once his heart began to pound like a bass drum in his ears. "What are you saying to me?" his deep voice grated. Leaving his place next to the desk, he made a move toward her.

Topaz stepped away and folded her arms across her chest. "I think we should break the engagement."

Alex's gaze narrowed, his expression one of hurt disbelief. "You're leaving me?"

Topaz could feel tears pressuring her eyes, causing her head to ache. "You've already left me."

"Topaz—"

"So many times you've left me and I've always bullied you back, pleaded and begged with you to let me help you when you were telling me how much you needed to do this alone."

"I don't want to let you go."

"But you know you have to."

Alex couldn't look at her then. He turned away, rubbing one hand against his denim shirt in an effort to quell the pain in his chest. He closed his eyes and massaged the bridge of his nose, shocked to find moisture wetting his fingertips when he pulled them away from his eyes. Yes, he did know he had to let her go—he'd always known it. After all, it was the reason he'd acted so coldly in New York. Hadn't he wanted her to move on and not waste any more time with him?

Still, he wanted to believe she could save him and he had no doubt about her conviction. But yes, he had to do this on his own—by himself. Not for Topaz or the possibility of a life with her, but for the possibility of finding the peace within his own life.

Topaz had stepped over to the desk. She rubbed her

engagement ring between her thumb and forefinger. Then she set the gorgeous pear-shaped diamond on the polished oak desktop. Her intentions to turn and walk away were thwarted when Alex caught her wrist. One massive hand cupped her neck, his thumb pushing her chin up as he took her mouth in a deep kiss. Lust, passion, love, and immense need were woven into the devastating act. Alex thrust his tongue repeatedly and more deeply with every stroke.

Topaz kissed him back even as tears puddled in her eyes and spilled onto her cheeks. Alex ended the kiss to catch the salty moisture with his lips. Topaz cried out softly when she realized he was kissing her tears away. Summoning her strength to pull out of his powerful embrace, she brushed her lips across his jaw and left the room.

SEVENTEEN

"This gang page was supposed to consist of over seventy-five ads. What happened?"

The spacious, fifth-floor advertising level was virtually silent. Only the soothing hum of the computers and vending machines down the hall lent any noise. Still, the group of thirty salesmen and women, who composed the classified advertising team of the *Queen City Happening*, were rattled. The group began to exchange uneasy looks once the question was posed.

"Well?" Alex persisted, watching one Gortex-booted foot swing back and forth as he perched on the edge of a desk. "What happened, Charles?" he asked the classified advertising manager.

Charles Black massaged the bridge of his nose while shaking his head. "Several of our advertisers canceled their spots," he replied in an uneasy tone, sounding as though he felt Alex already had the answer.

"And why would they do that?" Alex continued to probe, his voice retaining its normal level of calm.

Charles shrugged. "It was nothing personal, Alex. The market is still fickle, though, lots of businesses are still laying off—"

"Charles, tell me something I don't know," Alex interrupted, his voice never rising. "These cancelations tell me that these were weak sales," he surmised.

"And there I'd have to disagree with you," Charles retorted, his own voice becoming more firm. "My team knows what I expect of them. I have always stressed the importance of confirming *any* sale at least three times during the initial pitch. After the first conversation, my people follow up with calls to approve copy, layout, et cetera. There're no fluke sales here."

"And you expect me to accept that over twenty advertisers back out? Just like that? Just days before the final approval?"

Charles nodded. "It happens," he pointedly announced, doing an admirable job of masking his true frustration.

Alex responded with a cold smile. "I see."

"My team does a top job and I'll stand behind them," Charles decided, his hazel stare anger-filled.

Alex's smile widened. He glanced down at his agenda before looking out at the group. "Well, Charles, that's great and I'm glad you feel so strongly. That way, you won't mind too much standing behind your team in the unemployment line."

A hush blanketed the room and it almost seemed as though the machinery had gone a bit softer. Eyes were wide as the advertising staff watched their publisher leave his position on the edge of the desk.

"Meeting adjourned," Alex called over his shoulder as he left the sales floor.

Clifton Knowles arrived in the advertising department in time to hear the final minutes of the meeting. He watched the group disperse, stunned by what they had just been told. Clif had known Alex Rice for well over ten years and he had never seen the man behave in such a way. In spite of Alex's personal demons, he had always treated everyone—his *QC Happening* staff especially—with respect, consideration, and understanding.

"Blue-eyed nigga . . . who the hell he think he is? Forget this mess—"

"What's up, C.J.?"

Charles Black looked back to find Clifton standing just inside his office. "Man, where the hell you been?" he demanded, the subtle, reserved demeanor he saved for the office having disappeared. "Ya boy done flipped," he continued.

Clifton rolled his eyes. "I heard."

"Screw it. I'm 'bout to roll up outta here," Charles muttered.

Clif took a step forward, his hands rising defensively. "Come on, C.J., man, don't do nothin' hasty."

"Hasty?" Charles retorted, watching his boss with an incredulous expression. "Hasty, Clif? Man, that nigga just fired the entire classified ad team and you think *I'm* bein' hasty?"

"I'll talk to him," Clifton promised, taking a few more steps toward the wide oak desk positioned in one corner of the cluttered office.

"Don't bother. I'm tired of this crap—stress and tension all up the ying-yang," Charles complained, searching his desk for his car keys. "Your boy needs to recognize that it's the ad department—retail *and* classified—that keeps a paper alive. It ain't the editorial department, no offense," he added, flashing Clif a quick glance.

"C.J., man, just calm down. Tell your people they still got jobs," Clif said, turning to leave the office. "I'm goin' to find that fool," he decided.

* * *

Alex was back in his office when Clif found him. Alex was frowning furiously over last week's edition of the *QC Happening* and appeared oblivious of all else.

Clif stepped inside the room and closed the door softly. "You tryin' to decide who to go off on next?" he chided.

"You back to work or just stoppin' in to give me grief?" Alex muttered, his eyes still focused on the newspaper.

Clif chuckled. "The conference is finished," he assured Alex, referring to the three-week editors' retreat he'd attended. "It was a surprise to come back and find you tryin' to finish off the classified department."

"Deadbeats," Alex hissed, grimacing as he turned the news page. "Probably sit on their asses all day waitin' for the phone to ring, instead of goin' after a sale."

"Aw, man, please. You know you wrong about that," Clif argued, his dark eyes narrowing as he crossed the carpeted office floor. "You treated 'em like crap, talked to 'em like they were a bunch of nobodies. You know you were wrong."

Alex was still focused on the paper. "We lost over twenty advertisers," he shared.

"Aw, man," Clif replied with a quick wave, "hell, even the dailies don't produce gang pages of over seventy-five display ads unless it's a real special promotion or they join retail *and* classified manpower. This was an ambitious sale and for the group to come out with a fifty-five-ad spread is a lot to celebrate."

"And what happens when it's thirty ads lost or forty?" Alex challenged, then muttered soft curses as he continued to scour the paper.

Clif lost what restraint he had on his temper. "Hell, man, what the hell's goin' on with you?" he demanded, pounding his fist against his palm. "You don't fire half your ad team because some advertisers backed out of being on a page that was still a success. These are your moneymakers and you gone mess around and run your paper right into bankruptcy."

Alex looked away from the paper, but didn't make eye contact with Clif. "I don't need you tellin' me how to run my business," he said.

"Well, you need somethin', 'cause this shit ain't right, Xan. Hell, dog, why don't you just go see Topaz and—"

"Go what?" Alex retorted, his eyes riveted on Clif now. "Go see—"

"Topaz, you heard me. It's obvious you—"

"Clif?" Alex called, his voice still disturbingly calm. "Don't step into that, all right?" he advised.

Clif sighed and slipped both hands into his navy blue trouser pockets. "You seen her since I left town?"

"No."

"Almost a month . . . I know you miss her."

Alex began to massage the tense cords at the base of his neck. "Clif, man, did you hear what I just asked you? Don't step into this."

Clif wasn't put off by his friend's anger. "Y'all were pretty good friends before all that crap," he remembered. "Might do you some good to—"

"Clif, look, yeah, we were friends," Alex snapped, his voice finally rising a notch as his emotions began to weigh in. "We were friends, then we were sleepin' together, then we were engaged. The engaged part is over and we can't go back to the rest."

Clif shook his head. "And that's what you believe?" he asked.

"That's what's true."

"Man—"

Alex grabbed his keys and cell phone. "Why don't you stay and give your advice to the walls? I need to go," he decided and left Clif alone in the office.

* * *

"And if you'll just sign right there, I'll let you be on your way."

Topaz pushed her hands into the back pockets of her jeans and waited for the driver to sign next to the X marked on the sheet. Her gaze glided across the warehouse that was gradually clearing. Movers had been arriving in a steady stream since well before dawn. Topaz had managed to sell off what remained of her inventory. Thankfully much of her stock was kept in a warehouse across town and had not been damaged in the fire that destroyed her shop. As movers shipped off the products to their new owners, Topaz ordered herself to stifle the urge to cry.

"Topaz! Hey, Topaz!"

"Thanks," Topaz whispered to the driver as he returned her clipboard. Turning in the direction of the yelling, she looked toward the office level located several floors above.

"You got a visitor!" the warehouse manager announced.

"Thanks, Reggie!" she yelled back, already climbing the creaky staircase.

"Clifton?" Topaz was saying when she arrived from the ground floor. Surprise registered in her eyes.

"Hey, Topaz," Clif greeted warmly as he took both her hands in a firm shake. "Looks like things are clearing out."

"Yeah," Topaz sighed, looking over the ledge toward the lower level, "it was almost too easy sellin' off all that inventory."

Clifton nodded as he watched forklifts and cranes doing their jobs. "You deserve some easiness after everything you been through."

Topaz watched the busy scene a while longer, then

took a long breath. "So what's on your mind? I know this isn't a social visit?"

"It's Xan," Clif replied, his eyes still riveted below.

"Is he all right?" Topaz asked without hesitation. She took a seat in the nearest chair she could find and waited for him to continue.

Clif's hand tightened over the edge of the railing as he continued to look down. "He's all right physically—mentally is what I'm worried about."

"What's happened?"

"He's on some kind of power trip, Topaz. I don't know," Clif sighed, turning to lean against the rail and fold his arms across his chest. "Everyone at the paper's scared to walk within two feet of him. He's snapping at everyone, for everything. He fired half the advertising team over nothing. Some have even said they'd rather be unemployed than work for him."

Topaz's light eyes widened as she listened—part of her stunned, part of her not believing a word. "This is Alex we're talking about?" she softly inquired.

Clif responded with a smirk, "It's all true. I swear."

"Why'd you come to see me, Clif?"

"I figured you'd know."

"I do," she admitted, her eyes lowering to the oil-stained concrete floor, "but I think it's best to leave things the way they are between Alex and me."

"How can you say that after what I just told you? You know the man's history and how damaging this behavior can be for him."

Topaz sat nodding. "Clif, believe me, seeing Alex would do more harm than good."

Clif shook his head.

"Besides, this could very well be something that'll pass." Topaz tried to convince Clif—and herself. "I've never known Alex to be harsh with friends and especially not with people who work for him. He'll come to his senses soon enough."

Clif could see that Topaz had her mind set and he deflated a little. "I pray you're right," he sighed and moved away from the railing. "I pray you're right, 'cause I can only go off what I see, Topaz, and the way Alex is goin' . . ." He took a deep breath and headed for the exit doors. "I need to go, but I hope you'll change your mind," he said as he stepped past her.

"All right, everybody, be serious now. I have something to say," Topaz called, trying to keep her voice somewhat light as she tried to get the group's attention.

"You not our boss anymore, does that mean we have to listen?"

"Yes," Topaz pointedly replied, fixing Stacy Merchants with a firm look before she burst into laughter.

Former proprietor and personnel of Top E Towing and Mechanical met at a local seafood house that Friday for lunch. The meal was Topaz's treat and the guys couldn't have been more pleased to attend.

"Okay, y'all," Topaz sighed, while reclining in her cushioned ladder-back chair. "This *is* a celebration meal, but it's also a good-bye," she said, watching the men nod, their expressions growing solemn. "The inventory's been sold and shipped out and all the papers have been signed," she continued.

"That's all good news, isn't it, Paz?"

She smiled. "It's very good news, Claude," she told one of her brakemen. "But I still want to know what you all think about this," she urged, her gaze growing a tad apprehensive. "My decision to sell kind of came out of the blue. And with the fire and everything . . . it's like you guys had a job one day and then the next . . ."

"Topaz, I think I can speak for everybody here when I say

none of that shit was your fault," Darryl Groves was saying as he leaned closer to the table. "Yeah, things did happen in a messed-up way, but I for one am five figures richer and I ain't 'bout to complain," he said, earning a round of nods and voiced agreements from his former coworkers.

The lunch orders arrived and the food was as enjoyable as the conversation. Everyone spoke on their plans for the future, and Topaz was teased when she shared her thoughts on beginning a farm. The guys warned her of the risk involved, but Topaz wasn't easy to sway. She told them about Salamine Sentron, who'd owned the restaurant on Briarcliff. Salamine was thinking of returning to the business and thought it would be quite a selling point to boast that all the restaurant's ingredients were exclusive products of its own local farm.

". . . prime example of what I'm talking about is right on page one-A. This is clearly a story that belongs on page five-A—as a sidebar."

Alex sat only a few tables away from where Topaz enjoyed lunch with her crew. The *QC Happening* meeting, however, was far less lively. This time, the editorial department had fallen victim to what had become known as the "publisher's hot seat."

Clifton Knowles sat watching his friend/boss conduct the meeting. Clif's disgust was evident, and while he didn't relish calling Alex out in front of the rest of the staff, he believed it was the only way to take a stand against what was going on.

"I mean, for the past several weeks the front-page stories have been growing weaker and weaker," Alex criticized, his stare narrowed and cold. "Our readers aren't stupid. They can recognize a story that's been regenerated to the point that it's lost its appeal."

"Alex—"

"I'm not done," Alex informed Clif without so much as a look in his direction. "This mess has gone on for too long and I'm to blame for letting it go *this* far," he said, his voice gaining volume. "You people have been slacking off ever since Casey started making waves with his coverage of the buyouts. But now even those stories are old news and neither Casey nor anyone else has come back with suitable follow-ups."

Casey waited for a break in the speech, then cleared his throat. "With all due respect, Mr.—Alex, um, I think it's obvious that the public disagrees,.." he pointed out softly. "Circulation's up twelve percent over last month and fifteen percent over the month before."

The table of reporters swallowed in unison. Some reached for water glasses or napkins. Everyone waited for the inevitable explosion.

Alex leaned back against his chair and fixed Casey with a humorless smirk. "Mr. Williams, you're coming up on your first anniversary with us. I suggest you remember that, if you want to make it *past* that anniversary."

"All right, Xan, that's enough!" Clif finally snapped, slamming his palm to the table. "You're takin' this bull too far. These people do good work and you know it. They put out a prime read *every* week and I will not sit here mute and let you dispute that!"

Alex rolled his eyes, massaging his nose as he took deep breaths in an effort to quell his temper. It didn't work and he stood so quickly, his heavy chair crashed to the floor

"Screw it," he said and stormed out of the dining room.

The place was silent, everyone having overheard the conversation. Topaz's eyes were focused on her former fiancé. She was stunned, having never witnessed him lose his temper in a business setting over a simple difference of opinion. She couldn't help but remember her conversation with Clifton Knowles.

Topaz didn't waste time after her lunch with the guys. She drove right to the *Queen City Happening*. Marci Evans, Alex's assistant, stood behind her desk the moment she saw Topaz leaving the elevator.

"Ms. Emerson, this really isn't—"

"I know, Marci. I know what's going on. I know all about his mood."

"Mood," Marci muttered, "more like a metamorphosis. No one recognizes him anymore. One day he was just completely different."

Topaz shuddered, smoothing both hands across the long, clinging sleeves of her black knit wrap dress. "I've got to at least *try* and talk to him."

Marci shrugged and waved one hand toward the corridor. "Good luck," she breathed.

Topaz paused outside the door to the office. She could hear Alex beyond the closed door. Whatever was being said, it wasn't pretty. Still, she issued a tentative knock and jumped when he barked for her to come in. Bracing herself, Topaz twisted the knob and stepped inside the room. Alex was leaning against his desk, his back turned partially toward her. He was on the phone and he was yelling.

"What the hell good does it do to put out a paper if it's not bein' delivered, Rory?"

"There're only a few routes in question, Alex, and we're in the process of—"

"Only a *few* routes? You know how many papers we're talkin' about, man!" Alex asked the circulation manager.

"Alex, we're in the process of making changes to improve the present delivery system and I—"

"Do you know how many times we've had to improve

the present delivery system!" Alex thundered, his hand blushing crimson as it gripped the receiver. "Do these people have too much work on their hands?" he continued. "Is the work too hard on 'em?"

"No, Alex."

"Because I can take care of that if it is," Alex threatened, just as he glanced up to see Topaz standing a few feet away. "Get your department in order, Rory," he advised, his blue-green stare raking Topaz's body as he spoke. "Get it in order or I'll have to do it," he said, then slammed down the phone. "What are you doing here?" he was asking Topaz a second later.

Topaz cleared her throat, slipping a lock of hair behind her ear as she stepped closer. "I was hoping we could go somewhere and talk."

"Talk about what?"

"Anything. You . . . sound kind of stressed."

A muscle danced along Alex's jaw. "Stressed? How do you figure?"

Topaz responded with a short laugh, "It wasn't so hard to figure after the conversation I just overheard."

Alex shrugged, massaging his shoulder beneath his tanned shirt. "Business," he said.

"That's what has me worried," Topaz admitted, feeling a rush of cold when his gaze narrowed toward her. "You dote on your staff, Alex. It's almost like they can do no wrong with you, and now—"

"You know, I think you're confusing the way I run my business with the way you ran yours. My staff knows this is a business and there're things that have to be said to ensure that the business continues to thrive. Things don't always go so smooth round here as they did at Top E."

The remark caused Topaz to smart as though he had slapped her. "That was unfair," she whispered.

"Oh? I see, and you comin' up in here and telling me

how to run my paper when you don't even know what's up, *that's* fair?"

Topaz took a deep breath and forced herself not to meet his anger with her own. "Listen, Alex, all I'm saying is that this isn't like you. You hardly ever raise you voice."

"Damn it, Topaz, I'm handling business here!" he bellowed, rolling his eyes when he heard her gasp. "I don't have time for this," he muttered, focusing on the papers on his desk.

"I only thought we could talk about—"

"Hell, Topaz, I don't want pity from you!"

"Damn it, Alex, why are you doing this to yourself when you've come so far?"

"Hmph." Alex grimaced, then fixed her with a frosty smile. "Obviously not far enough for you."

"Alex—"

"Get out."

Topaz accepted that there was no way she could get through to him. She raised her hands to signal defeat and backed away. She left the office as quietly as she had entered.

Alone in the room, Alex bowed his head and massaged the tension at the base of his neck. "Damn," he whispered.

"Damn it to hell! Who decided to do that? Tell me who in *the* world called that dumb-ass play!"

George Scarborough sat pounding his desk. His light green eyes were glued to the ten-inch portable positioned beneath the counter. "You don't pitch to a guy who gets a homer on you every time. You walk him . . ." George sang in a matter-of-fact tone.

"Calm down, George, they'll make it to the play-offs."

George looked away from the baseball game and smiled. "Long time no see, man!"

Alex grinned as he leaned across the security counter to shake the guard's hand.

"What's been goin' on, man?" George asked.

Alex shrugged. "Workin'."

"I heard that. How's Miss E doin'?"

Alex stopped short. "Topaz?"

"Mmm, she runs in and out of here so fast these days, I hardly get the chance to speak," George explained, not noticing Alex's reaction.

Alex didn't know what to say. He was sure Topaz would have already told everyone the engagement was off.

"How the wedding plans going?"

"Plans?"

George laughed. "Yeah, that sounds about right. I know the feelin'. Man, I was so out of it when we were plannin' our wedding . . . felt like I was caught up in a tornado."

Alex shook his head, deciding it would be up to him to set things straight. "George—"

"Yeah, I was no good to my wife. Thank God she loved all the plannin' and all I had to do was show up," George was saying as he ushered Alex to the elevators. "Go on up, man," he instructed.

"Um, George, don't you think you should buzz in and let her know I'm down here?" Alex suggested.

"Don't worry 'bout it, I'll let her know you're on the way," George promised, clapping a hand to Alex's shoulder as he ushered him inside the elevator car.

During the ride up, Alex took several deep breaths. He hadn't felt quite so uneasy in a very long time. It had taken him almost a week to work up the nerve to go see her. He wouldn't back out now. She deserved an apology—a damn good one for the way he'd treated her.

She was amazing, he thought. She still wanted to help

him after everything else that had happened. She offered him an ear to listen and he thanked her by ordering her out. For a moment, he considered leaving—his courage slowly deserting him.

Just then, the elevator doors opened in the living room of Topaz's condo. Alex paused, hearing the affecting rhythms of the music filling the air.

"EPMD?" he whispered.

The classic rap CD was the perfect accompaniment during Topaz's workout. She had taken to her punching bag more frequently over the last few weeks. The bag creaked on the heavy chain that suspended it in the workout room just off from the living room. Topaz punished the bag with heavy kicks and fierce punches.

Alex stood motionless, just past the room's doorway. He watched her bounce, bob, and weave around the bag as she considered her next shot. Clearly, she had scores of energy and a lot of anger to burn. Of course, he could easily relate.

The forty-minute workout had reached its end. Topaz pressed her forehead against the bag and took several deep breaths. She then moved away as though she were reluctant to do so. On weighted feet, she dragged herself deeper into the condo—toward her bedroom. Alex followed unnoticed and unheard, thanks to the music that still pulsed throughout the house. His eyes never left Topaz. He watched as she moved down the dim hallway, removing articles of clothing as she walked. He paused in the bedroom of the doorway, looking on as she removed the tie from her ponytail and shook the lengthy black mass around her shoulders.

Exhausted, Topaz flopped onto the bed. Reveling in the feeling of being completely nude, she stretched on the bed. She reached for the remote lying along the shelf above the headboard. One click silenced the

music. Topaz sighed amid the quiet and indulged in another languid stretch as she raked her fingers through
her damp hair.

The unconsciously seductive act forced a tortured
moan past Alex's lips. Topaz shrieked, instantly alert as
she jerked up on the bed to crouch on her knees. A
pillow partially shielded her nudity from the unexpected
visitor.

"Alex!" she gasped, her eyes as wide as small moons.

"Shh . . . I'm sorry. I'm sorry," he said in a hushed
tone as he ventured closer.

"What are you—"

"George said he was going to buzz you. I guess you
couldn't hear over the music."

Topaz was still breathing heavily as she struggled to
calm herself. "George?" she parroted between gasps.

Alex nodded, easing both hands into his jean pockets as he studied the floor. "I guess he doesn't know
we're not engaged?" he prodded.

Topaz's lashes fluttered closed. "Alex, why are you
here?" she whispered.

"I came to apologize."

Topaz watched him approach the bed. Her fingers
loosened around the pillow and she waited for him to
continue.

"I'm sorry, Topaz. I had no right. I am so sorry I
treated you that way."

Topaz shrugged. "I guess I overstepped. As usual."

"No. You didn't do anything to apologize for," he told
her, closing what distance remained between himself
and the bed. He stopped himself from moving farther
when his gaze raked her body.

Topaz cleared her throat and clutched her pillow a bit
more tightly against her chest. "Thank you. Thanks for—
saying that . . . will you be all right?"

Alex's laughter was brief. "I hope so."

"How's the therapy coming along?" she asked.

Alex's vibrant stare hardened momentarily, before he shook his head. "I cut down on 'em."

Topaz looked away then. She pressed her lips together and stifled the desire to advise him to reconsider.

Alex also looked away, and then his striking eyes slowly moved back toward her. Topaz swallowed, noticing his stare focused on the pillow, which was doing a poor job of shielding her nudity. He studied her as though he were creating an image of her in his mind. Seated in the middle of the tousled bed, her lovely hair damp and clinging to her molasses skin, she was every fantasy he'd ever had.

Topaz scooted back on the bed when she saw that he was stepping closer. "Alex—"

"Topaz I . . . I just need . . ." He trailed away, his fingers reaching out to grasp a lock of her hair. When the tendrils slipped out of his fingers, he stroked her collarbone, shoulder, and down . . .

"Alex—"

"Please don't tell me to leave."

She blinked, the lost tone of his words draining her resistance. When his hand curved around her breast, she rose to meet him.

Alex trailed his lips from the corner of her eye and across her high cheekbones. He suckled her earlobe as his thumbs caressed her nipples into firm jewels.

"Alex . . ." she whispered, sliding her hands across the chiseled plane of his chest in search of the skin that lay beneath the opening of his shirt.

Alex's mouth crashed down upon her own as he followed her down onto the bed. His tongue stroked the deepest recesses of her mouth and he moaned each time hers did the same. His hands began a possessive descent across the flawless expanse of her body, stroking the dip of her spine and rise of her buttocks. When his fingers probed her most sensitive possession, Topaz shuddered and arched into the caress.

"Alex?"

"Mmm-hmm . . ." he soothed, cradling his face against her neck.

Topaz kissed his temple and threaded her fingers through his hair. "Please stay," she whispered, completely unashamed.

Alex rose above her and removed the linen mocha shirt he wore. "I was planning on it," he assured her.

Scott Woods and Cicely Grays's wedding day finally arrived after seemingly endless months of planning. Unfortunately, the special day arrived quite cold, overcast and rainy in many instances.

The weather conditions, however, went completely unnoticed inside the mason's lodge where the wedding and reception would take place. Damon Grays, Cicely's father, had arranged to have his organization's impressive facility booked for the three-day event.

The lodge was a virtual madhouse. Everywhere, guests and hired workers rushed about getting situated in reserved bedrooms. When Topaz arrived, she shamelessly used her feminine appeal to garner the assistance of a few gentlemen to herd her through the slow-moving crowd.

The would-be suitors, however, were taken aback and quite disappointed to discover the large, fierce-looking man who already occupied the quarters.

"Thank you, guys, I—Alex?" Topaz said when she stepped through the doorway.

Alex only nodded. A knowing smirk tugged at his lips as his eyes narrowed.

Topaz cleared her throat and smiled back at her assistants.

"Um, guys, thank you both so much," she said, ushering them out of the room and offering another quick thank-you before closing the door behind them. She turned back to face Alex. The two of them simply watched one another. There was no confusing what had happened. Obviously, the bride and groom had intentionally overlooked the room change after their friends informed them of the split. After a few more seconds of silence, the room was filled with their laughter.

"Hmph," Alex said, wiping a tear from the corner of his eye. "I better find Scott and see if he can get me another room."

"I'm sure we can share the room," Topaz suggested in a tiny voice. "It's pretty spacious," she added when Alex looked at her.

He smiled, his expression a mixture of humor and regret. "I think you know we can't do that."

Topaz watched the tip of her boot as she kicked it along the claw-foot of an armchair. "I was surprised to find you gone after, um, when I woke up," she softly stammered, referring to their night together two weeks earlier.

"Don't think that I didn't want to stay."

"Alex—"

"Topaz listen, um, what happened . . . let's not discuss it to death, all right?" he urged, hiding his hands inside the front pocket of his white hoody. "No apologies. I wanted it," he said.

"I wanted it too," Topaz admitted without hesitating. "I don't regret it," she added.

Alex bowed his head and grimaced. "But . . . to—to cling to whatever enjoyment it brought us would just make it all more complicated, you know?"

"You're right," Topaz managed to say once she swallowed past the emotional lump in her throat.

Alex gave a curt nod and grabbed his keys off a small

message desk. "I'm goin' to find Scott," he muttered as he headed for the door.

The following evening, Scott and Cicely celebrated with their family and wedding attendants at the rehearsal dinner. A local R&B group had been hired to perform at the party. The soulful ballads set the stage for romance and love. The performers took a short break to give the bride's and groom's fathers a chance to make their respective toasts. Damon Grays had the crowd laughing hysterically during his bodacious speech. Sanford Woods's words were a bit more prohetic.

"I think we can all agree that couples today have a lot more hurtles to jump than most of us older folks did back in the day," Sanford began amid a round of nods and soft clapping from the crowd. "Because of this, they got it a lot tougher than we did. But that's when love *and* trust come into play."

"Amen," someone called.

"See, these two things go hand in hand in marriage," Sanford continued. "You gotta depend on each other," he said, clenching a fist for emphasis. "This is what gets you through those tough times. You two remember that," he ordered his son and future daughter-in-law as he raised his champagne glass. "To Scott and Cicely!"

"Scott and Cicely!" the crowd roared.

"All right, y'all, we payin' these people good money to entertain us, so let's dance!" Damon Grays ordered.

Although Sanford Woods's wise words were directed toward Scott and Cicely, Alex and Topaz listened reverently. Neither could deny the truth of those words and how closely they related to their own relationship. The best man and maid of honor were seated side by side. They were the only two remaining at the table after Damon Grays ordered everyone to the dance floor.

Alex eventually offered his hand and Topaz accepted the unspoken invitation. On the floor, she decided it would be best to keep a measure of distance between the two of them. Her partner had other ideas. Alex's hands skirted her hips and he pulled her close. He toyed with the buttons at the base of her spine, before his fingers played a sensual dance across her skin left bare by the backless formfitting gold satin dress.

Alex relished the feel of the woman in his arms. He bowed his face to the crook of her neck and let his forehead rest on her shoulder. His wide hands cupped and molded to her hips and back as though he hoped to memorize her shape.

Topaz was just as affected. Her fingers skirted the lapels of the tailored silver-gray suit coat that emphasized the stunning breadth of his shoulders. He wore no tie with the crisp black shirt beneath the coat, and Topaz's gaze focused on the powerful cords of his neck. She allowed the intoxicating aroma of his cologne to carry her away on a cloud of sensation. The pleasure of his embrace was her undoing. She stood on her toes and brushed his earlobe with the tip of her nose. The soft sound Alex uttered in response brought a smile to her lips.

"Pathetic, huh?"

"Who? Your girl?"

"Your boy."

"Both of 'em fools."

"I agree."

"I thought that room mix-up might help."

"Obviously not. I think we've done all we can, husband-to-be," Cicely sighed as she arched closer to Scott on the dance floor.

"I guess you're right," he agreed with a grimace clouding his handsome caramel-toned face.

Cicely shook her head while studying the couple on the other side of the dance floor. "So much hurt in their relationship. If only they could work through it," she mused.

Scott gathered her small frame closer. "How 'bout this weekend, we pull out all the stops?" he suggested.

Cicely focused her wide, expressive gaze on her fiancé. "I thought we were already doing that."

Scott made a face. "I mean with the lovey-dovey stuff."

"I'm confused."

Scott lowered his head and pressed a kiss to Cicely's ear. "I suggest that we go overboard with all the kissing and hugging and makin' goo-goo eyes at each other. Maybe them fools will get the message."

Cicely smiled, even as her eyes twinkled with playful doubt. "I don't know if that'll work, but it'll be so much fun to 'go overboard' and show everybody how much I love you."

Scott's expression turned serious. "I love you too, Cice," he whispered, sealing the words with a kiss.

The wedding was a beautiful event. Every carefully planned detail came through without a hitch, including the last-minute arrival of the very broom Cicely's great-grandparents jumped when they married in 1900.

Everyone had a marvelous time and constantly complimented the newlyweds on knowing how to throw a party.

Topaz had been trying to find Alex ever since Scott and Cicely announced they would be cutting the cake shortly. She finally caught sight of him on one of the balconies that skirted the second floor of the lodge. He was easy to spot, since no one else had ventured out into the nippy, overcast weather.

On her way to the glass double doors, Topaz stopped midstride. "Damn it, girl," she hissed, closing her eyes as though she had just remembered something, "do you have a fetish for letting the man hurt your feelings or something?" she whispered fiercely.

I never thought I did before, she admitted silently. It was then that she recalled her last conversation with Alex's mother. *He was a man worth saving,* they had both agreed.

"Well, I certainly can't save him, but that doesn't mean I can't care about him," she decided, determination flavoring her steps as she headed out the doors.

"Alex?" she called, noticing him turn his head just slightly when he heard her. He sat in one of the cushioned armchairs facing the gorgeous expanse of the wooded property.

Topaz stepped up behind his chair and massaged his shoulders beneath the white tuxedo jacket. She indulged in the brief treat of toying with his gorgeous hair, before ordering herself to step away. She was about to take a seat in the opposite chair when he caught her hand and pulled her onto his lap.

"Alex?" she gasped, taken totally off guard by the action. "Alex?" she called again when he hugged her tightly. "Sweetie, what is it?" she whispered, after they'd embraced close to three minutes.

Suddenly, Alex cleared his throat and pulled back a little. "Sorry, um, I didn't mean . . . I have to tell you something."

Topaz was in no mood for high emotion or upset that day, but knew she had to give him this chance. "Go on," she said.

"It's about that day you came to see me at the paper."

"Alex, no," she blurted, knowing this was one thing she *didn't* want to discuss.

His hold tightened around her waist when she would have moved away. "Baby, we never discussed it . . . that night I came to your place."

"But this isn't the place or the time."

"I'd been in the worst mood for a long time," Alex went on, dismissing Topaz's words. "Clif thought it was because of what happened between you and me. . . ."

Topaz was puzzled, her own curiosity piqued. "What was it?"

Alex leaned back in his chair and braced his elbow on the arm. "I'd been tryin' to make a decision and I think I finally made it."

"I don't understand."

"I've been thinking about going to the police, Topaz."

"The police."

Alex studied the imprint woven into the material of Topaz's cream satin dress. "I told you that I never paid for any of the things I did . . . back then."

Topaz went cold as realization hit her like a spray of cold water. "Are you saying that you've been thinking about turning yourself in or something?"

"Not thinking about it anymore. I'm doing it."

"What for?" she snapped, leaning down to cup his face in her hands when he didn't respond. "Alex, what would this prove now? What about your therapy?"

"I don't feel it's working," he replied in a stubborn tone.

Topaz pursed her lips. "You don't feel it's working or you don't feel it's working fast enough for you?"

Alex pulled her hands away. "I have to do something. I think this is why I can't get myself completely together—guilt is a hard thing to be rid of."

"And you think going to jail for who knows how long would rid you of this guilt?"

"Topaz, I killed people. Do you remember me telling you that?" he pointedly asked, his gaze boring into her. "No matter how you slice it, it's murder, and murderers go to jail."

Topaz turned on Alex's lap and brought her face

closer to his. "Murderers go to jail to do time for the crimes they've committed, but most people who send them there also send them in hopes that they can be rehabilitated."

"Topaz, don't tell me you believe that crap?"

"I do."

Alex rolled his eyes. "Well, I don't. I got to find peace in my life. You don't know what it's like to live with this."

"And you think prison is the place to find this peace?" she persisted. "I always thought you were a smart man. I can't believe I was so wrong about that," she whispered, finally accepting that she could no longer watch him destroy himself.

"I guess you'll do what you want," she sighed, blinking back the tears pressuring her eyes. "You'll do what *you* feel is best. No matter how stupid it is. I can only hope you'll think twice about talking to the police and go to someone who can really help you." She sniffled and traced the sleek line of his eyebrow. "Whatever you decide, I pray it *does* bring you the peace you're searching for." She pulled his head to her chest and kissed his temple. "You take care of yourself, you hear?" she ordered, her voice breaking on a sob. Quickly, she pulled away, leaving Alex alone.

EIGHTEEN

Six months later . . .

". . . and a little grated cheese on the side."

"Thank you, sir. This won't take long, gentlemen."

Clifton Knowles nodded and passed his menu to the petite waitress. His eyes narrowed then, as he leaned back against his seat. "Well, I have to say I'm glad you decided to resume those sessions. Jails sure don't need another black man."

"I can only pray the decision I made was the right one."

"How many more sessions do you have?"

Alex smiled. "Five more," he answered, folding his arms across the front of his burgundy knit top. Aside from Lynetia Rice—Alex's mother—and Topaz, Clif Knowles was the only other soul who knew about the therapy. Topaz and Clif, however, were the only ones who knew about his decision to talk with the police.

"It helpin' any?"

Tapping his fingers along the side of his water glass, Alex gazed out over the crowd of lunch eaters in the dining room. "Yes," he finally replied in a firm voice as he thought back over the past five months.

Clif gave a satisfied nod. "Good to hear."

"Good to say," Alex shared. "The sessions must be helping, I've been able to really *talk* about the crap I been holdin' inside. I haven't had any of those damn crazy-ass dreams—"

"And you've handled the craziness of that paper without breakin' a sweat."

Alex chuckled. "Maybe, but, man, there was some shit that nearly drove me crazy. 'Specially during the three weeks you went off on that damn news editors' seminar."

"But none of that old . . . stuff came into play?" Clif surmised, tugging on the cuffs of his silver-blue sweatshirt.

"None of that 'old stuff' came into play," Alex confirmed, "I'm not sayin' I'm Mr. Nice Guy now, but the angry-at-the-world nigga I was is definitely tryin' to make his exit."

The waitress returned with the drinks and Clifton raised his cognac in toast. "All the best to you, man," he said and they clinked glasses.

Casey Williams was laughing, his arms outstretched as Topaz ran toward him.

Casey grunted in appreciation as they hugged. "I missed you so much," he whispered, giving her another tight squeeze. "You look so good, smellin' like the tropics."

Topaz backed away, a look of playful doubt coming to her lovely, dark face. "Is that good or bad?"

Casey's boisterous laughter returned. "It's definitely good."

They took their seats at the cozy table Casey had managed to snag before the lunch crowd began to descend.

"So how was it?" he asked, as they studied menus.

"I went back to New York for a while," Topaz sighed, smoothing one hand across her hair pulled back into a chignon. "Then we spent a couple of weeks in the Keys, then on to Jamaica. My parents went all out for the trip and we had the best time."

Casey was watching her in his usually probing manner. "I'm glad to hear it. You needed that."

Topaz shrugged, fiddling with the scoop neck of her emerald-green top. "I was just happy to see my parents having so much fun. Especially when they've been so worried about me."

"You're their baby and you been through a lot." He leaned forward, bracing his elbow on the edge of the table. "So . . . how are *you*?"

"Okay. Not great, but okay, and I'm fine with that. For now," she said, in an honest, refreshing tone. "The guys are planning some sort of party to celebrate the deal with Mecklen Gas. They've invited most of the old crowd from the block. I'd like for you to be there," she added, laughing when Casey began to clap his hands.

"Speaking of your guys, have you thought about re-building the shop?" Casey asked.

Topaz shrugged. "I thought about it, but I'm not really settled on a decision." She hesitated then. "I *am* in the process of selling the house."

Casey allowed his distress to show. "Yeah, I saw the sign. I guess you waited to tell me, 'cause you knew I'd try talkin' you out of it."

"Casey, I'm sorry," Topaz whined, extending her hands across the table, "I just think I need a change of scenery. Right now I'm staying at the condo."

"Change of scenery," Casey sighed, folding his arms across his chest. "Change of scenery from the neighborhood or change of scenery from Charlotte?"

Topaz would not answer. Her expression, however, provided a clear enough response.

"Does it have to be that way, Paz?"

Casey's soft question forced Topaz to shake her head. Weariness crept into her eyes for the first time that day. She thought about her last conversation with Alex. Knowing his plan to turn himself in overwhelmed her. Then, when Clif informed her that Alex had resumed therapy, she was even more overwhelmed. Desperate to escape the emotional whirlwind, she opted for another lengthy getaway. "I haven't seen him in almost six months and it still hurts," she finally admitted, "but that feeling is numbing slowly but surely."

"Well, there you go!" Casey bellowed.

Topaz grimaced. "I can't stay around here, never knowing when we may run into each other . . ."

"It may not be that dramatic, you know?" Casey pointed out, while tapping his fingers against the menu.

"We were engaged, Casey. Our entire relationship's been dramatic. How could this be any different?"

To that, Casey had no reply. He and Topaz sat in silence close to three minutes.

"So how is he doing?" she finally inquired.

Casey shrugged. "I don't know what the brotha's on, but he ain't nearly as closed off and scary as he used to be. I feel a lot more cool around him now," he expressed.

Topaz grinned. "I can believe that, 'specially since you're Mr. Big Stuff at the *QC Happening* now."

Casey chuckled, nodding slowly to accept her compliment. "It ain't just me. Hell, everybody up in that paper feel more at ease around the man now."

Topaz leaned back against the padded high-backed chair. The smile she wore relayed her mood. She found Casey's words refreshing, but bittersweet. Obviously, Alex was coming to grips with his ghosts. How she wished they hadn't had to let go of one another in order for him to do that. Still, as she'd often said, "Sometimes things just have to be a certain way." Clearly, this was one of those things.

"Might do you some good to see him," Casey suggested, focusing his brown gaze on the tabletop. "You'll see how good he's doing and it might help you put it all behind you," he added.

Topaz closed her eyes briefly, smoothing both hands over her sleek, straight hair. "Casey, that sounds so good. I miss him so much . . . but seeing him would do me no good. Casey, I think I gave Alex all I had to offer. I told him over and over again how much I wanted to be there for him. At first, I thought he didn't believe me," she whispered, her eyes misting with tears. "I thought that *he* thought I was just sticking by him because I pitied him. Now I know he couldn't accept my help because he didn't think he deserved it and, Casey, he didn't need to be bothered with that. He needed to concentrate on getting himself better." She spoke in a decisive tone, folding her arms across her chest. "I told him as much when I broke the engagement," she confided. "I won't lie that a part of me still hopes he'll come to me. But I can't let myself hold on to that."

"Shh . . ." Casey urged, brushing his thumb across her cheek when he saw a tear there. After a moment, he leaned closer to pull her into a hug.

Across the dining room, Alex's gaze was focused solely on Topaz.

After weeks of planning, the highly anticipated party date had arrived. Proprietors of the businesses that had once existed along Briarcliff began to arrive at Horace White's beautiful estate. Though the event promised to deliver more than one bittersweet moment, the group was determined to enjoy a wonderful evening.

Topaz arrived on the arm of Casey Williams. Also joining

them were Scott and Cicely Woods. The newlyweds were visiting from Raleigh.

"I'll be damned . . ." Scott breathed, his deep-set onyx stare narrowing. "Alex! Yo, Alex, man!" he called, having spotted his old friend among a crowd just outside the foyer.

Alex frowned and looked in the direction where he heard his name. His grin deepened when he saw Scott Woods waving and calling for him to join them.

Topaz muttered something below her breath and squeezed Casey's arm. "I see some people I want to speak to," she whispered close to his ear. She had no idea Alex would be there, then cursed her own stupidity for the oversight. Of course he'd be there! He knew everyone she knew! Praying fervently that she could enjoy the party without seeing or speaking with Alex, Topaz left Casey's side to find Horace and his partner.

Topaz had barely finished greeting Stan and Horace when they pulled her with them to the bandstand.

"Excuse me! 'Scuse us! Could we have everybody's attention please?" Horace called into the microphone.

"Horace?" Topaz whispered, dreading that she was about to be thrust—quite unwillingly—into the spotlight.

"Thank you, all. Just a few words please, and then we can get back to havin' a good time. Um . . . I think we all knew there would be some less than 'happy' moments here tonight. Well, this is one of 'em. This gorgeous lady here," he said, waving one hand toward Topaz, "she's decided not to rebuild her shop in Charlotte. She's movin' on to seek her fame and fortune elsewhere. We're gonna miss her a lot, but I think I can speak for everyone when we say thank you and we wish you nothing but success," he toasted, leaning in to kiss her temple. The rest of the group raised their glasses in a silent salute.

Stan ushered her close to the microphone, intending for her to say a few words. Topaz could barely see the crowd through the blur of tears pooling in her eyes. Overwhelmed by emotion, she could only whisper a hushed "excuse me" into the microphone. Then she fled the room.

She ran to the kitchen, grateful that the staff was out working the party. Relishing the solitude, she walked across the room to brace her hands along the stainless steel double sink. Bowing her head, she allowed herself to give in to the sobs swelling inside her chest. She stood there, until a knocking sound rose from some place inside the kitchen. Topaz cleared her throat and reached for a glass—pretending to get water.

"Topaz."

Alex's familiar, canyon-deep voice stilled her movements, and the glass almost slipped from her hand.

"Hey," she whispered, turning away from the sink. "I was just getting some water," she said, tossing her hair across her shoulder when she went to move past him.

Alex refused to move from the doorway. Instead, he stepped inside and forced her back into the kitchen. Topaz looked everywhere but his face.

"Was Horace telling the truth in there?" he questioned, his startling blue-green gaze boring into her. "You're leaving town?" he asked, closing what distance there was between them.

"Mmm-hmm. He sure was," she lightly replied. "Places to go, people to see . . ."

"What about your life here? Your friends? You're just ready to walk away from that?"

Topaz shook her head. "I just can't stay here."

The lost, defeated tone in her voice rendered Alex speechless. He felt his chest constrict as a sudden feeling of helplessness overcame him. She was going and he was powerless to stop it from happening. It had been over six months since they had been so close to one another. Of all the things that had changed, his feelings for her had changed most of all. Now he was even more in love with her.

"I have to go," Topaz was saying. She turned to set her glass aside, then left the kitchen.

Alex swallowed past the emotion that was surging up through his chest and causing his head to ache. His breathing grew labored, and after a while he reached for Topaz's glass and swallowed the tepid water.

"Sweetie, didn't you at least want to hear what he had to say? I don't think he would've come in there unless he wanted to change where things stood."

"Cice, I wanted to hear what he had to say so much. I don't know . . . with him standing there after all that time, I—I just couldn't . . ."

Cicely Grays-Woods lowered her wide brown gaze to the dining table. Her heart ached at the pain she heard touching her best friend's voice.

"The engagement is off. Maybe it was never in the cards for us. Maybe we were just fooling ourselves."

"Topaz, how can you say that after everything y'all been through?"

"I don't want to say it!" Topaz hissed, her light eyes glittering with frustration. "I don't even want to think it, Cice. It's been almost six months and I still don't want to face it."

Cicely reached out to rub her friend's shaking hand. "Honey, you know Alex better than anyone, but even *I* know the man don't say things he don't mean. If he said he loved you and wanted to marry you, I know he meant it. No matter what's happened, he wouldn't say those words lightly."

"I wanted to believe that, but now all this time has passed. . . ."

"Well?" Cicely challenged. "In light of that, don't you think someone should make the first move?"

Topaz pushed her hands into the bell sleeves of her tan sweater and looked down into her lap. "It's got to be Alex, Cice. *He's* got to allow himself to accept what I'm offering. I can't force it. I just can't."

Cicely leaned back in her chair. "Doesn't make sense," she said, chewing her thumbnail as she spoke, "but Alex Rice is a complex man and I don't have to tell *you* that. He seems to keep so much of his pain inside."

"And it's eaten away at him as a result. He's opened up to me before . . . maybe he can't do it again," Topaz softly acknowledged, her long hair curtaining her face when she bowed her head. Tears pressured her eyes when Cicely patted her hand again.

"Um, Cice, I'll be back, all right?" she said suddenly, leaving the table before her friend could reply.

On the other side of the Italian restaurant, Beck Gillam faced his most challenging patient.

"So you're just going to let her walk out of your life?"

"Hell no."

Beck offered a skeptical smile in response to the fierce admission. "Sounds admirable, but I can assure you she's gonna think that's what you want her to do."

"Is that your professional opinion?" Alex snapped, fixing the man with a sour look.

"Hey, we just had out last regular session this week. Today I'm speakin' as a concerned friend," Beck stated, using a clearly indignant tone.

Alex couldn't argue. The man had a made a valid point, and gradually his hard demeanor began to melt. "She's too fine a woman to go through all this," he sighed, massaging his square jaw while shaking his head. "The last thing I ever want to do is hurt her. Seems like that's all I ever do."

Beck leaned forward. "Have you ever considered that in your quest to keep from hurting her, you may be doing exactly that?"

Alex looked away from the man's hard, jade stare and muttered a curse. "After everything I told you, how I reacted to that damned offer Carlos made, how I decided to walk away from her—you can still ask me some mess like that?"

"Hell, man, you still human, you know? Any man would want revenge against someone who threatened the life of the woman he loved—and that's not my professional outlook either."

"I need more time before I go to her. . . ."

Beck nodded. "I see, and you just figure she'll be there once *you're* ready?" he probed, his heavy brows rising when Alex's head snapped up. "'Cause, news flash, brotha, women like Topaz Emerson don't remain alone for long."

Alex's stare narrowed, his features relaxing with confidence. "She loves me. In spite of everything, I know she still loves me."

"But you won't be around, remember? You off some place taking 'more time.' Look, Xan, you've bared your soul to this sista. You've probably told her things *I* don't even know about."

That was certainly true and Alex couldn't help but grin over the look of mock disapproval on Beck's brown face.

"Xan, all I'm sayin' is that the woman knows all this and she still wants to be with you. Now, you've done a lot to get yourself together. Maybe you can start thinkin' about what *she* needs and less about what *you* want."

Alex inhaled deeply as Beck's point drove home. He

spotted Cicely Woods across the room then and excused himself from Beck to go speak with her.

Topaz left the ladies' room with a sheet of facial tissue clutched in one hand. She had a feeling the tears would be more abundant in the coming days. She had already decided to spend a few days with Cicely and her husband in Raleigh. Then she would be off again to her parents in New York. Then . . . perhaps another nice long vacation some place far away from North Carolina and Alexander Rice, she thought. She was so absorbed in thought, she almost walked right past the man who was calling out to her. Finally, she tuned in and turned in the direction of her name.

"I'm sorry if I scared you, Ms. Emerson. My name is Beck Gillam, I'm—"

"Alex's therapist."

Beck grinned in spite of himself and took a step closer. "That's right."

Topaz pressed her lips together, debating momentarily before speaking. "I pray you can help him," she whispered, wringing her hands as she shared her concerns. "Something happened before we left New York after our . . . engagement party. Alex said it was business, but . . . I know there was more to it. He's been talking all this nonsense about talking to the police . . ." she continued, watching Beck through the fringe of her heavy lashes. She prayed she wasn't saying too much, but she felt too desperate to stop. "He shuts me out and I know he can't help it, these ghosts of his . . . I've seen the man behind them, Doctor. He's wonderful and I love him. I don't think he's fully capable of opening himself up to what that means, though. Just help him, 'cause he's gonna make some woman very happy."

Beck squeezed her hands then and Topaz looked

away, hating the fact that she'd allowed her emotions to affect her so. Across Beck's shoulder, she could see Alex approaching. Her heart flew to her throat, but she managed to avert her gaze and prepared to walk away.

Alex switched paths easily. He blocked her way. Topaz kept her head down, her eyes riveted on his hand, which smothered her wrist.

"Come with me," he said, tightening his grip when she tried to pull away. "I need to talk to you."

She couldn't speak.

"Topaz, please."

Finally, she cleared her throat, her eyes still focused on his hand. "Alex, it's over between us. Can't you just let it end where we left it six months ago?"

Alex's eyes narrowed to thin slits as he leaned close to her. "Is that what you think I really wanted?"

"Yes, and I think it's what you need. I think it's what *I* need."

"Topaz . . . please come with me."

"I'm here with Cice," she sighed, rolling her eyes in toward the direction of her table.

Alex glanced across his shoulder. "I just spoke with her. She promised to take care of your car."

Topaz looked up at him then. What she saw in his extraordinary eyes removed what little remained of her resistance. Slowly, she nodded and followed him from the dining room.

"Where are we?" Topaz asked, pulling a hand through her tousled hair and away from her face.

Alex was leaving his SUV. "Don't you recognize it?"

Topaz studied the dark, remote stretch of land along the rural road. Her expression was both curious and suspicious as she peered out the passenger window. "I haven't been here since that day . . ." she breathed, finally recognizing the area. "That day we took out my 'Vette," she recalled, when Alex assisted her from the vehicle. "Seems like that was a lifetime ago."

Alex watched her hair whipping against the night breeze. The glossy midnight locks appeared as strands of black ribbons against the moonlight. "It *was* a lifetime ago," he agreed, and caught a few of the tendrils between his fingers. "Topaz—"

"Why'd you bring me out here?"

"Will you let me talk?"

"And tell me what?" she snapped, putting distance between them. "What, Alex? It doesn't take much talkin' now that it's all over."

"Over?" Alex whispered, rubbing his hands across the small silky curls covering his head. "Is this what you want? You want things to stay this way between us?"

"No!"

"Then why do you keep sayin' it?"

"Would you just get to the point?"

"Calvin Fines is dead," he told her, tilting his head in anticipation of her response. "Do you remember the name?" he had to ask when she simply stared at him.

Topaz laughed as though the action were being forced from her. "It's pretty hard to forget the name of the person who wants to have you killed, Alex."

"You don't have to worry about that ever again."

The laughter stopped and Topaz shivered. Her palms turned clammy and she smoothed them across the seat of her jeans before easing them into her pockets. "He's dead . . . um, how . . . did he . . . ?"

"I was given the chance to handle it myself," Alex said, knowing what she was asking. "To silence the threat on the life of the woman I love . . ." he added, walking off to lean against the hood of the massive sport utility.

Topaz followed him with baby steps. "And . . . what happened?"

"What do you think?"

She blinked, her spiky lashes leaving trace amounts of water against her cheeks. "I'd say no to what I'm thinking, at—at least I pray it's no. Alex, you were so changed that night I saw you and—and I . . . you were talking about going to the police."

"Well, I decided against talking to the police," he said, noticing her relief. "I didn't kill Calvin, either," he confessed into the night air, never looking back at her. "I couldn't. But how I wanted to," he shared, closing his eyes as if to savor the pleasure that would have resulted from the act. "The rage came over me like that," he said with a snap of his fingers. "I was so mad that night, so mad I think I even scared myself. It was so bad, I finally helped myself to one of those damn pills," he revealed, sending her a quick grin across his shoulder. "They knocked me flat out with help from a bottle of bourbon. I slept it off in a crappy hotel in the city. The side effects weren't exaggerated a bit. I felt like warmed-over dog crap that day and I didn't want to come back to you that way."

Topaz was leaning next to Alex against the front of the truck. "So what does all this mean for us?"

Alex smiled and lowered his head. "You know, Beck said somethin' tonight that had gone through my head before but . . . I guess I never really thought about it. I been tryin' so hard to make sure you were safe, that *you* wouldn't be hurt, and truth is, I've been the one hurting you all along."

"Alex, no," Topaz whispered, her hand curving around a tassel from his hooded Winston Salem State sweatshirt.

"This is the truth, Topaz, and you know it. Hell, you

been sayin' it yourself. I guess it just never got through this rock head of mine till now."

"And now?"

For a moment, Alex shielded his face in his hands. "Topaz, I won't lie. The way I went off when the chance to snuff that nigga fell in my lap . . . I wanted it. I could've done it without a second thought. Sometimes, I think that whole way of livin' is just ready to be reclaimed and that *I'm* ready to reclaim *it*. I have to stop hiding from that fact and face it," he said, smiling down at her when she turned her face into his arm. "The way I treated you in New York and when we came back here—it could happen again and you don't deserve that."

Topaz moved, reaching out to cup his face in her palms. "Why do you put yourself down that way? Before you even know what'll happen?"

"Baby, I don't have the luxury of waiting for the outcome."

"And *I* don't have the luxury of being able to just completely forget about someone I love."

"Even if he's a monster?"

"But he's not a monster and I think you know that. If you didn't, you wouldn't be fighting this thing. Fighting and winning."

Alex's blue-green stare searched Topaz's sparkling amber one and he shook his head as if he was unable to believe how blessed he was to have her in his corner. "The last thing I need is a crutch. Especially a crutch as fine as you," he teased, drawing her into a tight hug.

Topaz snuggled into the warm embrace, nuzzling her face into his chest. "I don't think you need a crutch either. I believe you're doing just fine on your own. I'd only like to be there. Just to be there."

He kissed the tip of her nose and cheek. "I don't want you to spoil me," he whispered.

"Oh? Is that what you think I'm doing?" she taunted, favoring his jaw with an airy brush from her lips.

"Well, you cook like a master chef, my kind of music is your kind of music . . ."

"I can fix your car free of charge . . ."

Alex snapped his fingers as though he had forgotten. "What am I thinkin'? I can never let you go."

Topaz laughed as Alex pulled her high against his chest. "The man is finally wising up," she whispered against his ear.

Alex sobered, pressing his forehead to hers. "I love you so much. I don't want to lose this—lose you. Especially when I pray more than anything that you'll say you'll marry me."

Topaz looked up, her light eyes searching his for further confirmation that he was serious.

"Maybe this'll help you decide," he said, while reaching into his pocket. He extracted the pear-shaped diamond and slipped it onto her finger. "Take as much time as you need," he urged, pressing a soft kiss to the back of her hand. "I'll wait as long as it takes."

Topaz stood on her toes and hugged him. Alex closed his eyes, then opened them when the wind danced more frantically around their bodies. He watched the sand swirl in the moonlight, its circular motions resembling a mini tornado. In that moment, he felt as though more ghosts were being swept away from his heart and mind. Swept away to make room for the woman in his arms.

Dear Readers,

I thank you for taking time to read *In The Midst of Passion*. I hope you found it to be a novel full of sensuality and mystery. Moreover, I hope you found the main characters, Alex and Topaz, to be intense as well as stirring in their attraction for one another. I was first drawn to the story when the idea for Alexander Rice's character came to me. For me, this was *his* story—a testament of a man who desires forgiveness and solace from the demons of his past. I hope that in the midst of the dark elements prevalent throughout the story, the elements of light beamed just as powerfully. As always, I'm eager to hear your comments, whatever they may be. Please feel free to e-mail me at altonyawashington@yahoo.com.

Peace and Blessings,

AlTonya Washington

READER'S DISCUSSION QUESTIONS

1. Did Alex atone for his crimes? In what ways?

2. Was Alex's rehabilitation satisfactory or would it have been more acceptable had he actually served time?

3. Was Topaz so drawn to Alex because of the extreme circumstances of their relationship?

4. Was DeAndra's dislike for Topaz because of skin tone or for reasons that may have been more deep-seated?

5. Lynetia Rice, Alex's mother, said he was a man worth saving. Topaz believed that, too. Was his goodness a genuine part of his make-up, in spite of his work as a contract killer, or was it learned over time?

6. Alex said he justified his deeds by telling himself that the targets were bad people. As a contract killer, could he have fulfilled orders and murdered an innocent woman?

7. Was Topaz so trusting of Alex because of her attraction for him, or had he truly earned her trust? Should she have been more wary of him once he told her about his past?

8. After five years of therapy and medication, could Alex have killed Topaz in his dreams? Had he come too far to lose control like that, or were his fears justified?

9. Was Topaz the sole reason behind Alex's desire to get better, or was she simply the catalyst?

10. One possible theme for this story is that strength of mind triumphs over the demons of life. How does this relate to the major characters (Alex, Topaz, Simon, DeAndra)?

ABOUT THE AUTHOR

AlTonya Washington is a South Carolina native. She began writing in 1994 after graduating from Winston-Salem State University in North Carolina. After attending the HBCU, AlTonya had a desire to see more African American characters in the romances she'd come to love. Therefore, she began to create her own. When she signed her first contract in 2002, she had almost twenty manuscripts completed. *In The Midst Of Passion* is her seventh novel.